MASTERPIECE

www.**booksattransworld**.co.uk

MASTERPIECE

Miranda Glover

BANTAM PRESS

LONDON • TORONTO • SYDNEY • AUCKLAND • JOHANNESBURG

TRANSWORLD PUBLISHERS
61–63 Uxbridge Road, London W5 5SA
a division of The Random House Group Ltd

RANDOM HOUSE AUSTRALIA (PTY) LTD
20 Alfred Street, Milsons Point, Sydney,
New South Wales 2061, Australia

RANDOM HOUSE NEW ZEALAND LTD
18 Poland Road, Glenfield, Auckland 10, New Zealand

RANDOM HOUSE SOUTH AFRICA (PTY) LTD
Endulini, 5a Jubilee Road, Parktown 2193, South Africa

Published 2005 by Bantam Press
a division of Transworld Publishers

A catalogue record for this book is available
from the British Library.
ISBN 0593 05409 1

Typeset in 10.5/14pt Goudy by
Falcon Oast Graphic Art Ltd.

Printed in Great Britain by
Mackays of Chatham plc, Chatham, Kent

1 3 5 7 9 10 8 6 4 2

Papers used by Transworld Publishers are natural, recyclable products
made from wood grown in sustainable forests. The manufacturing processes conform to the
environmental regulations of the country of origin.

For Charlie

Acknowledgements

My heartfelt gratitude goes to Mum, Dave, Rosie, Liz, Daisy and Luke for daring to read for me and to Katie Owen for her razor-sharp insights. Thank you, also, to my late father David Leitch for his wisdom and support. Without Maggi Russell this book would not exist. Also to Charlie Viney, my agent and friend, for his passionate determination and belief in me. Thank you, also, Francesca Liversidge, for your exceptional talents, and Nicky Jeanes for your editing skills, as well as all the team at Transworld for making the publishing process so painless. Thank you, Simon Stillwell, for your hedge fund tips, and Henrietta Green for your wireless connection when it really counted. And last, but by no means least, thank you, Fen and Jessie-May, for letting your mum get on and write this book.

The good painter has to paint two principal things, that is to say, man and the intention of his mind. The first is easy and the second difficult.

Leonardo da Vinci on painting

In the room the women come and go
Talking of Michelangelo.

T. S. Eliot, *The Love Song of J. Alfred Prufrock*

MASTERPIECE

1

'It's not art,' I said, throwing the newspaper back across Aidan's desk.

My dealer glanced down at it, failing to disguise a smirk. There was a sketch of a boy on the front page, lying naked in a field, smoking a joint. The words 'Blow, baby, blow' appeared underneath – in my inimitable scrawl.

'Who was he, Esther?'

'Does it matter?'

'Of course not.'

'His name was Kenny. I can't believe his cheek.'

Aidan chuckled. 'You can't blame the guy – he just scooped three grand for a drawing. Have you got any more?'

I didn't answer.

'I bet your mum could unearth a few.' He ignored my scowl and tried to cajole me. 'Think of it as a pension fund – our future. If someone's stupid enough to buy an adolescent sketch by Esther Glass . . .'

'What other parts of me would you like to sell?' I asked defiantly.

'Well, we could begin with your legs.' Aidan's hands went up behind his head as he laughed. A case of cats' eyeballs stared straight back at me from the wall above him: Billy Smith's latest offering, just hung up. His private view was at the gallery in three hours' time.

'Do you reckon Billy would let you auction his dirty underwear?'

'Funny you should mention it: he's on the phone to his old ma right now, to see what she can dig out.'

'I thought we shared the view of art for art's sake. Regardless of its price tag.'

'We do, Est, but you've got to be realistic – we all need money to live.'

I held a lit match against my cigarette and sucked. Aidan beckoned me over but I ignored the gesture and instead concentrated on blowing smoke circles into the air.

'You've got to face it,' he said: 'they'll buy any bit of you that's for sale. You might as well benefit.'

The truth was, the sight of that sketch left me cold, but I couldn't explain why to Aidan – there wasn't a way. I had done it such a long time ago, so long ago, in fact, I felt like it belonged to someone else's history, a history I thought I'd managed to skip over, through years of active reinvention and determined shedding of skins. As I looked down at the paper what I saw was my own fatal error staring back at me. I had foolishly believed I could erase from memory those people who had run away from me in the past, because I had assumed they would never turn and run back in my direction. But I'd failed to take into account one critical factor: I had become famous, and with that fame I'd become a valuable commodity – if you had a piece of me to sell, that is. Crafty old Kenny Harper, I bet he couldn't believe his luck when he found that drawing at the bottom of some old box.

'Esther, are you OK?' Aidan's tone had softened and he observed me curiously.

'I guess so,' I said. 'It just feels weird to see something I did so long ago made public. You know, it was just a scribble, and now Sotheby's have gone and authenticated it as a work of art. It's crazy.'

'You've got to remember, Esther,' he replied gently, 'you've

2

encouraged the media's hysteria around you – and the public's obsession. Take advantage of it while you can.'

He had a point and we both knew it. My art was about 'the moment' – who knew when it would pass?

'Please, Aidan, can we let it lie?'

'Sure thing, Est,' he answered with a sigh. 'After all, it is your past; it's no one else's business.'

His words contained a subtle tug, an undercurrent which I chose at that moment to ignore. We both knew the issue of sharing information was a personal one – one that, before now, had never centred on my art.

I heard the gallery door click open and turned to see Katie O'Reilly click-clacking her kitten heels across the white space. She had a tray in her hands and I got up to open Aidan's glass door for her. She smiled sweetly as she passed me by and then, with her back to me, she enquired how I was – a touch uneasily, I felt.

Katie was a critical component in Aidan's staff, his most trusted employee and indefatigable PA. She was in her late twenties, a classy Dubliner with foxy-red hair, Emerald Isle eyes and a feline form; she was also super-efficient, super-nice and super-well-connected; and to top all that, she had somehow managed to keep me on track for more than five years. In fact she had become an indispensable aspect of the Aidan Jeroke Gallery team. Recently Aidan had invested heavily in his stable of artists, expanded the space and brought in two new exhibition staff to support Katie. The recognition of her respected role had had an amazing effect. She seemed even more confident and in control of the day-to-day running of the gallery than ever before. Katie knew as well as Aidan that I was suffering from a long-term creative block. Six months ago I'd committed to a deadline that was now looming large – and so far I had failed to deliver, even on the concept level. I'd been selected by Tate Modern to represent Britain in an international show of contemporary art. The backers were global, including

MOMA in New York, the Museum of Modern Art, Sydney, and the Kunsthaus in Berlin. My selection was tantamount to a public acknowledgement of all that not only I, but also Aidan, had achieved over the previous decade. If I didn't come up with something soon we'd both be losing face.

'Let's just say I'm not quite there yet,' I told her quietly as she handed me a coffee.

She nodded understandingly, then picked up the newspaper and began to gawp at the drawing. 'Who on earth was that?' she exclaimed.

This was the cue, I felt, to take my leave. I said I needed to get ready for Billy's opening and headed out into the afternoon drizzle. I mused over my predicament as the cab drove me home. Critics have often said Aidan's gallery is nothing more than a concept factory focused on money; a machine fuelled by PR stunts, price fixing and hype. I'd be the first to admit we've all ridden high on a wave of popular culture – and enjoyed the financial rewards that our ensuing celebrity has generated. But however bold and self-referential our artworks are, they're not limited to irony. We've all had more to say, about looking again – 'post-modernists with personality', as one critic described us at the start. But maybe our moment was passing: some of us were beginning to sell out. The idea hit a raw nerve. To me, the auction of my 'memorabilia' symbolized the beginning of the end. And if I had anything to do with it, my childhood was not about to form part of my artistic inventory. Sketches of my distant past weren't for sale – unless, of course, they were already in other people's hands.

My flat is my sanctuary. It comprises the top two floors of a warehouse, accessed only by my personal lift: no neighbours, no intrusion. One floor is the main studio, just a huge space, where, for the past two weeks, I'd also had my bed. In a desperate attempt to concoct a plan, I'd decided to immerse myself, live and breathe my art. I paced around up there now, surveying past props, trying to think things through.

What was wrong with me? Art had always come easily; it had always been a bit of a game, a bit of fun.

Mirrors run the length of one wall, a whiteboard the other; on the south side, a full-width glass wall looks out onto a roof terrace, then beyond over East London. Scattered around the space were a number of mannequins, camera equipment, lights and an easel. I observed myself critically in the mirrors; my hair was currently peroxide blonde, cropped to an inch of my scalp; the tone highlighted the paleness of my complexion and dark shadows were puddling under my blue-grey eyes. I knew I needed to clean myself – and the flat – up, but I had no energy to do so. Anyway, this wasn't the time; I needed to get ready for Billy's opening. I opened a bottle of wine and smoked a cigarette on the terrace while looking over the city, which was smudging to grey like charcoal on paper. It was early-November, getting colder, and a light wind was stirring.

The phone disturbed me. I picked it up and came back outside, expecting to hear the voice of my friend Sarah Carr; she'd promised to call about sharing a ride to Billy's show. But as soon as I heard the line I knew it wasn't Sarah. Someone was calling from a relatively long distance, or on an internal phone network. It clicked once or twice before the line came clear. I thought it might have been a marketing call, but then I heard his voice.

'Hi, Esther. How's it going?'

I felt a spasm twist inside me. The man on the line was affecting joviality, evidently aware, as was I, that there was no need for an introduction. Fifteen years may have passed but his tone hadn't changed – maybe worn just a little thinner, been drained of some of its richness, like an over-cropped field. I tried to think fast. I was in no way prepared for Kenny Harper's readmission into my life. My first temptation was simply to hang up, but I knew, as he must have known, that I wouldn't – indeed, couldn't. Kenny had one up on me, for this moment, at least. He knew why he was calling and I needed to find out.

'I wondered when you'd show up,' I said, trying hard to sound nonchalant, but the words came out too throatily to mask my anxiety.

'You've become quite the fancy artist, haven't you?' he answered, but beneath the jokiness I could hear his heavy breath. It was dense and moist. So he was uneasy, too.

'How've things been for you?' I asked, determinedly turning the tables away from my world.

'Not quite, how shall I put it, such a bed of roses,' he replied, laughing, but his underlying bitterness struck me like steel. He wanted something from me, I was certain.

'You must have been pleased with the auction,' I said, coolly.

There seemed no point in hiding from the facts, and I guessed the sooner we got down to the business of it, the sooner I could get him off my case. A touch of shame almost coloured his laughter. He gave a sort of snort-chuckle, akin to that of a schoolboy caught red-handed in some petty wrongdoing.

'Yeah, well, needs must,' he replied, once his outburst was contained. 'We aren't all as loaded as you must be these days.'

'Why are you calling me, Kenny, after all this time?' I asked a touch too aggressively, but my anxiety was fast turning to indignation.

There was a momentary pause. Then, 'I just thought it might be nice to have a chat,' he lied, unconvincingly.

I was still standing out on the terrace and suddenly realized I was shivering violently – and not due to the cold. I moved inside as I tried to think quickly. How much did he know – I mean about what happened to me after he left? Nothing, was the answer, as far as I was aware. So what did he want? But I didn't need to ask: Kenny was all too keen to fill me in.

'Some nice bloke got hold of me the other day – wanted to know if I fancied reminiscing about us – you know, about our—' he paused, 'affair.' The use of the term was obviously foreign to Kenny but had flattered him. He was probably still more one of your 'quick fling' kind of guys, not in it for the medium term, let alone the long haul. 'Seems we've got quite a high value,' he continued, sounding increasingly chuffed, 'to the tabloids, an' all that. But what we had was special and it don't feel right, sharin' it with the press, you know what I mean?'

I thought I might be sick. Kenny might be emotionally puerile, he might be uncultured, but he wasn't stupid and he knew exactly how to hook me in.

'Who was he and what did you tell him?' I said, coldly.

'Nah, nothing, Esther,' he answered with faux-innocence. 'Don't panic. I just said I'd have to think about it. I think he was called John – yeah, John Herbert, that's right, from that new red top, the *Clarion*.'

John Herbert had been after my blood for years. He was my most acidic critic, and the last person I needed digging around in my past. My anxiety rose higher.

'How much did he offer you?'

'Ten grand,' he said, proudly.

'Obviously, I think you did the right thing,' I replied, trying to sound unperturbed, 'but I'd hate to feel you were left out of pocket for your integrity.'

The puerile snigger returned. 'How thoughtful of you,' he said. 'You know, he asked about the other sketches, too.'

How could I be so stupid to forget? Over the pathetic week or so Kenny and I had spent together, I had drawn him endlessly, but I could remember giving him only one picture, the one he had just sold. However, there was no reason to believe Kenny was lying. Whatever he had, it was bound to be embarrassing, sexually explicit and far better kept under wraps.

'I didn't know you had any others,' I said. 'I'd love to see them. Maybe I could make you what they call a counter-bid.'

'Yeah, yeah, my thoughts exactly,' he answered, suddenly sounding more distracted, then his tone changed and his words began to spill out fast. 'Esther, I've got to go, but maybe we could speak again, same time, next week, hey? See ya.'

The line cut dead, like a switchboard had shut him off. I threw my receiver down on the sofa in disgust, as if he had left his germs there, and began to pace up and down my studio, rubbing my arms. I was shaking all over, yet covered in sweat. I had experienced many, many things in my rather chequered artistic career, but up till now blackmail wasn't one of them.

What did he really want? If it was just cash to keep him from talking to the media I had it, and if he had other sketches I'd buy them from him, too. But his call was more unnerving than that. It wasn't what he knew about my past that I was worried about, because, frankly, I was certain he didn't know a lot. It was the idea of the media beginning to delve deeper into my childhood and adolescence that I hated. I'd always actively kept my art in the present tense, determinedly retaining a distance from the history that had formed me. I'd left all that behind me at seventeen, when I'd moved to London, and I didn't want it following me around. Kenny came from a time I kept absolutely to myself, a time when many things had happened in my life, that had truly shaped who – or, should I say, what – I'd become. Essentially what concerned me was the ripple effect. Kenny was the stone, and now he'd been thrown into the water there had to be repercussions, the ripples would circle outwards – unless, that is, I could do something to curtail them.

I took a shower and began to get dressed. I had to cover the real me up: I looked a fright. So I put on a long black wig, painted my lips poppy-red, and dressed in a new creation by my best friend and designer, Petra Luciana. As I recreated myself I tried to think of a way to stop Kenny in his tracks, but nothing would come to me, other than one basic thought. In principle, if I could throw a much bigger stone into the same water I would create wider ripples, which would turn attentions away from his little pebble and back onto me, and by that I meant the me of today. If only I could think of a project that would blow a hole in his stupid little story about an adolescent love affair, then maybe the media's attention would be diverted for long enough for their interest in him and my past to run to ground. The phone rang again and my stomach lurched, but this time it was Sarah.

'We'll be with you at seven.'

'You sound breathless,' I said.

'I've just finished on the running machine,' she puffed. 'Been trying to get in shape for our next show.'

Sarah Carr and Ruth Lamant were two of my good friends. They were a double act, part of a popular new theme on the art scene: 'collaboration artists', doing the unit thing, like Gilbert and George or the Chapman brothers, but much younger and prettier than the former and without the latter's fix on sexual perversions. And, to my knowledge, they weren't in the habit of defacing old-master drawings, either. The girls had the added advantage that they could sing – more like cabaret artists than fine artists, perhaps – and their shows involved a good deal of acrobatics, too. Some people questioned their categorization as artists at all, but recently the media had all got muddled up – the boundaries blurred. Art, photography, film, fashion, the media: we'd all succumbed to the same melting pot. If we were talking about ethnicity, we'd be living cheek by jowl, fighting amongst ourselves but ignoring everyone else we passed on the street. Where the arts were concerned it seemed we were all busy trying to muscle in on one another's territory, stealing the best bits and leaving the rest to collect dust.

'You sound strained,' she said. 'Everything OK?'

'Yeah, fine,' I lied. 'Just a bit preoccupied, with my new project.'

'How's Aid behaving?'

'What do you mean?' I knew my tone was brittle, but I couldn't help it.

'He seemed pretty low when I saw him yesterday.'

I didn't like Aidan wearing our personal worries on his sleeve. I guess his depression could easily have been about the state of my art as much as the state of our relationship, but I doubted it. Since I'd been struggling to produce a new work, we'd been getting on badly. I'd hidden myself away, and a deep gloom had set in.

'There's a lot of pressure on him right now,' I said lamely.

'I guess so: he's invested heavily in your success,' Sarah replied with genuine feeling. 'But, hey, Est, remember, in the end you're the one who has to come up with the goods. He's just your pimp.'

When I rang off I finished dressing, then went back out onto the terrace to wait for her to arrive. Sarah had a point – about Aidan – but I meant more to him than money, or so I thought. I needed air, I needed to clear my head, to think. My phone bleeped again. It was a text from Aidan. I clicked to read.

Sorry I joked – I'd never sell you, Est; you're my masterpiece, Aidx

I contemplated a reply, faltered, read the message again, then snapped the phone shut and looked out over the terraces stretching the length of Bow. My gaze moved up into the night sky. I clicked the text open and read it again. *I'd never sell you.* Maybe there was something in these words, the start of a theme; everything about my art seemed to be focused on my value right now. Everyone wanted a bit of me: Kenny, Aidan, the media, collectors, the Tate, the public. Maybe that was what I was struggling to understand: my real worth. There had to be a way for me to throw the question into my next project. If only I could concentrate. Instead I felt jumpy and confused. I determined to push Kenny Harper from my mind, at least for the week. Presumably he'd be too intent on our next call to do anything else with the *Clarion* in the meantime. Surely he'd want to wait to see if I came up with a better offer. If I was right, that gave me seven days to plan a competitive attack. Maybe, if I could bear to look on the bright side of it, Kenny was doing me a favour of sorts. At least I no longer felt in a deep malaise. My mind was racing. I knew a solution had to be found, and fast.

2

Billy's view was evidently in full swing by the time we arrived; the narrow street outside was crowded with people who couldn't get past the doorman, drinking lager, smoking each other's fags. Sarah paid the driver as I sent Katie a text. When I got a response we headed out, Ruth on one side of me, Sarah on the other, arms interlinked. Faces turned to peer, a camera bulb flashed, then another, a whole bank. We were used to the attention and all enjoyed the rush it gave us. We smiled and giggled together as we headed for the private entrance. I felt better being away from the flat, there was safety in numbers and the party was crowded.

Wily as a fox, Katie appeared and ushered us straight in. Another door took us into the main gallery and we piled straight through and into view of one of Billy's exhibits; two crashed cars filled the space, lifelike bodies spilling out their guts from open doors, in front of one a rabbit, eyes frozen in flashing headlights. Tinny pop music was playing from the other car's stereo, the music almost drowned out by the noise of the private view. The guests were pressed against one another, looking away from the art into semi-lit space. No one was interested in the work on show; they were too busy watching each other's backs, swapping malicious gossip and dissing the latest deals. I spotted familiar figures, among them Lincoln Sterne, my old friend turned art critic, engaged in viperish chatter with two sculptors – old friends and gallery 'originals' – the privileged term given to those who'd been with Aidan Jeroke from the start.

I tapped Lincoln on the shoulder and he swung round, saw me and smiled coquettishly. As he aged, his pale hair and boyish looks became more pronounced. He could have passed off for David Hockney's younger brother.

'You promised me lunch,' I said.

He held his hands up by way of apology and made a mental calculation. 'I'm off to Milan. Perhaps next week: our regular haunt?'

I nodded. 'We need to talk,' I said.

He knew why but affected an innocent grin. Lincoln had filed a subtly critical profile on me a week earlier in the *Sunday Times*, without my consent. There'd always been a silent faith between us: he always asked first and I always gave him exclusivity over new stories about my work. The article broke our faith for the first time. I couldn't understand what he thought he'd gain, other than a new distance between us. Before he could defend his actions, someone grabbed my arm and hung onto it. I recognized Aidan's fingers, the precise measure of his touch, and turned.

He looked a little harassed but pleased to see me. 'You OK, Esther? Can I grab a minute with you upstairs?'

'Sure,' I replied.

'I'll see you in the office in a bit,' he continued. 'Billy's just threatened to head-butt some journo from *ArtFuture* who said the work was wank.'

He headed off as I took a glass of wine from Katie. Billy was always itching for a scrap. One day somebody would knock his lights out. I looked back round. Lincoln was now deep in conversation with a foppish young man in a striped suit – either he worked in the City or he was going for a look of post-ironic affectation. I couldn't decide which and I didn't really care.

For their part, Sarah and Ruth had started flirting with an artist from Dreamland Studios. Each had an arm draped around him, and they nodded in unison as he spoke. They used to have a space there, he was part of the act, understood the drama. They both wore T-shirts. Ruth's said *Bol*, Sarah's *Locks*. I could tell this was only the start of a big night. Sometimes art openings were like that. They stimulated us, got us energized, left us wanting more. Art was one of our most intensely coveted drugs. It was hypnotic, addictive and, when it was really good, gave the most incredible high. But right now I had other more pressing issues on my mind. Avoiding all eyes, I slipped past the crowd and headed up to Aidan's office to wait.

Eventually I heard the door click shut and the key turn and I smiled at the security measure. Aidan came and sat down on the desk. His eyes were dancing and he tapped his fingers in time to his words. There was a sheen to his dark skin. Obviously the party was going well.

'Esther,' he began, 'I just wanted to say I'm sorry. My words this afternoon were out of line. I understand you value your work, and I didn't mean to belittle it.'

I couldn't help but smile. For the first time in months the frost between us was thawing.

'But maybe you had a point,' I said ambiguously.

'What do you mean?' Now he looked confused.

'I don't know, but this whole value thing, I've started to see it has to form the basis of my next project.'

Aidan came around the desk and took hold of me, kissed me deeply. I responded in kind.

'We have to go back downstairs,' he said eventually, 'but promise you'll stay with me tonight.'

As everyone else headed off to party after the private view was over, Aidan and I slipped away in his car. Despite his professional East-Ending, for living time he prefers the affluence of North London. His place commands views high over the heath and across the night sky.

We both like big views, space outside the day-to-day detail of our lives. Standing together at the open window we breathed it in. Then we closed the world out and submerged ourselves inside a stormy darkness, roaming deep inside each other's bodies until at last our nerves were calmed. It had been weeks. Our recent emotional distance had made us both too afraid to share such physical intimacy. We had always done so in the past with pleasure. It was too frightening to consider coming together in pain. Afterwards, Aidan lay next to me, running a single finger up and down my spine, and spoke quietly through the darkness.

'You're not to worry, Esther,' he whispered. 'If you don't make a new work, we can submit *The Painted Nude*, or a range of former pieces you've already made.'

'It's OK,' I replied. 'It's coming into focus now. I'll come up with something really soon, I promise.'

I lay in the stillness and listened to Aidan's heartbeat slowing, his breathing become heavy, then even out. I wished I too could sleep, but my recent paralysis had now been replaced by a heady restlessness. My problems were lumbering clumsily around the corridors of my mind, bumping into things as they moved, shaking my memories up. Kenny's call was forcing me to think about big issues: like my real worth as an artist – and about how I was going to stem his interest in my world, too. It had to be through my next project. Why was I finding it so hard to find the next big idea?

I was in the business of making shock-factor art, the kind that causes tabloid headlines and soft-boiled intellectuals to row on the *Late Review*. But my increasing popularity had let a new genie out of my box. The public's gaze added an unanticipated weight to everything I said or did. Critics watched me, took my ideas seriously, or viciously cut them to pieces, and the public had started to want to understand where my true meanings lay. My last project, *The Painted Nude*, had really turned up the heat, made me into something of a household name.

For it, I'd painted my body with words and lain on a chaise-longue in the gallery for twelve consecutive days. It had been a trademark confessional piece, prose poems painted in henna on my skin: down my naked back, across my arms and along my legs, even on the soles of my feet. On each of the twelve days that I performed, new words were applied, their basis being metaphors for each month of the year, describing the way changing seasons make me feel. Film screens formed a backdrop, giving atmosphere – sun, rain, mist, storms. My whispered voice projected the written words around the space. Aidan had billboards made of me, hung them round the country like an advertising campaign. It worked. Overnight Esther Glass became a national brand – with teenage girls my greatest fans. Now they copied my ideas on their own skins, revealing their secrets in painted prose. Their response had made me uneasy; they were the first daughters to join my 'cult' and with them as my followers nothing could ever be the same again. Whatever I now did, I had to bear them in mind. My next project was a rare opportunity, a chance to teach them something more – about the value of womanhood and the value of art. If I failed, all they'd learn would be the cost of my fame. Because of them, I couldn't leave my flat without a disguise. Kids hung outside, scrawled notes to me on the building wall, followed me up the street. This week I was on the cover of OK and Hello! – just for showing up at a premiere of a new art-house film, though admittedly I was wearing a gravity-defying dress designed by Petra. We did one another favours when we could. It was all about sensation, about making waves; and with Kenny pitching up on the scene, the next project didn't only need to fulfil the qualitative criteria I had now set myself, it also had to be big – bigger than The Painted Nude series, bigger and more sensational than anything I'd ever attempted before.

I realized I was particularly freaked out by how familiar to me Kenny's voice seemed, even after such a chasm of time. Did we really never leave anything behind? Was our past stored in our minds like clean film edits, just waiting for a moment to be replayed? Kenny knew as well as I that the drawing had marked a critical day in my life, even if he hadn't been a party to the full repercussions. I guess no one else had. I remember precisely where and when I drew it, to the very hour. Because to me it represented a great deal more than a piece of 'juvenilia'. That drawing marked a moment in my life from which there'd been no going back.

For the first time in more than a decade, the fine details of Kenny Harper's rough-hewn face now nudged their way to the forefront of my mind.

I rolled over and tucked myself into Aidan's sleeping form, and closed my eyes tight to block Kenny out. But his face stayed etched inside my head and, even in the depths of darkness, I couldn't force it away.

3

Stirring slowly, deliciously heavy with sleep, I half opened my eyes and squinted at the Constable clouds scurrying through a pale-blue sky above. Dry grass prickled my back as a shadow crossed me. The figure who'd been lying quietly by my side sensed my return to consciousness and turned. Kenny moved on top of me now and flickered butterfly kisses onto my throat and cheeks. Then his lips sought out mine. He tasted warm and earthy and as sweet as the spring sunshine. I smoothed my hands down his warm, naked back.

'What's the time?'

He laughed gently. 'Gone six. You slept for more than an hour.'

I pushed him back off me and sat upright, pulling my denim miniskirt down over my hips as I glanced around us at the remnants of our afternoon's picnic. An upturned, empty bottle of cider, Kenny's Yamaha 'Fizzy' bike propped against the thick trunk of the old beech tree, my T-shirt in a crumpled heap next to a mustard-yellow espadrille. My sketchbook was open at a drawing of him lying naked on the rug earlier in the afternoon; pencils were scattered among the grass around it. My other shoe lay further away in the hay field, where I'd tossed it earlier in gay abandon. My pink knickers seemed to have disappeared in the excitement of what came next.

'Shit! Ava'll go mad: I'm supposed to be at her talk.'

Kenny chuckled and pushed me down under him again, smoothing my hair back from my face. 'You're even more sexy when you're worried,' he said.

His accent had a slight West Country lilt to it, a Hardy-esque resonance that had initially attracted me to him. It made me feel like Tess of the d'Urbevilles, with him one of the woodlanders. I liked to act, play characters, and Tess was my current favourite. She was on my English syllabus. I looked at the punnet of strawberries I'd bought as a result of Hardy's metaphoric fascination with wild fruits. We'd eaten a couple from each other's mouths, then discarded the rest to become warm and flaccid in the sunshine. They'd been enough to help move us on to ever-sweeter delights.

Kenny and I'd met at The Hobnails a few days before. It was an old local pub hidden inside dense beech woods, somewhere only locals knew about, a 'safe house' where Gabriel, the ancient publican, was left alone to practise his own laws, turning a blind eye on both under-age and after-hours drinking – all in the name of equilibrium. The beer came up from barrels in the cellar. Nothing was on tap, apart from personal favours. Everyone was on the make in one small way or another. Even Pete Sargeant, the appropriately named local bobby on the beat, was one of the more regular customers. No one wanted any trouble round here: everything was focused on sustaining an easy life and helping one another out of sticky spots. I'm sure Sargeant Sargeant could have expensed his pints – he got most of his tip-offs about the local troublemakers from late-night alcohol-loosened tongues in 'The Hob'.

Kenny had been standing over a cloudy, caramel-tinted pint, thick elbow balanced on the bar, talking quietly to Gabriel, with the pub's old sheepdog lying contentedly at his feet. He looked crafted from the countryside that encircled us, tall and thick-set as the trees, with a wide, expansive face, and a mass of long, thick, curling hair. He was natural, unpolluted, without manicure. Everything about him was slightly wild, particularly the look in his eye.

When he saw me approach, Kenny glanced up and Gabriel smiled in welcome, then introduced me merrily.

'Ah, Kenny: Esther Glass, one of my new regulars – from down at Ickfield Folly.'

Kenny eyed me with clear interest, nodded, then took a long, slow swig of his pint. He had broad hands with tattoos across the knuckles. On the right it said *power*, on the left, *glory*.

'Kenny's Mike Harper's young lad,' Gabriel continued, a touch wistfully. 'I miss his presence at my bar. We went back as far as the war,' he looked between us and chuckled, 'before you nippers had even entered the world.'

I knew who Mike Harper was, and I'd heard all about his wayward son. No one had seen Kenny for a couple of years. Rumour had it he'd been doing time. Meanwhile Mike had passed away. As far as I could remember, Mrs Harper had been out of the picture for decades. Their cottage had been left empty. I knew where it was: on the edge of the woods, the other side from the folly.

'It's good to have some of his flesh and blood back in the village,' Gabriel pontificated as he moved slowly off down the bar to serve another regular.

Kenny and I struck up tentative conversation. He told me he was staying at his dad's old cottage for a while and when I left I knew it wouldn't be long before our paths through the woods crossed again.

Now I could feel distinct pressure from his groin against my stomach. Wriggling sideways, I determinedly forced myself free and got up, shaking grass seeds from my hair. I picked more off my *Echo and the Bunnymen* T-shirt and pulled it on over my head. I hadn't been wearing a bra. I didn't need to: my breasts were firm, taut. Earlier I had wanted him to be conscious of my nipples protruding provocatively beneath the black cotton. The plan had proved effective.

As I began to gather up my sketchpad and pencils, Kenny accepted defeat and he, too, rose, put his own – still buttoned – shirt over his head. Then he lit a finely rolled joint, pulled from behind his ear. The smell of freshly burning marijuana blended perfectly with the rise of an early-evening breeze. I turned and watched him for a brief moment. Kenny was rough-shaven, broad-shouldered, with gorgeous long ringlets of liquorice-coloured hair – due, he had told me flirtatiously that first night in the pub, to his mother's gypsy blood. He excited me. He tasted of a different, foreign world, one disinterested in intellectual ideologies and the constraints imposed by the group living to which I was accustomed. He was focused, he had told me playfully, only on the ways of one individual, himself, and on the precise moment he inhabited. He was from the outside, a free traveller in life, never still, always unsettled and inconstant, a bit of a loner and, best of all, quite a lot older than I was. *Mature.* Twenty, in fact, just the week before.

'Come on, Est,' he coaxed me now, his jet-black eyes twinkling in the ripening sun, 'I'll give you a backy.'

I held his waist tight as we flew, helmet-free, between green streaks of hedgerow frothing with cow parsley, his old motorbike purring like a calmed cat. Above us a canopy of chestnut trees laden with flowering candles reached out across the lanes to touch one another's branches candidly. At his shirt's neckline, Kenny's skin was russet-blushed from its first contact of the year with the sun. I nuzzled my face into it and shut my eyes. My long dark hair flew out behind me. It was the end of May, I was sixteen years old and deeply immersed in a passionate, all-consuming love – and, more significantly, freed at last of my childhood. Kenny had taken it from me without coercion. In fact I had positively encouraged the act. As he drove me towards the folly, I revelled in this new feeling; I was now a 'real' woman. It hadn't even hurt. Admittedly, there hadn't been much pleasure in the experience – but maybe, I thought, that would come later.

The journey left me exhilarated, breathless. By the main gates I got off the bike and Kenny leant forward to kiss me, a deep, searching kiss that left me trembling, then he pulled back and smiled knowingly, pushing my hair away from my face once more. Eager to mark this moment between us, I tore the page from my sketchpad quickly and handed it to him.

'My thank you,' I giggled, then turned and ran along the edge of the path to the house, trying to avoid my feet crunching too noisily on the gravel.

The main hall was hushed. I tried to push the door open silently but knew exactly at which point it would creak. Predictably, as it did so, the audience, numbering thirty, (I knew, I had set up the chairs earlier), turned in unison to clock the late arrival. Bunch of losers, I thought, as I pushed my head high and sat down on the single spare black plastic chair at the back, crossing my long legs carefully, only now aware of my lack of underwear. I pulled a piece of stray grass from the seam of my skirt and twisted it between my fingers, then glanced up at the main speaker. Ava was already up on the podium with her glasses settled on the tip of her nose. She was looking up from the notes held in her right hand, staring straight back at me. I detected a slight frown on her brow as my eyes now focused, then locked with hers; I couldn't help myself and smirked, defiantly. Her kohl-lined eyes glinted at me, coldly, two perfect, polished opals. She had pulled her sleek grey hair back in a neat chignon and wore a duck-egg-blue linen dress, cut straight across at the neckline. No jewellery. Indeed, she was in need of no further embellishment. Ava was tall, slender-necked and narrow-wristed, as elegant as a swan – and, as I knew to my detriment, with a similar hiss if riled.

My father, Simeon, was looking directly at me too, but his gaze was far more weary than my mother's. He was leaning back in his chair at the front, which was set to look out towards the audience, next to Mum's podium. His long, slim legs crossed at the ankle; on his feet were soft beige leather mules. He was wearing old faded jeans and a plain white, cheesecloth shirt. His arms were folded behind his head and he was surveying the group with an air of quizzical interest. My father was always keen to gauge their response: after all, it was material for his next paper.

I imagine he had just completed Ava's introduction. Beside, yet below her, my father paled into insignificance, as did most people in her presence. It suddenly occurred to me that, on this occasion, he really did seem indeterminate, almost transparent. There was no energy around him, none at all. He was beginning to look old. I'd never noticed it before. But he was sixty-six now. Mum was still in her mid-forties, and although her hair was completely grey (she of course refused to dye it) her complexion was still flawless, her face almost devoid of wrinkles. Simeon'd been her sugar daddy – or drug daddy, should I say. He had really been the hand that introduced her to an alternative future. It was he who had acquired the tenancy of the folly, he who had invited the first few visionary people to join them there; an early shaper of this world that she had since come to rule with an aptitude none could have foreseen.

Ava practised her own brand of alternative philosophy. She was an academic with extreme feminist principles, which matched the liberal attitude of Simeon and his cronies. Ava was autonomous here. At this time, her relationship with Simeon was purely platonic. In fact, it had been, as far as I could tell, from the day I was conceived. They never shared a bedroom, let alone a bed. She was with John Cressfield, the poet, now. It seemed to mean something to them both, although I hadn't quite got to grips with the basis of their love affair. It seemed to have emerged out of a malaise. They'd been around each other for so long I couldn't figure out how their relationship could suddenly have ignited strong passions. It seemed unwholesome – and unnecessary. They were too old, I thought, as I watched her. I also felt their close-ness upset some of the equilibrium at the folly. It was always better when there were fewer obvious alliances. I think Simeon felt it too, but he'd never say. He was too busy being fair-minded to express a strong emotion like jealousy or rage.

Simeon had set up this week-long workshop for devotees to their naturalist beliefs, and, as ever, Mum had been rolled on as the keynote speaker to close the conference. It was pretty convenient, their double act. He literally provided the stage on which she could stand. And she, in turn, could always attract the audiences to keep the whole show on the road.

'Margaret Thatcher pronounces feminism a cause without virtue . . .' she began as my mind started to drift back to my lascivious afternoon with Kenny. I could still feel drips of his moisture between my thighs. Later, once this event was over, I would cycle back to the woods, meet him at the pub and, afterwards, we could do it all over again, maybe at the cottage, in front of a fire. This time I'd leave my sketchbook at home. I could hardly enter this personal project for my A level, after all. Imagine the examiner's response. I knew my drawings of Kenny were better than anything anyone in the class could dream of producing – even had a touch of early Klimt about them, perhaps. I might not be interested in more studious subjects at school, but I sure could draw – and act, too. My ambition was to take to the stage. Right now, I was practising 'demure'. Which was proving more difficult than 'Tess', particularly considering the length of my skirt, lack of knickers, and the nature of the thoughts running through my mind. But I would need to convince Simeon and Ava of my continuing innocence if I was to continue to enjoy the luxury of their liberal parenting. I knew that, if they thought I was making out with a gypsy in the woods, the gates would be closing firmly around the folly at night, my bike confiscated and locked away.

A massive thud interrupted my thoughts. I looked up at the same time as the audience seemed to surge to its feet with a collective 'Ohhh'.

Ava was already down off the podium and then I noticed him:

Simeon, lying on the floor, convulsions gripping his body. I found myself frozen to my seat, couldn't move forwards to help.

'Someone get a doctor,' Ava was instructing, her voice unusually high and breathless.

She held Simeon's head in her hands and murmured to him as he continued to fit, his face turning a deep, angry, explosive purple. It was then I began to hear him moaning, a low-pitched, primeval sound, like a wild animal caught in a huntsman's trap. Someone was trying to press their hands down on his chest. I think I heard them say, 'I am a doctor.'

After an interminable period of time, the moaning ceased and Simeon became still. A trickle of blood left the side of his mouth and flowed evenly down his face to form a small scarlet pool on the parquet floor. The pressure had been released – albeit too late. His brown eyes were staring up at the ceiling, open, but lifeless.

Now his moaning had ceased I could detect a second, more pitiful whimpering. It was Ava, shuddering over him like an injured dog, with her head heavy on his chest. Her hair had fallen from its knot, uncoiled down her back like a loose rope. People began to move away, their heads bowed, shoulders rounded, out of respect, not knowing what else they could do. Someone put their hand on my shoulder and I flinched at the touch, but it released me from my paralysis. I felt cold as I stood up and began to walk forwards. The crowd parted and I passed their watchful eyes, my own now fixed firmly on my destination: the inanimate form of my dead father.

4

Eventually I left Aidan sleeping and made my way home. I needed to be alone to think, to clear my head. I spent the day pacing my studio, scribbling notes and ideas on the whiteboard, but nothing seemed forthcoming. No one called and only Aidan texted, to say he'd missed me when he woke up. I responded with the words **Don't take it personally. Just had to work!**

Which I'm sure would have met with his approval. It was true Kenny had stirred me up, but the solution still seemed out of reach. By mid-evening I collapsed onto my bed and shut my eyes. For all my scrawling nothing seemed to have come to light. But then suddenly, from out of nowhere, I knew exactly what I needed to do. I sprang from my bed as if someone had given me magic shoes, and manically cleaned from the length of the whiteboard all the marks I had made. Then I grabbed my phone and clicked through my messages, until I came across the critical one that had triggered my chain of thoughts. I copied Aidan's words in large capital letters along the wall: I'D NEVER SELL YOU, EST; YOU'RE MY MASTERPIECE.

I stood back and looked at them long and hard and I knew the solution to all my problems was staring me in the face. The idea set like cement in my mind before I had a chance to think it through. Perhaps he'd just have to sell me – and the concept of me being a masterpiece wasn't such a bad one either. It was the most sensationalist notion I had ever had. I would get Aidan to auction me, to put me up for sale, as a living, breathing work of art. I was a performer, after all. My face was as famous as my work; in fact, to all intents and purposes, it *was* my art. I was a showgirl, my own masterpiece; the ultimate symbol of our culture's self-obsession. My value was in my flesh and blood – they were, after all, the only real tools of my trade. Forget childish doodles, forget Kenny Harper and his stupid little story: this way we'd all discover how much I was really worth. And I'd offer the news exclusively to the *Clarion*, too – with the proviso they dropped their offer to Kenny Harper. There was no way they'd refuse. I knew their game too well. The focus would change, I would be back in control and life could carry on as before. My heart was racing. I had to see Aidan, I had to tell him *now*.

He was at the gallery, working on papers, and looked surprised but pleased when I buzzed on the door.

Before he had a chance to speak, I blurted out, 'I've got it.'

He leant back in his chair, folded his arms and nodded for me to continue, a wry smile on his lips.

'I want you to sell me,' I said, a touch defiantly, and smiled in return.

Aidan's turquoise eyes narrowed. 'What are you talking about?' he said.

'Forget doodles from my childhood,' I replied slowly. 'Put me up for auction at Sotheby's, as a living work of art.' My heart pumped mightily. 'I want to know how much I'm really worth.'

Aidan's eyes held mine for a second more, then he looked away. 'It's ridiculous,' he said categorically, watching his foot kick at a piece of tape stuck to the floor.

'Why?'

He shook his head from side to side and kicked a little harder, then glanced back up, allowing his eyes to hold mine for a brief second. 'It's a stupid idea, Esther. Anyone could bid for you, any fucking madman. I won't let you do it.'

I felt panic, then a flame ignited inside me. 'Only yesterday you were blithely recommending we flog any old bits of me,' I said. 'Why not sell off the real thing? I'm sure you'll be up for a healthy commission.'

For a moment Aidan looked confused, then I saw silver shards cutting through his eyes, like broken glass. 'Is that really what this is all about?' He sounded deflated.

I almost wanted to say forget it, to turn the clock back. But I knew instinctively that the idea would work. I had to persuade him to support me. We had time to do it before I needed to deliver to the Tate. It solved so many problems, all in one go.

'Your response did trigger the idea,' I replied resolutely, 'but the more I think about it, the more convinced I am it's the perfect next project for me.'

'I thought I was the one who came up with the marketing pranks,' he said, uncharacteristically snidely.

'It's not a prank.'

'Well, then, what the fuck is it, Esther? A game?'

'This might prove to be the first project in my career that isn't a game,' I replied, my voice rising. 'I'm deadly serious; I want to question my value, the value of this whole goddam industry. I want to know how much I'm really worth.'

'I think you should sleep on it, Esther,' he said evenly. 'We can talk more in the morning.'

'If you don't want to take my next project on, then I'll just have to find an agent who does,' I shouted.

Despite his café-latte skin, I could see the blood draining from Aidan's face. He put both hands down on his desk and leant forward towards me. I could see he was trembling.

'Is that really what you want?' he whispered, tersely.

I didn't answer. There didn't seem much more to say.

Giving up, Aidan got up from his desk, turned on his heel and stalked out, slamming the door forcefully behind him.

I went back home feeling deflated. Aidan's and my lives were as embedded in one another as brushstrokes on a canvas. It was impossible to distinguish one mark from the next. I couldn't believe that I'd suggested breaking our faith, but then equally I also couldn't believe Kenny Harper had come back into my life. For however much Aidan and I shared the present, I'd never given him anything of my past. When we met I was already through art college, I was already set on my path, already making up stories to tell about myself through my art – that was the Esther Glass that Aidan had first got to know and I wasn't about to show him another me. I couldn't: it would change the ground we existed upon. I didn't know what would occur the next day. But I knew one heart-chilling fact. I was determined to see this project through, with or without Aidan's support. It suddenly seemed essential, not only to keep the media away from Kenny's door, but also to ensure I retained my place at the forefront of my profession. The idea was scintillating, it was extreme, it was sensational. In fact, everything about it was perfect for my current predicament and for me. I didn't feel I had a choice but to see it through.

The next day Aidan called me up and asked me to come back in. He was cool on the phone, gave nothing away. I had woken feeling defiant and arrived at his office ready for another stand-off. To my surprise there was no need for a fight.

'OK, Esther, I've decided to support the project,' he said definitively. 'But as your friend, I want you to know I think you're making a mistake.'

A wave of relief spread through me. I'd never worked without Aidan's backing. I wasn't sure I'd know how to. 'Thank you,' I whispered. 'You know I have to challenge the ground I'm standing on.'

Aidan was silent for a while, then he spoke. 'What I don't under-stand is why you feel the need to play this issue out on a public stage. If you're worried about your value, about the future, we should talk about it together, in private. The idea that I'm trying to exploit you is, quite frankly, an insult.'

'My art's always been a performance, Aidan. You know that better than anyone else. It's who I am.'

His eyes challenged me. 'Are you sure?'

'Sure?'

'That this is about your art?'

I shrugged. 'Something has to give,' I reasoned.

'Maybe I've been too preoccupied with the gallery, with the public eye,' Aidan murmured. 'I'm sorry if I haven't been a support.'

'No. It's your job to do that. I understand, but I don't know where my values lie any more. I'm not sure I ever have. I think this could be a way for me to step back and take an objective look.'

'At you, your art, or us?'

I paused and tried to find an honest answer. If I told him about Kenny's threat, maybe he'd begin to understand. But then I'd have to tell him about the rest of it, too. I couldn't do that. Our relationship had started because of my art, not my past, and the business of selling me had always been at the core.

'Aren't they all one and the same thing?' I said, finally.

'Est, don't confuse your work with your life. If you're determined to go through with this idea, try to remember you're not selling your soul. Keep a little left over for you – and for us.'

5

A period of détente set in between us after Aidan consented to taking my new project on. I left the gallery that afternoon saying I'd get straight on with developing the concept in detail and we agreed to meet four days later with Katie to talk plans through. He didn't call during that time, and neither did I. I felt anxiety and excitement in equal measure. Each morning I bought the *Clarion* and scoured it for stories, but none came to light. And each time the phone rang I jumped nervously before answering it, anticipating another call from Kenny. But none was forthcoming.

So I threw myself into the concept, and began working with a new ferocity and speed lost to me over previous months. It was as if this whole episode had lifted a massive dark cloud that had settled above me and I was seeing sharply again, through a bright, searing light.

The idea of being sold as a masterpiece was potent. But which masterpiece should I be? And once I was sold, what exactly would my collector get for the money? This whole art thing, it had started out as a game – a way to move on from the past and avoid the mundane. There'd been no great agenda: I'd happened upon my vocation like a child who has stumbled over a dressing-up box and excitedly tries on each costume in turn. Until now, each act had evolved seamlessly out of the last, none had taken long to contrive, and each had been more successful, more entertaining to see through, than the last. My main approach was to dress up, record videos of myself, and take photographs that told fictionalized stories about my invented past lives. But with this new project I wanted to take the idea further. Instead of acting out stories apparently about myself, I decided I wanted to tell not one but a series of stories about other women, women who exist in paintings, in masterpieces from the past.

I would get Sotheby's to auction me for seven days. And on each day I would perform for my collector, as a different work of art. The starting point for each act would be a masterpiece, a portrait of a woman. I would try to reassess their values from a contemporary perspective and so tell a revised art history, one perceived through female eyes.

Museums across the world are filled with masterpieces and that's literally what they are: master pieces – artworks commissioned by men, painted by men and mostly intended for men to view. The reason for the higher worth of one painting over another often has more to do with who financed and owned it than the qualities of the work of art itself. Until the past thirty years women really have only registered in the art world as sitters inside the frames – with a few exceptions, of course. So the past has one critical element missing: the woman's view.

Once I'd worked out my premise, I spent the next three days trawling through museum catalogues, leafing through books at the V&A in search of the perfect partners. I wanted to choose portraits of women to whom I could readily respond, women who seemed to have something more to say underneath the surface of the canvas-watchers' eyes. I wanted to discover their secrets and tell the true stories of their lives. I came up with twenty portraits very quickly, but struggled to reduce my shortlist from twenty to ten, then finally from ten to seven. But on the morning of the fourth day I made my choice. There was no time to lose and I felt I had the perfect catch.

I arrived at the gallery a few minutes early for our meeting. Aidan was at his desk and I noted he looked tired. He was cool towards me, businesslike. I suppose it was what I expected, but all the same I couldn't help but be excited by my plan. The project details had fallen into place with such ease that I knew it was right, that it was going to work. And I had thought through every angle. It was watertight. I couldn't see how he could criticize the series. Soon Katie joined us, her eyes twinkling with anticipation. She must have been relieved to see me coming up with the goods. And so the meeting began.

I described the project and showed Katie and Aidan reproductions of my seven chosen portraits. I was a seasoned performer, and my performances were what people had always paid to see. I video'd my pieces to turn them into permanent works. But the live aspect of what I did was critical. I liked to perform to an audience. For me, that was where the magic lay – somewhere in the space between the artwork and the viewer. So, for this particular week, I suggested I should plan seven ten-minute acts for my collector, one for every day I was owned, each a view that could be held in private or public, depending on its nature. We'd ask Petra to collaborate on my costumes. Petra and I were old college friends and she'd made many outfits for me in the past. She was currently working in Paris. Aidan and Katie agreed and we left a message on her voicemail, asking her to call.

I would film each performance and produce a series from them for the Tate. Once the exhibition tour was over, the purchaser would own the complete work. I'd need to plan precisely what those performances would mean, but for now I knew only the over-riding theme: it had to be possession, in its widest – and wildest – senses. I just needed to find some vehicle to pull it all together. I thought of the crumpled cars downstairs and hoped my project wouldn't end in a crash.

Aidan flicked through his address book as we talked. Katie threw in the odd question, then typed up the details. Four hours later, and we had it all fleshed out. There was an auction at Sotheby's at the end of

February. We had sixteen weeks for me to plan my sale and for Aidan to find a cash-rich collector. Aidan agreed we could invest £40,000 in the development of the work. That would give Petra £20,000 for the costumes, me £20,000 to spend on travel and accessories. In order to break even, we'd worked out I needed to sell for £60,000. It seemed, to me, a reasonable price.

I had chosen paintings from seven different collections around the world, giving the project a historic and geographic reach. I would have to go and see the pictures, each one in turn, before the auction. Katie agreed to plan my itinerary. With everything that was going on in London, it would be good to have an excuse to spend some short trips away. The research would take me on a whistle-stop tour of six cities over twelve weeks, starting here in London, then heading to Paris, on to Nantes, back to London, then over to New York, Vienna and, finally, Venice, returning just in time to prepare for the night of my sale.

Aidan listened in without interjecting as Katie and I brainstormed details.

I was pleased that the concept so obviously had Katie hooked. Her enthusiasm was bound to imbue Aidan over time. When she'd finished he scanned the document, looked up over it and gazed at me. I smiled and, despite himself, he reciprocated. It was a certain kind of smile, loose and general, unless you knew how to read beneath its surface, like Braille. Katie saw it but was blind. The smile is one he reserves only for me, and the sight of it made me feel reassured.

'I'll set up a meeting with Sotheby's,' he said, slowly. 'We need to get you in their February sale – that's if they'll have you. I think that's it for now.'

He closed his diary and Katie took her leave. The meeting was over. Once she'd gone I sat forward.

'There's one more thing,' I said, as casually as I could.

'Go on,' Aidan answered.

'I want to give exclusivity over the project to John Herbert at the *Clarion*. I don't want the journos fighting against us on this one. Lincoln's been double-crossing me and I think we need to switch allegiances – for this project only. I reckon we should aim for as wide a media hit on it as we can, to get the message out, find appropriate collectors. It has the widest circulation of all the newspapers – and, like me, it's the most sensationalist.'

Aidan eyed me suspiciously. 'What's really going on, Esther?' he asked calmly. 'What have they got on you?'

I could feel a blush rising, and tried my best to contain it. 'I don't know what you mean,' I answered, avoiding his eyes. 'I just think it's best. And I'll call John Herbert myself. Then you and Katie can sort out details on price, OK?'

Aidan leant forward across his desk and looked at me hard. 'I don't know your real reasons for doing this project,' he said quietly, 'but you know my view and it won't change. So you go ahead and direct the process, Esther. Whatever you want. And I'll just sit back and concentrate on my part, on the business of selling you.'

As soon as I got home I called John Herbert.

He sounded pleased, rather than surprised, to hear my voice. 'How are you, Esther? Long time no speak,' he said, his voice rough as the gutter dirt embedded within it.

'Good, good,' I answered, 'and I've got a proposition for you. Have you got time to talk?'

'I've always got time for you, Esther. Now tell me, what's on your mind?'

I trod carefully, making no mention of Kenny or his sketch, but by implication I made it clear I knew that offers had been made in that respect and John made no attempt to deny the fact. I told him I had something bigger and better to give them, an exclusive on my next project, explaining that it was sensational and newsworthy, but that the story would come at a price and, I added, as if as an afterthought, with one proviso – that the little auction of my sketch and the person behind its sale wouldn't be appearing in the *Clarion*'s column inches for the foreseeable future. At this John laughed knowingly and readily gave me his promise. I didn't trust him as far as I could throw him, but I had to take my chance. 'So, how do I get the details of your new art-work?' he asked enthusiastically. I told him to call Katie but that I would prefer him not to discuss the little issue of the sketch with her. He agreed readily and I hung up confident that, at least in the short term, John Herbert would respect our agreement. I was worth too much as a media personality right now for him not to want me on his side.

I had one more night to wait before Kenny's promised call. He was the last fix I needed to make and, so long as he was playing ball, I hoped then to close this whole sorry episode and get on with the real business of my life, the business of making art. I had colour copies of my seven chosen portraits hanging in a row along the studio wall. I lay back on my bed and watched as the fading light reduced them to spectres and wondered what our shared future held in store. They seemed to be eyeing me expectantly, as if anticipating orders. I was dying to get on with it, to breathe new life into them – with a contemporary twist or two, of course. But first I needed to get Kenny off my back, and, second, I needed to introduce them to my one live collaborator. Who else but Petra could help me get this one off the ground? She'd agreed in principle to take the commission on, and we'd made a plan for her to make a quick trip to London for the weekend to talk it through.

I got undressed and into bed. I was restless and edgy, thinking about Kenny's impending call. When I finally dozed off he was roaming around in my mind and my dreams took me straight back there again, into the heart of the matter.

6

I tapped lightly on the door and slipped inside the large, gloomy bed-room. Ava was sitting on its far side, at her mahogany dressing table, her back to me, attaching large silver hooped earrings to her lobes. I could smell Cacharel in the air, like fresh rain sprayed over a cool morning. I couldn't remember the last time she'd worn scent.

'Are you ready?'

'I won't be a moment,' she said falteringly, a fraction above a whisper. She was wearing a long, blue-green, silk dress, the fabric shimmering like kingfisher's wings, and around her shoulders a lime-green, crocheted shawl threaded through with fine strands of gold. Her hair was piled up on top of her head, held in place with a large, shiny, mother-of-pearl comb. She resembled an exotic, tropical bird.

As Ava glanced up at me now, I caught her eye in the reflection of the glass. Immediately, she looked away. Her eyes were free of tears, but beneath them her skin was uncharacteristically pale and puffy. I approached the table and held out my hand. She turned and took it between hers. They were icy.

'Simeon loved you very, very much. You do know that, don't you?' Her words sounded fragile. I didn't reply. Instead I looked away to the floor. This didn't seem the right moment to talk about me.

*

Everyone was assembled downstairs in the main hall, waiting for us. As Ava and I descended the main stairs together, all heads turned to watch and the hushed conversations faded to a dense silence. Like Ava, everyone else was dressed in a colour from the rainbow – as Simeon had requested in his will. Apart from me, that is.

I wore black: black plimsolls, a black bead ankle bracelet and bangles, a long, black crepe skirt, my black *Echo and the Bunnymen* T-shirt under a black shirt with black buttons, a black cloak with a fox fur hanging around my neck – and, for contrast, a white cotton ruff and cuffs – black eye make-up, black lipstick and glinting jet-black stud earrings – oh, and to break it up a bit, a pair of soft, beige kid-leather gloves. I had scraped my hair back from my face and wore a black velvet cap over the top of it. Fuck their hippy shit. I felt black. It was, after all, my father's funeral.

'Holbein would have been proud of you,' Ava had whispered in my ear, smiling gently, as we left her bedroom.

I knew she'd recognize the references. It was our secret, our shared painting. Simeon had loved it, too. There was a poster of *Christina of Denmark, Duchess of Milan*, fading and curled at the corners, in his bathroom, tacked to the wall. We'd bought it for him the first time Ava had taken me to the National Gallery, about five years before. We'd chosen her together as our favourite work in the collection. Ava said there was something about her that was like me, but she couldn't put her finger on exactly what. Simeon had agreed.

As dusk fell, the most senior male members of the commune carried the body of their former leader, mentor and friend out of the library on a simple stretcher. It had lain there in wake since Simeon's death five days earlier, while all the formalities were put in place. Today they had wrapped him in layers of natural hemp. The parcel looked vulnerable, too small to contain the body of a man.

We followed after the bearers, through the folly's wide oak doors, first Ava with John by her side, then me, with Kay and Jo, my commune allies, by mine. Behind us the rest of our clan came, eighteen of us in all; adults and children alike joined in collective mourning.

We crunched down the gravel driveway. At the end, some three hundred or more other friends and supporters joined our procession. They looked like they'd gathered for one of our infamous festivals – everyone dressed colourfully, only the mood implying the unusual nature of the event. From here, we took a left along a pathway cut for the occasion through the wild-flower meadow, redolent with the heady scent of sweet peas and hollyhocks and humming poignantly with Simeon's honey bees, frenziedly feeding from the early-evening nectar. Next we shuffled, single-file, along the edge of the thriving vegetable gardens, the bier precariously raised ahead of us to avoid collision with the hedgerows. Our track then took us on into the cool darkness of the small copse, past the tree house and well-worn rope swings where the commune's children normally played. Here candles had been lit and silk ribbons of various hues hung prettily from branches, like bunting heralding the imminence of a village fête. Finally, we passed through a handcrafted wooden gate into a small stone-walled garden: Simeon's final resting-place.

The garden lay at the edge of the estate, next to adjoining farmland. It contained two apple trees and a pear tree, a weeping cherry and a small round pond, full of flowering white water lilies, all planted by Simeon over the previous two decades. The scent of the lilies permeated the garden: sickly sweet and intoxicating. A few of the commune's pet animals had been interred here during the intervening years, but Simeon was to be the first human lowered into this secular ground. It was fitting that he should be the first one, particularly as he was the founder of our community and the greatest champion of the human right to natural burial.

It took a while for everyone to crowd into the garden. Ava and I were at the front, poised precariously next to the narrow, deep hole. I wished Kenny were there. Kay and Jo sang an old folk song as

Simeon's body was lowered into the ground. I felt myself swaying forwards, as if there was a curious magnetic pull on my spirit to join him there. Ava clutched my arm and pulled me back. Then John read a long, rambling poem composed for the occasion and I felt my mind bleaching to white. As the sun smouldered, then set in the sky, one of the children played a flute and we each threw handfuls of red rose petals from a large basket into the grave, followed by a handful of moist, rich earth. Afterwards we turned slowly and, in reverse order, made our way back through the fast-fading light towards the folly. The air felt damper and despite all my clothes I was cold. It was time to get inside, time to celebrate Simeon's life.

Three hours later and I had had my share of spliff and reminiscences. As the band began to play I slipped upstairs and removed my mourning clothes. I left them in a heap on the floor, put on my jeans and a jumper, then sneaked back down and left the folly by the scullery door. I skulked across the lawn to the barn, grabbed my bike and wheeled it quietly down the edge of the drive, avoiding the gravel. Then I pedalled like mad until the lights from the folly's windows no longer lit up the lane. Now only the glimmer of a half moon and a sprinkling of stars highlighted the white petals of wild flowers along the hedgerows. I cycled faster. The air was fecund, fresh and very damp. I sucked it in too fast and the effect made me dizzy, but I continued to push hard on the pedals, too intent on my destination to care. I couldn't wait to see Kenny, to feel his arms around me. But when I got to the cottage it was shrouded in darkness. Over the previous three nights Kenny had left the outside light on to help me find my way. I leant my bike against a tree and crept up to his bedroom window to peer inside. Maybe he was already sleeping – or perhaps he was still at the pub? But it was already past midnight. I had told him I'd come when I could. Each night since Simeon's death I'd slept there, soundly, in the big old, damp double bed, locked inside Kenny's comforting embrace. No one from the folly noticed my late-night disappearances, or my failure to emerge for breakfast. They were too preoccupied with the occasion of a death to contemplate the surreptitious antics of the living.

But now, as my eyes acclimatized to the darkness, I realized that the cottage was empty, the bed was made. Kenny wasn't there. I took a slow walk around, glancing in through each of the cobweb-covered windows in turn, just to be sure. It was only after I'd gone full circle that I noticed the white envelope, propped up on the kitchen windowsill. I picked it up and saw my misspelt name written in slanting capital letters on the front. I ripped the envelope open. It took me a while to read what was within. The light was so dim I had to turn the paper up to the moon and wait for a clear beam to guide me through Kenny's scrawl. It was the first and last time I would see his handwriting.

Esta,
    I'm sorry I didn't get to say goodbye, but the road beckons and I had to go. Me and my old bike can't settle anywhere for long. If I hadn't met you we'd have cleared out of here Monday. I'm sorry about your dad, it's a real shame. You take care and keep drawing!!!
Kenny xx

My hands were shaking. Suddenly the woods seemed very deep and dark and forbidding, full of hidden meanings and memories, the ancient roots of whistling trees stirring inside the timeworn earth, earth where Simeon now lay, sleeping his eternal sleep. I felt my legs give way and I crumpled in a heap on the stone doorstep in the pitch dark, my head finding my hands. And for the first time since Simeon's death, I wept.

I awoke to a bitterly bright summer dawn, the birds shrieking through the trees with cruel delight. It could have been no more than three or four in the morning. I forced my stiff limbs up from the ground, got on my bike and cycled back to the folly.

Ava was perched on the front porch in her peacock-coloured clothes, a thick rug about her shoulders, head lolling to one side against the red brickwork of the house. When she saw me she stumbled to her feet and began running down the drive towards me. Her grey hair hung in tangles around her face, her eyes were haunted, sleep-devoid. I dismounted and she flung herself into my arms, breathing fast, tears coursing down her face: two deep rivers of woe.

'I thought I'd lost you, too,' she moaned.

In some ways she was right, if a touch premature, to mourn my passing. I left the folly later that summer and I never went back, not once.

7

I was dreaming about falling when the phone rang. I glanced at my bedside clock. It was 8 a.m. I had never been an early riser and found myself grappling with the receiver.

'You still in bed?'

Kenny's words woke me with a start. They seemed too familiar, too intimate. I didn't know this person any more and he gave me the creeps. But I needed his buy in for my offer: I had to try and sound pleased to hear him.

'Just waking up. How are you?' I asked.

'All right, yeah.'

I sat up and hugged my knees to my chest. 'Can I buy the sketches from you?' I asked quickly. 'I'd love to have them back.'

Kenny chortled. 'You know,' he said, 'after I left that summer, after your dad an' all that, well, I came back to see you.'

My heart began to sink. So the sketches were just the start of it. I remained silent. I was going to have to hear him out.

'Funny thing was, you'd upped and left. No one seemed to know where you'd gone.'

'I came to London,' I said quietly. Suddenly I felt deeply melancholic. 'There didn't seem much to wait around for.'

'Well, I knew that much,' he carried on slowly. 'See, remember

Gabriel? Well, he told me where you were, and I came lookin' for you.'

I felt stunned and confused. Gabriel used to know everything about everyone, his pub was the heart of our village community, but I didn't think anyone knew where I'd gone, not even him.

'He told me you were rumoured to be at a certain address,' he carried on, ignoring my silence. 'Some flat near Paddington station. Maida Vale, I think it was. So I came up on my bike, but when I got there some African bloke opened the door. I remember it really well because he had a spliff in his hand. Anyway, he told me some girl called something posh like Emmeline lived upstairs, and that she was up the duff. So I guessed I'd got the wrong house, bought some dope off him, and left.'

'Yes, you must have done,' I said drily.

'Imagine my amazement,' he carried on, 'when I saw your face in a newspaper a few years later – Esther Glass becoming a famous artist. Imagine how I laughed.'

'What do you want from me, Kenny?' I asked quietly, coldly. I was hating this conversation and I wanted him to go away. 'I don't go in much for trips down memory lane.'

He laughed. 'I don't want anything really. Just thought I'd tell you my story – you know, I s'pose that would be the conclusion if the paper ran it, wouldn't it?'

'They're not going to run your story, Kenny,' I replied resolutely. 'John Herbert spoke to me yesterday. He's changed his mind.'

Kenny faltered. Obviously he was unaware that I'd struck my own deal.

'But as it is,' I continued, 'I do want to buy those sketches, and I'll add some, what should I call it, compensation, I suppose, for that wasted trip to London all that time ago, and the missed chance with the *Clarion*, too. What do you think?'

'That would be a help, Esther,' he answered slowly. 'Yeah, that would be a help.' He cleared his throat, 'Ummm, how much did you have in mind?'

'Twenty-five thousand pounds,' I said frigidly. 'Cash.' I hoped it would be more than he was expecting. I wanted him to feel I'd done him proud. Luckily I'd just got a commission cheque for *The Painted Nude*.

He hesitated a moment and I could hear the phone clicking some more. Where was he calling from? When he responded, he couldn't disguise his mirth.

'I knew you'd see it from my point of view, Esther. You were always understanding, I'm pleased nothing's changed.'

'How am I to get the drawings?', I asked. I wanted it over with. I wanted him off my phone for good.

Kenny gave me a Clapham address and asked me to go there the following Thursday at 3 p.m., cash in hand. I agreed readily and before I rang off blatantly said I didn't expect to be hearing from him again.

'Don't worry,' he replied. 'I'll be off on a long trip come the end of the month.' And then, as with the previous call, suddenly the phone clicked off and he was gone. I crawled back under my covers and shut my eyes, feeling dirty and abused.

8

The *Clarion* ran my story on its front page the next morning. The headline read ESTHER SELLS HERSELF and the story detailed my project plan. The paper compared my possible sale price to a number of other products – from cut diamonds to a loaf of bread, and also listed the five most expensive masterpieces ever sold. It made a pun about reward points and seven-for-the-price-of-one deals, but otherwise the tone was generous, the editorial supportive, and it contained no mention of the sale of sketches, or of boyfriends from my past. I couldn't really have asked for more than that. When I rang John Herbert to thank him, he sounded smug, told me to remember where they were and promised the paper would be watching my progress all the way to the auction house. I wasn't sure whether I should take that as a compliment or a threat. I decided on the latter and checked myself that, however confident I might feel I could get rid of Kenny Harper, I would have to continue to watch my step.

As far as the *Possession* series was concerned, the cat was out of the bag. By 10 a.m. Katie said she'd already had twenty calls from the media and requests for information were flooding in. I had arranged to have lunch with Lincoln. I would have some explaining to do, I knew. Then Petra was flying in and we had planned to work through the evening on my plans. I was pleased to be busy: it gave me less time to think about yesterday's phone call. All contact with Kenny made me feel violated. I needed to block his influence out.

Petra called as I was getting ready to go and meet Lincoln. She was at the Eurostar terminal in Paris, waiting to board the train, and said she had breaking news that couldn't wait. She was in love – yet again, but this time it was the real thing. He was a German composer, an emerging talent who spent half his time in Paris. She was certain he was the one. I half-listened, amused. Petra's love affairs were always intense and short-lived but she believed in every one as if it would last for ever. I scrutinized myself in the mirror as she talked on. I was tall, shaped like a pear, with hips almost as wide as my shoulders, ice-white skin, coal-black pubic hair. Up closer, my eyes were cloudy and my protruding bottom lip dry. I licked it and ran fingers through my hair. It was all parched out. I looked terrible: this whole Kenny drama had really taken its toll. The studio was strewn with debris from my previous week's mad planning: postcards and cuttings on painted female faces; newspapers and books; dirty clothes; coffee cups; take-away remains. In the midst of it all there was a showroom dummy, black wig on.

As Petra divulged further details of her new romance I put my black bra and knickers on, painted my lips murder-red, then rescued my jeans, top, keys from the floor. As I had a quick clean-up of the flat, Petra continued to chatter. I found her voice reassuring and began to feel cheered. I had internalized so much recently, I needed to be brought out of myself. If anyone could do that, it was Petra. I was pleased she was coming to town. Finally I rang off and, wrapped in my thick fake fur, pushed the call button and the lift door slid open. It was time for lunch. As I hit the street there was a familiar whirr, a series of sharp clicks. Two snappers were huddled under the bus shelter, trying to avoid the rain. As I got into my cab I threw them my best Mona Lisa smile.

Lincoln was waiting for me, sitting at a table on the far side of the restaurant, grazing on the *Evening Standard*, dressed in Jermyn Street.

There was a sudden hush as I crossed the floor. The diners were watching my back. Their silence disturbed him and he glanced up, then quickly rose from his chair. Everything about Lincoln Sterne is beige – apart from a pair of cricket-green eyes. He's diminutive, faun-like, with a velveteen quality: the twenty-first century's Quentin Crisp.

'Esther, darling, what on earth are you cooking up?'

'So you saw the *Clarion*,' I murmured as we kissed air.

'I feel mortally offended you didn't give me first bite of the cherry,' he replied, pulling out my chair. His spirited tone failed to mask his unease.

A dark-haired waiter approached with menus. Lincoln smiled flirtatiously as he took one. We were doing lunch at St John's, Clerkenwell – low-key but high-profile. Today Rupert Murdoch was picking up the bill.

'Maybe you should have spoken to me before filing your last piece,' I said, smiling as I sat down. 'Most unlike you to take a swipe at me. I wasn't sure what I'd done to deserve it.'

'I was only remarking on how ubiquitous you've become,' Lincoln replied, pouring me water, 'and now, with this self-auction idea, well, my God, Esther, what do you want people to think? No one's talking about anything else.'

'I hope they're not baying for my blood.'

'Not this time, no,' he replied, 'I think most people really want to see you pull it off. But it may be your last chance. After selling yourself, what's left? You're right, they'll be demanding a public execution next.'

'Come on, Lincoln. Your last article about me did nothing but fuel ignorance of contemporary art. I expect more from you.'

'Now I'm flattered. How so?'

Annoyingly, he'd always enjoyed being chastised.

'Your skill's in revealing lateral connections, not comparing contemporary art to the celebrity world of "fame and fucking", or however you put it,' I said, deliberately misquoting him.

'Fornication, Esther,' he corrected pleasantly, then dabbed his lips with the napkin to mask a smirk.

In the past he'd been one of my greatest confidants. Lincoln attended the Courtauld with Billy Smith when I was at St Martin's, and had always championed the work of both of us with terrier-like determination. But the ground was shifting. We were all growing up. He wielded critical power now – and his last article was written to sell papers, not to please me. Sadly, from that moment on I knew I had to keep an eye on his activities too.

'How about the fillet of beef?' he suggested. 'I'm not in the mood for brains.'

I nodded. 'I could do with the iron,' I said.

He swivelled his eyes once more at the waiter. 'And make sure it's bloody bloody.'

Catching my eye, the waiter scribbled our order down.

'I wasn't denying that your work has intellectual depth, Esther,' Lincoln continued blithely. 'I merely said you've become bigger than the sum of its parts. That's a new phenomenon. The artist as the celebrity, the work with the secondary value.'

'But that's not true. I might aim to entertain my viewers, but the real value's in my art.'

Lincoln snorted dramatically. 'Not from the public's perspective, it isn't. To them *you* are the art, my dear.'

I suddenly became aware of a growing stillness. I glanced round to see lots of heads return to their plates. If we weren't careful, stories about a 'row' would feature in the next day's diaries.

I lowered my voice. 'I've never shied away from publicity. The fame thing's part of my overall theme.'

'Maybe I wrote the article as a warning to you, Esther.'

'Go on,' I urged, genuinely interested in what he had to say.

His eyes shimmered like oil. 'You fly so close to the flame. I'd hate to see you become Icarus.'

I wondered if he meant it, or if, like most people, what he'd really enjoy would be to watch me burn.

Our food arrived and we cut into the meat. I guessed it was time to turn tables and get what I wanted from him.

'I assume Katie got in touch from the gallery?' I said.

'Yes. She caught me yesterday. I wish you'd told me earlier.'

'You've been in my bad books,' I said and sipped the water. 'What you wrote has been playing on my mind. It's one of the main reasons I'm doing this project at all.'

'How so?'

'Well, you said I'd become a brand. It made me wonder how much I'm actually worth.'

Lincoln's eyes narrowed. He loved being in at the start of things. 'And what exactly will the buyer get for their cash?'

'Me.' I grinned. 'For a week – and the series I produce from the experience. Once the tour has finished with it, of course.'

'The theme?'

'Possession.'

'Go on, tell me more,' he urged, smiling conspiratorially now.

He listened intently, interjecting with a positive comment here and there, as I proceeded to fill him in.

'What particular values do your subjects represent?' he asked once I'd run through my list of selected portraits.

'Different aspects of value,' I explained. 'They were all different kinds of possession – whether sexual, aesthetic or financial. And none of their stories are skin-, or even oil-, deep. Whoever buys me, metaphorically speaking, is purchasing seven subjects, and me, as their willing medium.'

Lincoln chewed slowly on his beef as I talked. I could see the idea had him hooked. I was pleased. Aidan had urged me to do this lunch, the only media intrusion I would have to face, he promised, until the week before the actual sale. His hope was that Lincoln could stir up international interest, so stimulating new collectors to come out from under their gold-encrusted rocks. Whoever bought me would want value for money. This needed to be an exceptional project, under-pinned with foundations of steel: a piece to put Lincoln and all my critics to bed by.

Lincoln carefully put down his knife and fork and leant forwards. 'And what do you hope to learn from this, Esther?' he enquired, his green eyes sharp as shears.

I paused to think. 'In the first instance,' I replied finally, 'by selling myself I'll find out my current financial value; and by being owned for a week, perhaps I'll get an insight into what it feels to be a valuable work of art.'

He wagged his finger judiciously. 'But art doesn't feel, Esther.'

'Performance art does,' I replied confidently, 'and the women sitting inside their frames did.'

He put his hands together under his chin, in quasi-prayer. 'Ah, now I see. So that's how the women fit in.'

'I want to seek out the hidden depths from beneath their painted surfaces,' I told him. 'They're all symbols of value. Each, as an artwork, is a possession, and as women they were, too – although valued in a range of ways by their owners.'

His face lit up. 'Can I quote you?'

We used to be able to discuss this stuff as friends. I felt sad to appreciate that I now had to tell him when something was off record. He accepted my admonishment with unusually good grace and asked what he could do to help. I could see this was my moment to demand a favour.

'Well, you can support me, for a start. The media's response is going to make or break me. We need it to fly if we're going to find a big money buyer.'

'No problem,' he replied, eyeing me greedily. 'We'll fight for exclusivity over the night of your auction.'

51

Aidan would be very pleased with me, I thought. But as ever there was a bargain to be struck. Lincoln revealed he'd already been on the phone to a mutual friend at Channel 4. They wanted to do a documentary on the build-up to my sale and cover the auction, too – all, of course, with Lincoln at the helm. His tone became more businesslike with every word. And he, too, had chosen the perfect moment to ask something of me. He knew I needed his support, but he also knew I never did personal interviews.

'You know that I don't talk about my childhood or my family,' I warned him evenly, once his sales pitch was exhausted.

'Of course,' he replied, affecting a renewed gravity. 'But what about the history of your art?'

We'd finished eating. I lit a cigarette and flicked the ash into the bloody juices smeared across my plate.

'Give me forty-eight hours to think about it,' I said.

I called Aidan on the way home and filled him in.

'Well done,' he said, the words devoid of feeling. He understood how useful it was to have Lincoln on our side but it was clear he hated the fact that I'd colluded with the *Clarion*. He saw it as a step down, in media positioning terms, and I knew he still didn't trust my reasons for going to the paper. He knew I was hiding something from him but was too proud to keep asking for an explanation. The conversation was short, but before he rang off he mentioned that my mother had called the gallery. If I accepted Lincoln's documentary idea, inevitably he'd drag her into it. He'd known Ava since we first started hanging out together. He knew she'd leap at the chance to put her side of the story over – especially if Channel 4 was involved.

The media's always been disproportionately interested in my 'alternative upbringing' and Ava's never happier than when she can expound her feminist theories – and criticize my reinterpretation of them into the bargain. She'd taken a back seat in her own career over recent years, and with the extra time on her hands had fostered a renewed, acute interest in all that I did. I found her focus intrusive. She always had something contrary to say. We played cat-and-mouse with each other; it had been like that for a while. I didn't know how I would reconnect with her now, but I realized I needed to get to her before Lincoln did, and I didn't trust him to wait for my permission. So when I got home I called her straight back. But as soon as I heard her, I knew the call was a mistake.

'Esther, what on earth are you cooking up this time?' she said.

'How do you know about it?' I asked. It was unlikely that Ava would have read this morning's article in the *Clarion*.

'Dear Lincoln called,' she replied, smugly. 'He wanted my advice on a little documentary idea.'

He must have spoken to her before we'd met for lunch and my hackles rose.

'Don't waste your energy, Ava,' I said stonily. 'I'm not doing it.'

'Calm down, darling. I didn't say I was encouraging him. I just wondered what it was all about.'

I counted to three before replying, calmly, 'Don't you worry, I expect the press will be hanging on our coat-tails for the next couple of months. I'm sorry if they bug you. But I'd prefer it if you could just pass them on to the gallery.'

'I see. And not give my opinion?' she said. Her tone had changed to waspish.

'That's up to you, Ava.'

'I was surprised to hear that you're working with Petra on this project,' she continued lightly. 'You've always been so—' she hesitated for emphasis, "competitive".'

My stomach tightened. 'Petra's a fashion designer, I'm an artist. We work in different worlds.'

'I didn't say professionally, Esther. I meant personally.'

I chose not to react. It always ended this way between us. But I was determined not to be brought down. I wouldn't let her words tarnish the evening that lay ahead.

Finally it was she who filled the gap. 'Anyway, when am I going to see you? It seems like months.'

If I didn't go, she'd feel she had carte blanche to dabble with Lincoln. I knew it and I knew she knew I knew it. But the last thing I needed right then was an audience with my mother. It always threw me off course. Luckily I had an excuse to hand.

'I have to go to Paris next week,' I told her, 'to see a portrait. I'll come over when I get back.'

It was time to get ready for Petra's arrival and I spent my pent-up rage at my mother cleaning the flat. Ava's words played in my ears – *'You've always been so competitive'* – and turned my thoughts to Petra. Her career had really taken off since her move to Paris. We were both forging ahead in our own worlds. Competition between us was not an issue. Not now. When we first met we had recognized the same sense of daring in each other, though, of that I'm certain. But looking back on it, I think we had different reasons for our risk-taking. Mine was clearly to do with defining my own identity away from the communal world I had inhabited as a child. By contrast, Petra had enjoyed a rarefied upbringing replete with all the trappings affluence could afford. Within her was an urgency to prove that despite the family funds she still had her own values. She was a visionary and, not only that, someone who always got things done.

Finally she arrived and buzzed up. With rising anticipation I sent the lift down to get her. When the door slid open and Petra emerged she was confronted by the seven faces appearing slowly out of the gloom, like memories of things once known, now half-forgotten. Wanting the introduction to be gentle, I'd deliberately left most of the lights off. We embraced quickly. She smelt cool and slightly salty, like a sea breeze infused inside an expensive perfume There was a new confidence in her demeanour too. Paris was polishing her up. Quickly, she brushed me to one side, and the back of her blonde head nodded up and down slowly as she absorbed each portrait in turn, moving from one to the next. When she got to the end of the line she turned and looked at me. To my relief her coral lips were turned upwards, into a crescent moon. I switched the full studio lights on and opened a bottle of wine as she attempted to name each portraitist in turn: 'Ingres, Holbein, Manet, da Vinci, Whistler, Klimt, Raphael . . . but I can't be sure about this last one, Esther. I do declare you've caught me out.'

I laughed but didn't help her. This was an age-old game – Petra and I trying to outwit one another with our superior knowledge of the history of art – that went back to our shared student days at art college. Back then, the National Gallery provided us with an endless supply of practically private views, and many hours of impassioned adolescent analysis too, all absolutely for free. Together we'd mapped out our ambitions before the great masterpieces of the past.

Petra slipped out of her embroidered gold sling-backs. She shrugged in defeat and curled up like a Persian cat on my pink sofa.

'The last one's a Titian,' I informed her smugly, as I handed her a glass of wine.

'No wonder,' she replied dismissively. 'I've never liked him. Now, tell me how you went about choosing them.'

I'd scrawled new notes across the whiteboard. To anyone but me they read like nonsense verse, a series of drawings, words, scribbles, crossings-out and lists. I used them for reference as I began slowly talking her through my plans. More than anyone else, it was essential to me that Petra understood the concept clearly. As I'd explained to Lincoln, I'd chosen each woman for her specific, unique symbolism: politics, beauty, power, purity, sex, aesthetics and myth. I intended to find out all I could about them in turn, then devise a performance for each that would highlight their key attributes and say something more about their personal story. I also wanted to put them in the context of their financial value, both when they were painted and now, as priceless works of art.

The more I explained, the more engaged Petra became. Sketches were already emerging from her mind, and she began scribbling drawings on a pad with a pencil, both scooped from her pearl-encrusted bag.

At last I felt I'd explained enough. 'So. What do you think?' I demanded, collapsing on the sofa next to her.

Petra chewed on the end of her pencil, then eyed me sideways with a smirk. 'I think it's *très* Baudrillard,' she said.

It was an old joke, an in-joke, another one we'd shared since college, where we were taught about post-modern art. Her words were reassuring: I knew she was on board and I knew she'd got the idea. After all, jokes aside, the *Possession* series was clearly Baudrillard-inspired. His philosophy was that contemporary art could do nothing more than steal material from the past and give it a contemporary twist to provide new meaning. Petra's analysis was spot-on.

'I want to get on with it now.' She said impatiently. 'When can I start?'

We ran through the budget as we finished the wine and Petra enthused about a couple of art trips on which she'd like to accompany me. With her presence here the threat of Kenny Harper felt less frightening. I almost told her about it, but like Aidan, or anyone else, if I began I'd have to tell her the whole story and that was inconceivable. So I kept quiet about my recent brush with blackmail and let her visit alter my mood for the better. Soon we were on our way to a private view in an old theatre in South London, where we glanced into porcelain loos filled with glitter, and met up with a bunch of old art-school friends. We ended up at our old local on Brick Lane and stayed after hours, with doors shut, blinds pulled down. By now everyone was buzzing. Petra had been away for a while and it felt like a home-coming of sorts, a celebration of who she'd become. But some things never change. She still had the knack of making party wheels spin out of control.

9

The weekend passed in a haze of parties, drugs and, on Sunday, catch-up sleep. Petra finally left on Monday morning and I rather gingerly made my way to Sotheby's, where Aidan had planned our first meeting with their client director, Jacqueline Quinet. Dark, sleek and French-polished, she personified Euro-chic from her couture charcoal suit to the Chanel No. 5 emanating from her slender wrists. I was alarmed to see Aidan slightly aroused. He's always liked to play with players. Maybe they'd have a fling, I thought, in a panic. We hadn't done that to each other, not for a very long time, but things had become so cool between us, maybe she'd slip through the chink in our armour.

Our first meeting was only intended to be a 'preliminary chat'. However, it left me uncertain. Thinking about it now, I'm not exactly sure whether it was Jacqueline's immediate impact on Aidan, or the commercial nature of the discussion that I found more unnerving. Either way, it was hard to grasp what I had really let myself in for as I sat next to my dealer in her office, discussing the terms of my impending sale.

Jacqueline began before we even sat down.

'Congratulations on a really sensational idea. You're the most important lot we've had in the contemporary sale for years,' she exclaimed, her walnut eyes fixed hard on me. 'You may not command the highest price, but you'll get the most media coverage in the entire calendar.'

Instinctively, I didn't like Jacqueline, yet I couldn't help but feel safe in her hands.

'Tell me,' she continued warming to her theme, 'what's the basis of your idea? I'd like to feel on the inside track, so we can market your sale appropriately.'

I was aware that I would need to please Jacqueline if I were to get her complete buy-in. She leant forwards with her neat elbows poised on the desk, her small, fine hands interlinked under her chin, as I began to explain about my seven subjects, my performance plans, the contents of the sale. I was getting one hundred per cent of her attention.

'It's a wonderful idea,' she said categorically once my description was completed. 'I can't wait for the night of your sale: it will be the talk of London and New York.'

I had a feeling that if she was the determining factor, then such an outcome was sure to occur.

'And what about prospective buyers?' interjected Aidan mildly. Our chairs were pulled close together opposite Jacqueline's, a leather desk dividing clients and client director. I could feel the increased pressure of his thigh on mine. At least he seemed pleased with this performance. While I had been speaking, Jacqueline had kept her total attention on me. But at his question she redirected her gaze and held his for a tenth of a second – no more. Simultaneously I felt his pressure on my leg release.

Aidan unfolded a piece of paper and slid it across the table, like an opening bet, fingers spread flat. 'I've three or four interested parties so far,' he told her, uncharacteristically softly.

I watched as Jacqueline registered his hands before perusing the list slowly.

'A healthy start,' she said finally, nodding, before turning to eye me up and down dispassionately. We were back to the business of money. 'It seems the British are gaining a second wave of international interest. But, Esther, where shall we begin with you?'

I held her stare but remained silent.

'We can't afford to let her go for less than two hundred thousand,' interjected Aidan, pressure growing on my leg once more.

Jacqueline glanced across at him wryly. 'I was thinking more of a reserve price of 150k.'

'I know we can get two-fifty from the Germans.' Aidan replied, sounding determined.

I felt like reminding them that we weren't yet at the auction, but I've learnt over the years that at moments like this it's best to keep my mouth shut and let him lead the deals: he always gets a better price. Jacqueline nodded again, more keenly now. Money seemed to animate her too. In that respect, she'd met her match in Aidan. It was strange, I thought obliquely, that she had no personal effects on her desk, not even a family photograph.

'Let's keep our options open for now,' she replied nicely, her smile widening, but not, this time, to her eyes, 'and see how interest builds towards the sale day.'

'So, Jacqueline, what else are you expecting to see sell well?' Aidan asked, evidently aware it was time to move to a more general topic.

As she ran through a list of famous names Jacqueline began to rise from her chair, smiling knowingly, her hand proffered. The meeting was drawing to a close. As I shook it I felt my heart beating fast. How could I compete with a Lucian Freud on one side, a Francis Bacon on the other? For the first time since I'd come up with the idea I wondered if the *Possession* series might in fact be a huge mistake. Maybe I had reacted too swiftly to my fears over Kenny? Maybe I could simply have paid him off without spinning to such an extreme solution? But it was too late to regret it now. We all laughed and smiled together, but inside

I was feeling scared. There was excitement around that table which seemed to have nothing to do with art and everything to do with money, lots of it – which should have been great, but I had one major concern: this time, I was the object for sale.

10

'Aidan says you should go ahead with it,' Katie said.

I groaned down the phone. 'Can't I cancel? I've got to go to Clapham to meet someone for my research. It's critical.'

'Hold on. I'll buzz through,' she replied and the phone clicked.

To my annoyance, Aidan had been 'busy' when I'd called. I was set to do a repeat piece from *The Painted Nude* that night, inside Selfridges department store. It was Thursday and the last thing I needed after my cash drop. Time would be tight.

'You owe Selina a favour,' Aidan said blankly when he finally came to the phone, 'and it's good pre-publicity for the auction, too.'

Selina was an independent exhibition organizer with whom I'd had a run-in a few years before. I'd been the key artist in a show she'd planned and I failed to deliver a piece for her, messing up not only the exhibition but also affecting the sponsorship she had managed to raise. This was my chance to set things right. I could see I wasn't going to persuade him. It was a way to heal an old wound and since I'd taken on the *Possession* series Aidan's stance was toughening up.

'Are you coming along?' I asked.

'No, no. I can't,' he replied.

'Maybe afterwards?' I cajoled. 'Like before? To help me wash the henna off?' I hoped the reference to a happier time would warm things up, but Aidan's tone remained distant.

'I'll see if I can make it over. Call me when you're done. Oh, by the way, Lincoln promised he'd be there, cameraman in tow. Said he wanted footage for Channel 4's documentary. It's a perfect opportunity to get some new frames.'

I ordered a car to take me to Clapham. Having transferred the twenty-five-grand cash through two of my accounts and then out in wads of fifty-pound notes, I now had it stored inside an old red suitcase. I felt uneasy in the back of the cab as we sped southwards towards the given address. I didn't know what to expect when I got there. Kenny hadn't made it clear. Worried I was going to be duped, I hoped upon hope that he hadn't set me up. I was taking a risk, without back-up. The only measure I had taken was to leave a note with the address on my kitchen table at home. Should something happen to me, at least they'd know where I'd gone.

My car pulled over outside an ordinary terraced house in the middle of a suburban street and I asked the driver to wait. It was mid-afternoon, quiet and humdrum. I was wearing a hat and sunglasses in order to avoid recognition, and made my way quickly to the front door, rang the bell and waited. I saw a net curtain twitch and then the door opened slowly, halfway. A mousy-looking young woman of about my age peered around the door. A toddler leant against her, clinging to her knees. She appeared more nervous than I felt and I immediately felt oddly sorry for her. She'd obviously been around the block a few times, and it hadn't been much fun. There were worry lines around her eyes and her hair needed a wash. Old torn jeans and a cropped T-shirt revealed she was scrawny and there was a fake diamond stud in her navel.

'I've got something for Kenny,' I said quietly.

She nodded and handed me a large brown package. I wondered if I should open it before passing her the case, but decided there was little point. I had taken a high risk; I had now to see it through. She avoided eye contact as I handed her the money, then the door snapped shut before I could utter another word. I turned and got back into my cab and directed the driver to take me to Selfridges.

On the way I opened the package and pulled out three drawings. Seeing my old sketches there before me gave me a very strange feeling. To my surprise Kenny had obviously taken care of them: the sheets were pristine, the discoloration minimal. I'd made them such a long time ago and yet every line was familiar to me. They were utterly authentic. I had been going through a Klimt-inspired stage of working with fine, sharp pen-and-ink lines, and I had been inspired by his sexually explicit subject matter too. The content of my pictures was uninhibited: they showed Kenny and me having sex from three different angles. I let out a sigh of relief: at least I had avoided these meeting the public eye. It felt right that I had them back, they were mine, and I was pleased that Kenny Harper and his girlfriend no longer had the freedom to ogle them.

The car pulled up outside Selfridges and I took the package in with me. It seemed a strange coincidence that tonight I was going to strip off for my public and lay myself bare.

Katie met me at the staff entrance.

'You're doing November,' she said, reading from her notes, as we hurried inside. 'Lettie Sykes will start with an extract from her book, then you'll be on, then there'll be a book signing.'

'Can't I sign them first, then get going as soon as the performance is over?' I implored.

'I'll see what I can do,' she promised.

Lettie Sykes had been following my story for a volume in a new series being published on contemporary British artists. The store was launching the book and the series, and they were paying for the party. It was an odd new venture, a department store co-publishing the series with a fine-art publisher and with the Tate's endorsement too. Everyone was trying to understand the new phenomenon of high-street interest in contemporary art, keen to see if they could collaborate with commercial businesses to increase sales. It was a test-bed for future marketing enterprises between them all.

A slack-faced security guard led us to the temporary 'gallery' that had been constructed the day before. My familiar scarlet chaise-longue was waiting for me in the middle of a raised white platform, next to the 'teen clothes' section. It was late-night shopping. The idea was that consumers would still be there when the launch was taking place and could get a look-in on the 'real stuff' of the contemporary art scene. Tinny pop music fluted around the space and a few nosy shoppers were milling about, picking up copies of the book, which had been arranged in a huge pyramid. A toddler with a rashy face and snotty nose was careering about the platform, and seemed to be making a beeline for the chaise-longue. At this point I spied Selina's skeletal form lunging forwards: a slick vision in violet. She was just in time to stop him from wiping mucus-stickied fingers onto the scarlet silk.

By seven I'd signed two hundred and fifty copies of the book and was positioned naked behind a white curtain, on my chaise-longue, painted in verse. The mood of the day suited the most depressing month in the series:

> ghastly drizzling rain
> bald street
> breaks blank day
> eat my fat
> sweet coffee skinny latte
> lick my lips
> down my spine
> rain's my pain
> let me sleep
> missed again

The weather videos were running behind me and my soundtrack was ready to roll. But I could hear a lot of commotion on the other side of the curtain. Lettie Sykes was trying desperately to carry out a reading from the book above the noise. Evidently no one was listening. Katie was pacing around in front of me, shrieking down her phone to Aidan. 'There are hundreds of people out there – it's madness!'

Between the publishers, their PR company and our gallery, nearly a thousand people had been invited to the opening. It seemed most of them had decided to attend, along with shoppers who'd appeared from the maze of aisles. Everyone was getting impatient, wanting to 'see' something and the booze had already run out. To make matters worse, Katie had arranged for five security guards to protect the stage but so far we had only one and he appeared to be more interested in chatting to a blonde sales assistant than taking care of me.

Finally the situation came under control and a hush descended as the curtain was pulled back. Luckily my back was to the audience, so I didn't have to look at them, but I could feel the cameras and eyes exploring my body. As the crowd chattered excitedly I lay quietly and shut my eyes. I'd done this enough times to cut off from the scene and, as they absorbed me, I allowed my mind to drift to the *Possession* series. I could hear a scuffle breaking out and ignored it. Then the noise levels began to rise again and the curtain was swiftly pulled shut.

I was stiff and cold. Katie appeared with a face like a fist.

'Someone's just landed a punch. We'll never get involved in stuff like this again.'

'Don't tell me, tell Aidan,' I said.

'And Lincoln and his cameraman are having a field-day,' she muttered as she helped me put a dress on over the tattoos. 'God knows what their documentary will expose. More than your flesh, that's for sure.'

*

Katie was heading off to the Groucho Club with Lincoln, Selina, Lettie and the PRs. I refused the invitation, so she arranged for a security guard to escort me out to a waiting car by the back door. Just as it was leaving, Katie rushed up.

'Sorry,' she said. 'I forgot to give you this.' She shoved an envelope into my lap. 'Some guy gave it to me for you. Probably fan mail,' she continued. 'But he said it was urgent and I should make sure you got it.'

I tore the envelope open as we set off into the night. Inside was a short note.

Dear Esta,
You're just as gorgeous as all those years ago – at least from the back! Sorry I couldn't be there earlier. I hope you liked the drawings. Thanks for being so understanding. It's time I took off again now.
Kenny xxx

The kisses turned my stomach but the sentiment was a relief. It was odd to think he'd been there tonight, watching me perform, and I was curious to know why he hadn't been around when I'd dropped off the money that afternoon. In any event, I gauged from the tone and content of the note that Kenny was planning to go away with the cash and, it was to be hoped, this time for good. I felt I had got away by the skin of my teeth. The money was painful to give up, but the loss of it wasn't the end of the world. And the sketches . . . well, actually, to me they now seemed worth the price.

I called Aidan from the car to ask if he was coming over. I desperately wanted to see him now, to try to make amends. There was no answer and I felt depressed. I hadn't come up with this project to break us up; yet the centre seemed to be crumbling, and I couldn't see how to stop it, certainly not until the *Possession* series was complete. But when I arrived home I was pleased to see his car parked outside. He'd already let himself in, held a glass of Scotch in his hand, and was perusing the seven portraits hanging along the wall. His attention had been drawn to the third one in the row, a portrait by Jean Dominique Ingres. Entitled *Madame de Senonnes*, it was of a voluptuous beauty dressed in red velvet.

I wandered over and stood just behind him. 'What do you think of her?' I asked.

'She's utterly compelling,' he whispered slowly. 'Erotic and full of hidden meanings.' He turned to me. He looked relaxed, happy even. 'And her dress is perfect for the night of your sale.'

I had already decided that Marie de Senonnes would be my partner for the auction. What better metaphor for a woman putting herself up for sale than a lady adorned in red?

'How did it go tonight?'

'Oh, fine,' I replied, the performance already forgotten, 'but now I'm starving. I bought sushi on the way home.' I moved over to the sofa, and dropped the sketches and my bags. 'Do you fancy some?'

Aidan turned his attentions back to the painting. 'I've already eaten,' he said distractedly.

'With whom?'

'Er . . . Jacqueline Quinet,' he answered, a touch too casually. 'She wanted to run through details.'

I didn't answer. Instead I plonked myself down on the sofa roughly and opened the first tray of food. I stabbed a salmon roll with the end of my chopstick and put it in my mouth, then savagely gorged on the rest. He was interested in her, I was sure of it.

'Jacqueline's very keen on you, you know,' he said eventually. 'She thinks you're going to be a massive success. She's had some enquiries – two from China, a couple from New York. And I spoke to Greg Weiz today, too. He says he's got a couple of collectors considering a bid.'

Greg was Aidan's old playmate in Manhattan; in fact, Aidan still had a minor share in the Greg Weiz Gallery on the Upper East Side. They'd done a few small deals on my work there recently and Aidan was keen to get me promoted across the pond. But right now my focus remained purely personal.

'Where did you eat?' I asked, not even attempting to mask my annoyance.

'What?' He turned squarely on me, his eyes glinting, incredulous.

'You and Jacqueline, where did you eat?'

'Christ, Esther, why does it matter?'

'It doesn't,' I replied coolly. 'I just wondered.'

Lips pursed, he picked up his bag and started rifling through it for something. His lack of disclosure was characteristic. Aidan didn't like being put on the spot. He'd always refused point-blank to truck with what he called my 'petty neuroses', said I had to learn to live with life and not always expect things to be clear-cut. He had a point, but in general the shades of grey to which he referred existed in the other relationships I held – with the media, friends, critics. Until recently our affair had been pretty well-defined, if, for many years, actively clandestine. There had been a couple of cool periods in the early days, when we'd both had other, casual affairs, but we'd been open and honest about them. It had been a way of controlling the terrifyingly intense involvement that was growing between us at a time when neither had wanted such heavy commitment. But during the previous three years our relationship had become fairly well set. As far as I was aware, that was. The appearance of a possible rival on the scene only intensified my anxiety that we were beginning to fall apart.

'She gave me something for you,' he said, applying an air of non-chalance, and flipped a small black paperback over to me: a Penguin Classic. He placed his hands on his hips and watched for a response.

'I need a shower,' I said, dropping the book casually onto the table and heading for the bathroom, 'to wash these bloody tattoos off.'

*

When I reappeared, half an hour later, Aidan was lying on my pink sofa reading Jacqueline's gift. He looked up at me and smiled tentatively. 'Are you OK tonight, Est?' His tone was gentle. 'You seem uneasy.'

I had decided in the shower to let the issue lie. It wasn't going to help matters to have a major row.

'I'm just a bit preoccupied, I guess. It's the project. I need to immerse myself.' I answered, sliding down onto the floor in front of him. Aidan began to massage my shoulders. Against my intentions, I found myself beginning to relax. However, after the Jacqueline issue and everything else that had happened today, I was determined to go to bed alone.

'The performance has washed me out,' I lied after only a few minutes. 'I need some sleep.'

To my surprise, Aidan didn't protest. We both rose and I watched as he put on his denim jacket. Then he kissed me gently on the cheek and quietly took his leave.

I went to bed and closed my eyes. Once more I dreamt of the tail end of that summer for which I had just paid out £25,000 in protection.

11

'Miss Glass?'

I looked up over *Vogue* at the receptionist.

'Consulting room 4. This way, please.'

As I got up I couldn't help but glance furtively at the others waiting: five or six women hiding their faces and their shame inside well-thumbed magazines, their hearts, no doubt, like mine, thumping in their throats, trying to get out. One allowed her eyes to flicker up and connect with me for a millisecond, before retreating to the relative safety of a recipe tip or agony aunt's advice column. But it was too late for that – or for reading horoscopes either. By the time you found yourself settled into one of these blue-nylon-covered chairs, the damage was already done.

'That's all as it should be. You can get dressed now.'

Mr Nicholls had turned his back to me. I could hear slapping sounds as he stretched each digit out in turn and pulled the rubber gloves off his chubby fingers. He opened the pedal bin with his left foot as he surveyed his ruddy reflection in the mirror, systematically dropping the gloves into it. The lid fell shut with a metallic ping that echoed in the white silence of the room. It was a routine procedure and he'd had years of practice – day in, day out, fingers in, fingers out.

I swung my legs round and sat upright on the examination table, feeling slightly giddy, then reached for my lemon-yellow knickers and began wriggling them back on, up over my knees.

'Come through when you're ready,' he said evenly, without a backward glance, then disappeared out through the curtain.

'Good. Now, Esther, are you absolutely clear about the procedure?' asked Mr Nicholls as we stood in Reception.

I'd finished filling in the forms, had signed my foetus away and handed the papers back to the nurse who was perched like a ring-dove at a small desk in the corner. She was young, I thought, not much older than me. What a weird job to have when you're seventeen years old. How do you come to wake up one morning and think, 'Yep, a Harley Street abortion clinic, that's the life for me'?

She was quite pretty in a Barbie kind of a way, neat and blonde with pink lipstick, white tunic and beige tights. I'd never worn beige tights – or a uniform, not really. The closest they got us to that at school was a pale-blue T-shirt and navy-blue skirt. Mine had always defied the rules on length – which, perhaps, was partly why I was here in the first place. 'Break the rules, face the consequences,' that was what Mr Drewell, the head, would say every time I found myself back in his office to be scolded for another minor wrongdoing. Well, he was right this time. I couldn't deny it.

'And will you have someone coming along with you?' enquired Mr Nicholls with insincere sensitivity. 'You might find it helpful, before and afterwards, to have some emotional support.'

Ava's face appeared fleetingly in my mind. In her mind there was no question that I should keep Kenny's baby. She had taken control of the situation with an efficiency and emotional detachment verging on the clinical. I think she was still in a state of shock over Simeon's death, her sentiment all used up. Before I knew it, she had set the wheels in motion, was even paying the bill. Of course, Ava was a leading light in the woman's right to abortion movement and had championed the change in the laws a decade before. We'd even gone along on marches together, banners held high – albeit with me too young to understand what it was we were shouting for. I just knew it was the rights of women and I understood that we were both members of that particular club.

'You have your whole future ahead of you, Esther,' Ava had said definitively when I divulged my predicament. 'Too many women's lives have been destroyed by having unwanted children too young.'

There had appeared to be no point in arguing with her. Evidently there was no alternative emotional line to take. It did seem vaguely ironic at the time, though, considering the circumstances surrounding my own birth. After all, I'd hardly been planned. I thought of asking her why she hadn't left me in a bedpan. She and Simeon had made it perfectly clear that they had never been in love, that I was the result of a single, no doubt drug-induced night of passion. They seemed to see some romanticism in the idea that I was a pure 'love child' of the early Seventies, and Ava had never exactly been the epitome of maternalism. I was an addition to her life, the life of the commune, but her work had always been central. If I hadn't come along, I got the feeling she wouldn't have ever 'tried' for a child. She was too engaged with feminist theory to have chosen to muddy her hands with practice. But I had thought better of questioning her. Like it or not, I had needed her help.

She had offered to come with me that day to 'see it through'. But I felt that was one intimacy too far. This was something I had to get over and done with on my own. Although I felt a little bit shaky, I nodded in the vague direction of Mr Nicholls again, lied and mumbled that, yes, I would be coming with a friend. My tongue was sticking to the roof of my mouth. I could taste the acid there, sticky and impossible to displace. It had arrived a few days after I missed my last period, two weeks after Simeon's funeral and Kenny's disappearance: a portent, perhaps, of the calamity to come.

Appointment made for the following day, I walked out into the July heat wave and took a deep glug of thick London air. Then I turned the corner onto the Marylebone Road and promptly threw up in the gutter. Anonymous faces watched me from the top deck of a number 18 bus. They probably put it down to drugs.

It took a year for me really to get over the experience. During that time, I couldn't return to Ickfield Folly and I refused to see anyone from there either. Much to everyone's surprise, Simeon had left me a significant sum of cash. I guess communal living cost very little and he'd never owned any property. The fees for his seminars had added up to a fair few bob. I suddenly found myself to be quite comfortably off for a seventeen-year-old girl. Through the *Evening Standard* classifieds I got myself a bedsit in West London: one large, high-ceilinged room with a sink and a Baby Belling in the corner. Initially it smelt of boiled cabbage and stale cigarette smoke, which only served to make my nausea return. But the room had a large balcony looking out over a leafy park and cost just £20 a week. It didn't take me long to add a theatrical touch, with cheap velvet drapes and pots of herbs bought from Church Street market.

The guy downstairs was a neat-faced, leather-skinned Moroccan called Ahmed, a small-time dope dealer and DJ at the Astoria in Shepherd's Bush. He took me up as his cause, called me 'little sister' and helped me through those first few months with free spliffs and late-night confidence-boosting chats. I spent the first few months hiding away there, sketching madly. Then I got myself an easel and some oils and the odour of cabbages became overlaid by the pungent aroma of oil paint. That cavernous, damp, aching, threadbare house proved to be my lifeline, embracing as it did a community with a spirit not so unlike that of my past, although no one there was beholden to one another so it felt freer, fairer. The key difference was that you just gave what you wanted to and shut the door when you didn't feel like giving at all, so there was no false philanthropy on display.

Ava had begged me all year to come home, to finish my A levels, to be with her and John, to make amends. But for me the bubble of innocence had burst the day Simeon died and there was no way I could have spent another night under that roof. Ava didn't understand, *couldn't* understand, and I'm not sure I did either. But she didn't fight me over it, only made me promise to call her every day. And so I was free of them all, free for the first time in my life to do what I wanted to do, without eighteen pairs of eyes watching over my every move.

My new friends included an out-of-work actor called George, who lived upstairs, and, a few months later, his agent-cum-lover, Clara. By a stroke of pure luck she was a part-time speech coach at RADA. It was my chance meeting with her that changed the course of my future. Through Clara I found myself sitting in front of the examination board for an assisted scholarship into RADA the following autumn. Of course I seized the chance to show off my theatrical skills. Before I knew it, I was into my first term, full grant paid, as an undergraduate of the performing arts.

It was soon too late to go back to the commune anyway. With Simeon's demise the owner stepped back in and reclaimed the property. Suddenly the idyll was over. The tenants were given twelve months to clear out. I was pleased to have avoided the fallout. It was like setting prisoners free. They were disoriented and miserable. I felt more determined than ever never to return and didn't make the farewell party. It was now Ava and John who found themselves packing their bags and heading for London. Without ever having really planned it, we had all decamped to the city.

Paradoxically, London turned out to be a breath of fresh air. Let me rephrase that: it was precisely the opposite, which was why I loved it so much. London was the opposite of everything I had known before. And yet somehow, reassuringly, it felt totally like home.

12

I knew instinctively which masterpiece had to be first in the *Possession* series. The Duchess of Milan had been my talisman too long to be ignored. Ever since Ava had first introduced me to the painting I felt that she had belonged to me – spiritually speaking, of course. I had returned to her at various times during my first year in London, and less frequently over the following ten years too. Hers was a face to immerse myself in when things in my own life seemed unfathomable. There was something intangible about her look that I found curiously heartening.

Oddly, perhaps, I'd never before wanted to look beneath the surface features of this young girl captured so fully in paint. Perhaps I was afraid I might discover something tragic about her life, something to make me fear my sense of affinity with her. But now, for the first time, it seemed essential that I did get to grips with her personality, that I did experience again what it felt like to be sixteen years old. It was time to get under her skin.

Luckily her permanent residence was only two miles away from my flat. And, even more fortunately, she currently shared her address with Billy Smith. Billy had a year's residency in the vast studio behind the National Gallery's public spaces. A taxidermist with a bit of a coke habit loose among the nation's masterpieces might, on the face of it, sound like a recipe for disaster. In fact he was in his element, reshaping ideas from the past into a series of new works to be shown in the National's Sainsbury Wing the following spring.

He claimed to have the inside story on my Christina of Denmark, aptly defining her as a potent symbol of political possession. After graduating from Goldsmiths he'd studied art theory at the Courtauld – alongside our wayward art-critic friend Lincoln Sterne. Hans Holbein the Younger had been one of his special papers. It was a while ago now, but he said he was happy to dig out his notes. His enthusiasm was reassuring. To avoid press detection, I took a leaf out of Christina's historic sartorial book and dressed in veils to make my visit. In the painting her garments cover most of her body and head. I'd gone a step further, donning a black burka, with a veil over my face, a neat way to disguise my true identity. As I had begun to cloak myself in black the past began, once again, to nudge its way forwards in my mind. I should have anticipated that, by selecting Christina, it would creep back up on me. After all, she'd been with me all the way. Perhaps, subconsciously, I was ready to address the cobwebs of my youth; maybe that was what this project was really all about. The last time I had dressed like her was sixteen years earlier. But the situation had been completely different, had had nothing to do with disguise – and I hadn't been acting.

The Muslim burka is as omnipresent in London's streets as Levi jeans and as I headed across Trafalgar Square no one gave me a second look. I knew the route through the National Gallery's labyrinth towards her so well that I could have found her blindfolded, and reached my destination with ten minutes to spare. Christina hangs at a right angle to *The Ambassadors*, Holbein's other great masterpiece, but today I didn't afford it a cursory glance. Instead I gazed straight up at my first subject; she seemed to respond with an equally appraising eye. My heart was fluttering in my chest. This, after all, was the true beginning of things. For me the possibility of a new work is like the start of a love affair, it leaves me elated. And this time, I realized, the idea was more compelling than ever.

Christina is formidable, challenging, partly because she's painted to scale and so feels strangely real. Perhaps that was what had always drawn me to her? The fact that she represents timelessness, immortality. I looked long and slowly across her surface. She's willowy and elegant, yet surprisingly plain, and, most significantly, she looks extremely young. She's removed a pair of soft, beige leather gloves and her ivory hands, peeping out between folds of black velvet, are crossed passively over each other, her left hand displaying a single ruby on a gold ring. The multi-layered fabrics and jewels emphasize this glimpse of her flesh, so hinting at a subtle sensuality. Soft fur lines the coat and a clean white linen ruff adds contrast and definition to her neck and wrists. Her gown engulfs her slight, fragile frame. Light shimmers across the garment's silky surface, producing sensuous patterns, hinting at opulence, even in sorrow, referencing the fact that her husband, the Duke of Milan, had recently died.

Christina's skin is translucent, sparkling with youth. Her hair's scraped back under a black mourning cap, throwing her almond-shaped face into stark relief. She has a broad forehead, fleshy cheeks, a square jaw and a lusciously full peach-toned bottom lip. That was one characteristic, I thought, that I'd emulate with ease. Her scale and shifting expression make her seem as alive and communicative as if she'd been painted in a studio only the day before. In fact the painting's almost five hundred years old.

'Sorry to keep you.'

I swung round to see Billy's chunky form striding towards me, dressed in decorator's blue overalls. For the first time I noticed flecks of grey dancing in his curly black hair. White paint speckled his hands like freckles on an eggshell. He looked more like a painter hired by the National to touch up the walls than a leader on the BritArt scene.

'How did you recognize me?'

He smirked. 'No one else is dressed in a tent.'

I laughed and he put his arm around my shoulders. I shrugged him off.

'Don't do that, Billy,' I pleaded under my breath. 'You'll give the game away.'

He held his hands up in compliance and we turned together to look at the painting as he began to fill me in.

'I want to know what she was worth – as a political possession, a woman and a work of art,' I whispered.

'Essentially,' Billy explained, 'Holbein's portrait was a sixteenth-century passport photograph: this lady was for travelling. In her day she was a commodity with a high price, to be bartered, bought or sold when the price was right. The artist had painted her while on a business trip around Europe, recruiting possible brides for Henry VIII. She'd modelled for Holbein in Brussels for three hours while he sketched her. The time and date of painting are unusually precise: one p.m., 12 March 1538.

'Holbein returned to England with his drawings, painted them up, then used this, the resulting picture, as a taster for the king: kind of the sixteenth-century equivalent to internet dating, something for Henry to scan, see if she took his fancy. Apparently he clicked "buy" on sight. But Christina had other ideas, allegedly conceding that if she had two necks she'd have happily given one to Henry. Instead she chose to marry François, Duc du Bar. When he died in 1545, she became Regent of Lorraine. So she managed to keep her perfect head and inherited a kingdom into the bargain.'

'More by luck than judgement?' I asked.

As we studied her face for clues I could taste her vulnerability on my tongue. She was the same age as me when I'd done that scribble for Kenny Harper. How different our adolescent lives had been. I couldn't help but wonder if there were any experiences other than that of an early death that we'd shared.

'So, how do you feel about the first woman in your pack?' Billy grinned over the top of his Styrofoam cup. We had retreated to his studio. It was such an accolade, this big white space, hidden inside one of the world's greatest museums. Four rabbit skins were hung around a hat stand next to a large canvas propped on an easel, on which was marked a grid in streaks of burnt umber.

'I can't help but be mesmerized by her,' I said slowly. 'She's always left goose-bumps on my skin, ever since I first saw her with my mum. I couldn't have been more than twelve years old.'

Billy looks like he belongs in a boxing ring, but when he smiles a thousand creases scrunch around his eyes, revealing a gently purring spirit that would only strike out if provoked. He used the smile on me now and I grinned back. I thought fleetingly about the scuffle at his recent opening.

'What do you think of my idea?' I asked.

'I like it, your sale and all that,' he answered pensively, 'but there's something cynical about it. I don't know, like you're throwing in the towel on the business of making art that really counts. Is it really all about the cult of personality and celebrity for you now?'

I felt stung but I knew he had a point. I stroked the rabbit skins, discovering their fur was thinner than I expected, yet incredibly soft.

'You know,' I replied finally, 'that's part of the point, really. I want to confront face-on the reality of what we do. I know it's extreme, and I could fuck up. But there's a seed of an idea here that I think could grow into a big statement. About my value, the value of my chosen women.'

Billy, continuing to smile, picked up a brush and traced it along the lines on his canvas. 'I was pretty jealous when you got offered that international gig,' he confessed, 'but at least I got the residency at the National. Kind of squares things up. I want you to succeed, Est, you do know that, don't you?'

In recent years we'd both received nominations for the Turner Prize, but neither of us had won. It no longer seemed so critical as it once had. Ever since Martin Creed had gained a prize for switching off the lights, no one seemed to care much about it any more. It had become synonymous with back-of-the-cab chatter – a way to pass time outside the congestion zone, an alternative topic to the weather, and equally uncontentious. But to us, Billy's residency and my show both meant more.

'What about you? What do you want next?' I asked.

The brush stopped in its track as he concentrated on his thoughts, then he stepped back and put it down. He shoved his hands deep in his overall pockets and exhaled air from between his teeth, shaking his head.

'Well, I think I'm going to have to close the club. It's a total fuckin' mess.'

I felt sorry for Billy, although I never fully understood why he'd ever got involved in a venture outside his essential creative domain. Even Aidan had tried to persuade him against it. 'The Site' had been open for three years now. He'd caught the celebrity/culinary bug, thought he could add a bit of anarchy to the Modern British cuisine, shake it all up a bit and make some money at the same time. Instead his private dining rooms and bar had suffered a chain of chef resignations and staffing crises. The generally held view was that he hadn't put enough of himself into it, had thought he could run it on the phone while continuing to make his art. He'd also taken four months out last year to spend time in New Zealand, planning a film with a young antipodean director. The film hadn't materialized but he'd come home with a cool designer wife. They were now expecting a kid. It was changing him.

'What are you going to do instead?'

He looked furtive. 'Carrie and I've bought a farm, outside Bath.'

I shook my head in disbelief as he laughed.

'Maybe I need some cow shit under my feet. Rearing animals instead of stuffing 'em – it might breathe new life into this old git.'

*

As I left, Billy handed me his old research papers on Holbein. Once I got home I sat on my pink suede sofa with a pot of tea and waded my way through them. Christina continued to hold my full attention.

It transpired that, once she had rejected Henry, his search for a bride recommenced. The king soon commissioned Holbein again, this time despatching him to Germany to produce a portrait of Anne of Cleves, the Protestant princess. Henry fell in love with the artist's impression, hitting 'purchase' on sight once more. This time his proposal was readily accepted and the new commodity soon arrived in England, marriage contract in hand. But what the king saw in the painting was definitely not what he got in the flesh. Holbein had provided him with a false likeness of Anne. Henry protested he'd been duped into marrying a 'fat Flanders mare' and soon got shot of her. A few years later Holbein was dead of the plague. I expect Henry believed God had struck him down on his divine behalf.

That evening I rang Billy for more stories. He promised to ask the curators at the National for further snippets about Christina. Before I rang off he reaffirmed his enthusiasm for what I was trying to do, adding that he hoped his earlier words hadn't been taken in the wrong way. I think he was being sincere, and, judging by his possible plans to leave London, it seemed we weren't going to be such head-on rivals on the scene from then on. A bit of breathing space within our art circle would be a good thing. No way was I was heading out to the countryside. It was where I began, and what I had run away from – as soon as I, like Christina, had turned sweet sixteen.

True to his word, Billy phoned me the next day with more information about Holbein's masterpiece. One of the curators had given him the low-down on the movements of the painting after Henry VIII had died. Christina's painted history, it transpired, was as intriguing as her personal story.

Over the intervening centuries Holbein's picture had passed

through a number of aristocratic hands until, in 1909, it finally entered the public domain. But only after a drama that could have lost *Christina of Denmark* to England for ever. At this time she was owned by the Duke of Norfolk, who had loaned her to the National Gallery for her protection – it was the most secure place for a valuable painting to be guarded. But the duke fell on hard times and decided to sell his masterpiece. He quietly hired Colnaghi's, the illustrious art dealers, and they duly sought out an American millionaire with a consuming passion for the painted lady. A deal of a hefty £72,000 was agreed for her sale. It seemed our enigma was heading across the pond. But there was one proviso: the Duke of Norfolk offered the National Gallery one month to come up with a counter-bid.

The duke, however, had underestimated the public's passion for this young girl – or had presupposed it and was playing a high-risk political game. Within a week the affair became a national scandal, with articles in the press and questions raised in Parliament. How could Christina be saved for the nation? A total of £32,000 was raised by the National Arts Collections Fund to hang on to her, but there remained a huge shortfall. It seemed all was lost, but on the canvas Christina retained her composure. I guess she'd been through this before, but last time the issue was between kings; this time, it was between the public and private purse. She continued to project her knowing smile and, it transpired, with good reason. Only minutes before her boat was set to sail, the rest of the balance landed in the bank, donated by an anonymous female. And so *Christina of Denmark* got to stay on the walls of the National Gallery. In the end, it seems, it was a woman who really understood her worth.

Billy was pleased with himself for finding out so much. It gave him a role in my project and kept us level. Not only that, now he, too, wanted to work with Christina. She was one of those women whom, he said, it was impossible to get away from once she'd ensnared you. He was including her as a subject in his response to the National

Gallery's permanent collection. But, unlike me, he was more interested in the fur lining her cloak than the thoughts circulating in her mind.

I was feeling quite pleased with the way things had started out. But then I came across a second portrait of Christina in Billy's notes that chilled me to the bone. It was painted five years later, when she was yet again in mourning, this time for the loss of her second husband, the Duc du Bar. She was wearing the same style of mourning clothes as in Holbein's masterpiece, only this time she was painted only to her waist and was holding a prayer book, not gloves, in her hands. Her fingers are heavy with rings. Christina's innocence seems to have evaporated. Had this Flemish painter failed to capture her enigmatic spirit, or was her passion for living really already extinguished? Apparently, like Holbein before him, Michael Croxie painted Christina at a remove. In fact, he never saw her in the flesh. I hoped he had just misread the sketches. By this point, she was widowed with two small children in tow – and she was destined to spend the rest of her life alone. I found the information devastating. Why did I feel so embroiled in her life? And why did her experience make me feel so fearful for myself?

I couldn't help but try to find comparisons between us. My relationship with Aidan had taken quite a knocking over recent months. I guess it was, to a large degree, my own fault. I often hid inside my work and had been furtive recently about that whole blackmail thing, and it was stridently clear to Aidan that, although our love affair was central to my life, my art came first. That was all there was to it. It was an active, necessary choice. For me, like Christina, over the years self-possession had been a useful and necessary defence.

I decided that, in my reinterpretation, Christina's would be a remote performance, a virtual introduction to the *Possession* series for my collector. It would be filmed and played live online for his or her own personal consumption on the day of my arrival. Christina would stay at one step removed, in keeping with the original painting, but with a contemporary, technological twist. And one veiled in layers of uncertainty. She was, after all, young and evasive, as I had been. She seemed isolated and I now saw that was the attribute to which I had so naturally responded in my youth; I had felt the same way. Her identity was not yet set: she was looking outside of herself for answers. Every time I looked into her face, I saw something of myself floating back, an innocent me, a sixteen-year-old with an uncertain future ahead of her, one who would need to define her own identity, in order to break through and succeed.

I would ask Petra to design me equivalent yet contemporary funeral clothes and to source a set of seven translucent veils for my face and a pair of the softest pale kid gloves. I resolved to find an antique prayer book, and copies of Christina's rings, so that the later part of her life could be added to my performance too.

Taking advantage of Christina's ephemeral identity, I would use her to introduce all seven women who would inform the project during my own week as an aesthetic commodity. I knew there was going to be a significant difference between my collector's experience of perusing me for the first time and that of Henry VIII when he first laid eyes on his painted possession. In my instance, the physical as well as the artistic purchase would already have been made. What judgement on my own value would my collector reach from this virtual, solitary performance? My deeper message would be unravelled only as the week progressed. Christina would simply be a taste of things to come.

13

In every village once a year all the girls of marriageable age used to be collected together in one place, while the men stood around them in a circle; an auctioneer then called each one in turn . . . and offered her for sale, beginning with the best-looking and going on to the second-best as soon as the first had been sold for a good price. Marriage was the object of the transaction. The rich men . . . bid against each other for the prettiest girls while the humbler folk, who had no use for good looks in a wife, were paid to take the ugly ones, for when the auctioneer had got through all the pretty girls he would call upon the plainest, or even perhaps the crippled one, to stand up, and then ask who was willing to take the least money to marry her – and she was knocked down to whoever accepted the smallest sum. The money came from the sale of the beauties, who in this way provided dowries for their ugly or misshapen sisters.

Herodotus told lots of stories and many of them were tall. I hoped this one about Babylonian wives had been spun by a creative pen. I was reading this extract from the *Histories* while sitting on a Eurostar train, destination Paris, purpose an audience with the next portrait on my list. Jacqueline had turned over the corner of the book's page for me for quick reference. The note that accompanied it said simply:

Esther, I've searched high and low for references to auctioned women since Aidan first approached me with the idea of your sale. This was the most interesting one I found. Good luck with the research.

JQ.

There had to be an underlying message in the story. Maybe Jacqueline was implying that I might not sell, and hence that this could be a useful method for getting shot of me, a duff leftover, once the real masterpieces had gone under the hammer. Or maybe the story was a kind of metaphor. Perhaps she was thinking of a take-over bid on a more personal front.

I snapped the book shut and forced my attentions away from her and onto Victorine Meurent. She was the only woman on my list who was rejected on the grounds of her looks, or, should I say, look. When she was first put on show no one wanted to touch her with a barge pole, let alone be paid to take her away. In fact, when Edouard Manet tried to sell his first nude painting of Victorine at the Paris Salon of 1863 it caused such a furore that the picture was rejected out of hand, never even hung. It reappeared under a new title, *Le Bain*, at the Salon des Refusés (Rejections Exhibition) two years later. Today that picture is better known as *Le Déjeuner sur l'Herbe*.

What was all the fuss about? Well, of course it wasn't caused by the two fully clothed men with whom she was sharing a bite to eat. The worry was what a naked woman was doing picnicking with them in the first place. Could it be that Manet had painted a whore? At the Refusés, Manet valued his precious Victorine at 25,000 francs and although he didn't actually have to pay anyone to have her, in the end he did accept an offer for a spit of the price. A contemporary singer, known as Faure, picked her up as part of a job lot, along with two of the artist's earlier paintings, all for a mere 3,000 francs. A severe slap in the face for the artist – and his model, too. I wonder if she felt undervalued, or whether she accepted her going rate as being all that she was really worth?

Victorine was the second woman on my list. I had chosen her because I wanted to emulate a life model. After all, it was where my own art career had really begun, lying naked while artists painted me. Victorine had a look of defiance about her that I found both appealing and intriguing, a hard outer shell that would be difficult to crack. When I thought back to my time at St Martin's, I could see that, like her, I had been quite impenetrable too – at least, on a psychological level. The key difference between us was clear: unlike Victorine, the artists with whom I slept along the way hadn't paid me for the privilege.

I looked down at the second reproduction of her I had brought with me on the train. The same year that Manet painted *Le Déjeuner sur l'Herbe*, he used Victorine again, this time in the classical pose of Olympia. Around this work I felt an even greater affinity with the model. After all, earlier in the year I had spent days in the same pose. The painting had many revered precedents, not only the Velasquez *Rokeby Venus*, the inspiration for my last project, but Titian's *Venus of Urbino* and Ingres' *Odalisque with a Slave* too. Manet's version was shown at the Salon des Refusés in 1865. The curator insisted on placing her high up above another painting on the wall. But it wasn't enough to divert attention. Again, viewers were outraged. One critic even claimed that crowds thronged around the gamy Olympia as if at the morgue. It's easy to imagine why it had created such tension. It was one thing for Parisian men to visit tarts late at night in the streets of Pigalle, quite another to go gallery visiting *en famille* and find one staring back at you from the wall.

The classical term 'Olympia' held other connotations in 1870s Paris too. Indeed, the title was a subverted form of flattery. 'Olympias' were the labels used for the most desired whores in town.

I had read all about this painting before I left London. By 1898, Manet was dead and Victorine was living out her days in a sea of absinthe. But her painted value had risen sharply. The collector Etienne Moreau-Nelaton had bought *Olympia* and *Le Déjeuner sur l'Herbe* from Druand-Ruel, the pre-eminent dealer of the age. Moreau-Nelaton bequeathed his entire collection to the nation, and so on his death in 1907 Victorine became the property of the state, housed in the Musée des Arts Décoratifs, where she remained until her move to the Louvre in 1934. But by then, for Victorine, the show was over. In 1927 the woman on the canvases had died, poverty-stricken, in Montmartre, all too aware that her artistic value had far outstripped her personal fate. Now her paintings hang in the Musée d'Orsay, the nineteenth-century annexe to the Louvre. And that's where I had arranged to meet Petra that day.

The rain stopped as soon as I left London. In Paris the day was curaçao cooled with a chunk of ice. The cab hurtled me south towards the river and then we were across, the old train station that is now the Musée d'Orsay looming impressively on the Rive Gauche. I was early but it really didn't matter. In fact I was pleased to be there first. I wanted a moment or two alone with Victorine before having to share her with my friend.

The gallery was surprisingly quiet. I bought my ticket – only to discover Victorine's face printed in miniature on the back. I put her straight in my pocket – I was too close to the real thing now to waste time with bland copies – then I wandered into the main hall, where statues stood evenly spaced along its length, like a platform of solitary travellers waiting to board the next train.

The d'Orsay's ceilings stretched high above me and I could see shadowy figures scuttling between galleries behind the glass end-walls. I glanced at the nineteenth-century collection – Delacroix, Courbet, Ingres: France in the final throes of realism. I felt I needed a moment to get my bearings before going off in search of Victorine. But she wasn't where I was expecting her to be, upstairs alongside the other Impressionist paintings. Instead she was installed in a small side room on the ground floor and so I happened upon her without time to prepare myself at all.

No wonder Victorine was thrown out of the Salon, I thought, as I stared at her. Her look's indecently bold, unashamed – confrontational even. You can almost smell the attitude in it. Evidently she's meant to be appraising a newly arrived client, someone standing just outside the painting's frame, where I found myself now. Manet's *Olympia* seemed to eye me directly, and immediately I was ensnared. My eyes moved from hers and travelled across the canvas. She's lying on a bed, on an embroidered ivory shawl spread over a creased white sheet. Her calves are crossed and a gold and blue silk slipper dangles provocatively from her right foot – she's allowed the left one to fall, has made no attempt to replace it. Two large square pillows are propped behind her copper-toned head and her face is slightly flushed. She might have just yawned. There's a flower tucked coquettishly behind one of her ears, and she's tied a black velvet ribbon in a bow at her throat. She's wearing a thick gold bangle on her left wrist. Other than these trinkets, she's naked. Victorine's body is extraordinary and unusual. There's no romancing of her flesh. Her torso's jaundiced, her stocky body muscular and inelegant, her breasts full. She's surprisingly androgynous and there's a maleness to her overt display of sexuality.

By contrast, a servant woman with polished mahogany skin offers Victorine a blousy bunch of freshly cut flowers, while a sleek black cat stands eyeing her archly from the foot of the bed.

The most transfixing feature of the painting is Victorine's stare, but the second is her large, lifeless left hand. It rests across her lap, central to the painting's composition. Perhaps, by avoiding showing what was underneath, Manet hoped to retain a modicum of respectability for Victorine, and avoid backlash on his own account into the bargain.

Essentially, in the *Olympia*, Victorine represents two themes: sexual possession and art in transition. She had been painted to shock, as one of art history's first modern aesthetic experiments. Manet knew exactly what he was attempting to achieve when he put her in that pose. And once she'd appeared on his canvas, all painting that had gone before became historic. And all art with any true value created since has had no option but to be modern.

I tried to imagine what her world had been like and how intimate Victorine and Manet had been. I wondered, also, how aware she was of his theoretical intentions. I hoped she had been committed to his bigger idea, that she was a party to his plans. Otherwise the public and critical reaction to her work might have come as a horrible shock. I wondered if she preferred the physically painful process of sitting for an artist to her alternative way of making money, from fucking strangers, which no doubt was a faster and in some ways less difficult task. And then I speculated as to whether she had slept with Manet – before or after a sitting – or not at all? I wasn't of course the first, and wouldn't be the last sitter who ended up sleeping with the artist who was painting her. This reflection made me think back to the start of things, to the seeds that launched my own career in the contemporary art world.

14

My neck was beginning to ache. I was naked on a wooden chair, my legs crossed, right elbow resting on left knee, head at a 45-degree angle to my body. It was my fourth and last pose of the sitting. Outside, someone shouted and a car-horn beeped, then another; road rage at 10.45 on a Thursday morning. Covent Garden was waking up. Intermittently, ten pairs of eyes flicked up to concentrate on my body, then back down to their sketchpads to depict the image.

While they worked quietly, I'd been scrutinizing the student in my direct line of vision. She was about twenty, slim-framed, with blonde dreadlocked hair; a wide mouth, thin lips and chiselled cheekbones; possibly Scandinavian. Her face was clear of make-up, her complexion milky smooth with a smattering of sun-kissed freckles on the bridge of a neat little nose. She had eyes the colour of the sea, viridian one moment, azure the next, before shifting to granite, depending on the momentary effects of shadows that fell over her as clouds passed by the studio's high Victorian windows. She was wearing a pair of jeans, patched all over with cotton transfers of fish and shells, below a garment made from one long, thin strip of violet-coloured gauze that she had somehow wound up from her waist, round and round her body, to form a halter-neck top. On her feet were a pair of (prerequisite) trainers, cerulean blue, with magenta laces, like something Matisse would have painted if he were working today. I would like to paint her, I thought, which was ironic considering it was she who at that moment was sketching me.

The stillness in the studio was broken by the appearance of a dishevelled, middle-aged man in old faded brown cords and a checked red and blue flannelette shirt, open at the neck to display a few curling salt-and-pepper hairs. On his right wrist was a copper bracelet; on one finger, a thick, platinum ring. As eyes lifted to register Jeff Richards' appearance, the intense concentration of the moment dissolved and the art students began to pack up their stuff. I turned my neck round and round and from side to side to loosen up, then, as I rose from the chair, pulled my black T-shirt dress on over my head.

The shellfish girl was talking to Jeff. I approached them, then hesitated.

'I'll be lecturing on Baudrillard at four in Theatre 2,' he was telling her, his tone unassuming and warm. 'Maybe you should come along.'

The girl nodded and smiled lopsidedly. She found him attractive, I thought.

Jeff noticed me loitering and turned to acknowledge my presence. 'Hi. How did it go today?'

'Fine,' I said evenly, avoiding his gaze. 'Same time next week?'

As he nodded he smoothed one hand through his hair. Don't give the game away, I thought. We both knew that in fact I'd be seeing Jeff later, back at his studio after the lecture to which he had just referred.

Another student approached, so I made to leave. I got to the door at the same moment as the shellfish girl.

'Hello,' she said, eyeing me with clear interest and opening the door to let me pass ahead of her.

In her pronunciation her whole history could be calculated. There was a 'u' in the 'e', and a drawn-out 'owe' at the end. She was a middle-class chick with art-school overtones – laced with the slightest hint of an otherness, too, an inflexion away from standard English. I might be right about the Scandinavian link, I mused.

'I haven't seen you around college,' she continued. 'I'm Petra.'

'No, I don't study here,' I replied casually. 'I just model for Jeff's classes. I'm training to be an actress.'

Petra's face lit up. 'Intriguing,' she said. 'Fancy a fag?'

Petra and I spent a satisfying afternoon together inside the National Gallery, wandering past the old masters, pausing occasionally, but not concentrating too hard on the artwork. We had blatantly been far more interested in finding out about each other than the art. Petra, it transpired, was taking combined study in fine art and fashion. She had a heady, wayward laugh and an acutely dry sense of humour. In her I knew instinctively that I had at last found a friend, and on her invitation accompanied her to my first ever art lecture.

'The philosopher Jean Baudrillard coined the term "the simulacrum", which sums up the central philosophy of most post-modern artists. The fundamental key is that nothing they do is new, and everything is open to reinterpretation – or reappropriation.'

Jeff paused and glanced up at the audience. I was quite impressed. The National Gallery's main lecture hall was almost full. I hadn't been to an academic address since I'd last seen Ava's tragically interrupted performance, and that had been over two years ago. My first term at RADA had been almost all practical, and the few classes we had tended to be in small groups in regular college rooms.

'And they see representation and reality as overlapping,' he continued slowly. 'Therefore, to make their own works of art worthwhile, they subvert the surface value of what they see with unexpected juxtapositions or contexts, where the meaning shifts.'

I glanced sideways at Petra and she arched her eyebrows. I stifled a giggle. This Baudrillard lark was a bit pretentious. 'I can't believe you persuaded me to come,' I scribbled on a piece of paper and pushed it across for her to read.

Petra scanned the note, then added a more lengthy reply and pushed it back to me. 'The lecture might be boring, but you must confess it's worth it to watch Jeff. Don't you think he's sexy (in a perverse older man, Bryan Ferry kind of way?!!!)'

I considered replying, but then thought better of it. Best not to confess to all my sins on our first day of meeting.

After the lecture I made my excuses to leave. But before we parted company we arranged to hang out together again after the following week's figure-painting class. And I also managed to get a commitment out of Petra to allow me to paint her.

I had taken up the modelling job at St Martin's following a chance meeting with Jeff Richards in Cornelissen's, the traditional suppliers of fine-artists' materials near the British Museum. I was halfway through my first term at RADA and was struggling to get to grips with an energy-draining depression that had set in when I first came to London. The doctor blamed it on my hormone levels changing, but I wasn't so sure. Something inside me felt empty, bereft. It was probably the result of all that had gone on in the previous year. Maybe, I had thought, it would help to start painting again. Since I'd started at RADA two months previously, there had been no time to do so. That Saturday I had decided to use pretty much the last of Simeon's inheritance to buy six quality oil pastels. I wanted to make a small abstract picture that reflected the feeling inside me, in varying hues of red, from the palest rose blush, to the deepest blood-orange.

Setting me free in an art shop is like offering a huge box of chocolates to a child and I was kneeling down amid the trays of pastels, deeply absorbed in the process of choosing, when I heard a man clear his throat.

'This one will give you a more intense tone,' he advised in a low, even voice.

I glanced up from the tray of reds to see a lopsided but generous face smiling down at me, the man's finger pointing at a subtly different hue from the pastel I held in my hand.

'And that one,' he continued with growing enthusiasm now he knew he held my interest, 'will provide you with the many translucent qualities of flesh.'

'Right. Thanks for the tip,' I replied, swapping my choice for the two he'd recommended. There was something subtly suggestive in his choice of words and I felt my interest quicken. We exchanged a know-ing smile and struck up a whispered conversation among the endless trays of colour, as Jeff helped me whittle the rest of my choice down from the initial hundred reds on offer to a perfect six for the picture I had planned in my mind. During the process he divulged he was an artist and lecturer in fine art and I found myself happily telling him all about RADA.

'I'd love to see the resulting picture,' he said, and handed me his card as I paid for the materials. 'I'm looking for a new model for my students' life class, too. Perhaps you'd be interested?'

I took the card. I needed the money and was flattered to be asked. I was also attracted to Jeff. Since the episode with Kenny I had steered clear of men. But he was different. For a start, he must have been close to forty, more than twice my age, and that in itself felt strangely reassuring.

I started modelling for Jeff's students' life class the following week and, predictably, within a fortnight I was also modelling privately for him too.

Jeff's studio was hidden away in an old industrial estate in West Hampstead, surrounded by pretty, overgrown allotments. Inside, the arid smell of charcoal dust, mingled with the slightly sweet, heady aroma of linseed oil, provided the perfect partner for the studio's dense silence. A large, blank stretched canvas was waiting when I arrived for our first session. Over the following months I committed two nights a week to the painting, and as Jeff worked an erotic tension grew between us, culminating eventually in the first of many frenzied sexual encounters. As the painting of me evolved, so did a pattern to our affair. At the end of each session we would indulge in more physically creative pursuits and I learnt many things – not only about painting, but also about how intense the relationship could be between artist and sitter, and, equally, about how obsessed one could become with the practice of art.

Over the following months, as my friendship with Petra grew, I began to hang out at Central Saint Martin's, and we spent more time together looking at paintings and hatching creative plans. In the meantime I continued to model, both at the college and privately for Jeff. Inevitably our affair faltered, then failed, a fizzling-out of things without clear punctuation, an unfinished paragraph in my life without need of a conclusion. But the end of our fling opened up a new chapter to me. Through Jeff I had met Petra and through Petra it became clear that my future would not be in performing on the stage, but in the performance of art.

I completed my foundation stage at RADA then immediately made the switch to fine art at Saint Martin's – a true follower of fashion, and, latterly, of Jean Baudrillard. From the start I did not mix only the past masters with present thought to create new meanings. I also used myself and my fictional histories to bring my works to life. In so doing, it seemed I had happened upon my natural vocation.

Kenny Harper had a good memory. He may have got some of the facts wrong, but he had evidently, by hook or by crook, found his way to my flat in London that summer all those years ago. I changed my name to Emmeline when I left the commune. I wanted to be someone else, and I wanted to hide. Obviously the name change had only just been enough to throw Kenny off my scent at the time, although perhaps he saw through it and it was really the idea of my being pregnant that sent him scampering away again. But when I got into Saint Martin's I decided to revert back to Esther. That year was over and all the horrors that went with it – including, I now see, a deep, morose depression that followed my pregnancy – were gone. It was time to be a new Esther Glass, to be a better me, and time to take a very different, forward-looking path.

15

Voices broke me from my personal reverie before the portrait of Victorine Meurent. Shimmering in sea-green, Petra was gliding towards me, a stranger in tow. She drew her arm through mine, and spoke with enthusiasm. 'Esther, let me introduce Guy Coligny.'

We shook hands. He was a French curator or maybe an art historian – I could tell from his general demeanour and the fact that he was utterly at home here – with an easy yet stirring character. Only museum people and artists can achieve that measure of ease inside these impressive halls of fame. And he was wearing classic curator-style clothes too: a tweed jacket, thick wool trousers. A slim volume stuck out of his pocket, something old, red leather-covered.

'Guy works as a curator at the Louvre and specializes in French nineteenth-century painting. Isn't that fortunate?'

Petra's a skilled people-finder. And I loved her turn of phrase. I could immediately tell that she was scheming – and not about art.

'What luck,' I replied. 'Maybe you can supply me with some facts about the elusive Victorine Meurent?'

Guy wasn't much taller than I was, maybe five foot eleven, with a broad frame, olive skin, thick dark hair worn slightly long and messy. He gave a Gallic shrug.

'If it's something I know I would be delighted to help you,' he replied with an attractively gauche smile.

We all turned our attentions back to the painting. I tried to concentrate. I wished I knew whether the finished picture mattered to Victorine, or whether she treated Manet with the same dull disregard as her more regular clients. Did he pay more money or less for the privilege of painting rather than fucking her? But now I felt distracted by the unexpected company – I couldn't do Victorine justice with this shared glance across her surface. I resolved to come back on my own in the morning.

Guy led us from the museum, around a corner and down a quiet street, to a hidden courtyard sheltering Le Café des Lettres. It smelt of well-thumbed pages, fresh coffee, warm chocolate.

'You've provided me with an impossible challenge,' Petra complained as we ordered.

Guy nodded enthusiastically. 'Whatever can she design for you?'

It was true. Victorine's nudity was a bit of a hurdle to overcome. But I'd already decided, I had to use her, as Olympia.

Guy lit a cigarette for me, his searching eyes fixed on mine. I took a drag. In his mid-forties, I guessed. Did Petra consciously set this up?

'You'll have to take inspiration from her body,' he said quietly.

Guy turned out to be a font of knowledge and Petra and I pressed him for details as we drank coffee and I smoked more of his cigarettes. For a start, I asked about Victorine's left hand; it seemed to be painted from a different palate – was grey, dead flesh.

'At the time it was considered obscene to paint pubic hair,' he replied, glancing between Petra and me, 'and Manet was conscious he could push the Salon only so far. He didn't want to idealize Victorine, but he didn't want to be accused of obscenity either.'

Guy was naturally comic and now amused us with anecdotes about the rise of the pubic hair in art; how, for example, the police closed a

Modigliani show in 1917 because his reclining nudes 'had hair', and not on their heads. But there were earlier exceptions, such as Courbet's *The Origin of the World* – which, he told us, was also hanging in the d'Orsay.

'It was commissioned for a private patron's erotic enjoyment, so no one knew of it for one hundred years,' he explained conspiratorially. 'The painting shows the isolated torso and parted thighs of a naked woman.'

'So, virtually pornographic?' I asked, amused by his dramatic storytelling.

He nodded, thick eyebrows raised.

We walked alongside the Seine together in the late-afternoon sun, ending up by Notre Dame as the sky bruised to mauve, burnt with an orange crust. Petra took a phone call, then excused herself – something, she said, to do with a man from Japan in Paris for a day, selling nineteenth-century silk shawls. She had the bit well between her teeth, said she was determined to reference a copy of Victorine's scarf. I didn't believe her but decided to let it lie. Maybe her new German lover was in town. So Guy invited me to eat with him in a small restaurant off Place des Vosges. I was pleased to have someone to talk to about Victorine, so I accepted and we wandered slowly together towards the Bastille.

We ate in a small, intimate bistro where Guy was well-known. He lived just above it and said it was his kitchen during the week. We ordered red wine and, on the waiter's recommendation, shared a huge pot of bouillabaisse. As we ate, Guy deftly turned the conversation to my world. He was well-connected, knew the curator of my next show as well as a number of other players in the London market. I promised to meet him next time he came to town, even though I could sense he might be troublesome – personally, I mean. But I didn't want to focus on my life right now, I was desperate to find out more about Victorine. She'd taken hold of my mind and I didn't want to lose the moment. As soon as it felt appropriate, I guided the conversation back to her.

'Victorine's personal life seems shrouded in secrecy,' I reflected. 'I've found it impossible to unearth facts about her. It's as if the Establishment not only rejected her but somehow ensured her voice was silenced too.'

'You're right up to a point, but there are some interesting anecdotes,' he divulged – 'how true I don't know. For one, in old age she paraded a monkey on a chain in the streets of Montmartre to earn a *sous* – though the paintings of her were worth thousands.' He shook his head at the irony.

'No one's ever said there's a fair relationship between fine art and money, Guy,' I replied pointedly.

'Let's hope there will be in your case, Esther. Anyway, I have a theory for why Manet painted her so flat on the canvas.' His knowledge was compelling. 'I think he knew her well from photographs,' he continued, 'as well as in the flesh.'

'He must have painted her from life,' I interjected. 'I read how Manet scratched through the surface of her flesh some fifteen times before he achieved exactly the right hue for her skin.'

Guy didn't contradict the story, but he explained that there was more to Victorine's career than modelling for Manet. 'She mixed with artists, photographers, entertainers and musicians, and she'd discovered a very modern way to make money too. Not only did she paint and play the guitar, she also posed for pornographic photographs.'

I was intrigued. Guy had now warmed to his topic, speaking quickly, but with authority.

'Delacroix painted her from some. When you see *Le Déjeuner*, or *Olympia*, imagine how early photography flattened dimensions, skewed perspectives. People were seeing reality twisted through a lens for the first time, then recreating these new perspectives on the canvas.'

I was taken aback by these new facts. Guy registered my surprise. 'A friend of mine, a private collector of erotic art, owns three rare photographs of Victorine. I'll see if I can get hold of them for you to see.'

He sat back in his chair and smiled. I guessed the tutorial was over. It must be inspiring, I thought, to be one of his regular students. No doubt his lectures were always oversubscribed.

He signalled for the bill as my mind worked overtime. I could see my performance of Victorine coming to life before my eyes. She was a work of art and a sexual possession – in many senses.

'Esther, are you ready to go?'

I refocused on Guy. Victorine slept with her clients and they paid her in kind. I wondered what Aidan was doing in London, whether he was with Jacqueline tonight. Guy had been very generous with his knowledge, had added huge value to my project and he was a very useful and very attractive man. I was tempted to go home with him. I felt lonely without Aidan and his coolness towards me was dispiriting. But I knew I had to retain my faith in him, in us, or none of this would be worthwhile. So, a touch regretfully, I thanked Guy for dinner and took a cab back to Petra's, alone. His face told of his disappointment but once I'd left I knew I'd done the right thing. My phone began to bleep in my pocket and when I picked it up I heard Aidan's voice.

'I just wanted to say goodnight,' he said quietly.

16

My phone beeped and the gallery assistant frowned. It was a text from Guy. **Lunch now? I have access to the photographs!**

I was standing before *Olympia* again. I'd been observing her for more than an hour. She was a high-wire act and I wasn't sure I could produce a performance worthy of her extraordinary impact on the canvas. I could honestly say Victorine blew me away. I eventually took my leave of her, wandered outside into the sharp sunshine and texted Guy back.

We were to meet by the Pyramid, in front of the Louvre. I perched on the side of one of the fountains and waited. Within five minutes Guy was striding confidently across the colonnade towards me. He quickly led me away, across the Seine, to a bustling restaurant in one of the narrow side streets off St Germain des Prés. Noisy and packed with Parisians enjoying their midday meal, it smelt of richly flavoured stock and roasting meat. We ate *coq au vin* and drank more red wine in the course of which Guy announced gleefully, 'My friend has delivered the photos. They are quite extraordinary. Almost bestial.'

'Can I see them?'

He nodded enthusiastically and took a mouthful of food, chewed on it thoughtfully, then said, 'I read Lincoln Sterne's article this morning. He says you have become a global brand.'

Now it was my turn to be surprised, 'Where on earth did you see that?'

'It has been translated in *Paris Match* – did you not see your photo on the cover? The paparazzi have their eye on you, even if you have not noticed them.'

I glanced around; there was no sign of the pack. But I immediately felt as though I was back on display.

'What was the picture of?'

He had a glint in his eye. 'You and your boyfriend in London, in a car. He is holding your hands, kissing your fingers.'

I could feel myself blushing again. He ignored my embarrassment and adroitly changed the subject. But the news alarmed me. Right now the last thing I needed was the press on to Aidans and my case. We'd always been so careful, but we must've been snapped at Waterloo, before I caught the Eurostar the previous day. I always forget, snappers never sleep.

'Esther, don't worry,' he said reassuringly. 'Now, shall I take you to see Victorine's photographs after lunch?'

There was something almost avuncular about Guy; he kind of took control of things and was inexhaustibly knowledgeable. I hoped we would become friends.

He took me to his small fourth-floor office in the Louvre, packed with leather-bound books of essays and art criticism. His desk was awash with papers, a laptop, a full ashtray, an assortment of pens and a picture of his family. He beckoned me to sit down on the only chair in the room, behind his desk, and I waited patiently while he made a call, his French too low and fast for me to understand. He pulled the blind down, so the room was semi-lit. Before long, there was a tap on the door and a neat girl with brown eyes and sharply bobbed hair handed him an archive portfolio and left. He carried it over to his desk, gesturing for me to move the ashtray away, then pushed all the papers to one side, opened the desk drawer and pulled a pair of white gloves onto his wide hands. I watched as he removed a second plastic sleeve from inside the folder and laid it flat on the desk.

It was a daguerreotype, blurred around the edges, the size of a six-by-four print. There she was, sitting on the second rung of a wooden stepladder. And it was definitely Victorine, the resemblance to Manet's portraits was striking, even in half-shadow. But her face looked uglier, her mouth twisted slightly, her eyes deeper set, angrily dark at the centre. She was wearing a lacy bodice top, undone to her navel, her full breasts spreading across the centre of the image, pale nipples soft and unaroused. Her legs were spread wide apart.

Guy laid out the other two photographs. They were similar in content. I suddenly saw what Manet had so ingeniously captured on the canvas. In all of these images Victorine Meurent retained a certain dignity, indeed emerged victorious. She had a healthy disregard for her viewer's intentions, a sense, in the grand scheme of things, of the triviality of her flesh. Its abuse, after all, had been long in the making. She was a whore who protected the thoughts in her mind from the necessary actions of her body. Remember, in *Olympia*, how Manet had depicted Victorine with a black lace bow around her neck? The metaphor was now clear. What her body did enabled her to have what her mind desired, whether it be another bottle of absinthe, medicines for her ailments, or even coal for her fire to keep her flesh warm.

I had been afraid that my idea of the woman who was fast becoming my favourite subject might be destroyed by these images. In fact the photographs reinforced her stoical, working-class *hauteur*. In Manet's paintings I had seen further than a bland reproduction of Victorine's daily life, into a proud spirit determined to survive, at all costs and against all odds. In the photographs she still remained a priceless possession, a masterpiece in my mind. I walked to the window. Down below, people were emerging and disappearing from the edges of the Pyramid. It was getting dark: time to head back to London. I was ready to go home, but dreaded what I might find.

There was nothing to fear. There was no sign of Kenny, no stories about him and me in the *Clarion* or anywhere else, but in my absence the press had refocused its attentions away from the *Possession* series and onto the photo snapped of Aidan and me at the Eurostar terminal. When I next came into his office, Aidan showed me the clippings with, I detected, a wry smile on his lips.

'This project has reignited their interest in you big time, Esther, which, I imagine, was the whole idea. It's no surprise they're now zooming in on your private life. It was only ever going to be a matter of time. How would you like to respond?'

Aidan's tone was cynical. He wasn't going to let me off lightly for sparking this recent flurry of media attention and I knew he was right to point the finger of blame at me. But I didn't really care what they said about us, so long as they continued to keep their interest on the me of today.

'What's the media saying about the project?' I replied, ignoring his attack. 'Can't we try to keep their attentions on that?'

'They all want a piece of you,' he replied distractedly. 'The US press is picking up on it, too. Katie's just been on the phone to the *Washington Post.*'

'That's great,' I said, trying to mask my concern. The expectations were growing. Aidan's expression shifted and he eyed me blankly. 'At least from a PR perspective Esther Glass fits into the art-market pages as well as the arts sections now. You must be pleased: you're a double hit.'

I ignored the sarcasm and flicked through the pile. My eye caught Martha Bloom's byline above a newspaper profile. She was one of Ava's cohorts. I skim-read the all too predictable argument.

... Glass is championed as the woman's artist. She comes from an impressively feminist background. Her mother, Ava Glass, one of the leading exponents of the women's movement, includes among her writings the Sixties' best-seller *Raising Women*. But what, in fact, has she reared? Is her daughter, the artist, finally selling out on her mother's ideals?

Glass actively embraces hype – using it ironically, she says – but has her fame become disempowering? She recently declared, 'The feminist fight belonged to my mother's generation. Now we look outwards and forwards from it, into a different kind of world, where the issues are broader, the male–female struggle only one factor.'

Maybe it's too soon to demote the original issues in this way? Equality is still on the agenda. There remains disparity in male and female pay; a continuing, pernicious sexism in the media.

If the current trend of chick-lit and fairytale films tells us that all a woman really wants is a man, then the daughters of Ava's Revolution will be applauding the fact that Esther has ensnared such a valuable one in her handsome dealer. Perhaps what they should be celebrating, however, is his apparent ability to win Ms Glass junior over. Otherwise, if she's such a powerful role model for the present generation, what lessons will they learn from this revelation? That, in a perfect world, the moneyman should also be the sleeping partner? In this context it will seem to them that Esther has won the ultimate art prize.

A word of warning, Ms Glass: don't underestimate your influence; and use it responsibly. Otherwise you may be selling short not only yourself but the work your mother's generation put in to give you the chance of independence and the generation that follows you the path to true emancipation.

I threw the paper back down.

'And we haven't seen what Ava's up to with Lincoln yet,' said Aidan.

Lincoln and his 'film crew', which turned out to be Dylan, an effeminate guy with a handheld camera, had just spent the day after I came back from Paris with me at the studio, and I'd talked them through some of my plans. They were about to fly to Paris to see Petra. Before they left, Dylan let slip that they'd already paid a visit to Ava. Lincoln brushed the event off in his typically laissez-faire way. I refused to be riled, but I determined to go and see her myself, as a damage-limitation exercise. I'd been keeping a wide berth. I knew she'd have more opinions about my sale that I wasn't sure I wanted to hear. However, I also knew all too well that information was modern-day power.

'Oh, and talking of Lincoln,' Aidan continued, 'he's on his way in to see Katie. Wants to take copies of all your old catalogues and press releases, for research.'

I decided it was time to take my leave. There was only so much media I could cope with in one day.

I went back to the flat and absorbed Victorine's impact on me. What was she to be? She was charged with meaning, a sexual possession who'd been subjugated and perverted, and in addition, she marked a critical turning point in the history of art. I knew where and how I wanted to represent her in my series. I would show all sides of Victorine in my performance – the street performer, the artist's model, the painter, the whore, the musician and the impoverished elderly woman begging for change. And I would do it through mime. Victorine's would essentially be a private view but, as in her life, it would take place in a closed yet public space. Anyone had had the opportunity to watch Victorine – at a price – in a photograph, in her bed, playing music or even parading the monkey. I would ask my owner to arrange a private view, in a gallery, with a pay-per-view invitation for his or her selected guests, and I would create a screen with peepholes between me and the audience, for them to watch me through as her various lives unfolded behind. Then they would all learn how it felt to take brief possession of a woman and an artwork for themselves. I hoped that they would walk away understanding that possession is often only in the eyes of the beholder. In the end, like Christina, the real Victorine was self-possessed, with only her artistic character in the ownership of the state.

I found a company in Tokyo that made traditional Japanese and oriental screens, which were all the rage in mid-nineteenth-century France. I decided to commission them to custom-make a very special example, based on *The Pleasures of Life* by Armand Seguin, a well-known and pertinent semi-abstract design from the times comprising rich colours and vague figures in an embroidered series of shapes and patterns. The screen itself would comprise four wood panels, made of red oak and birch, covered in three layers of Japanese handmade rice paper, painted by hand in acrylics and watercolour. The frame would be manufactured from black lacquered poplar and have a hand-stamped and engraved solid brass trim. It was to be six feet tall by eight feet wide and it would contain ten concealed peepholes.

Petra's research had produced equally fruitful results – she hadn't been lying, after all. She had commissioned a Japanese silk shawl to replicate the one on which Victorine lies in *Olympia*, and had sourced a pair of antique slippers in the style of those she is wearing, one off, one on, too. In addition, I decided that each of my women would be in possession of a book which would tell or show something more about them. Christina had her prayer book; Victorine would have a traditional Japanese 'pillow book', a photographic diary of an erotic affair, showing only my naked body, abstracted and ambiguous. I wondered if I should ask Aidan to take the pictures for me, but right now the faith between us was fragile. Our love affair had begun in an unusual and intense way. I'd never known him as anything less than both my dealer and my lover. Perhaps that was why we had come to this crisis. Perhaps we needed to find a way to separate the two if we were to gain a future we could share. I had met Aidan because of my art. In fact, I recalled now as I sat staring at my reproduction of Victorine, it was the reason he had come looking specifically for me.

17

'Who's that?'

I shrugged.

Petra arched her finely pencilled eyebrows and flickered her mascara'd eyelashes at a man in a charcoal-grey suit, who was staring at one of my video screens with apparent absorption. He was about thirty, Latin-looking, or maybe even Asian, at least six feet tall, with very short-cropped dark hair and elegant, almost feminine, features. It was apparent he was out of place amid the hurly-burly of the crowd at the graduate show's opening. For one thing, he was the only one concentrating on the exhibits; for another, he was the only person in the place not wearing trainers.

'He sure isn't a student or a tutor,' Petra surmised. 'Looks foreign – and like he could have serious money.'

'Trust you to spot affluence.'

'Money attracts money,' she replied, winking.

I watched as she now turned on her spiked heels and shimmied through the crowd towards him. The man proffered a hand. Their heads were soon bent together, the conversation evidently intense. It seemed Petra had taken it upon herself to be his guide, directing him now from one of my exhibits to the next. She was dressed in a seventies British Airways uniform, had cut out her dreadlocks and her hair was now done up in a neat bun, her false eyelashes complemented by over-painted lips: a perfect pastiche trolley-dolly. The man seemed to pay a lot of attention to my work. Maybe Petra was trying to flog it to him. That would be typical of her. Petra had a nerve, and a charm that could be deadly. The poor guy would probably be coerced into making an acquisition he didn't really want, one he would regret in the cold light of day.

For these pieces for my finals show Petra and I had collaborated on a series in which I'd dressed up and told anecdotes through five different versions of a fictional 'me' – as a child, an adolescent, a young, a middle-aged and an old woman. Petra had designed me a range of costumes. Although the pieces were always apparently about 'Esther Glass' – my history, my personal relationships – they were confessionals with a highly creative spin. Indeed, the fictionalized Esther bore no relation at all to my real world. She was a one-person soap with a dark underside. First we filmed the scenarios and then, as estheris.com, we had placed them on the web. Just like that, I was globalized – and virtualized.

Now I noticed Petra turning and pointing in my direction. For a split second my eyes met with the stranger's. His expression was polite, but mine was one of embarrassment at being caught observing him. I quickly averted my gaze. Moments later I watched as he shook Petra's hand once again, before turning to force his way out through the crowds. He didn't seem interested in looking at any of the other students' works. Petra caught my eye across the room and smirked wickedly. It was extremely hot and noisy and it took her a while to fight her way back.

'I think I've got you a dealer,' she hissed when she finally reached me, mischief shimmering in her eyes.

18

Ava lives in the armpit of Kentish Town these days – a far cry from Ickfield Folly – but she says it suits this stage in her life, is resolute that she has no intentions of moving on. I guess cheek-by-jowl living makes her feel she's at the heart of the matter. Her bell's the top one of four; all below are labelled with crossed-out names of past occupiers. It's not a place where people usually stay very long. But Ava's been ensconced for over ten years now, as much through choice as necessity.

There was no response to my ringing. She's always been a movable feast. It's part of her game, keeping people waiting. And much against their better judgement, wait they always do. I pushed the bell again, impatiently this time, then stepped back and arched my head up at the sitting-room window. Her cleaner glanced tentatively out. It was drizzling again.

The front door finally opened. Desiree's no more than nineteen, a West Indian girl from the neighbouring estate. She's slim-hipped and round-bottomed and was wearing unflattering blue leggings and a murky red sweatshirt, Nike emblazoned across its front. Dusty feet sported a pair of greying white trainers, laces untied.

'Your mum's gone shopping,' she said lazily.

'I thought she knew I was coming?'

She chewed the question over with her gum. 'She went down the High Street.'

So I went looking. Plantain and sweet potatoes vied with hot chilli peppers and knuckles of ginger for customers' attention. Ava was head and shoulders above the crowd in a finely cut (but moth-eaten) tweed coat, with the black DKNY trainers I'd sent her for Christmas peering out underneath. She was pushing a trolley ahead of her like a shield, her grey hair flying out in the wind like an untamed mane. Maybe, I thought, I should suggest renting her a place somewhere a little more uplifting. But I knew she wouldn't concur – would call it dirty money. She was getting closer. I tapped urgently on the taxi's window. Ava glanced in and spotted me. Hesitation wrinkled her brow. When she saw I saw it, her expression shifted and she produced a cautious smile.

She brought the damp air with her as she shuffled into the car, the queue behind beeping as the driver forced the shopping trolley into the boot.

'I thought you said eleven.'

I didn't disagree.

When we got back I hoisted Ava's plastic bags up to her front door. Desiree leant against the hall wall, watching, as I took the shopping through to the dimly lit back kitchen. Ava went straight to the front room, Desiree dog-like at her heels. She sat herself down in the faded floral armchair beside the lit gas fire. Desiree, duster in her hand, began polishing the book-lined shelves. A leafless plane tree and a telegraph pole broke up the view of a dreary grey sky beyond the velvet-draped windows.

I sat down in the armchair opposite.

'Desiree, would you mind putting the kettle on? Would you like tea?'

I nodded as Ava talked, at a pace. She seemed particularly anxious. I wondered what she'd been up to with Lincoln. Dread settled in my knee-high boots.

'John's coming for tea. I bought some hot cross buns – in January, can you believe! Buy one, get one free. Two packets for just 75p.'

I laughed with a degree of affection and she smiled knowingly. She'll never shake off her natural asceticism, however high her royalties rise in the bank.

'Don't you ever think about moving on from here, Ava?'

She shot me a look of steel. The generous moment between us had passed. 'Think I can't bear too much reality?'

'I didn't mean that.'

'We can't all live in glass towers.'

'I just think the stairs, the crowds, might not help you write.'

'Write?' She laughed hollowly. 'What is there left to say?'

'I don't believe you mean that for a moment.'

She looked absently into the fire for several moments. 'Maybe what I really mean,' she said finally, 'is that there seems to be no one left to listen.'

Desiree reappeared, tray in hand, teacups rattling.

I tried to relieve the tension by asking after John as she poured the tea. When the commune finally broke up they'd stuck together. Must be fifteen years now. They lived separately, but otherwise were knitted together like steel wool.

'He's well. Writing a regular column for the *New Statesman*, of all things. Feels he's sold out, to a degree.' She was wistful. 'But we all need to earn a living.'

My tea was weak – but scalding.

'We're thinking of going to his house in France for the spring. But I wouldn't want to miss your sale.'

Clever old Ava: she'd found a way to it.

'Don't worry. I'm sure you can read about it in the press.'

'But it's causing such a stir. I've never known such media hype.' She glanced at a pile of clippings next to the fire. 'Lincoln says it's going to be the biggest art event of all time.'

'Has he been hassling you?'

'Darling, to the contrary. It's been a lot of fun. He's only asked the obvious questions about our past, what it was like being a feminist raising a wild child.' She smiled a touch sanguinely. Ava loved to be mistress of her own myths. My dread deepened. 'But he really hasn't been interested in your art at all. I suppose he can get all that from Katie.'

'Be careful,' I answered coolly. 'Remember they're cutting film – a second here, a second there. When they replay it the meanings can come out upside down.'

She smirked, evidently enjoying the game. 'Messages often get mixed, don't they? I mean, really, what on earth was that Martha woman talking about? And where did that dreadful sketch come from? I remember the Harpers but I had no idea that biker son of theirs was one of your boyfriends.'

Ava saw me pale and for a moment she faltered. In that second she learnt something she must have wanted to know for the past fifteen years: it was Kenny's. No words needed to be exchanged on the matter now. It was resolved.

I swallowed my tea and offered her a cigarette. She refused and I lit one.

'I guess Martha has a point,' I said, intentionally turning the conversation to a safe topic. 'If the public thinks I've become Aidan's puppet, I'll lose their respect as an independent voice.'

Ava looked confused for a moment, then concentrated her attention and followed my line of argument. 'Respect?' Irritatingly, she suppressed a snigger. 'Surely, after all you've done, that's the last thing you care about, respectability?'

'What do you think of my latest project, Ava?'

She interleaved her fingers through the string of red beads hanging from her neck and turned them. 'To be honest,' she replied slowly, twisting them tighter, 'I don't understand what you think you're going to achieve. Is it just a media stunt?'

'Of course not. I'm raising serious issues about women, art and their perceived values.'

'Oh, I see: selling yourself is a form of self-evaluation.'

'On one level, yes.'

'Surely empowerment should come from within,' she retorted, letting the beads go, 'not from augmenting your public and financial status.'

'I'm an artist, Ava.'

'What – because your messages don't translate into the regular language of us mere mortals?'

'No. Because I am an artist who uses herself as her subject.'

She looked pensive and to my surprise, a touch sad. 'You use yourself? And who might that self be, Esther?'

I didn't answer; instead I blew smoke into her fake fire.

'You don't really want to know what I think,' she said with a sigh.

'Actually, I was hoping for some words of support.'

I hated the way she triggered self-pity in me. I never understood what that was about. But I did know that every one of us needs the self-less love of a parent. How could that equate with a mother on a quest for the emancipation of all our gender? I'd only narrowly avoided combining motherhood with my art. Unlike Ava, I believe women can try to have it all, just not at the same time.

'Esther, the one lesson I hope I've taught you in life is that you are self-determining. It's not for me to judge what you do.'

I swear that sometimes she could read my mind. The conversation had emptied me out. I glanced at my watch. 'I'm meant to be at an opening.'

She looked at me wearily and smiled. 'Off you go, then. Do you mind awfully if I don't get up? This damp's got into my bones.'

'Are you OK?'

'Of course. Just tired.'

She'd got in a quick twist of guilt to season my retreat. I kissed her on both cheeks. They felt surprisingly old, powdery and soft.

'Send my regards to Aidan,' she said.

*

We'd been invited to the Serpentine Gallery. Aidan said he'd collect me at six. After seeing Ava I didn't feel up to an evening with him, or the public or the press. So I called to try to wriggle out of it.

'You can't miss it, Esther,' Aidan remonstrated. 'The *Sunday Times* and *Hello!* are both sending photographers specifically to shoot your arrival – and the PA to the director of Tate Modern has just called to ask if you're attending.'

I didn't answer.

'Esther?'

'So much for no more media intrusion before the sale,' I said.

I could sense his frustration sizzling down the phone.

'What else did you expect, Esther? The idea was yours.'

'I know,' I replied. 'But I thought you were here to shield me, not feed me to them like carrion.'

'It's a chance for you to get a feel for how the concept's going down with one of your real commissioners,' he answered tersely. 'I'll see you at six.'

The truth was, I was nervous of encountering the curators who were planning the show. So far the press were enjoying the idea, but how did the suits really feel about it? I knew that they liked to keep a closed shop, but there was always going to be a curator or exhibition organizer keen to shake things up a bit, particularly if the gossip concerned an artist not in their own particular favour. So far, though, I had heard nothing negative from my sources. Maybe everyone was waiting for my actual sale before they threw an opinion into the ring. The Serpentine show was a group affair, ironically with the general theme of playfulness. I thought it sounded a little bit soft, but knew I should reserve judgement until I saw it for myself.

Aidan spent the journey talking on the phone to a sculptor. I got the feeling he was making it clear that I was not the only thing he had on his mind. As the car pulled up I realized this would not be the night for looking at art. The crowds milling around Hyde Park proved that the social pastime of private viewing had become a London obsession. Everyone with an invite must have shown up. Not so long ago galleries were pulling out all the stops to get attendance up: sushi canapés, famous patrons. Today none of that was necessary. In fact, like budget airlines, private views were often without refreshment of any kind – apart from champagne reserved for the VIPs.

Before we got out of the car, I braced myself for the press. It surprised me that I didn't have a flashlight constantly going off in my brain. I couldn't move, it seemed, without a camera in my face. I had loved the attention in the early days and had always accepted that the media's interest in me was essential to my art. But since the Kenny episode I realized I had really begun to fear them. Tonight I wished I could hide my head under a raincoat and escape from their prying eyes.

'How would you feel about chairing a panel at Tate Britain in February? We're running a symposium on Personality in Art. You seem to be the perfect candidate.'

The Tate Modern curator had congratulated me on the sale idea; she didn't seem displeased with my project plan, but was keeping her cards close to her chest. Part of the curators' skill and power lay in their ability to hide their real opinions and deflect any leading questions.

'In principle, of course I accept,' I replied, smiling evenly.

'Get someone to phone Katie at the gallery to confirm the date,' Aidan interjected, his hand resting on the curve of my back. 'Esther's on a tight agenda. She needs to put all her energies into preparing for the sale.'

'Of course,' she replied. 'We'd all hate anything to come between Esther and this particular commission.'

We left shortly afterwards. I stood for a photo call before we got in the car. Aidan hung back, but the paparazzi seemed to know about us and called out for clarification of our affair. I refused to be provoked. Aidan, too, remained silent, but the fact was we left together.

'Well done, Esther. You handled it well,' he said surprisingly kindly as we headed east.

'Which part? The press or the curators?'

'Both,' he replied. 'But you know the press aren't going to leave us alone until we make some kind of statement.'

'It's all got too complicated,' I said. 'I just want to concentrate on the project.'

Aidan looked out into the night, remaining silent for the rest of the trip home, then left me at the front door.

19

In preparation for our 'next stage', as independent artists, after Saint Martin's Petra, Billy, Sarah, Ruth and I had taken up residence as squatters in a disused fruit warehouse just off Shoreditch High Street. It was a Victorian building, four storeys high, with metal windows – and no central heating. But it was summer and we didn't care. Billy had rudimentary plumbing skills and he and a friend had managed to connect us to the water mains. Now there was an old bath sitting in the middle of each floor for very immodest bathing, in scaldingly hot water. Another friend had also managed to re-rig the electricity. For as long as it lasted, this was our playground. We nicknamed it the Eastern Palace.

Petra and I shared the second floor and within a few weeks of being there we'd transformed our space into a creative oasis. My easels and video equipment took up one quarter, Petra's sewing machine, work-table, fabrics, costumes and mannequins another. In the middle was the bath, overhung with a candlelit chandelier from which, Crivelli-like, we had hung plastic fruits: apples, pears, melon slices and bunches of grapes. At the other end were our sleeping and rudimentary eating quarters, each separated by dyed lengths of muslin hung from long metal rails found in a skip.

There was always music playing at the Eastern Palace and our world became the social centre of the local artistic community. All our mates had moved to East London and every night we'd get together and party. We created Nineties 'happenings' in which we'd perform, show off our latest projects, talk about art and future schemes. Petra also held regular fashion shows, using the length of the room as her catwalk. Afterwards she held sales of her clothes. I occasionally made objects to sell, too, to help pay for food. We were broke and happy. My money from Simeon was long gone, and Petra was going through an 'I don't want funding from my family' phase, refusing to plunder her personal fortune rather than earning a living.

Often, very late at night, I would do a performance from the *estheris* series, each time adding another layer to my character's life, building up her fake history through the performances. The films were downloaded daily onto the web for a virtual view. On one particular night the crowd had grown to around thirty people and there was an air of anticipation. Word had got round that I was preparing for a 'big scene'. Esther's story was at a critical point: she was about to confess to the childhood murder of her brother.

Petra and I had spent the day preparing me for my show. In it I was twelve years old, and for the act I was wearing a red checked gingham dress, long white cotton socks, old-fashioned brown lace-up shoes and an auburn wig, plaited down each side of my face, topped by a straw boater replete with crimson bow. I was going to use a skipping rope as a performance prop. I intended to skip and sing, and through the verses of a nursery rhyme the story of my brother's murder would be revealed both to myself – who until now had blocked out all memories of it happening – and to the audience, who in previous performances had been led to believe the death had been caused by a swimming accident. There was to be an eerie contrast between the sweetness of the tune and the macabre confessional eased out in the lyrics.

And to add to the sinister nature of the performance, we'd spent ages lighting my corner, so Esther's childish figure threw long shadows against the walls. The video equipment was set to roll and, for the first time, the performance would be downloaded live onto the web. We had closed the muslin curtains to hide me and the space and Petra had rounded up the guests. The performance was set for twelve. Eventually, everyone squatted or sat in a huddle in front of the area and, on the stroke of midnight, Petra pulled back the curtains and I took the stage.

I held my opening pose, gazing directly into the middle distance, ready to begin. And there he was, looking straight back at me: the man from the finals show. I'd forgotten all about him since that night. Even though he had told Petra very little about himself, she had been convinced he was some hotshot collector who was going to buy up all my work. I'd taken her fantasizing with a pinch of salt. It was every undergraduate's dream – and Petra had wanted it so badly for me she'd almost willed it to happen. More than two months, however, had passed, and we hadn't heard from him again. My mind was working overtime. How had he known to come? Tonight's performance had been noted on my website in the form of an open invitation. He must have seen it there and followed it up. I felt a thrill but didn't want to feel distracted by his presence. So I closed my eyes for a moment and when I reopened them I recast my gaze away from his face. Then I began.

Petra had planned a mad after-performance party. A couple of her friends from Stockholm had flown in with their weird take on rave music and the decks started to spin as soon as I had finished. The show seemed to go down quite well, although everyone was so high it was hard to gauge a true critical response. The great thing about videoing the work, however, was that I had it recorded to review in the cold light of day and I was a dab hand with the editing tool. Something good could usually be made out of a performance, even if it required a series of clever cuts and a new voiceover to add atmosphere or a further level of meaning.

I quickly changed out of my costume and back into my jeans, then made my way into the party. I scanned the room for the stranger, but, to my disappointment, he had already disappeared. Petra was furious to have missed him, claiming she had not even been aware of his presence. She hated to feel left out, and tried to convince me he had been nothing more than an apparition, a symbol of my subconscious desire to find a dealer.

The next morning she was proved wrong. I woke up amid the debris of the night before to the sound of insistent knocking on the door. Petra had gone off somewhere after our party and hadn't returned. I pulled myself upright and wrapped a sarong around me, then made for the door, expecting to see one of the Stockholmers arriving home before her. Instead I was confronted by the stranger in the suit. But this time he was wearing jeans and a black T-shirt. He looked very clean. I felt scum-encrusted. I hadn't even bothered to remove my make-up when I'd gone to bed; I'd simply crashed out at the end of it all.

'Hey, I'm sorry, I didn't mean to wake you,' he said. His accent carried baseball and diners, yellow cabs and sidewalks, in its measured stride.

Realizing it was already too late to apologize for my appearance, I instead dragged my hand through my hair, stood back and gestured for him to come inside.

'I saw you last night,' I said as he followed me into the room, 'but you disappeared before I got introduced. Here, have a seat.' I shoved a load of stuff off the sofa to make a space.

He ignored the invitation and remained standing. 'I decided to go before I ended up staying all night. I'd just got here from New York and the jetlag was kicking in.'

I perched on the arm of the sofa and watched him. 'Ah, so I have one truly American fan,' I said. 'Does that mean to say someone's actually seen my stuff on the web?'

'Sure does. You've got quite a following in downtown New York.'

'I have?'

'Yep. There must be, oh, at least ten of us engrossed in Esther's world.'

I felt a stirring of excitement. It was kind of wild to think that by some means or another my work had attracted the interest of a circle of people thousands of miles away whom I'd never even met. The web experiment had evidently worked.

'And what do these people get up to when they're not searching for weird projects on the web?' I asked.

'Well, that's why I'm here,' he replied with a confessional shrug of the shoulders. 'I'm an art dealer, and it's a crowd of my artist friends who found you for me.'

'Do you have a name?'

He laughed and stretched his hand towards me. I took it, noting slim, fine fingers, smooth ochre skin. 'I'm Aidan. Aidan Jeroke.'

The unfamiliar sound of his name scattered through my being like shingle thrown up a beach by the seventh wave, before settling like sand in the pit of me.

'Strange name,' I said, letting go of him.

'Half Croatian, half American.'

'Ah ha,' I said. 'And what may I do for you, Mr Jeroke?' I liked the taste of his name on my tongue.

'Sell me everything,' he said casually.

'Everything?'

'Sure,' he replied.

Studied casual, he smiled at my evident surprise. This wasn't the first time he'd made such a proposal, I was sure. Maybe I should find out more about him first, get a lawyer, or whatever you were supposed to do. But there was a genuineness about Aidan, and I trusted him instinctively.

'OK,' I said. 'What's the deal?'

Over the following hour he explained. Aidan's ambitions were focused on London. He was intent on making a move over here, to set up an art dealership.

This, it seemed, was my big break. Aidan promised that, within a year, he'd put on a show of my stuff, along with 'three or four others', in a warehouse somewhere down here in East London. He was still to work out the finer details. He confessed he'd been watching the emergence of a new crowd on the British scene for a while now, and that he wanted a part of it. The more he talked, the more enthusiastic I became.

But there was more to Aidan than met the eye. I could sense it without having to ask. He had other reasons for coming to London that had nothing to do with art. He was running away from something – or someone. And I knew it would only be a matter of time before I worked out what or who was lurking behind his intense turquoise eyes.

20

I set off for Paris the day after the Serpentine show. I intended to spend a night with Petra before heading on to see *Madame de Senonnes*. The moment I had first laid eyes upon Marie Marcoz I, like Aidan, knew she had the perfect personality for my sale. After all, she knew all about her value and how to project herself to ensure everyone else understood it too. And so, apparently, did Jean Dominique Ingres. She was an impeccable model for his canvas. When the Vicomte de Senonnes commissioned him in 1814 to create a masterpiece of his beautiful wife, the painter must have whooped for joy. Madame de Senonnes had secrets. I could sense it. I had to go and meet her to find out what they were, and that meant a trip to the Musée des Beaux Arts in Nantes.

Petra's apartment is extremely chic, a glass house skewed on top of a traditional French apartment building down a winding side street. It looks over the jet-black Montparnasse tower to one side, and the cemetery where Sartre and de Beauvoir lie to the other. Apart from the lilac-shuttered high windows everything is white: the walls, floors, furniture. It's all embellished by a mass of accessories: coloured glassware, richly intricate Eastern wall hangings, thick-woven rugs, stained-glass doors and sculpted vases, embroidered throws, even a canary in a gilded cage – and chandeliers with sparkling crystals hanging from the ceilings.

This art deco flat was added during the 1920s, one of many studios erected in the sky by the artists who had been forced to move across the river when the rents in Montmartre crept too high. Petra had 'inherited' the property from a distant Italian aunt who'd worked for a perfumery in Paris in the Sixties. There was never a shortage of money or property in Petra's family. Her brother had a flat in Rome, her younger sister a house in LA. They were both pursuing creative careers, the former as a painter, the latter as an actress. Neither had a salary to afford the keys to their comfort. But I liked Petra too much to feel embittered about her financial security. I too had more money than I needed these days. In some ways, perhaps, Petra's money simply made her more confident to go and get the things she needed. And that included men.

'Guy's coming over this evening for an aperitif,' she announced breezily as I walked through the door.

I moved past her towards the living room and the breathtaking view from her roof terrace; Paris rising and falling elegantly from east to west like a fairytale princess stretched out in sleep. I let myself out and scanned the panorama, Sacré Coeur to the north, industrial towers curling their smoke along the Seine further east.

'What did you say to Aidan about Guy?' she called.

I didn't answer. At this moment I was more intrigued by Petra's motives for introducing me to him than how I was going to handle the repercussions with Aidan.

'Charming, isn't he?' she urged, reappearing with a tray of coffee and petits fours. Petra has always relished complications, mine just as much as her own.

'I'm surprised you didn't want to keep him to yourself,' I replied, a touch snidely.

She ignored my tone. 'Not for me. I prefer the more extreme types. It's you who always falls for the bourgeoisie.'

'Petra, what do you mean?'

She put the tray down. 'Aidan's hardly a member of the avant-garde, is he?' she replied, rather saccharinely. 'He simply fuels its fires.' She sat down on the white sofa, lips shimmering like mother-of-pearl, neat little hands cupped under her mermaid chin. As ever, she was intent on stirring things up.

'Petra, what are you trying to stoke up?' I asked point-blank. We'd known each other long enough for me to ask.

She laughed. 'I think it's healthy for you to see other people right now, honestly.'

I felt unsettled by her words. 'It seems you revel in the prospect.'

'Maybe. Only because I think you've depended on Aidan too much. You're going to need to strike out on your own for this project to work. You can't hide behind your dealer's coat-tails – and, anyway, I think it would be good for him not to be so sure of you for a while.'

I sipped my espresso and looked at her curiously. 'How so?'

'You're extremely valuable to him, Esther. You've outstripped every-one else at the gallery. He needs you: you practically support the business. And it's all getting more intense with the build-up to the auction. I think some distancing's healthy.'

'Do you know something I don't?' I wondered if someone in Paris had linked Aidan with Jacqueline.

'No.' She seemed genuinely surprised. 'No, but I'm sure this auction's going to be bigger than you think. You should be careful and keep in control of your art; don't let him manipulate you, or it. It's a brilliant concept, but it will only work if you fiercely guard your independence. I don't want to see you fail.'

I sat down next to her. 'Thanks for the advice, Petra. It has been on my mind. Aidan hates the idea of my sale. But sleeping with some French curator wouldn't really be my way of creating distance. All it would do is stir me up. Aidan and I might have had our ups and downs, but we are faithful – or, should I say, I think we both are. Things have been tricky enough between us recently as it is. This would just add another chink. And if the press got hold of the story, they'd have a field-day.' To my surprise, I felt tears smarting in my eyes.

Petra seemed oblivious, or chose to ignore my moment of self-pity. She sighed and turned her attentions to a portfolio case on the table. 'OK, honey, but don't say I didn't warn you. Aidan's keen on the cash. I told you that the first time we met him.'

Almost a decade had passed since we'd first come into contact with Aidan, and he and I had been together for most of that time. I found it a little arrogant that she now seemed to think she had a greater insight into his character than I did.

'Thanks, Petra, but on this one I think we should agree to disagree. And just to set the record straight, I seem to remember the first time I met Aidan it was you who told me you could smell his affluence. It didn't seem he was gold-digging back then.'

'OK, OK,' she answered. 'But things move on. You don't seem to appreciate how iconic you're becoming. You'd better start acting the part if you want to keep a handle on it.'

As she moved to the table and a pile of drawings I thought of Ava's words about competitiveness. Maybe what she really meant was ambition. I was beginning to think that, of the two of us, Petra had always been more clear about her objectives. She was determined to succeed. I had made my art for fun, as a kind of displacement therapy, and it had come to mean more to me as time had moved on. I hadn't actively started out wanting to be recognized, and when I began to gain a reputation I'd used celebrity as a theme to explore – the concept of shifting identities had been a powerful, recurring one. These things happened despite, not because of me. I began to see how, in Petra's case, her future had always been contrived, was one that would work even better against a backdrop of fame.

'Now, come on, babe,' she urged. 'Let's not waste any more time on your love life. Here, take a look at this lot.'

Petra came from a family whose members all succeeded. She had learnt the key principles at a very young age. The upside of this characteristic was that, if Petra promised to do something, she always delivered, and on time. I was about to discover that the *Possession* series was no different from any other joint collaboration we'd had in the past. She was already well and truly ahead of the game.

I moved over to the table to join her. One after another she spread out her initial designs and we ran through them in turn. All seven women had been stripped bare and she was beginning to reclothe them in her inimitable style. Her ideas were far-reaching and adventurous, the most complex and evocative I'd ever seen. Petra was on a creative roll, possibly at the height of her powers. I felt my mood rise to the challenge.

In the weeks that had elapsed since the project began, she and her scouts had been tireless in their search for authentic fabrics and accessories to incorporate into the designs of my women's costumes. And she'd been busily commissioning Thierry le Comte, a hip new jewellery designer in Paris, to produce contemporary paste jewellery referencing that worn by all seven of my subjects. While I was busy trying to get under the skin of my women, Petra had applied herself equally intensively to their surfaces.

We worked happily for hours with a focus that reminded us both of our student days. By the end of the session I'd forgotten the anxieties caused by her earlier words and felt reinvigorated to carry on.

As promised, Guy dropped by early in the evening and I was relieved he greeted me with the ease of an old friend. It was a Friday and so, he announced happily, he was *en train* for the country – a weekend with his wife. With his words I began to relax. But when I explained the purpose of my visit to Nantes, he looked knowing.

'Ah, the sensual *Madame de Senonnes*. I understand why she appeals to you so.'

'Am I right to assume that there's more to her gaze than meets the eye?' I asked.

'Oh yes,' he replied with apparent amusement. 'But on this occasion I am going to leave you to find the missing piece of the jigsaw. It will not be hard and I think it will amuse you to discover for yourself her inner life.'

I had to confess my research into the painting so far had been scant. I'd selected *Madame de Senonnes* at face value. I loved Ingres' paintings and knew that, of all his portraits, she was best suited to me. I hadn't needed to fix on details. I'd decided upon Marie for her calm, her worldliness, and I was sure she would be capable of handling the most complex of situations. She appeared totally at ease with her opulent status, perfectly content as the possession of a very wealthy man. And I was delighted to discover that, at the time of painting, she too was thirty-one, exactly my age.

And yet, as with all my selected collaborators, I could sense that there was more to Marie Marcoz than her surface suggested. Was it self-doubt, a wariness that sat in her eyes? Or was it simply a lack of questioning, a languid disinterest in the world around her, the common effect of an overindulged life?

In the hope of finding answers, the next morning I took a two-hour high-speed TGV to Nantes. As soon as we hit countryside I opened one of the monographs I'd brought for the journey and the first mystery readily resolved itself. No wonder Guy had been keen for me to source her history for myself. Damn right Madame de Senonnes was not quite what she seemed. The date of the portrait, 1814, was the first clue to her true identity; the date of her marriage, 1815, the second. What's the deal with French men and mistresses, I wondered, as the train picked up speed, tearing past fields blurred to streaks of green. Marie Marcoz (1783–1828), a native of Lyons, was no aristocratic bride. She was clearly well below the Vicomte's station, a true bourgeois, the daughter of a draper. At the time of sitting for Ingres' portrait, her aristocratic status was far from confirmed. There was, indeed, a promise of marriage but, so far, no ring.

Her story was quite simple. Marie had been betrothed to a Frenchman whose textile business brought the couple to Rome. They divorced in 1809, and within months she'd established herself as Senonnes' mistress. Alexandre de la Motte-Baracée, Vicomte de Senonnes, was a wealthy collector and amateur artist living in Rome. A committed patron of the arts, he later in life became the Secretary-General to the Royal Museums and a member of the Académie des Beaux Arts. Understandably, the portrait is commonly known as *Madame de Senonnes*, or the *Vicomtesse de Senonnes*. So, for the majority of viewers, me included, her status as his wife has been duly accepted. But now the real story altered my perspective on what I was about to see.

As the train approached Nantes station my anticipation grew. That the painting had become known by Marie's married title was unsurprising, particularly when one considered how its value had risen astronomically as time moved on and Ingres' reputation became etched in stone. *Madame de Senonnes* was a relatively early work – Ingres was only thirty-four when he painted it. Nevertheless, she's considered one of his finest portraits. No one would want to suggest that the subject of the painting was in any way *déclassé*, that there was any smear on the character of one of Ingres' finest masterpieces. Later I was to discover that I was right on this point – but only to a degree.

I intended to spend two days in Nantes: go and see Marie, pass a night digesting what I had absorbed, then pay her a second visit the following morning to cement my view. This was a suitably bourgeois city for such an upwardly mobile young lady. As he drove, my cab driver explained proudly in broken English how Nantes was becoming 'the new Paris', the preferred domicile for young professional families who had had enough of the high rents and chaos of capital-city living.

I could understand why. Over the centuries Nantes has preserved the assets of its maritime and river-based history. We passed a series of eighteenth-century ship owners' residences overlooking the river Erdre, with 'mascarons' – sculpted stone masks – and wrought-iron balconies, then drove on around a dynamic port which runs the whole length of the estuary linking the town and river to the Atlantic ocean. Having crossed one of the many bridges braceleting the town, we then headed into the medieval centre, concentrated around the cathedral, the château prominent in its southeast corner. The Musée des Beaux Arts is situated between the château and the botanical gardens. *Madame de Senonnes* is the undisputed jewel in their crown.

My phone rang as I walked into the museum's immense, elegant white marble foyer.

'Hi, Esther. It's Guy.'

I was surprised to receive a call from him *chez famille* in the Loire but he sounded quite at ease.

'How's it going?'

'I now know all about the vicomtesse's infidelities,' I replied.

He chuckled. 'I'm pleased. Now, Esther, I have arranged for one of the curators at the Musée to call you. I hope that's OK. She is responsible for *Madame de Senonnes.* Can't tell you more.'

I thanked him but I was keen to see this painting alone. After trying to share Victorine with Petra and him, I recognized the value of a private view. But no sooner had I hung up than my phone began to ring again. I hesitated, then answered.

'I am Sandrine Macon. A friend of Guy's.'

She offered to come and meet me, apologized that, as it was a Saturday, she was not currently at the gallery. I suggested we have tea at my hotel later in the day. By then I would have had time to meet Madame de Senonnes on my own.

So now I traced the museum map towards her. She was easy to find:

up the grand marble staircase and through the first main gallery to her own private quarters in a small circular room at the end. All paths converged on the masterpiece. Great paintings are like famous people. They seem to draw you naturally towards them, but, on meeting, are frequently less impactful than anticipated in your mind. This was far from true of Marie Marcoz. Her seated portrait did not disappoint. Standing a metre high, she makes her presence felt. My immediate response was one of surprise. Her indolence was disconcerting. Unlike Christina or Victorine, who seemed to want to communicate their thoughts to you, clearly, in direct contrast to her provocative pose, Marie Marcoz was cautious of forging a relationship. She didn't want to share her past, or indeed her present life. I felt an immediate affinity with her stance.

She's a dark-haired beauty, seated at a slight right angle, her head turned to look straight at the viewer. It's an enlivening pose, popularized first by Leonardo da Vinci in the *Mona Lisa*, and appropriated by portraitists ever since. But in this instance, Ingres has tilted Marie forwards on sumptuous golden cushions, so forcing her waist in and her chest out, enhancing the fullness of her breasts. It's an overtly sexual pose that contrasts starkly with the closed look on her perfectly oval face, reminiscent itself of a vanity mirror. There's a dream-like quality to this portrait, emphasized by the mirror-image of the back of her head, enabling Ingres to show the ruby and diamond comb in her hair.

She's dressed in deep red velvet. The folds of the fabric are slightly faded in parts, suggesting that this signature dress has been worn before. Ingres was painfully aware of detail, and fanatical about replicating the fashion of his times. But I wondered whether, on this occasion, he was also hinting at the 'second time around' of the woman as well as her attire? The dress is decorated with puffs of silvery grey-white satin, in imitation of the sixteenth-century taste for slashing the upper layer of the fabric to reveal the contrasting garment beneath it.

Her right arm is curiously lengthened and distorted, curving snake-like to her lap.

Around Marie's neck is a triple-layered ruff of delicate 'Blonde', a silk lace that was *à la mode* at the time. It froths like champagne spray, contrasting with and enhancing the smooth, almond quality of her skin. Attached to it is a translucent silk chemisette, superficially covering her chest and shoulders, giving her bosom a scintillating, pearlized sheen. The cleft between her breasts is emphasized by three long jewelled chains, one carrying a small perfume container, the others a cross and a cluster of jewels, a jade at its centre.

She was the ideal vehicle for my first performance, I decided. Madame de Senonnes' body oozes sexuality. I would be for sale and needed to pull out all the stops. The red dress is a perfect metaphor, her overt sensuality and lavish adornment suggestive of high value and availability – but at a price. She is also wearing a surfeit of jewellery, which I assumed were love tokens from the Vicomte. There were a few too many for good taste. Marie Marcoz wasn't completely top-drawer. And neither, to be frank, I thought, was I. I wondered what the Vicomte's snobbish family would have made of her. I noticed she had pierced ears, too. Piercings and slashed fabric: hardly the trappings of the aristocracy – at least not in public.

Marie's right hand holds a white linen handkerchief, drawing attention to the seven rings on her fingers. Her right arm is set back on the cushions, and an Indian silk shawl unravels from behind her and out of the picture frame, like a stream in mid-flow. One more specific element caught my eye. In the mirror behind Marie are tucked a number of calling cards, one of them signed with the artist's name. These were not the devices of aristocracy; they were a definite reference to her more humble roots. I decided to find a way to incorporate these props into my performance.

In the *Possession* series, I'd already planned that Madame de Senonnes would symbolize beauty, metaphorically displaying wealth and sexuality, but now I could see the hidden meaning. She was also a touch disingenuous, a woman hedging her bets. She was playing to win and – as her later history confirms – win she did.

'I feel privileged to meet such a renowned artist.' Sandrine Macon was in her early fifties, with tight grey curls and tiny round specs on the end of her neat little nose. She was as small as a mouse yet moved with an air of serious intention. Her smooth doll-like hand settled lightly in mine. 'We are proud to have you staying in Nantes.'

I think the sentiment lost something in translation, but I smiled in return. A friend of Guy's is a friend of mine. We drank black Earl Grey tea in the hotel's soulless dining room. Sandrine, it transpired, was a consummate storyteller, and she now generously told me more about Marie.

'When the Vicomte announced he was to marry his mistress, his family was horrified,' she began with high drama, eyes sparkling. 'She was hardly considered suitable to join the family – either morally or socially. Regardless, marry her he did. Their union lasted until her death fourteen years later, in 1828. Seven years after that, the Vicomte remarried and at this point decided to remove the painting of his former wife from his home. Marie was duly handed to his elder brother, but his distaste for his younger brother's first wife had not been lessened by her death. Rather than hang her on the wall, he locked her away in the attic. At some point over the following few years, someone climbed up there and slashed her with a knife. No one ever confessed to this murderous crime – or hazarded a guess as to why anyone would want to deface such a precious artefact. Perhaps, high on venom, the Vicomte's brother had cut her up, inspired by the piercings and slashes Ingres had placed on the surface of the canvas. Till this day the mystery remains unresolved.'

My hotel room was small and nondescript. Late that night I lay awake listening to the hum of the air conditioning and thinking about Marie.

My initial impressions of her as a successful, self-satisfied wife had now transmuted into something more complex and paradoxical. The painting was still very fresh in my mind and I absorbed its meaning behind closed eyes. Marie was conscious of her beauty, was more confident about it than her status or social worth. Ingres had captured this dichotomy of spirit: an outward confidence yet internal uncertainty. How would this affect my performance as this masterpiece? I realized, nervously, that it reflected my own current psychological state all too closely. In this project I was putting myself at the mercy of the public. Like Marie, I was conscious of a superficial admiration, based in my case on past projects and my now absurdly high celebrity status. But inside I was struggling to come to terms with my true values, both as an artist and a woman. I wouldn't need to try too hard to put across a similar mix of availability yet unease on the night of my sale. I hoped to project Marie's enigmatic spirit, but I worried the public might be able to smell my fear.

As a symbol of possession, Marie, I could also now see, was multi-faceted. She was initially loved, for her beauty and character, by the patron; for her aesthetic attributes, by the painter. But as a possession in the hands of the Senonnes family she was shunned, both as a woman and a work of art. Ironically, today her portrait is priceless and the Senonnes family all but forgotten – other than in her name. Even their sinister slashing of the canvas has been rendered invisible to today's admirers by the craftsman's art.

I had just drifted off to sleep when the phone rang. I expected Aidan but got Petra. She sounded gravelly from lack of sleep. Anxiously, I switched on my bedside light.

'I've been surfing all night, trying to source some original First Empire scarlet velvet for Madame de Senonnes' dress,' she said.

'Christ, Petra, it's four in the morning.'

'I know, but listen. It's so valuable most collectors refuse to allow rolls to be purchased for cutting. It's deemed unethical.'

'Never mind,' I reassured her, wondering why this required a middle-of-the-night call. 'We agreed it wasn't essential. We can always use contemporary manufacture.'

'I know, Esther, but that's not what I'm calling about.' Petra sounded triumphant. 'I've found her shawl.'

'What do you mean?'

'It's an original: exactly the same colour, design, everything. The website actually references the painting.'

I pulled my legs round and sat upright. 'That's extraordinary.'

'Go online. I've sent you the address. Buy it now, before anyone else gets their hands on it.' Her enthusiasm was infectious.

'OK, OK! I'll mail you when I've had a look.' I switched on my laptop and clicked through to her mail, then hit on the URL supplied. Sure enough, pixel by pixel, a photograph of Madame de Senonnes' ivory shawl started to download onto the screen. I glanced at the reproduction of her in my book: Petra was right, it was identical. I eagerly read the supplied information from antiquetextiles.com, based in some obscure corner of the United States.

A collector's treasure! Rectangular shawls with solid ground and patterned borders were the signature fashion accessory of the Empire period. This shawl is fashioned with an ivory silk twill weave ground, surrounded by applied borders and stylized flowers. It measures 19.5″ wide by 96″ long, including the fringe.

I nervously clicked the 'buy' button and, sure enough, $2,000 later I was promised shipping of my Ingres shawl within forty-eight hours. I called Petra straight back.

'I've bought it.' I didn't mention the price. 'Let's hope it's authentic.

What else have you found? How about Victorine's boudoir: any way we could source original objects from that?'

Petra laughed. 'The shawl was more luck than judgement. I spoke to Caroline Jones at the V&A last week. She says originals from the period are extremely rare.'

'Let's hope this one's not a fake,' I joked. 'Now, go to bed.'

'Oh, one more thing,' she added, casually: 'Madame de Senonnes' cuff and collars, they're made of Blonde Lace. When you get a chance, have a look at the second URL I sent you. In the eighteenth century it was manufactured in and around Caen, in Normandy – two hours or so from Paris. I've sourced an antique-lace dealer who lives near there, in Bayeux. He thinks he may have some originals. Might be worth a visit. Guy's keen to go see it – do you fancy a trip out there on Monday?'

'What's Guy's interest?' I asked suspiciously.

'Well, it is his period, darling.'

'I'll think about it. Now, go to sleep.'

Having told Petra to go to bed, I now found I couldn't get back to sleep. So I followed her advice, hit the URL and read about Madame de Senonnes' lace, which helped to turn my thoughts away from Guy.

Blonde Lace is a bobbin lace made in France in the eighteenth century from unbleached pale beige Chinese silk. Subsequently, the term 'Blonde' was extended to cover lace made of bleached silk (white blonde) and black-dyed silk (black blonde). Blonde Lace was made in France at Bayeux, near Caen, and Chantilly in the mid-eighteenth century and also in England (Dorset) c. 1754–80.

Before the Revolution of 1789, Blonde Lace was light and decorated with flowers. This style later gave way to a heavier 'Spanish' style. A revival of Blonde, including earlier styles, took place in France in the nineteenth century. According to the Duchesse d'Abrantes,

who married in 1800, Blonde Lace was a must-have summer lace
and it was plentifully used to trim the gowns of her trousseau.

I never thought I'd be awake at five thirty in the morning reading
about antique lace, but I was fascinated. As dawn nudged its jaundiced
light into the January sky I looked up at Madame de Senonnes. She
and I were about to face the greatest challenge of my career. We were
going to walk together through Sotheby's before the world's media and
the art world's high and mighty. And someone was going to put a price
on my head. I knew that any original piece of her I could take along
with me would be somehow reassuring. I couldn't explain why. I wrote
a quick email to Petra before heading back to bed.

Must get the lace. Suddenly seems imperative I wear some original stuff. Don't
mind about the velvet if the rest's antique. E
PS: Happy if Guy comes along. Maybe he can help authenticate any
purchase?

The sun pierced through a gauzy mist rising across the fields of
Normandy. Guy hurtled along the autoroute from Paris – Miles Davis
loud, shades on, windows half down – towards Bayeux and the antique-
lace dealer with a promise of original Blonde.

Petra coloured the trip with stories of recent finds: a fur stole hunted
down in Prague for Isabella d'Este, and, she boasted, her pièce de
résistance, a Queen Elizabeth I prayer book, made in the 1550s, for me
to carry with Christina. I was impressed. It was a particularly relevant
choice: as Henry VIII's daughter, Elizabeth had come to the throne
during Christina's lifetime.

The lace dealer's bony fingers handled the tiny pieces of lace like
jewels, laying each out on a small table covered in black velvet. The
'blonde' was the colour of crème fraîche, whipped to a silky sheen,
fragile to the touch. With Petra's prompting, he allowed me to try on

the ruff and it settled easily around my neck, gently tickling my skin. Guy looked on, entranced, then spoke in low tones to the dealer. We struck what appeared to be a fair price. A young girl, apparently his daughter, then emerged silently from the shadows and folded the lace into a midnight-blue velvet sleeve, before sliding it into a black box tied with a purple ribbon.

Guy smiled broadly as we stepped out with our prize into the sharp brightness.

'We must celebrate. It is quite perfect. There is a gourmet restaurant, in an eighteenth-century château, only twenty minutes away. It is exactly where Madame de Senonnes' circle would have convened.'

He was right. It was like stepping back in time two hundred years. The magnificent dining room hummed quietly as a handful of diners talked in low tones over their meals. Its floor-to-ceiling windows looked out across ornamental gardens, set with topiaried trees, gravelled pathways and a small fountain spraying water through the ever-sharpening sunlight outside.

We ordered local delicacies: fresh oysters, chicken poached in Calvados and cream, a Petit Livarot cheese and pear-infused sorbet. All washed down with citrus-laced Sancerre.

I raised my glass. 'To my friend and designer *extraordinaire*.'

Petra smiled, Guy winked, and we drank.

It was already dark when we arrived back in Paris and Guy dropped us in Montparnasse. There'd been a mounting tension between us all day. He asked if I would like dinner.

'It's not that I don't want to, but I shouldn't. Thanks, anyway.'

He nodded understandingly, but his expression was hangdog. As we embraced he pressed a small package into my hand.

I opened it as soon as we got inside Petra's flat. It was a long, jewelled chain with a small glass perfume container hanging from it, pendant-like. Petra scrutinized it, eyes bright, then retrieved my Ingres monograph.

'It's a replica of Marie Marcoz's necklace, known as a *cassoulette*,' she said.

A small piece of paper was rolled neatly inside the glass vial. 'A lucky charm for the night of your sale, from a very charmed Parisian, G.'

21

Aidan had a face like thunder. 'Have you seen the *Clarion?*' he asked angrily.

My stomach lurched and I forced myself to peer down at the cover. Thank God the story was about Guy. There was a picture of him kissing my cheek outside Petra's flat the night before. So much for loyalty. John Herbert had promised to inform me of any unsolicited stories they ran on the lead-up to my auction. Nevertheless I couldn't help but let out a short burst of laughter in relief.

'So what's the deal between you?' asked Aidan, archly.

'He's a good friend of Petra's,' I said, determined not to be drawn. 'I kind of like him. He's funny and educated – and he's been an enormous help with my research.'

'Is that all?'

'Aidan, come on. Please don't do this possessive thing.'

'Est . . .' He sounded frustrated.

'It wasn't deliberate. We were just getting out of his car. He came to Normandy to source some very rare lace for my performance. Petra was there.'

He raised his eyebrows and lit one of my cigarettes. He hadn't smoked for years.

'Maybe the timing's quite good. For people to question whether or not we're together, I mean,' I said, tentatively.

He took a drag.

'You know, when I go up on that stage I don't want the audience thinking I'm being sold off by my art dealer "pimp" for a week. I want them to understand the value as being mine.'

'So how is implying that you're sleeping with some French curator going to reinforce that?' he asked bitterly.

Petra's words floated through my head. 'It wasn't intended and I promise I'm really not interested in him. All I'm saying is the press's interest in him may dampen the focus on you and me – and just before the sale, I think that might be a good thing. In fact, that dinner at Tate Modern, when you're in New York next month, maybe I should invite Guy to accompany me.'

'Do you think he's stupid enough to allow you to use him in this way?'

'Aidan, he's a happily married man.'

'At the moment. You wait till the media's got to him. Let's hope he tells his wife before you get him involved.'

'You're being dramatic.'

'Esther, I know you like to play the media at its own game but they're tougher and nastier than you. Much nastier.'

'I take that as a compliment,' I answered. 'Anyway, when are you going to New York?'

He wasn't keen to change the subject, and remained silent.

So I tried again. 'How's it going over there?'

'It's getting interesting,' he replied sulkily, stubbing out the cigarette. 'I plan to leave Monday, stay for three weeks, meet some possible buyers for you, and talk to Greg about the future in general. Also see as much of Sam as I can.'

'And Carolyn?' Why did I feel the need to ask about his ex-wife?

'Of course. I can't see Sam without seeing Carolyn, can I?' he replied. 'She *is* his mother. Are you coming over?'

'I've got to go to the Frick in two weeks. I was planning to do it just before the Tate dinner. In what sense are you and Greg going to discuss the future?'

Try as he did, he couldn't disguise his excitement. 'There's definitely potential for us to strike a more intimate collaboration. We need a direct pipe to the collectors over there. Europe just doesn't cut it for the majority of our artists.'

I wondered how much the outcome of my sale would influence this ambition.

'You're the lucky one.'

'Well, thanks, Aidan. I thought it was more about judgement than luck?'

'I don't mean you haven't made your own luck, but you understand the business as well as anyone. This sale idea, well, I have to concede, it's shot you right up there in the celebrity stakes. If you pull it off it will be good for everyone. I'm just trying to help you stay on top. For all our sakes.'

'I understand that, but it's not just about money, you know.'

'Esther, without money who's going to fuel your creativity? You don't do things on the cheap.'

I hesitated. Where I was concerned I'd never heard Aidan to be so economically aligned. 'Just so long as the cost's not too high, Aidan.'

'What do you mean?'

'I guess I mean that I don't want to lose sight of my aesthetic principles. Lose sight of myself. The money side – it unnerves me.'

He faced me squarely now, as if he'd been waiting to hear me stumble.

'Well, you were the one who came up with this idea, remember that.'

I felt serious, impassioned. 'Yes, but for me it holds artistic purpose.'

'I know, and that's why I'm here, Est, to take the strain of the commerce out of it. You don't need to worry.'

'But the pressure's there for me to succeed.'

'That's different. That's about you exploiting your artistic skills to their limit. The money gives you the freedom to do that.'

'I hope you're right.'

'Are you worrying about the sale?' He sounded surprised.

I didn't answer. I wasn't going to give him the benefit of seeing me falter. But I was pleased he seemed to be warming to the project, if a little alarmed by the level of wheeling and dealing that seemed to be following in his trail.

I realized I was beginning to get jittery. I didn't want to be laughed off the stage, my reputation reduced to common farce. I wished Jacqueline Quinet hadn't given me the Herodotus. The concept of knockdown prices for the unwanted had really hit a raw nerve.

'Where shall we sleep tonight?' Aidan asked suddenly, quietly.

I was surprised. 'The press is everywhere,' I answered gloomily. 'There's nowhere to hide.'

He took a set of keys from his pocket and dangled them before my eyes.

'What are those for?'

He looked smug. 'I've got us a bolt-hole.'

'What, in the country?'

He laughed. 'No way. Thought you might like a trip with me down Memory Lane, to a time when no one knew or cared who you were. Also, it's easier to be anonymous in the heart of Soho than anywhere less crowded. I think we need to spend some private time together, don't you?'

I took the keys from him and read the address label. It was just around the corner from his original flat in Beak Street, off Soho Square.

'I seem to have a sixth sense with these portraits,' I said.

'How so?'

'When Marie first got involved with the Vicomte he was married to someone else.'

Aidan looked wry.

'Their affair was, to say the least, clandestine,' I continued. 'When Ingres painted her she wasn't his wife, she was his mistress.'

'It was all a long time ago now, Esther. I want to go public about us. I want the world to know how much I love you.'

I was taken aback by this change of heart. 'What about Jacqueline?' I asked gingerly.

He looked bemused. 'What about Guy?'

'I promise, Aidan, there is no one in my life other than you.'

He pulled away from me and sought the truth in my eyes. He put his hands under my elbows and held tight, the whites of his eyes looked brighter than I remembered, his pupils sharp as pinheads. 'Perhaps we needed to start trusting each other a little more. Stop this insidious rot from gnawing through our roots,' he said.

Late that evening I slipped through the crowds unnoticed and into the Soho flat. The size of a shoebox, it nevertheless contained a shower, bed/sitting room and tiny kitchenette. The entire space was painted magnolia. On the wall above the bed Aidan had hung one picture, a black-and-white photograph of the two of us, taken many years before by Ruth, or was it Sarah? We were on Waterloo Bridge, at sunset. I set up my cameras at the end of the bed, then lay back and thought about Aidan's extraordinary ability to forgive – and then about the complicated ghosts of our shared past.

22

'Esther, I've never known you like this about someone.'

Petra and I were submerged top to toe beneath a mass of bubbles in our enormous bath, smoking spliff. We had lit all of the candles in the fruit chandelier, but the studio was otherwise in darkness. We liked to think we looked like two muses. It was the Sunday after Aidan had come and bought me up.

'When he's near me, I can't concentrate on anything he says. I'm utterly overwhelmed by his presence,' I reflected.

Petra arched her eyebrows and took a drag of the joint.

'Every movement of his body seems in tune with my own, like we're implicitly involved in a choreographed dance.'

Now she began to snigger.

'I'm conscious of the angle of his arm in relation to mine, the way our heads tip together, of the movement of the air between us – the atoms seem to bounce and fizz.'

Petra giggled and soon I joined in, until we ached with laughter. No doubt the combination of hard love and soft drugs had unleashed my more lyrical side. But I was telling the truth. Aidan held me utterly captivated.

I'd never met anyone quite like him. For a start, he was a lot younger than my most recent boyfriends – especially Jeff. Aidan was no more than thirty, and he was passionate and energized by life. He saw a future he wanted a part of and was in a hurry to get to it. And he was foreign too, from somewhere that was intangible to me, yet iconic. I'd never been to the US and New York was a fantasy that had always filled my mind. It was the city where Andy Warhol had his factory, where Peggy Guggenheim had set up her gallery, where Yves Klein had created The Store. The MOMA was there, and the Frick, collections that could stick both fingers up at most others on the planet.

To me Aidan was a living, breathing symbol of it all. He was also as obsessed by art as I was and easily as knowledgeable about its history. The key difference was that he wasn't a practitioner. Indeed, his commercial zeal was worn proudly on his sleeve. That was another distinctly un-British attribute. He was up-front about my financial worth, and the marketing potential of our scene in general. He liked to party, but steered clear of the drugs. And for the first year after we met he hopped between New York and London on a weekly basis with the nonchalance of a home counties commuter boarding a daily train. He was intensely charismatic too. I guess that had something to do with his natural dynamism. He seemed to spark excitement in everyone he met.

True to his word on that day we first met, my first group show took place within the year, and soon he'd bought up Billy, Sarah, Ruth, and a number of other artists from our graduation year too. London was a hotbed and he was helping to fuel its fire. In the beginning he didn't try to sell the work. He hung on to it, watching its perceived value rise. By the time he started putting us up for sale, our values had risen tenfold on his original purchase price.

For all his up-front tenacity in business, Aidan was far more reticent when it came to his personal life. We spent a lot of time together over that first year, but I found out little about his story the other side of the Atlantic. Aidan expected me to take him at face value and often said he liked to live for today. It was a policy I was happy to share. After all, I was equally unwilling to drag the ghosts, howling, from my closet.

When our relationship finally moved into top gear, the experience was far weirder than I could ever have imagined, even though I had been certain it was going to happen from that first morning when Aidan had dropped by the studio and found me in a dishevelled heap. I had felt patient and unconcerned by his reticence to make any move on me. I wasn't looking for a relationship, I didn't want commitment, but the easy closeness that grew between us was already implicit in everything we did together, like an unspoken pact.

He had hired an old antique shop, just off Tooley Street, as a makeshift office and storage space. As the months passed we spent increasing amounts of time together. I helped Aidan get other artists on board and he began planning our first group show. When he went to New York I would throw myself back into my work and hang out with my friends as before, but as time moved on I found those weeks harder and harder to deal with. I felt physical withdrawal symptoms when he wasn't around me. Aidan didn't know this and so far nothing had occurred between us. And he kept his activities in New York to himself. I began to suspect that there must be another woman over there, some kind of relationship he was in the process of resolving. But I felt too fragile around him to ask.

On the day he was due back after one of his New York trips I went to his office and waited for him to arrive. We had known each other for about ten months and this time he'd been away for four weeks. In his absence I had worked with a ferocity that frightened me. I'd never been one for toiling; I had always made my art with passion, but in a fairly relaxed, low-key way. But this was different. I felt I was doing it for Aidan and I wanted it to be right. I was pleased with the results and couldn't wait to share them.

I watched from my camouflaged vantage point on the office steps as he walked down the cobbled street, case in hand, head hung low. I was alarmed by his demeanour: something was seriously wrong.

When he saw me a half-smile spread over his face, but his eyes remained clouded, like a mist over the sea.

'What happened?' I asked gently.

'I've had a rather tricky few days,' he replied ambiguously and let us inside.

I'd been to the supermarket and now I emptied out the contents of a carrier bag onto his makeshift desk, pulled the ring-can and passed him a beer. He smiled ruefully and took a swig, then sat back on his chair, let out a big sigh and shut his eyes.

I didn't demand detail, but instead offered to give his back a massage.

'I didn't know you could,' he said.

'What did you think they taught me at that commune?' I asked and moved behind him. I placed my thumbs at the base of his neck and began to turn them in gentle circles. I had never touched his bare flesh before and this initial contact made me light-headed.

His muscles felt knotted and it took a while for me to loosen them up. I lost track of time as I slowly worked my way down to his shoulder-blades. At some point, Aidan reached back and took hold of one of my hands, and kissed my fingertips lightly. Then he turned, his eyes still closed, pulled me onto his lap, and held me close to him. A fine, pure current flowed between us. Slowly, but certainly, our bodies melded into each other until, hours later, we had played each other out. When we finally reconnected with the world around us we were lying together on the dusty floor, amid the cardboard boxes, installations and canvases crammed into the space. Aidan slowly sat upright and put his head in his hands. He was breathing deeply. I lay and watched him, uncertain of his thoughts. Finally he turned and looked back down at me, raised his hand and with one finger stroked my cheek. I smiled sleepily up at him. I felt happier, more complete, than ever before in my life. Like I had arrived at the centre of myself.

'I didn't mean this to happen,' he said thickly.

The words pierced me like a knife. It was only then that I saw Aidan's expression. He looked haunted, as though he'd just dived into the deep end of a swimming pool and remembered he didn't know how to swim.

How could I have misinterpreted the signs so completely? My tongue stuck to the roof of my mouth and my heart burned in my chest. I couldn't speak. I scrambled to my feet and grabbed what clothes I could find. Aidan tried to stop me but I had to get away. I ran from the office, away through the cobbled street and out onto Tooley Street, and I didn't stop. I ran down to the river and over Tower Bridge, through the sleep-silenced City and on. Finally I fell through the doors at the Eastern Palace.

It was only then I realized I hadn't stopped to put on my shoes. My feet were black and bleeding. Petra found me there and called Billy. Together they carried me up to our floor and laid me on the bed. Then Petra ran me a bath and helped me into it. She washed my hair, soaped my skin, and slowly eased a confession from me amid the steam.

I felt I had stumbled into an abyss, like I had laid myself bare. I thought of Francis Bacon's portraits and for the first time in my life I understood the horror in them. If Aidan wanted to, I would let him cut me in half and pull out all my organs, one at a time, analyse each in turn, then dissect my brain, read every channel, understand every nuance, follow every line back to its root. I would sacrifice myself to him and wish for nothing in return. The vision terrified me. I felt vulnerable and alone. I lay on my bed but sleep wouldn't come. Sometime in the middle of the night he rang.

'Esther, I'm so sorry,' he whispered.

'What happened?' My voice sounded disconnected from my brain.

'I'm carrying so much baggage right now. I don't want it to break you.'

'It's too late,' I replied quietly. 'I'm already yours.'

He was silent. I listened to him breathe.

'Can I come over?' he asked finally.

'Why don't I come to you?' I said. 'Petra's here.'

At dawn I rang the bell of his tiny flat in Beak Street and he buzzed me up.

Without speaking I undressed, got into bed with him, and we lay together listening to Soho coming down after another night of cheap Chinese food, gay clubbing and illicit sex. And as light strained to get in through the blinds, Aidan told me all about New York.

'I've been married for six years,' he explained quietly, 'to a woman called Carolyn. She's a beautiful, brilliant lawyer. And we have an even more beautiful and brilliant four-year-old son called Sam.'

Dread clamped its hands around my heart and squeezed. I shut my eyes. 'What's gone wrong?'

Aidan paused before he replied in a small voice: 'Last year, Carolyn told me she couldn't live with me any more. She'd met someone else.'

'I'm sorry,' I said. The stranglehold loosened.

'And there's more. She'd fallen in love with a woman. Carolyn said they were deeply committed to each other.'

'Does that make it worse?'

'I don't know – sometimes yes, other times no. But for Sam, well, it's been devastating. We were all so close. Now everything's had to change.'

'Can you forgive her?'

'Of course. But it's complicated. She's a well-known commercial lawyer. Her reputation could be affected by her sexuality.'

'So it's a secret?'

'Our close friends know, but no one else. And Sam's too small to understand. They live alone now, in our apartment.'

'What happened to the girlfriend?'

'Carolyn's affair came to an abrupt end. Her lover couldn't handle the deceit – she's married too, has kids, has stayed with her husband.'

'So Carolyn, what's happened to her now?'

'Nothing. That's what I find so hard. There's no one else. She's sad and lonely and I miss her – and how it all was. But there's no going back now. It's over.'

'Did you hope there could be?'

Again he was silent for a while before he replied. 'I love her, and Sam, more than life. I've found it very hard to accept. But Carolyn confesses she can't love me the way I need to be loved. She never will. We have to get over it, we have to move on. And do what's best for Sam.'

'Do your families know?'

'Carolyn comes from a family of lawyers. Republican white America can be unforgiving. She doesn't want Sam to lose them, so for now she'd prefer to keep the issue private.'

'So why do they think you split?'

Aidan laughed, albeit a touch sourly. 'That's part of the problem. Because there's no apparent motive on her part, they figure it must be my fault. And I love her and Sam too much to come clean. So I have let them point the finger of blame and moved away so things can calm down.'

We stayed silent for a long time and then, slowly and deliberately, we made love again.

We didn't wake again until late afternoon. But when we did I asked Aidan what he wanted to do.

'When I came to London to find you I wasn't looking for an affair,' he said, 'and I certainly didn't think I was ready for a committed relationship. I wouldn't want Sam to feel his dad had left him for someone else.'

At that point I didn't care what the constraints on us would be. All I needed to know was that we could carry on.

'I understand,' I said. 'I don't mind if no one knows about us at all. So long as I can be with you, I don't care about anything else.'

'Are you sure?'

'Let's just take one day at a time,' I continued. 'You have to put Sam's needs first. It's the way it has to be.'

Like Madame de Senonnes, thereafter I only very occasionally wore our secret on my sleeve. I was terrified that if I did I would lose him. But there were moments when I looked at Aidan and the intensity of my love for him must have been apparent in my eyes. The rest of the time we behaved in public like any other artist with their dealer, and except among our closest friends that's the way it stayed. We had developed a pattern that seemed to suit the design of our lives.

Over the years, as our relationship grew and Aidan's emotional damage healed, he began to spend more time back with Carolyn and Sam together, as a family, and they pulled their relationship round. Now, it seemed, they were very good friends. She often called to ask his advice. And although Aidan kept his own apartment in New York, when he was there he spent as much time living with them at her place as he did at his own. He was a determined father who spent at least a week a month with Sam. For years I accepted this double life he led. His absence always gave me a chance to feel free, independent. Surprisingly, it was often when Aidan was away that I produced my best work.

In the early years, we did have a couple of brief splits, though, when the pressure of the gallery, my high-spiritedness or his wrangles with Carolyn got too much. Partly those splits were about fear, on both of our parts: fear of accepting the very real yet fragile nature of what we had together. But I found it hard to 'be' without Aidan, and we had always come back together again in the end. In those early years Aidan had opened the door for me to talk candidly about my own errors of early adulthood, but I had not been able to find the right words or occasion to explain my past to him. As time had gone on, it seemed the stories became out of reach, and inconsequential, so they remained unspoken.

23

The new flat proved an unqualified success. Aidan and I fell into a new routine that seemed, temporarily, to pull us back together. I felt happier than I had in months. The project was going well, Kenny had, it seemed, gone to ground and Aidan and I were reigniting all that had made us so good together in the past. Over the following few nights we made a pillow book for Victorine. I could imagine her life more readily as I headed for the flat, past young girls framing paint-chipped doorways, neon flashing above their heads. I realized I was losing myself through the lives of the subjects in the *Possession* series. Inside the flat Aidan took Polaroids of me naked, then we developed the images before they were set, allowing light to bleed into the process. The results were random, semi-abstract. In contrast to the pornographic photographs I had seen of Victorine, these were poignant and suggestive yet remained ephemeral, lyrical even.

From these nights of erotica in the heart of London's sex district, I would wake up, put my burka back on and thread my way through knots of tourists in Leicester Square to the back entrance of the National Gallery. I was currently also absorbed in the identity of my fourth subject, a woman whose values could not have contrasted more with my nighttime activities in the name of Victorine-Louise Meurent. And yet, she too had qualities to which I was anxious to try to relate.

There had to be a mother figure on my list. I wanted to explore my complicated and unresolved feelings towards my maternal instincts – as a woman, daughter, and almost mother. I had an inherent fear of ever repeating the experience. It was a sticking point between Aidan and me. He had occasionally hinted at a desire to become a parent again, was keen to be a full-time father. He wanted me to give him another chance at it. But I felt differently. I expect I still hadn't come to terms with what had happened before – and, to make matters worse, I hadn't even been able to tell Aidan about it.

The Madonna of the Pinks is an all-engaging portrait of motherhood and a symbol of pricelessness, both in spiritual and artistic terms. Mary is endlessly reproduced and reinterpreted yet remains pure and perfect. She's been painted more times than any other woman, mythical or real, and in this example she's currently more valuable per square inch of oil paint than any other masterpiece on the planet. As I investigated her core values, I fast realized that I needed an adviser to tell me more about Mary. Although she symbolizes purity, she had the most complex range of perceived values of any of the women on my list. I swallowed my pride and called on Ava. I knew she was friendly with a female priest, someone she'd worked with on a book about feminism and Western religion a few years earlier. Jennifer Crossland was one of the first deacons to be appointed and had risen smoothly through the Church of England's hierarchy. She now controlled a whole diocese and was also a keen amateur art historian who occasionally wrote articles for some of the more pedestrian art magazines. She sounded delighted when I called and readily offered to meet me and so help me define Mary's core qualities.

As a middle-aged female vicar and an apparently Muslim woman wandering through the National Gallery early on a Wednesday morning, we raised eyebrows. Even the invigilators stopped staring at the middle distance to take us in. Jennifer was one of those rare, wrinkle-free people who had no need for miracle creams. Evidently God had made her to be good. By contrast, being with her made me feel more unclean in thought and deed than ever before, particularly when I thought of my recent preoccupation with Victorine Meurent. Jennifer crossed one hand over the other as we wandered slowly through the galleries towards our subject, her head slightly bowed, as if she were wandering through a church. In contrast, her thoughts moved swiftly to my critical theme. She talked evenly about Mary's coexisting roles in art and religion, and I listened attentively.

'On one level, Mary is a symbol of purity and ideal maternalism,' she said. 'But she's also the embodiment of the Church itself and, perhaps most interestingly of all, she's recognized by all three monotheistic religions: Judaism – her own faith – as well as Christianity and Islam.'

'How so in the Muslim faith?' I had never heard of the link before.

'The Koran devotes a whole chapter to Mary,' she told me enthusiastically.

As we passed through the galleries, Jennifer pointed out the range of depictions of Mary that adorned the walls. Through the centuries the Mother of Christ has been painted as everything from courtly queen to peasant girl, from the apocryphal moment of her own Immaculate Conception to her posthumous crowning as Queen of Heaven. The painting I had selected marked a turning point in the way she was depicted. Raphael was one of the first painters to truly humanize the Madonna.

We were aware of her presence long before we could see her, owing to a huddle of tourists crowding us out.

'Is that really her? She's so small,' declared a neat-haired woman with a nasal twang.

'Kinda pretty,' observed her identikit daughter dully. 'But fifty million dollars – is she really worth it?'

Thankfully they drifted away, leaving *The Madonna of the Pinks* to be revealed to us in all her infinite glory.

My recent nights with Aidan had forced my emotions to the surface. I found tears welling in my eyes as I looked at this mother gently holding her child. I glanced across at Jennifer, who was gazing beatifically at Mary. She too was utterly absorbed. At times I might have sniggered at such devotion. But there was something about Raphael's Mary that stopped me in my tracks. Her selfless love imbues this minute canvas with a spiritual radiance as rare as pearls in used oyster shells. I closed my eyes to block the crowds out, and breathed her in. Then I opened my eyes again to look long and slowly at Mary. She had an extraordinary pull on my spirit. I could see how, when Raphael painted her, nearly six hundred years ago, she must have been equally captivating.

The Virgin is settled on thick, golden cushions, the naked Christ child playing on her lap. They're in a lavish bedchamber; behind them sage bed curtains are looped back, and in the right-hand upper corner a small window gives out to a sunny landscape, a typically sixteenth-century device to create depth and dimension. They're playing with pinks, or carnations, as we more commonly call them today.

'The flowers symbolize marriage,' Jennifer explained in low tones. 'Mary's not only the mother but also the bride of Christ.'

Raphael appears to have captured an eternal yet everyday moment. Mary's posture and intense concentration on her child's activities heighten the themes of selfless love and mutual adoration.

The Madonna of the Pinks has been subject to such keen public and media scrutiny in recent times that she's been set within a whole wall display of information about her value. But hanging in my mind, I had my own private image of her. There she was on the wall of a small white room, alone, with an oval window sending shafts of sunlight over her during the day, darkening her surface at night. In the National she seemed in need of escape. In my mind I saw the tiny monochromatic paintings I had made endlessly in my bed-sit when I first came to London, the flat, deep hues reflecting my own emotional solitude, and I realized how bland they were in comparison with this gem of a painting. I forced the memories away, and now read on the walls around her about the drama that surrounded her fate. Until a few years ago Raphael's painting had been left to languish in a dusty corridor of Alnwick Castle. For years Mary's identity was very much in doubt, her aesthetic qualities dismissed as pastiche. But when a curator from the National Gallery visited the owner, the Duke of Northumberland, in 1991 and established her true paternity, the Madonna of the Pinks' fortunes changed overnight. The duke was advised that Raphael's sacred woman and her son would be ripe for kidnapping if left in his castle – and that their priceless value now rendered them uninsurable. Hence the canvas, like Holbein's before it, was put on permanent loan to the National Gallery. With a government indemnity and a safe house for their protection, the mother and child would be secure. The full authority of the state added weight to the curator's verification. Some would say the support was better, even, than a positive DNA. And the duke knew that authentication was the necessary stamp to ensure a continuing rise in the value of his masterpiece.

The National Gallery has seven other Raphaels but *The Madonna of the Pinks* quickly became the centrepiece. But when the duke died suddenly in 1995, his son put his hand in his pocket and discovered a hole. Disregarding any promises made between his father and the gallery, he determined to get shot of Mary on the open market. Extraordinarily, she now suffered a similar tug of war to that experienced by Christina of Denmark almost a century earlier. So much for artistic respect: in both instances, when push came to shove, the woman's greater value was deemed, by their owner at least, to lie in their financial worth.

Before the National Gallery got a look in, the Gettys had committed $50 million and *The Madonna of the Pinks* had a one-way ticket to California. Enraged, London set its mouth in a line and confiscated

Mary's passport. Months of bargaining with the public purse ensued and, amid much contention, she was 'saved'. But saved from what exactly – and for whom? As I was quickly learning, eyes and spirits will admire the Madonna, whosoever and wheresoever they may be.

I went home and took a long bath, to scrub my body clean of Victorine before sleeping through the afternoon. I wanted to find a new blank canvas in my mind, one I could fill with Mary. Victorine needed a period of sleep. Jennifer had pointed me to an essay about the role of art in defining Mary's core qualities to a modern audience. When I woke again, I read it. During the Middle Ages devotional images evolved within closed religious communities as a window into God's domain, heightening religious communion. By the thirteenth century, new monastic orders, such as the Franciscans, were forging more open relations with the secular world. Lay people began to adopt certain aspects of religious practice, such as daily prayer and silent meditations, and they were quick to embrace imagery to stimulate and enhance religious experience. Art could teach ordinary people how to pray – and the focus of these images soon fell on particular stories from the Bible, particularly those relating to the lives of Jesus, Mary and the saints.

Mary's unfixed status ensured that she quickly became the subject of a hundred reinterpretations. As the mother of Jesus Christ, she was the saint to whom all could pray for emotional salvation. But by the sixteenth century some religious leaders worried that Mary was actually overshadowing religious devotion to Christ himself. Much to their consternation, Mary had gained cult status.

In my series Mary was meant to symbolize purity: one clear aspect of womanhood. As to possession, it seemed to me that there was a dichotomy: on the one hand she was priceless and yet on the other everyone felt they had a share in her – and that they could make of her whatever they wanted. In this respect her symbolic value was far from pure. Visual art had a significant role to play in this idolatory; at least in that respect we shared common ground. Each day now I received letters from my fans, and Katie told me girls kept showing up at the gallery in the hope that they might catch a glimpse of me, get a photograph, even persuade me to write my signature on their skin. I was gaining a cult status, one that I worried had little to do with my true identity or the messages I intended to convey. These teenage girls writing their deepest thoughts on their flesh – were they liberating a part of themselves or conversely just displaying their innocent naivety? I feared for them, and for what I might have unleashed: not a new freedom, but increased vulnerability.

I finally came up with a plan. Mary's was going to be the hardest performance to pull off – and could easily be a total failure. I decided to stipulate in my sale contract an audience with my collector in a religious environment, and then I would dress as the Madonna and tell the story of her 'life'. I would attempt to describe the rise of the cult of the Virgin and the impact image-making has had on her perceived value; how it has rendered her far from 'pure'; how she has become the composite of her worshippers' different, deepest desires. I would finally allude to her current aesthetic value in dollars. I would be dressed in robes that mirrored those worn by Mary in *The Madonna of the Pinks*: a beige silk bodice over blue silk skirts, a fine veil over blonde hair. I would carry a spray of pinks and *The Book of Hours*, a prayer book in which the section *The Hours of the Virgin* was devoted to her.

I knew that there was one critical aspect to Mary that I had wanted, yet failed, to confront: her simple role as a mother. It was something I knew I ought to work on. But search as I did, I couldn't find a way to penetrate that part of her – or, indeed, of me. It seemed I had turned a lock on that aspect of my own life and mislaid the key.

24

When Aidan left for New York I had felt bereft – rudderless, even. For two days I couldn't work. My concentration on the role of Mary had been draining. She mystified and compelled me in equal measure, and I found it very hard to move forwards from her as a subject. She also made me anxious about what I was planning to do. Who would be watching my performances and what would they think of them? Ultimately, what would it all mean? The first four scripts were almost complete, but I still had three to go. And the combination of nights with Victorine and days with Mary had already stretched me wide across the spectrum of womanhood, from Madonna to whore and back again.

Each of my women had values to which I could readily respond, but what could they really teach me, or the public who followed my ideas, about artistic possession, women's aesthetic values or our financial worth? One thing was for sure, they reaffirmed the fact that the experience of womanhood was extreme and diverse, that we are definitely much greater, more powerful and more complex than the aesthetic view of our individual parts.

I had a few days to spare before heading to New York. Billy and his wife, Carrie, had invited me to visit them in the country. Much against my anti-rural principles, I found myself on a train heading for Stroud.

Perhaps a break would do me good. Artists tend to hunt in packs. Everyone was there. Sarah and Ruth had driven up the night before, as had Billy's builder brother, Jamie, with Louise, a Californian friend of Carrie's. Saul and Joachim, two sculptors from Aidan's gallery, were showing up later that night. It seemed everybody was getting high on the fresh air. Billy had bought an old Land-Rover and was escorting his guests around the 'estate' – a series of muddy fields and barns – with a new-found vigour. I was concerned that the fresh country air had made him slightly crazed.

I spent the weekend observing my friends with a dispassionate reserve. They loved Billy's place and were plotting with unbridled enthusiasm a collective 'return to basics'. Ruth and Sarah shot off to the local property agents, keen to investigate cottages for sale in the area. It transpired that Louise was an events planner and she'd come up with the idea that Billy and Carrie host an alternative art festival the following summer. To be honest, their enthusiasm reminded me too much of my childhood to get me excited. It was like history repeating itself, but without the political ideologies of my parents' generation. And, unlike them, this lot had loads of money. Their rural idyll was the twenty-first-century designer upgrade, accessorized with organic food and parking on-site for their four-wheel-drives.

I escaped on an early train back to the capital. In one respect, at least, the weekend had been a success, diminishing Mary's grip on my spirit. And I now felt ready to tackle my next subject. Mrs Frances Leyland was waiting for me in New York. I was confident, at least, that she wouldn't have such a pull on my emotions.

Petra was coming to meet her with me. She was struggling to come up with designs for her dress and wasn't sure why. I suggested that maybe she needed to meet her in the flesh to work the concept through. And I was pleased to invite her to New York with me for another reason. I didn't relish the prospect of being there alone with Aidan, Sam and Carolyn. It was too much of a family thing for me to cope with. Their intimacy made me feel fragile – and in the past it had sometimes resulted in bad behaviour on my part when I was in their midst. I had rowed with Carolyn's friends, or indeed with Aidan, over petty differences, refused to go to dinners and often left early to go home alone when we met at social events.

When I arrived in Paris I went directly to Petra's studio in Republic, where she promised a final fitting of Marie de Senonnes' velvet robe.

'You look like a fucking stick,' I found myself snarling as soon as I saw her. I felt anxious about the trip – and at the prospect of trying on the dress. It was critical to the success of the sale. Petra, I could see, was also on edge.

'Food can come later. I only have time to work,' she answered coldly.

I was truly shocked at her appearance. She'd lost at least a stone since we went to Bayeux four weeks ago. She took a cigarette from my pack and lit it.

'And you don't smoke,' I added tartly.

'Fuck you,' she said and struck a match.

We stared each other out, before descending into hysterical laughter. Her three assistants watched on, confused. The air immediately felt thinner, better.

'We're not allowed to lose the plot,' Petra warned. 'It's hard work all the way now. Just keep cool.'

Her workspace is more like a dance studio than a design place: a circular white room with wooden floorboards and mirrors interspersed with floor-to-ceiling windows giving out onto metal-webbed narrow balconies. Her assistants brought all seven prototype costumes out, one by one, and pinned them on me while she circled us silently, as watchful as a shark. Each was in a different state of preparation and I appreciated this was not the moment to pass comment. Petra gave precise orders in immaculate French and the assistants concurred efficiently. I smiled at them encouragingly. By contrast Petra's face was giving nothing away.

Finally the assistants tied me into Madame de Senonnes' corsets, then her silver satin underdress, finally slipping her red velvet robe over my head. I could feel my personality shift as I took on the air of my subject and saw my reflection in the mirrors from all angles. The dress followed the contours of my body, the claret-coloured velvet moulding to me like a second skin. The fabric was cut on the bias, slashed along the inside of the sleeves, allowing the silver satin of the lining to peek through – the style imitating and reinvigorating the earlier Renaissance fashion that Marie's original dress had mimicked. In addition, the velvet was slashed from my heart down to the centre of my stomach – a reference to the painting's sabotage, her posthumous murder.

Petra placed our newly acquired Blonde Lace around my neck and wrists, then added the *cassoulette* from Guy.

'Now we just need the shoes and the rest of the jewellery,' she murmured, a pin sticking out of the corner of her mouth. 'And the skirts need to be seven millimetres shorter, don't you think? We have to glimpse your ankles as you walk.'

Beneath her serious veneer she was pleased with the result, I was sure. As I observed my reflections I could understand why.

'Can someone get my bag, please?'

One of the assistants brought it to me and I asked him to retrieve a package and give it to Petra. The original antique shawl had arrived from the US and was rolled inside. It was a perfect example, the cashmere as light as air, the embroidery as delicate and intricate as in the painting. Petra hung the shawl around my shoulders. I walked forwards and looked properly at my reflection in one of the full-length mirrors, turning full circle. The costume performed its function with precision, referencing the past yet ingeniously bringing Madame de Senonnes into my present with the contemporary twist to its styling and the extravagance of the fabrics. I could see Petra's face reflected in the mirror. She was staring at my back, her face lit in an exhilarated smile. At last it was time for me to pass comment.

'It's perfect,' I said.

The fitting left me reassured. However my actual performances went down, the costumes were magnificent, the effects would be startling. In each instance I was going to be transformed into someone else – someone grander and more valuable – into a series of true art icons. That alone would be enough; any drama that my performances could add, I now saw, would be icing on the cake.

Sometimes Katie does her job inimitably. We managed to slip into JFK unnoticed by the media. The heightened post-9/11 security ensured our passage through the terminal was well handled, the press kept at arm's length. Within half an hour of landing we were on our way into Manhattan. The wind-chill was minus twenty and the streets deserted. This was a whirlwind trip. We only had forty-eight hours in the city.

Aidan was waiting for us at his apartment in a nondescript block on the Upper West Side. He was on an unusual high when we arrived, and embraced me with a candour that Petra had never before seen. I caught her eye behind him and she made a face as he now paced around, talking quickly, a bottle of beer in one hand.

'There's real interest growing over here. And I spoke to Jacqueline yesterday: she says she's got three collectors flying in from the East.'

I forced myself to ignore his reference to Jacqueline, asking instead, 'Who are the Americans?'

Aidan's expression shifted. 'There are two or three possibles, but it's not worth divulging details right now. It may all come to nothing.'

'Don't get all businesslike with me, Aid.'

He threw himself down on the sofa, laughing, and beckoned me over. Petra had gone to take a shower. I sat down on his lap.

'I've missed you,' he murmured.

'Don't change the subject. What can I do to secure their interest?'

'Like what?'

'I don't know . . . like meet them, for example.'

Aidan stroked my hair. 'Don't be so absurd. This is business: you never get what you haven't paid for.' His fingers started to caress my neck. 'I've really missed you. Do you need any more help with the project?'

I knew he was referring to the pillow book. I shook my head slowly. 'I think I've pretty much got Victorine sewn up.'

'No room for improvement?'

'Any more work on that performance and I'll need to retire from exhaustion – *before* the sale. And you're changing the subject. Tell me more about these possible buyers.'

'Don't be so impatient. I'm not prepared to get your hopes up until we have more absolutes.'

He kissed me so hard I had to give up.

'What shall we do tonight?' I finally asked.

His reply was studiously casual. 'There's a dinner, at Carolyn's. Sam's looking forward to seeing you.'

I didn't respond but Aidan could read me like an open book.

'Esther, it's about time you guys got to know one another a bit better. For Sam's sake as much as anything else.'

'I didn't say a word.'

His tone was gentle but coaxing. 'He's getting older now, wants to know more about you. Maybe he'll start coming to spend time in London with me for the vacations soon.'

The last thing I wanted tonight was to have dinner with Aidan's ex-wife, and I felt uncomfortable around his son. He made me feel . . . What was it? Unmaternal? No, it wasn't that: he made me feel inadequate, like I'd failed.

'Why don't you want to go?' Petra whispered, curled up in a towel on her bed.

'I just don't like being around Carolyn.'

'They've been divorced for eight years, and she's a lesbian, for God's sake. There's no chance of a reconciliation, is there? And they've got Sam to consider.'

'Sure.'

'Don't tell me you're jealous of Sam?'

'Of course not.'

The truth was, when Aidan was with Carolyn and Sam I felt like an outsider. I knew his devotion to them was right, but it was hard to bear, particularly when things between us were strained. His relationship with them was pure, had nothing to do with his work. I lay back on the bed and shut my eyes, feeling light-headed and disembodied. The effects of the jetlag were coming over me.

There were at least twenty people milling around in the drawing room of Carolyn's uptown apartment, sharing small talk, drinking cocktails handed around by a uniformed waitress. Carolyn was in their midst and rushed to greet us. I was wearing a short, purple velvet dress and a wig with long, russet-coloured ringlets. In fact it was the wig I intended to use for my performance as Mrs Leyland. Petra was keen I give it an airing, so she could get a feel for the look. I knew the contrast to Carolyn couldn't be starker, with her short blonde bob, beige-toned clothes, peachy complexion and surgically de-creased eyes.

'How are you?' she enthused.

'Good, thanks,' I replied, forcing a broad smile and accepting a drink from the tray. I knew I had to learn to relax around Carolyn; she meant no harm. There was no basis for my rabid jealousy but it was like a mental block. For Aidan's sake I had to try and I so wanted things to be OK.

Aidan gave her an affectionate hug and introduced Petra.

'I've heard so much about you,' said Carolyn.

To my annoyance Petra seemed charmed and they fell into an easy conversation. Sam now appeared from nowhere and leapt up at his dad. They embraced. Aidan loved that kid more than life. He would drop me like a stone if Sam needed him.

Sam turned and eyed me quizzically. 'Hi, Est,' he said happily. 'Your hair looks kinda weird.'

There was no need for a response: Sam had already moved on.

'Can we go watch a DVD, Dad?'

'Hey, in a moment, but first there's someone I want Esther to meet.' He nodded towards a figure whose back was to us on the far side of the room, and Sam made an enthusiastic beeline towards her.

'It's Sonia. Come on, I'll introduce you.'

On Sam's demands the woman turned to greet us. I recognized her immediately from press photos. Her face was a perfect round, her skin pale and flawless, her age indeterminate. She had cropped jet-black hair and was wearing a severe thunderstorm-grey suit. Beneath her ice-white shirt she looked as fragile as a porcelain doll, like she might shatter if you so much as touched her. She'd always reminded me of someone but I could never think whom.

Sam had now got his arm around her waist. Smiling, she held out a small, cool hand and shook mine lightly.

'Hi. I'm Sonia Myrche, one of your transatlantic followers. It's good to see you in New York.'

'I'm thrilled to meet you,' I said, 'but I'm afraid it's only a flying visit.'

'I heard about your sale. We can't wait.' She glanced at Aidan and smiled. 'It would be wonderful if Esther could end up in Manhattan for the week.'

'I'm working on it,' said Aidan.

Their eyes locked. Then they both laughed, seemingly at some private joke.

'I hear Jacqueline Quinet's coming to town,' she said. 'I've met her before.'

Aidan glanced at me. I returned the look coolly.

'She may come over to meet a couple of Esther's prospective buyers,' he said.

Luckily for him, Sonia swiftly moved the subject on. 'So what are your plans while you're here, Esther?' she asked with keen interest.

'I need to go to the Frick tomorrow and look at a painting. It's part of the project,' I said.

'How exciting. Which work . . . No, no, let me guess. Mrs Leyland?' Her words took me aback. 'How did you know?'

She shrugged and glanced sideways. 'It's the one I would choose.'

The night ended in disaster. I drank far too many cocktails and when we got home I challenged Aidan about Jacqueline's apparent trip.

'It's not even confirmed,' he answered evenly.

'Who will she meet? Would it help if I were introduced to these prospective buyers, too?'

'I've already explained, Esther, you never get what you haven't paid for. *You* worry about producing the work, *I'll* worry about selling it. With Jacqueline's help if it's required.'

We rowed late into the night. Maybe it was the proximity of the sale that had put me on edge. There were only a few weeks to go. I had the feeling Aidan was acting particularly harshly to teach me a lesson. After all, he hadn't wanted me to undertake the *Possession* series. But once he'd conceded, it seemed I'd offered a red rag to a bull. Already on this trip I was beginning to see he was now hungry for its financial rewards, was intent on pushing the auction price as high as it would go, maybe at any cost. But he refused point-blank to be drawn on his dealings. Finally, all acrimony played out, we lay in bed together in an unresolved silence while New York rumbled around us like retreating thunder after a violent storm.

'To be quite frank,' I muttered before stumbling into a confused sleep, 'I don't really care what's going on here. It's the last place I want to end up. I fucking hate New York.'

I was relieved the stay was short and that my flight home left the following evening. A quick trip to meet Frances and I'd get the hell out. I felt claustrophobic and threatened in Aidan's city and I couldn't wait to get back to London.

25

The next morning Petra and I trudged across Central Park to visit Frances at the Frick. Snow had fallen on Manhattan and was now turning to a colourless sludge. The day was bright and the sun flushed its surface with a rose-tinted glow. A muted New York City lay all around us, slightly abstracted and curiously still. I was silent and Petra didn't push me to chat. I guess she'd heard Aidan's and my fight in the night. The apartment walls were thin.

Although Frances Leyland had ended up in Manhattan, she was painted in London between 1872 and 1873, at the same time Manet was working in Paris on *Olympia*. But she's modern in a very different way to her French cousin. Unlike Victorine and her uncompromising confrontation with the viewer, Frances turns her back to us, glancing away to an unseen place. So we see only her profile, and not the look in her eyes, not what she's thinking.

We dodged the traffic on Fifth Avenue and approached Henry Clay Frick's magnificent mansion. He was one of America's most successful steel and railroad barons at the turn of the twentieth century and used his wealth to build this powerful art collection. Part of its charm lies in the way the works are hung, by aesthetic rather than historic association, along the mansion's winding corridors and narrow stairwells.

Frances resides in the East Gallery, the final room you enter on a logical trip around the museum. Petra and I wandered slowly past the many other great masterpieces in silence, trying not to hurry towards our destination. But we were both equally distracted by the thought of our meeting, unable to give the dozens of other works the attention they deserved. We passed a Holbein, Titian, El Greco and Bellini with barely a second glance. Then a Constable, Ruisdael, Corot and portraits by Rembrandt and Velázquez. We did stop to pay homage to Piero della Francesca's *St John the Evangelist* dominating the Enamel Room – the only large painting by Piero to have made it to North America. It gave me a moment to prepare for the purpose of our visit. I knew that Frances was waiting in the next room, in the good company of Goya, Turner and Degas.

I spotted her as soon as we entered the East Gallery. There was no one around except for one person, who was standing before our destination painting. Ignoring all other artworks as we passed them by, we were drawn towards Frances like moths to a flame. As we got close, the viewer turned and I was taken aback to see that it was Sonia, wearing jeans and a leather jacket, looking less severe than at Carolyn's apartment the night before, yet still uncannily familiar. She took a tentative step forward to greet us.

'I was working at Weiz,' she said, her tone touching on apologetic. 'It's only a block from here. I remembered you said you were coming at eleven.'

I wasn't sure whether I should feel flattered or suspicious.

'Have you got a show opening?' Petra asked with unbridled enthusiasm.

Sonia glanced at me before she answered, searching, I surmised, for consent. I turned my lips into a smile. 'Not for three weeks, but there are going to be twenty screens. It's a technical challenge, to say the least.'

We all refocused our attentions on the painting. I checked myself. I thought I liked Sonia and really shouldn't mind sharing the picture with her. After all, I had brought Petra with me: I'd never intended this view to be one on one. And I knew for certain that both women shared my aesthetic sensibility. Their presence could only help me in my quest, and there was no one else in the gallery, no one at all. So I turned my attentions to Frances.

Viewing the masterpiece properly, I was struck by its fragile beauty. Frances was definitely painted as an aesthetic experiment, Whistler reducing her to a subtle series of off-white tones. Even her face is simply a remixing of the same colours as her dress, the wall, blossom, and matting beneath her feet. It's one of the first stirrings of true abstraction on canvas. In fact, the palette's so muted it's almost singular in tone. Mrs Leyland's robe makes her look saintly. It's like a priest's gown or a christening robe, or even a simple wedding dress, with its long, elaborate train, embellished with gold brocade and small, embroidered golden rosettes. The abstract, basket-weave patterns of the matting at the base are repeated on the frame, offsetting the naturalistic flowering almond branches to the left, and reflecting Whistler's deep interest in Japanese art. The work's signed on the middle right-hand side with the artist's emblematic butterfly, a design based on his initials: JMW.

I realized that Petra had turned from the painting and was observing me long and hard. At her request I again had on the wig I'd worn at Carolyn's party.

'Your wig's far too red,' she judged. 'The overall tone of the painting's really quite pink. The hue perfectly offsets Mrs Leyland's auburn hair.'

I watched her admiringly as her critical eyes returned to the painting. She was concentrating hard.

'I've made her clothes too white,' she murmured finally. 'They need a hint of rose. We'll have to get the fabrics dyed.'

I too was struck by something new I could see in the painting, but it wasn't to do with tone. Whistler may not have bothered to paint a likeness of his model, but he succeeded in capturing something far deeper than her looks. Like Holbein's *Christina of Denmark*, I realized, this canvas was imbued with a quality of knowingness. Whistler, like Holbein, had captured the sitter's essence. Frances, indeed the entire surface of the canvas, displays a sentiment I couldn't recall seeing so intensely in any other portrait. She resides in deep solitude. The reduction of the model to an almost abstract series of hues only serves to intensify her lonely meditation.

'I bet on my life that she was miserable when she sat for him,' I found myself saying aloud and with unintentional vehemence.

Sonia glanced sideways at me, dark eyebrows arched. 'Mrs Leyland may have been rich, but you're right, she was really unhappy,' she agreed.

'Why?'

'Her marriage was failing.'

'What more do you know?'

Sonia gave me an enigmatic smile and began to fill us in on her favourite painting in the Frick.

'The pre-Raphaelite painter Gabriel Dante Rossetti painted Mrs Leyland first, then introduced Whistler to the family,' she said. 'Her husband was a shipping magnate from Liverpool. Whistler was then commissioned to paint the second portrait of her, but when Rossetti saw it he claimed it looked nothing like her. That seems ironic to me, considering Rossetti's painting idealizes her as a pre-Raphaelite beauty and he made no attempt to show her individual character.'

'I don't know the painting,' I interjected.

'It's called *Mona Rossa*,' she answered. 'I think it's in a private collection.'

'And how well did Mrs Leyland get to know Whistler?' I pressed.

Sonia shrugged. 'Mr Leyland was one of Whistler's greatest patrons, but they fell out. I don't think there was much of a relationship between any of them after that.'

I nodded but didn't believe that was all there was to it. There were undercurrents rippling beneath this painting's surface, a knowing sensitivity here that, from personal experience, I felt sure hinted at something deeper and more complex between the artist and his model. I glanced sideways at Sonia, but she'd already turned back to the painting. There was more to her presence than met the eye, too. I wondered if she'd been sent to check me out, evaluate me, even, for Greg Weiz, or Carolyn, or someone else, perhaps. After the sale was over I might find out. What were we all really looking for? Right now, Aidan, for one, wasn't keen to clarify the undercurrents of New York's scene.

I spent most of the flight home mulling over the ripples left behind me in New York, and not just under the surface of Frances Leyland's canvas. When he was in Manhattan it felt like Aidan didn't belong to me at all. He had a family there, a neat little family, albeit an unconventional one, as well as a collection of committed old friends, most of whom, it seemed, I didn't even know about. And there were a father and mother he saw regularly in upstate New York, and two brothers who both lived further up the East Coast. I suppose I'd never asked much about them; I hadn't really been interested before. I was starting to realize, however, that Aidan's reasons for wanting to live with me in our 'today' were very different from my own. Unlike me, he had not chosen to reject his yesterday. He simply didn't feel the need to share it.

I looked down at the reproduction portrait of Mrs Leyland in my lap. She was looking backwards, towards something – a happier past when she had no regrets? Suspended in a jet stream midway between two cities my attention turned from her towards our destination, my home town, London. I could visualize myself there, see myself from the outside: running too fast to take stock, hiding from cameras, darting between my public and private worlds, obsessing about my art. And I could see all too clearly how intensely I had guarded my private life as my public persona had grown, how secretive I was about my past, and how awkward I had allowed my relationships to become – with Ava, Aidan and even, to a degree, with Petra.

I had been naïve, and so had Aidan. Between us we had courted the media, encouraged their interest, my projects becoming more and more sensationalist as time had gone on, until now I had their mad, relentless eye on me at all times. With this latest project, I realized, I was beginning to fear them like a demon. My work had been a way of disguising who I really was; by hiding inside fictionalized identities I had avoided confronting my own reality. But I had reached the point where I felt naked in the eye of the media. Since Kenny had sold that sketch I knew it was only a matter of time before they would ruthlessly strip me bare of my artifice.

Out of the blue I thought of Simeon. I wondered what he'd have made of all this, of what I was becoming? He'd been dead for over fifteen years already and as I flew home I missed him with a depth of feeling that surprised me. My father had always despised media intrusion into our private lives, into the life of the commune. Whenever they had tried to penetrate the sanctuary of Ickfield Folly Simeon had stridently guarded it – and us. There had been times when the police were called to remove spying reporters in pursuit of stories of rumoured lascivious behaviour inside the estate's walls. When I was young I had been intrigued by their interest in us and thought Simeon was boring for so determinedly keeping them away.

So much happened to me immediately after Simeon died that I didn't grieve properly for his passing. I thought of Mrs Leyland, looking back over her shoulder with an expression of regret, and realized I felt regret and, to a degree, shame for giving little consideration to the life of my father. I had not allowed myself the privilege of missing him; instead I had shot on ahead into my own independent adult life,

HOLBEIN's *Christina of Denmark*

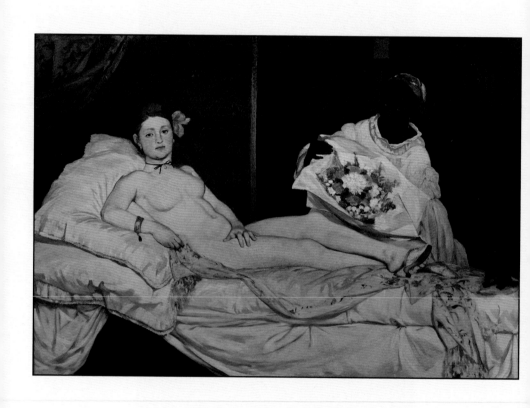

Manet's *Olympia*

INGRES' *Madame de Senonnes*

RAPHAEL'S *The Madonna of the Pinks*

WHISTLER's *Symphony in Flesh Colour and Pink:*
Portrait of Mrs Frances Leyland

LEONARDO DA VINCI'S *Isabella d'Este*

KLIMT's *Judith and Holofernes II*

LEONARDO DA VINCI'S *Mona Lisa*

believing I no longer needed parental input. But at this point in my life his advice would have been invaluable. He would have been sage about my career, but not harsh on me in the way that Ava was. He would also have given me wise advice about the future of my life with or without Aidan as my dealer or lover. I wished he were here.

Sometimes I dreamed that he knocked on my door, and when I opened it he said, 'Esther, why haven't you been to see me?' Each time, before I could respond, the words would send me on a spiral towards regaining consciousness. And there, in the cold light of day, it came home to me that I rarely thought about Simeon. I had never understood where his value for me really lay – and now it was too late to show my appreciation. I thought about the way Aidan looked at Sam the previous night, and how fiercely he had always protected his relationship with his child. It hit me then that not only was there nothing of my childhood left, but somehow I'd quashed most of my memories of it too.

My mind was beginning to drift again, back to the one place I refused to let it go, to that year when I left the folly, the time when my past and a possible future evaporated together. I had embraced a new existence, one that was about discovery, being young and free. But maybe I had made a grave mistake. Maybe I'd ended up creating a series of fictions that would result in my never being able to find permanent ground on which to fix my feet.

I looked back down at Mrs Leyland. What was Whistler trying to say about her? What was I missing? Or was I looking too hard for hidden meanings? Perhaps all that was there was a romantic notion on the artist's part, which in turn imbued the painting with its deep-set melancholy. Or maybe I was simply seeing things that weren't there at all, things that reflected my own emotional solitude. I had become engrossed again. I wanted to know more.

Over the following week I researched my subject hard, looking for clues to the artist's relationship with his sitter. James McNeil Whistler was a prolific correspondent and, remarkably, some 7,000 of his letters are now archived at Glasgow University. Yet again the internet came into its own. Within hours of discovering their existence, I had all of his correspondence with Frances up on my screen. There were at least a dozen personal letters from him to her. And they revealed a clear intimacy between artist and model, the depth of which took even me by surprise.

Whistler began the portrait of Frances in 1871, at her home, Speke Hall, near Liverpool, and continued to work on it over the following two years. When it was exhibited in his first one-person show of 1874, the artist declared it still unfinished. During these years he became a regular visitor to the Leylands' home. He had also become a devoted aide to his sitter during her trips to the family's London residence at Princes Gate, generally when her husband was occupied with business commitments up north.

I discovered references to rumours that had abounded in London of a liaison between the artist and Mrs Leyland, and of plans they had made to elope. Frances herself declared them without foundation. Strangely, Whistler was also, for a short time, engaged to Frances's younger sister Elizabeth. Was this, perhaps, I wondered, an attempt on his part at emotional displacement? Or was I guilty of trying to turn fact into fiction? Frances later said her sister was 'pretty but not the wife for him, and it was a good thing that the engagement was broken'. Good thing for whom, I wondered. For her? I also knew that, at around this time, Whistler had begun conducting an affair with his new model, Maud Franklin, who would sit in when Mrs Leyland was not available. Maybe he fantasized that she, too, was the real thing?

Whatever the nature of their affair, Whistler's letters show that theirs was an emotionally intense union, for a time at least. In his communications, the depth of the intimacy between artist and muse may be couched in formal language but, as in the masterpiece, the undertones cannot be ignored. And in one of his letters his attachment could not be more clearly expressed:

> For nearly all day long you are recalled by your absence! . . .
> Princes Gate is so lonely and so dismal without you that as I
> work and labor through the dreary silence I cannot well over-
> come the sense of being left by you all – and I miss you and
> miss you dreadfully!

For me it is that sense of longing exuding from the canvas which has the viewer in its thrall. Artistically, Mrs Leyland may have been in Whistler's possession, but emotionally she always remained out of reach. Some time after the painting was completed Mr Leyland ordered his wife to cut all ties with Whistler, and it wasn't long before the marriage ended in divorce.

How was I to use this information in my performance? What were Mrs Leyland's critical values, in life and in art? On the canvas she remained, essentially, an artistic experiment, but one that examined how paint could communicate the depth of human emotions as well as complex aesthetic ideas. Who possessed Frances? Her husband paid Whistler £210 for the painting, but perhaps during the commission he had also lost her heart to the artist? That would have been a heavy price to pay for any painting.

I resolved to use Frances on day five of the *Possession* series. Hers would be an enigmatic performance, abstract and solitary, simple and fragile. The act would need to be played out in a social context – a private one, with only my purchaser and his or her close family or social circle present, at their home – during tea, perhaps. Who would she be feeling an emotional attachment to at the event, I wondered. Maybe no one – only time would tell.

26

'Esther, it's me.'

I was sitting on my sofa surrounded by a sea of papers about Mrs Leyland. Aidan was still in Manhattan but the line was so clear he could have been next door.

'How's it going?' I asked casually.

'Why haven't you called me?'

'I've been immersed. You know, I think Whistler was in love with Mrs Leyland.'

'Come on, Esther, that's not why you haven't called.'

'Is Jacqueline there?'

'Jesus Christ.'

'Is she?'

'Actually, yes. She flew in yesterday. But it's business, Esther – you know that, goddamit.'

'Ah ha.' I felt fragile, very fragile.

'You know, Esther, your behaviour right now is crazy. Things were going so well back in London.'

'That's before I came to Manhattan and realized I hadn't been seeing the whole picture.'

'You have given me the job of agenting this project, so why are you now not letting me get on with it?'

'Because for some weird reason I feel you're being furtive. It's either got something to do with Jacqueline, or the project. So tell me, Aidan, which is it?'

'You're acting like a spoilt child.'

'Where's she staying?'

'I'm not going to indulge you,' he said.

'So why are you calling?' I asked, cool as ice now. I felt hurt, but also strangely distant.

'I just think . . .' he faltered.

'What?'

He didn't answer.

'Go on,' I urged.

'You haven't been honest with me about this project, Esther,' he replied quietly. 'It's not me who's being secretive, it's you. I'm just doing my job and you better let me get on with it. I'm doing the best by you I can. I'm not divulging details because nothing is clear, and on the night, well, hey, who fuckin' knows how it's going to go. I said at the start that any crazy guy could put in the highest bid for you and that's a fact. All I can do is try to find you the best purchaser and try to keep you safe. Because, believe it or not, I love you.'

I felt my cheeks burning with the shame of my behaviour.

'I don't want to fuck things up with you any more, Esther,' he continued, 'but I also can't handle your spoilt rages.'

I felt my entire body begin to shake. 'Fine,' I found myself answering, dispassionately, despite my true feelings. 'If I need anything I'll call Katie at the gallery.'

He sighed audibly. 'OK.'

I felt like my insides were imploding and I could hardly breathe. Once I'd calmed down enough to speak I called Petra and tried to tell her what had happened, but I couldn't control my tears.

'The project is taking its toll because, for the first time in your life, you're putting yourself at the heart of what you do,' she insisted. 'Everything you've done before has been a bit of fun, story-making. This work might be masquerading as a project about seven master-pieces, but actually it's the real story of Esther Glass the artist, the adult woman. It's a grown-up work. No wonder it terrifies you and no wonder it's put such a strain on your relationship – about time, too.'

'That's not what I intended at all.'

'Are you sure?' she asked curiously.

'I think so.' My answer was tentative.

'I think you need to reposition yourself,' she replied gently, 'and I understand why. Mixing work and pleasure is very difficult. If you guys are going to get to the next stage together, then what you're doing now is essential. You couldn't have chosen a more appropriate subject for the work: possession. My God, Esther, doesn't that say it all?'

I had the feeling that Aidan had decided that if he couldn't beat me he'd join me, square-on. This project was about more than art or money. Whatever he said, I knew it had turned into a battle of wills.

27

'It's so good to see you.'

Guy sparkled with good will. He smelt sweet and southern, of a sharp, lemony cologne. I knew I shouldn't be doing this but I needed help and he made me feel safe and good about myself. There was something paternal in his considerations, and he played a role I had recently begun to see I missed in my life, one that in my early adult life had been filled with lovers like Jeff Richards. By avoiding this mistake with Guy, I could now appreciate how invaluable he could be to me as an experienced friend. Guy had dismissed my warning of possible media interest in us out of hand and readily accepted my invitation. Was I using him? For me his wedding ring rendered the issue irrelevant. I enjoyed his company and I needed the companionship of a friend. I was surprised how pleased I was to see him. I knew that the only chance I had of getting through this project now was if I pushed Aidan and my problems to the back of my mind. Guy was not only a good distraction, he was excellent company into the bargain. When I saw him ambling out of customs at Waterloo, I felt my mood lift.

The dinner was being held in the restaurant on the top floor of Tate Modern. The ten artists involved in the project were invited from all over the world. As our car slid past the Millennium Wheel, which was turning slowly, almost imperceptibly, beside a choppy Thames, Guy asked about my progress.

'Five down, two to go.'

'So who's next on your list?'

'Isabella d'Este.'

'Ah, the first lady of the Renaissance. You share fame in common. Will this require another trip to Paris?'

I was aware that there were two depictions of Isabella at the Louvre.

'I'm afraid my chosen portrait of her is in Vienna,' I lamented.

'Ah, the Titian. Of course, it shows a flattering likeness of Isabella as a young woman,' he pontificated, 'but the Leonardo, although it's only a cartoon, I would argue is the essential image.'

'You don't have to try and sell me art to get me to come back to Paris,' I teased. 'Petra and I have a fitting next week. I'll go and see the da Vinci then, I promise.'

He shook his head a touch conspiratorially. 'If you want to see the real thing, Esther, again you will need me. The da Vinci drawing is not on public display. It has to be protected from the light. I will have to arrange another private view.'

'I appreciate your efforts on my part,' I said with a laugh.

'All roads, including da Vinci's, lead to Paris,' he replied knowingly.

I slid my arm through Guy's as we sauntered casually past the pack of photographers hanging outside the jaw-wide turbine entrance to the museum. I forced myself to smile gaily at the cameras and posed for photographs with Guy. We were then escorted to the lift. Inside the restaurant on the top floor the atmosphere was competitive, with invitees milling around clasping cocktails or talking to their partners in low tones, looking out over the Thames toward St Paul's, which was lit up against the backdrop of the retreating city. The group hadn't melded yet. Intentionally, we were the last to arrive and I could tell they'd been anticipating the moment. Sideways glances connected around the room; conversations faltered. Even the curator in charge of the exhibition raised a hand in welcome and immediately excused herself from a highly acclaimed Spanish artist to come and greet us.

'So pleased you could make it.'

Jane Smithson is a global art player who teaches at the Royal College of Art and guest curates significant international shows. She smiled broadly at Guy. 'How good to see you here,' she said. 'Last time we met was at the reopening of the Palais de Tokyo.'

I was relieved Guy was in familiar territory. We were soon seated at a long table down the middle of the restaurant, which had been closed for the occasion. I was placed between the curator and Guy at the centre, opposite a German photo-artist and his Parisian boyfriend, who of course both also knew Guy.

'How's the project coming along? We've got tickets for the sale,' said the German languidly.

'I'm nearly ready,' I replied with caution.

'So is the project, to all intents and purposes, going to be completed before the week begins?' interjected Jane.

'No, but the seven performances I'll be making have to be carefully prepared, the costumes designed and so on.'

'Ah, I see. So will you be filming the performances as the week progresses?'

I nodded and took a sip of wine. Her interest reminded me, once more, why I started out on this project in the first place. Jane had her own investment in me. If I didn't pull it off, she wouldn't fulfil her own brief. She knew reviews of my work would impact on her attendance figures. Hence, in my failure would lie hers. The money was on the door.

'The seven films will form the centrepiece of my room,' I said to reassure her of my good intentions, 'supported, of course, by my overall response to the auction and to a week of being "possessed".'

'So the performances are–,' she paused to clarify her thoughts, 'thematic vehicles from which you will take your lead.'

'You got it,' I agreed, determinedly avoiding eye contact with Guy. Jane is great, but her worthy curator-speak makes me want to laugh. I could imagine those words on the catalogue blurb, or even on the gallery wall, in three months' time. But she looked pleased with herself, nodded approvingly, then took a sip of water. Meanwhile the German looked fashionably bored.

'Where's Aidan Jeroke tonight?' he asked me, pointedly turning his eyes on Guy, who was now chatting animatedly with Jane.

'In Manhattan, on business,' I replied guardedly.

'Oh yes, of course,' he replied. 'I heard Jacqueline Quinet flew over to meet some possible bidders.'

I felt panic. He smiled slyly. I only knew this guy by reputation. How did he know so much about me?

'I'm represented now by Greg Weiz,' he continued. 'I just got back from a visit. He happened to mention you, the sale.'

I hated feeling sidelined. Maybe I should have hung on in New York, gone to Weiz myself and met up with Greg, tried to patch things up with Aidan. I'd met Greg Weiz a few times in the past, but hadn't paid him much attention, and neither had he me. Everyone seemed to be involved with that gallery these days, not least Sonia, and now this guy. What were they scheming for me? I couldn't believe Aidan's big plan didn't involve my future – professionally, at least.

No one drank too much and the conversation was purely work-oriented – very different from a gathering of British artists, which always ends in some kind of riot or showdown. This was far more serious and intellectual and much less fun. We left as soon as coffee was served and Guy dropped me home before heading off to his room at the Charlotte Street Hotel.

28

Isabella d'Este could teach me a thing or two. In many ways this Renaissance queen was an outsider in my mix of women. Unlike the others, who were all painted by and for men, Isabella was, to a high degree, self-determining. She was a cool customer who spent a lot of time alone and she was both a patron and sitter – as well as a symbol of political power. I'd done my research into her in the few days that had elapsed since Guy had come to town and I was fast engaged in her rich and historic world.

Isabella was the first lady of sixteenth-century Italy, the Jackie Kennedy of her age, and she liked to be in control. She was the personal friend of kings and popes and had witnessed many political upheavals. These included the French invasion of Italy, the sack of Rome and the coronation of Emperor Charles V. A high-powered intellectual who could translate Greek and Latin, she moved in a circle of distinguished writers including Machiavelli, Castiglione and Ariosto. She was also a prolific correspondent. Around twelve thousand of her letters are still preserved in Mantua's Ducal Palace today.

I was pleased to discover that Isabella was also an obsessive collector. She commissioned thousands of artefacts to adorn the two private rooms in her palace, the Studiola (Studio) and Grotta (Salon). Her studio was decorated with friezes and her own coat-of-arms was engraved on all the wardrobe doors. Later these were replaced by a series of allegorical paintings by Mantegna. For the Grotto she commissioned the Mola brothers, who inlaid architectures of imaginary cities and palaces, musical instruments and graceful court scenes on wooden panels. In this room, Isabella gathered all kinds of masterpieces: small bronzes, precious manuscripts, musical instruments and a globe on which she followed Columbus's voyages. Only three of the 1,600 pieces she commissioned remain today.

As a child I had squirrelled objects under my dormitory bed like nuts tucked away for winter sustenance. I would pick these up at local jumble sales for a penny or two: old chipped china plates painted with flowers and edged in gold leaf; glass paperweights with flowers trapped inside; silk scarves with geometric Fifties designs; necklaces made of red and green glass beads; strings of pearls and old black and white postcards with other people's personal messages written on their backs in inky italics. I was furiously protective of my meagre possessions, never wanting to share them with the other kids. I suppose it had a lot to do with the egalitarian, sharing, caring mantra of our world. As a child I needed to stake my claim to something other than a big idea. I created my own emblem, a six-pronged star, with each letter of my first name set within a point, and in the centre an open eye. I marked my bed head, my cupboards and the inside cover of my books and even some of my clothes with this insignia, and I hand-painted shoeboxes, with my stamp in the centre, to store my collections inside.

I flew into Vienna on a day-return ticket. I had little time left for research and felt that a single visit to Titian's canvas should give me all the additional emotion I needed to drain from Isabella. She already seemed pretty clearly set in my mind. I arrived at the Kunsthistoriches Museum's reception desk and asked where I might find her. An enthusiastic student inadvertently directed me to a coin cabinet on the second floor; when I peered inside, I found a beautiful state medallion of Isabella from 1505. This unintentional introduction seemed surprisingly appropriate. The coin showed a bust of the first lady of the Renaissance in profile, as stately in pose and with the financial authority of any Roman emperor or king. It was apt that the coin dated from her early life. The surviving portrait by Titian, painted thirty years later, was an attempt to recapture what the coin showed her to have been in her youth.

She may have owned much, but in life she was owned, too, by her husband, at least for a time. Isabella was engaged at six years old to the Marquis of Mantua. They married when she was sixteen, he twenty-five. By reputation the Marquis was ugly yet honest, and an effective fighter – key attributes to success in sixteenth-century Italy, a country then racked by violence and power struggles between the great landowners, foreign invaders and the Church.

But on reading about Isabella I couldn't imagine how he could ever really have possessed her. She was far too clever. It's rumoured that he took unkindly to her political interventions on his part, although they were always to his advantage – at one point she even managed to negotiate his way out of prison. When he died in 1519, their nineteen-year-old son, Federigo II, became Marquis, but the indomitable Isabella retained the real power as regent. So, I suppose you could say that, however hard they tried to possess her, Isabella never let anyone override her true ambition to control.

Isabella championed the arts, systematically pursuing the leading Renaissance artists to paint her portrait. Mantegna, Correggio, Perugino and Lorenzo Costa all took up her commissions, but Leonardo da Vinci produced for her only the sketch now hanging in the Louvre.

At the age of sixty, Titian, the greatest Venetian painter of the age, painted her twice. The first was a contemporary portrait of her in late middle age; the other recreated her youthful beauty. Of the two, only the latter remains. It was for this that I had flown to Vienna.

I finally located the masterpiece, which Titian had painted during 1534 and 1536, only two years before Holbein painted Christina of Denmark. But Titian's portrait of Isabella is cut off below her waist and she's wearing fur and densely embroidered clothes. Back home, Petra was already revelling in the designs. Isabella's head and body are painted at a slight angle, so she glances past the viewer into the middle distance. Her young, soft features are serious and she appears pre-occupied with her own interests. She's lofty and foreign, distant and determined, with maybe a touch of Jacqueline Quinet's controlling personality.

Overall, I felt the trip was a disappointment. The austerity of this cool, well-mannered Austrian city seemed out of keeping with Isabella's hot-blooded Renaissance character. Or, at least, what I had understood it to be. And, somehow, so too did Titian's representation. But maybe these feelings once again had more to do with me than with my subject. For whatever reason, the model just didn't speak to me.

I was keen to get back to London to take stock. However, Guy's words kept playing in my mind: 'Leonardo's sketch may be slight but it is essential.' I had to concede that perhaps, for character, the lesser-known work might provide me with a greater insight than this formal portrait.

As I left Isabella behind, I conceded it was time to ask Guy for one more favour.

'Come now,' he ordered. 'Don't bother to go home first. You might as well catch a flight straight to Paris.'

I took his advice and boarded a different plane, then went straight from Charles de Gaulle to the Louvre, where he was waiting for me. I was anxious to clarify my view of the Renaissance queen. Guy led me to her without preamble. And as soon as I stood before the drawing I knew the detour had been well worthwhile.

Together we stood quietly before her in the semi-lit room. A simple black chalk sketch, heightened with red for her hair and skin, yellow pastel for her robe, it shows Isabella in profile. As I took her in I now understood the term 'masterpiece' in its most elementary form. Guy couldn't have helped but see the intense delight that spread across my face. I was sure he was trying hard not to appear smug.

'The colours are unusual,' I whispered.

'The addition of yellow makes it the only "pastel" remaining by Leonardo,' he replied. 'That fact alone makes the drawing unique.'

I looked long and hard at her. What was it I found so compelling about this simple sketch?

Isabella's shown in a classical pose, in contrast to the more lively approach adopted later by Leonardo for the *Genevra de Benci* or, indeed, the *Mona Lisa*. Isabella sits, torso front, head turned away to profile, a touch inclined, just as she had in the coin I'd seen in Vienna. She has strong features, a prominent nose and wide eyes. Her mouth is set in a gentle, unchallenging line. She has long, thick hair and displays one fine hand crossed over the other.

'Was she pregnant?' I asked inadvertently.

Guy shrugged. 'The timing suggests she could have been. Some critics say so – indeed, they say the sitter in the *Mona Lisa* could have been too. In the case of both pictures they point to the rounded face and figure, and to the fact that neither woman wears rings.'

I determined to check the dates. There was definitely earthiness to the drawing, however 'dry' it might appear to be on the surface, and there was a human quality too: her hair seemed thick and silky, her flesh warm. I already knew that Isabella had been desperately keen for Leonardo to paint her and this was as near as she got to a portrait.

'For four years she harassed Leonardo to that end,' Guy told me. 'You can see how this drawing has been pricked, prepared to be transferred to canvas. Leonardo obviously intended to do it, but he had a reputation for never completing things.'

'I expect he was too busy trying to get Mona Lisa to smile right.'

Guy laughed. 'I hope Isabella came to appreciate that in this sketch masterpiece he had already fulfilled the brief.'

I'd commissioned Petra to design an outfit based on the Titian oil and still felt it was the masterpiece that formed the basis of my act as this independent spirit. I spent the next few days with her as she worked on the costume. The chestnut brown wool/cashmere mix pencil skirt and tailored jacket were richly embroidered in russet with a repeat pattern of Isabella's insignia. It was beautiful, a haute couture suit with a fur collar and cuffs, accessorized with a woollen hat shaped like an anemone. I could easily imagine Parisians strutting up and down the Champs Elysées in such next winter, poodles in matching coats trotting at their heels.

I had invited Lincoln Sterne and the cameraman to come over for the final fittings. All were now ready – but for Klimt's *Judith*, which would not be finalized until my meeting with her in Venice. I allowed Lincoln a sneak preview of all of the costumes, save for my pièce de résistance, Marie Marcoz's sumptuous velvet gown, hanging in darkness, awaiting the day of my sale.

The greatest treat of all was Petra's design from Frances Leyland's robe. She had left New York at the same time as I had, with a portfolio of reproduction sketches we'd discovered at the Frick: preparatory drawings for the dress. It had come to light that Whistler reckoned himself to be a fashion designer as well as an artist, and he'd designed Frances's outfit himself. It can loosely be described as a 'tea gown', a style of garment that was flourishing in the US and England in the 1870s. It was a more comfortable alternative to the tight corsets and highly structured fashion of the time and reflected a link with a history rooted in modernity.

The series mapped Whistler's creative process. They included intricate sketches for the rosettes that stud the dress, and numerous restylings of the robe itself, some with an elaborate train, the palette wider, incorporating ivory, pale yellow and tangerine, the flowers at times almost blood red. Mrs Leyland herself is unlikely to have sat for the sketches; her head is either left out or rendered featureless. Petra discovered that the robe was styled to the paintings of Watteau, the French eighteenth-century romantic painter. In the final portrait it has been simplified, but still harks back to a past age of elegance, to a courtly style: the long train hanging from the shoulders, the gathered sleeves and ruffles around the neck. In the sketches Whistler seemed to have tested a number of poses, too, finally deciding to show Frances from the back, so displaying the train in all its magnificence, while providing the viewer with only the wistful side profile of the sitter. On some of the sketches for the rosettes, instructions are written in French. Much to Petra's delight it appears that Whistler had intended the dress to be made in Paris. There are references to the dress in letters between Whistler, his mother and Mrs Leyland, but the robe itself has been lost to time. Now Petra had well and truly resurrected it.

Once back in London it was to my reproduction of the Leonardo drawing that I returned daily for inspiration. Meanwhile I had contacted the state archives in Mantua and discovered that, three years after her death in 1542, an inventory of all Isabella' s possessions inside the Ducal Palace was drawn up. A complete facsimile of this manuscript had recently been published and copies were available for sale. Never one to miss an opportunity to get closer to my subjects' lives, I ordered one and, with uncharacteristic Italian efficiency, it was delivered three days later. The illuminated manuscript ran to forty-eight pages, inscribed in sepia ink and bound in imitation leather bordered in gold leaf. The two hundred and thirty-six items catalogued inside intimately revealed Isabella's taste and opened my eyes to the true extent of her obsessive collecting.

As a performance, hers was the one I most looked forward to, as it would be my most flamboyant and needed to be played out in public.

I hoped for the chance to play her to a crowd. I would stand and read from her inventory, hand out replica coins to mark her financial worth. After all, Isabella's way of imprinting her value on her people was through financial, intellectual and artistic ownership.

29

'Last time I was in Venice it was a hundred degrees,' Petra moaned from behind next season's Dior, masking Scotch-shot eyes as she shivered in the wind. My mind flicked back to the last Venice Biennale. I was tempted to mention her exploits in Peggy Guggenheim's cloakroom with a certain Italian sculptor, but seeing her pallid countenance I decided this probably wasn't the moment. As the launch swept us past distressed *palazzi* lining the Grand Canal, I too felt distinctly queasy. We were heading for the Ca' Pesaro, a magnificent baroque palace on the island of Santa Croce, home to this floating city's modern art museum. It was a murky February day. Venice was eerily shrouded inside an impenetrable fog, lights flickering from its ancient villas onto the mysterious waters below, providing the perfect atmosphere for a meeting with Judith, my final subject and a potent symbol of myth and murder.

We'd flown in from Paris. I thought back to the reason for our vicious hangovers, a late session in a bar off Rue du Faubourg St Honoré – with Guy and 'the German' – discussing, among other things, my impending sale. As the night wore on, the discussion had inevitably turned to the final subject on my list.

'Gustav Klimt's *Judith*?' the German had asked with affected astonishment. 'We must all be afraid.'

'Of what?' challenged Petra, giggling, arm hanging loosely around his shoulders.

'A man entrapped by a femme fatale faces ultimate ruin,' he had replied, gesturing to Guy and running a finger across his throat.

'It was all in Klimt's mind,' Guy quickly retorted, raising a glass of vodka. 'He was obsessed by sex and death.'

I was having more fun than in ages. Staying in Paris had been a tonic; it had helped me to push my problems with Aidan to the back of my mind. It was great, too, to be around people who knew about my project, as this released the tension in me and for a moment it felt like the responsibility was shared.

'Judith used her sexuality to overthrow a general,' I had informed them sagely, 'but Klimt made her intentions sexual, which, according to the myth, they never were.'

The German tried to focus on me but the vodka was beginning to get the better of him. 'So is his Judith the male fantasy of what drives woman to extremes?'

'Absolutely.' Now Guy looked at me clearly, spoke slowly. 'It's too terrifying for men to acknowledge that women might rationally commit murder. Better to believe Judith was driven to it by unleashed sexual passions.'

'I would say Esther and Judith share something,' the German said. He was definitely slurring now.

Before I could defend myself, Petra fought my corner for me. 'She might take risks,' she asserted, 'but Esther doesn't decapitate her enemies.'

'No,' he replied, truly forceful now. 'I mean they're both Giocondas.'

Guy failed to suppress a laugh.

'But it's true.' The German now took a long swig from his glass. 'Mona Lisa was the archetypal femme fatale.'

'Whoever said I was the model for my myths?' I replied.

*

I thought about Judith's mythical bad behaviour as we travelled across the waves towards her. Five of my seven choices have been real women: Christina, Isabella, Marie, Victorine and Frances. The other two symbolized man's most extreme representations of the female sex in art: Mary, the pure, and finally Judith, the sinner.

I wanted the project to go full circle. Klimt had dragged this Old Testament tale into the twentieth century and reinterpreted the story to suit the culture of his times. He was an Austrian Secessionist, painting at the turn of the twentieth century, who was obsessed by eroticism; even his landscapes seem imbued with a feminine sensuality. Klimt's themes were fashionable in Freudian Vienna. The concept of the femme fatale found a receptive audience but the painting caused outrage in some parts of Viennese society, most particularly among middle-class Jews.

The original legend describes the deeds of Judith, a young Jewish widow from Bethulia, an Israelite city under siege by the Assyrian army. When she hears that the city's learned elders are about to surrender to Holofernes, the Assyrian's despotic leader, she determines to save the city herself. Dressed provocatively in fine clothes, adorned with exotic jewellery, Judith goes to the enemy's camp and offers herself as his slave. A few evenings later, 'desirous of intimacy', he invites her into his tent. On her encouragement, Holofernes drinks 'more wine than he had ever drunk on any one day since he was born' and falls fast asleep before any sin could be committed. Judith then seizes his scimitar and with two strokes cuts off his head. She quickly summons her maid, puts the head in a sack, and returns with it to Bethulia, where she orders the Israelites to display it on the battlements of their besieged city. Soon afterwards the Assyrians flee. She declares she was acting on an order from God. There's no suggestion in the original text that she has enjoyed the experience, let alone gained sexual gratification from it.

Klimt reinterpreted Judith twice, first in 1901, then, again, in 1909.

The earlier painting is as sexually charged as the later version, but lacks its iconic qualities. The first sitter was clearly a contemporary Viennese model, probably Klimt's muse Anna Bahr-Mildenberg. Characteristically, the artist embellished the picture with gold leaf, melding flat planes with three-dimensional figurative painting to produce an idiosyncratic mix of the traditional and contemporary. Judith is wearing a fashionable and expensive gold dog-collar necklace and she holds Holofernes' head, almost absent-mindedly, in her hand, eyes half closed, mouth half open, implying a state of sexual ecstasy.

In Klimt's second interpretation, Judith is imbued with more symbolic warrior-like attributes and exudes an extreme sexual energy which both outraged and antagonized Vienna's Jewish bourgeoisie. In fact, the picture was often retitled 'Salome' by those who assumed Klimt to have mixed up his myths, inadvertently defaming Judith in the process. But Klimt knew who he had painted and why. He wasn't out to please the crowds; like Whistler and Manet before him, this artist vehemently believed in art for art's sake. I couldn't wait to meet her.

We alighted, after only a few minutes' ride in our smart launch, onto a small wooden jetty outside the Renaissance *palazzo* and walked a short distance down a silent, cobbled alleyway, bordered on one side by a narrow canal, to the wide entrance of the museum. In contrast to the winding alleys on its outside, through the gates the pale stone court-yard was expansive, with a deep well at its centre. We entered the museum through a cavernous foyer, then were directed up a wide stone staircase to the main collection on the first floor. The galleries them-selves were unexpectedly small and intimate. The extraordinary frescos on their ceilings, in various states of disrepair, were more compelling than most of the art on the walls.

Judith and Holofernes II is as famous in reproduction as Manet's *Olympia*. Details of the painting have been reproduced and Klimt's work exploited to sell everything from chocolate to lingerie. But even in its poorly curated position on a dividing wall in the middle of a gallery, the actual work is far more arresting than reproduction can ever project. Judith's a visual feast. Like Christina, she's painted full-length, the picture having been constructed specifically to emphasize her height. The thick, gold frame appears to slice into the scene so we seem to catch a glimpse of the dynamic subject as she strides past an open doorway, mind fixed on murder. Her breasts are bare, dark hair glistening behind, and there's a post-coital sheen to her olive skin; intricately patterned gowns and flamboyant jewellery adorn her lower body and wrists, and she wears chains that imply she'd been tethered but has now broken free. And she has Holofernes' bloody, lifeless head gripped tightly in talon-like fingers. The energy projected by the painting is particularly extraordinary considering how thinly Klimt painted the canvas. In reproduction, its jewel-like qualities had made me anticipate a far more thickly painted surface.

Klimt had taken advantage of a myth to suggest men were powerless in the face of a woman's sexual magnetism – and that empowered women are a force to be reckoned with. Maybe this was a little warning of the shape of things to come? The year was 1909, after all. It wouldn't be long before Emmeline Pankhurst chained herself to the railings outside London's Houses of Parliament and female suffrage became a Western crusade.

From a purely theatrical perspective I was looking forward to re-enacting the drama of Judith. She was as equally extreme a representation of woman as either Mary or Victorine, if not more so. Hers would be my final performance, once my week had played out to its last act. I drafted a short script for Judith, whispered thoughts about her manipulative wooing and the ensuing murder. The ideas were stable but the performance would depend on the collector. I wanted to leave the details to chance. The act would be a private view, the nature of the performance influenced by the nature of the viewer – whether man or woman, and with or without a sexual dynamism – after a week that might or might not have proved a critical and personal success. Judith was my loose cannon, sensual, unstable and dangerous. I would be able to use her to draw conclusions, to sum up what had gone before and with her bid a fond – or not so fond – farewell to my owner.

Like Ingres and Whistler, Gustav Klimt personally designed the costumes for his sitters. They were not reflective of the contemporary vogue for froth and frills; rather, they were symbolic metaphors for the characters on his canvas. Judith was overtly sexy. And Petra was making a dress for her to go to town in. She'd designed a fabric inspired by a combination of the two paintings: made of woven silk, it was composed of pink, green and orange coils and square, oval and circular motifs, picked out intricately with gold thread. She'd used it to create a kimono-style dress. But its overt modesty belied the underlying reality. Concealed ribbons at the front of the kimono undid to display an inner robe, cut just to cover my nipples, before plunging to my navel, then rejoining the outer robe below. With it, I would wear an encrusted gold choker and countless chains around my wrists and ankles. Klimt's women often appear with the soles of their feet on display, and mine, like theirs, would remain bare. The result was an outfit that seamlessly married the battleground to the boudoir.

The end of the project loomed. There were only twelve days to go until the auction and the excitement of everyone involved was tangible. I felt a mixture of elation and relief that the planning was almost complete. A new stage in my career was about to open up before me. My anxieties regarding Kenny Harper had calmed. He had not been in touch again and the press seemed to have forgotten about the auction of my sketch. Maybe, in a perverse way, I owed thanks to Kenny. His re-emergence had reawakened my senses. I felt more edgy, more alive, since he had struck fear into me; my nerve endings had become more intuitive. I felt ready to go back on display. The time would pass in a rush of press conferences, meetings, dress rehearsals and filming. The characters in my plot were fixed, the scripts written and the props were in place. It was time to put them away and concentrate on the art of selling myself. There was only one critical factor that was still not in place. Before I could go anywhere near the stage at Sotheby's I needed to have a dress rehearsal and somehow I needed to make amends with Aidan.

30

The assistants hauled Petra's bags out of the lift and into my apartment. Aidan was arriving back after lunch and Katie and Lincoln were on their way over, film man in tow. Sarah and Ruth were coming along, and Billy too. This was turning out to be a truly public private view.

I had spoken to Aidan only once since our last row, simply to confirm when he'd be home. I felt sad, but resigned. I couldn't afford to let our problems overwhelm me and the closer I got to the sale, the more focused I became. I began to realize that, although I loved him, Petra had been right all along. This was one project I had to see through alone. It was only one more week, then we could sort out our differences – if that were at all possible – and move forward again.

Everyone had to sign a confidentiality agreement before being allowed into the studio, and we made it clear we'd sue Lincoln's ass if anything got into the media before the sale took place in twenty-four hours' time. I'd hired a sound engineer to ensure today's recordings were perfect and my cameras were set up to film the performances. If the real things screwed up during my week of Possession, at least I'd have a back-up.

We cleared my studio so there was a space in the middle of the floor, on which I'd laid out a large white square. I intended to use it as the base for all my performances. It was made of a new, spongy fibre, designed for NASA, that rolls up into a tiny tube, making it easy to transport. The seven costumes were stored in separate marked cases and the assistants lay them in a row, directly under the gaze of the relevant reproductions. I took a moment to film them, genies lying quietly inside their boxes. Victorine's screen was packaged next to them. It was the one prop that would have to be sent on to my destination under separate cover and it was ready to go.

'I have one more surprise,' announced Petra as she helped haul a huge cardboard box tied with string out of the lift.

I went over to help and was surprised by its weight.

She handed me a pair of scissors and I knelt down to open the packaging as she explained, 'It's a gift – from Dior.'

I ploughed through styrofoam until I could see the edge of a large, antique-leather trunk inside. It had bulbous brass buttons and metal bands running from front to back. Leather straps crossed the top from the back and then fastened down the front.

'It's called a Jenny Lind, and it's the correct size to store all of the costumes,' Petra enthused. She was standing back, watching, hands on hips, then she pulled a piece of paper from her back pocket and handed it to me.

I unfolded it and read:

Made in 1860, this trunk's named after the Swedish soprano Jenny Lind, whose purity of voice and natural singing style earned her the nickname 'the Swedish nightingale'. She made her American debut at the Castle Garden Theatre in New York City on September 11, 1850. The appearance inaugurated a 93-stop tour organized by entertainment entrepreneur Phineas T. Barnum. The tour came on the heels of a fantastically successful string of appearances in England that gave rise to the term 'Jenny Lind fever'.

I glanced up at her. 'September the eleventh: I hope that's not an omen.'

She shrugged apologetically. 'Mere coincidence, I promise. Go on, open it up.'

Everyone was standing around expectantly. So I lifted the top.

The inside of the lid was inlaid with eight panels, seven of them detailed with exquisite miniature copies of my seven masterpieces. In the eighth section my name appeared and, underneath it, the words 'The Possession Series' printed in gold leaf. Across the top of the trunk sat a wooden tray containing seven small compartments that varied in size. Each had a lid with its own key and a lock. And on each one my initials appeared, intertwined with the name of each one of my collaborators in turn. These were the insignias I had designed for use in the labels of the costumes, and on the calling cards that I would hand out – as Madame de Senonnes at the auction, and, in Isabella's case, imprinted in the fabric the clothes I would wear for my performance.

'Each compartment is made to the correct size to store the jewellery for its associated costume.' Petra had knelt down next to me. 'Take the tray out.'

I peered inside. There were three packages, wrapped in red tissue. I opened the first and out fell a rubber mould of Holofernes' head, long, brown hair flowing, eyes shut. It was so lifelike I found myself shuddering. Then I glanced at Petra. She looked dangerously mischievous.

I now undid the second. Inside it was a black velvet jewellery box, containing an exquisite ruby and gold ring which perfectly fitted my left index finger. I turned it over to find my Christina insignia engraved on the inside. It was a perfect match of the ring she was wearing in Holbein's painting.

'Dior commissioned it in-house,' Petra explained gently.

'Is it on loan?'

'Esther, of course not. Go on, open the third.'

I tore the tissue paper away from the final package. Inside a further box was a silver key. Petra was good at this suspense business. I looked up at her questioningly.

'You don't have to use the trunk,' she said, sounding very practical, 'but it's the exact size you need to transport all the costumes and there are boxes to hold each day's costumes to put inside. If you do take it, don't forget to lock it now, will you?'

There was no way I was leaving this behind. I could picture the trunk now, sitting on the stage as I went under the hammer. Marie and her dowry – ready to roll.

Petra got hold of the inventory and with the assistants' help meticulously checked the details, painting by painting. As ever, the assistants were quietly efficient, bringing each piece forward for inspection as she asked to see them before I tried on each in turn. Suddenly, as we focused on the real work at hand the atmosphere seemed tense again.

31

Evening Standard, Arts Diary, 24 February

As we gear up for the big night of Esther Glass's sale tomorrow, we wonder who's going to take a punt on her. In her personal life there seems to be a new fight for ownership – the much lauded French curator Guy Coligny was her escort at a Tate Modern dinner last week, then was spotted showing her round the Louvre a few days later. Meanwhile, Aidan Jeroke, her dealer and intimate friend, was caught out dining with Sotheby's client director, Jacqueline Quinet, in New York on Tuesday, before they headed back to his Upper East Side apartment for a late-night business meeting – or more? We wonder who will be leading Esther to the slaughter tomorrow – and who will get the heftier commission on her sale.

'Did Lincoln plant it?'

I shrugged and took a drag on my cigarette. I was wary of having a conversation with Aidan tonight about our personal life. The sale was less than twenty-four hours away. He had arrived at my rehearsal straight from his flight. We hadn't spoken since our horrible phone call a week earlier and when I saw him my chest had tightened so much I had struggled to breathe. But there were so many people around I could do nothing but accept his gentle embrace as if everything was fine between us, then carry on with the rehearsal. I used this emotional trigger to imbue the performances with as much intensity as I could muster. The reaction of my observers was positive and I now had all seven women captured on film. It had been close to midnight before Petra and her assistants had finally left, satisfied that all last-minute alterations were complete, my costumes ready to go. All but Madame de Senonnes' robes were now carefully stored away in the trunk, awaiting collection by Sotheby's in the morning.

Aidan and I were left sitting at opposite ends of the sofa, me in my dressing gown, feet up, the newspaper he'd brought lying open between us amidst the cushions. I felt washed-out but distinctly edgy. I could have done with forty-eight hours' pure relaxation before the sale. But time had run out. And despite my better instinct I found myself challenging him.

'What were you doing at your apartment with Jacqueline?'

'Are you having an affair with Guy?'

'You're the last person I expect to believe what you read in the papers.'

He sighed and lay back, eyes closed. 'You were so wired in New York.'

'I was wired? *You* were the one acting weird on me.'

He sat back up and turned to face me. His eyes were shining with anger. 'Esther, read my lips. There's nothing going on between me and Jacqueline Quinet. She stayed at my place, that's all. Why does it always have to be about you?'

'Well, if it wasn't about me, what was it about? I just want to know what you're really doing over there.'

Aidan took my hands in his. I let him hold them, limply. 'We'll talk about it after the sale, OK?' he implored me. 'I'm nearly through with Greg – and I've done everything I can to keep you safe with this goddam crazy project.'

'Go on,' I said.

He paused for a moment, then spoke quietly. 'Let's just say I think we may have a buyer,' he couldn't help but smile, 'one who's been thoroughly vetted.'

'Have you fixed my sale?' I said. I know I sounded nervous.

He remained silent.

I got up from the sofa and stood above him, shaking with rage. 'Aidan, what the fuck is going on?'

To my amazement, he looked up at me and began to laugh. 'Esther, calm down. Let's just say I've found a buyer who I'd like to see adding you to his collection. But this is an auction; he could easily be outbid.'

'You'd better not have fucking rigged my sale,' I hissed, turning on my heels. I felt confused and unbalanced. But it was too late now to talk about it. I needed to save myself, reserve my energies. There was only one thing left to do. 'I'm going to bed,' I said.

32

Catalogue

<small>LOT</small> 143
The *Possession* Series*
'Beauty, Politics, Power, Religion, Sex, Aesthetics, Myth'
by Esther Glass

A work of art in collaboration with
Marie, Christina, Isabella, Mary,
Victorine, Frances and Judith

Costume designs by
Petra Luciana

The purchase comprises
the process of creation
and
ownership, once completed, of the *Possession* series

Status, Desire, Wealth, Subjugation, Purity, Ambiguity, Danger

*The series has been committed to loan to the International Contemporaries Touring show for a
period of eighteen months following its completion.

Terms and Conditions

The purchaser will take ownership of Esther Glass, hereafter called 'the artist', for a week, immediately following her auction, and will provide the following performance environments for her completion of the series:

Virtual View
A Public Show
Spiritual Place
A Private View
Tea with Family/Friends
Dinner for Two

The purchaser will provide the artist with:
First-class travel
All insurances for her protection
A suitable, secure environment for her to inhabit
All standard daily living expenses – food, etc
The seven aforementioned environments for the development of the series

The artist will comply with all demands deemed 'reasonable' but retains the right to refuse to comply with any requests that she judges to be outside the scope of the project.

I closed my eyes and whispered each of my subjects' names in turn, like a mantra, then I opened them again and nodded to the security guard. As he opened the doors, the sound of chattering receded and the audience turned to acknowledge me. I fixed my gaze above their heads and glided down the central aisle, my expression set in a half-smile. It was definitely worth the hours of practice; my composition felt just right. Perspiring bodies inhaled and exhaled the fuggy air around me. Jacqueline Quinet certainly had jammed them in. When I was halfway through the first room, my pace slowed and I glanced across the crowd, left, then right. I paused every few steps to hand out calling cards, each carrying my signature and insignia, printed in jet-black italics, interwoven with the name of one of my seven subjects, penned in red. People grabbed them eagerly, aware they'd have a future value of their own.

The press had been second-runged, forced to watch the main event on a plasma screen. I knew it was advantageous, that film rendered me more 'aesthetic'. Passing by the entrance to their side room, I caught the sound of braying journalists penned in like cattle jostling for feed.

'. . . she's a contemporary Mona Lisa.'

A laugh.

'No . . . a high-class hooker . . .'

A snigger.

'. . . More like a Toulouse-Lautrec call girl.'

I was familiar with their game: scribbling ideas, stealing sound bites, hurrying to file before nine to catch Sunday's first editions.

I moved swiftly on into the main salesroom. The mood here was more reserved, the audience wearing its self-importance on its sleeve. There'd been no way to beg, steal or borrow a ticket for a view of the main event; unless you were someone special you wouldn't get past the door. Jacqueline had deliberated long and hard over the seating. As if planning tables for her own wedding feast, she said she'd aimed for 'the perfect balance – stimulation and provocation without the risk of a full-scale fight'. Again it seemed she'd got it spot-on. European and American dealers rubbed shoulders with only the most influential curators on the circuit; and for the first time in this category, three Asian collectors had flown in for the sale. Everyone knew tonight was seminal: the young Brits were in a take-over bid for the contemporary art scene.

Finally I had arrived and stepped up onto the stage. I positioned myself in the middle, a foot to the right of my waiting trunk. It felt like my anchor; stabilizing and strong. Inside lay the histories of six other women, who depended on my success for their own re-emergence out of the gloom of the past. The pressure was palpable. I glanced across at the audience. Did I detect discomfort? I expected it was hard for them to address what they could see: this woman-artwork was for sale tonight. Who among them would buy living, breathing flesh? I was intent on projecting charisma, aloofness, sexuality. Petra had excelled: I felt like the perfect combination of implicit historic reference and overt contemporary daring.

My satin underskirts had rustled as I passed down the aisle. Now I could feel eyes absorbing me hungrily, first flitting across my dress of exquisite velvet in full-bodied claret, sitting high on the waist and pouring down effortlessly to the ground. Minute silver diamonds shimmered across its surface like shooting stars.

Their focus quickly shifted to the bodice, cut dangerously low beneath a diaphanous veil that implied – but did not achieve – a modest cover for my breasts. Above it a triple ellipse of Blonde Lace encircled my neck. Like Marie Marcoz before me, I held a white linen handkerchief in my right hand, drawing attention to thirteen emerald-encrusted gold rings decorating my fingers like high-class trinkets on a festive tree. Three gold chains dangled from my neck to my waist: one carrying a cross; the second, Guy's tiny scent bottle, his message curled inside; the third, another emerald, in a cluster of diamonds. In my ears were blood-red rubies, flanked by more diamonds. They sparkled tantalizingly under the artificial lights. I batted thick false eyelashes, contact lenses flickering fake blue. It was getting hotter – I hoped I could hold out. A camera crew knelt low before the stage, like web-spinning spiders waiting for me to fall. To their far right I spotted Aidan's familiar figure, shadowy in the wings. His presence made me feel strong – strong enough to conquer them all. I'd sent him home the previous night, and refused to come to the auction escorted by him. I needed, for the time being at least, to believe I was doing this alone.

But now I was standing there in the spotlight, I was reassured to know he was close by, waiting for me, beside the stage.

The audience's focus shifted as they heard the heavy thud of the auctioneer's gavel. Fourteen minutes late, exactly as Jacqueline had planned, it was time for me to go under the hammer. The first half of Sotheby's sale had achieved good figures and the auctioneer was warming to his task. He glanced at his checklist, verified his staff were in position, the phone team ready, then he cleared his throat with dramatic intent.

'Now for lot 143. The sale of the artist Esther Glass . . . Sorry, I mean the *Possession* series.'

It was intended theatre. The audience knew it and laughed. For a moment the pressure valve released.

'The purchaser will own Ms Glass for a week,' the auctioneer continued, more seriously now. 'Full details can be found in the catalogue, and have been well documented in the press.'

Laughter again fluttered across the room, like a dance of butterflies. Who could have missed the build-up to the art event of the season?

He threw me a quick sideways glance. I smiled back fleetingly, then he called for silence and the noise level subsided. At last, as my heart thumped in my throat, it was time for my sale to begin.

Marie's heavy velvet dress was not suited to such intense spotlights and I felt faint from the heat, but this was no moment to weaken. I was ready and waiting, in position, by my trunk on the stage. The audience was set, too. They were absolutely silent now, settled back in their seats.

'We have a reserve price of £100,000. Do I hear 120?'

A lone card was raised slightly at the left side of the room.

With a brief nod the auctioneer was quick to bank the figure. 'I have 120 bid.'

I knew Carl Ziegermann, the corpulent, middle-aged dealer from

Switzerland, and attempted to mask my surprise. Aidan hadn't mentioned he'd be in the running. Perhaps he was a plant, put there by Jacqueline to get the ball rolling?

A new bid was raised before I had a chance to think the probability through. Yes . . .

'140 in the middle.'

I eyed the woman but my look wasn't returned. She was businesslike and close-faced. A touch more tantalizing, this was: I thought I'd prefer a week in the company of a female stranger than one prey to Carl Ziegermann's 'avuncular' whim. My mind flicked back to Christina's anonymous female financier. Or maybe this was a buyer with someone else's tastes and cash? I turned my attention back to the auctioneer as he raised the figure higher. Ziegermann was still on the case and I wondered if Aidan had put him up to it. The night before, I'd tried to persuade him to tell me who was on his shortlist, but he had refused to be drawn, arguing that there was no point in predicting, that it was better to let the sale take its due course.

'One hundred and fifty taken.' The auctioneer cast his eye back to the woman. 'Do I hear £160,000?'

She nodded curtly. Before the auctioneer had a chance to confirm it, Ziegermann raised his card again.

'I have 170,000 to the right.'

She came straight back to him.

'And 180,000 in the middle.'

Finally Ziegermann hesitated, looked down at his lap.

'One hundred and eighty thousand in the middle,' the auctioneer repeated.

Now Ziegermann calmly glanced up at me, smiled slowly, then raised two fingers tight together.

The auctioneer noted the gesture and was quick to commit him. 'I have £200,000 bid.'

For her turn my female friend didn't hesitate, just shook her head briefly. I couldn't help but feel disappointed. I would have liked to know who she was.

The auctioneer waited, looking around carefully, chiding the audience. 'I have £200,000 bid. Do I hear an advance?'

There was a pause that seemed to weigh heavily on the room. I was tempted to glance at Aidan. But before I could the pressure was broken by the auctioneer's voice.

'I have 220,00 bid.'

The release of collectively held breaths sounded like wind whistling through tree branches. Sure enough, the late bid had come in from a sales official, ear-piece in. The auctioneer immediately returned his focus to Ziegermann, who raised his card and allowed a slip of a smile to pass his lips.

'Two hundred and forty thousand is bid,' the auctioneer reiterated. 'I have 240.'

The response was immediate.

'Raised now to 250 on the phone.'

Ziegermann's eyes fixed steadfastly on me, then he shook his head slowly, acknowledging defeat. I wondered if Victorine had felt the same relief when particularly loathsome clients couldn't afford her price.

But who was the other bidder? Was this Aidan's man? I was known as a risk taker. I'd put my life on a plate for my art, and I wasn't about to start shying away now. I returned my full attention to the auctioneer, adrenalin coursing through me.

'I have £250,000 bid.' His tone was more urgent. 'Do I hear more?'

It was the guestimate price. If that was it, he was keen to move on to the next lot. He raised his gavel ready to seal the bid.

It was only then that another phone assistant nodded, almost imperceptibly.

'I have a late bid, at £275,000,' he said, raising the audience's blood pressure considerably higher.

All eyes were on the two sales officials. No one was now looking at me. For the moment they'd actually forgotten I was human. My experiment had worked: in their minds I'd become purely a valuable aesthetic commodity.

The first sales official was talking furtively into her mouthpiece. Now she glanced up briefly and nodded.

The auctioneer banked the bid. 'I hear £300,000.'

An expectant silence prevailed as he turned once again towards the other. All eyes were on him. The official was holding a calculator and keying in numbers rapidly as he listened to the caller's instructions. He hesitated, then whispered something in the auctioneer's ear, before passing the calculator over. As the auctioneer glanced at it a momentary frown furrowed his brow. Was there a problem? The audience edged forward on their seats.

Finally the auctioneer spoke quickly but clearly, his tone triumphant: 'I have one million dollars bid. That translates to £665,000.'

The audience rose up as one, like a coiled spring released from its box, and then they paid me their absolute attention once again.

I knew what this meant: in their eyes the figure had changed me into a higher being, something untouchable, iconic and, they knew, from now on, out of their reach. For my part, I had finally been thrown completely off balance.

Evidently, the bid had brought the deal to a finite conclusion. The auctioneer took one more look around, then exclaimed above the noise: 'I formally close the bid at £665,000.'

No one heard as the gavel hit his desk.

Mobile phones rang and text messages bleeped in a surging noise level, but my performance wasn't over yet. First I had to get out. Turning slowly, I at last acknowledged Aidan, who was still loitering to the left of the stage. He coolly raised an arm and escorted me down the steps. Having draped the Ingres shawl around my shoulders like a security blanket, he guided me out of the auction room. The ovation grew in volume as I departed; the audience needed to let off steam. Journalists stampeded after us and we stepped outside into a bank of flashing lights and microphones thrust in my face as the police attempted to hold the media back.

'Who bought you, Esther?'

'What's the deal?'

'Where are you going next week?'

I glimpsed a reporter from the BBC and, remembering it was wise to give the nationals the best bites, turned towards her mike and camera-man. 'I'll be at the whim of my purchaser for a week from tomorrow,' I said, my voice sounded disembodied, 'for him or her to do with me what he or she pleases, so long as it's legal' – I could hear laughter – 'and with my consent.'

'Who's the purchaser, Esther?'

Aidan interjected. 'I'm afraid we can't disclose details until the auction house has authenticated the sale, just like with any other lot.'

'Esther, how does it feel to be worth a million dollars a week?'

'I think it's best I use the International Contemporaries show as my mouthpiece,' I replied. 'Once I've taken stock.'

My response brought a swarm of new questions hurled into the cold air, where, it seemed to me, they circled like gathering bats around a single lamplight.

Aidan ushered me into the back of the waiting limo. And just before a policeman slammed the door I heard my recent confidant, John Herbert from the *Clarion*, shout out, 'You're not worth it, Esther. You're a fucking fake.'

And for a split second I thought of Kenny Harper.

In the back of the car, I found myself shaking uncontrollably. Aidan put his arm around me and kissed my hair.

'Who was it?' I asked. 'Who spent such a crazy amount?'

Aidan grinned widely and held me tighter. 'We'll have to wait for Jacqueline to call,' he said. 'They'll be verifying the details right now. Best to wait, Esther, until it's all agreed.'

'Come on, Aid. Was it your man?'

'I'm assuming so, but he wasn't planning to go nearly that high.'

Before I had a chance to challenge him my phone began to ring. Petra was fizzing down the line.

A private party had been organized back at the gallery, and a sound system was throwing music out across the empty warehouses all around. The press arrived before us, and there was a scuffle as Aidan and I fought our way out of the car and into the building. Here I hooked up straight away with Petra and together we continued my performance – of sorts. A red carpet had been laid down the centre of the gallery and we paraded along it, to the applause of our friends and colleagues. I handed out more calling cards, as mementoes of the night. Among the invitees I spied Guy and his wife, then Lincoln with the cameraman hanging on his arm.

The words 'The Possession Series' were printed in black along one wall of the gallery. Underneath them, in neon, a projection of one million dollars had now been illuminated in pink. Those who hadn't attended the sale had watched the auction on a screen stretching across an end wall of the gallery and it was now replayed so I could see the action for myself. The experience was surreal. Watching myself, I could see Marie Marcoz staring back. I wondered how she would feel from the other side of the grave. I felt vindicated that her value was now publicly recognized, even if the audience didn't yet quite know whom it was they had been so admiring.

Aidan took a call, then told me that Jacqueline had said that, as the figure had gone so high, Sotheby's needed to verify the purchase before they'd pass on the details. We wouldn't hear the outcome till morning.

'So there's no point in worrying about it. You might as well let your hair down, enjoy the party,' he said encouragingly, before disappearing into his office and talking on the phone for the next half an hour.

I felt in a state of limbo, but the buzz of the evening kept me high. First I retired with Petra and she helped me to change. I removed the wig, spiked my hair with gel and put on a daring little black dress, designed, of course, by Petra for the event. The contrast was suitably startling. It was sad to realize that Marie's time was already up. Petra's assistant carefully laid the costume to rest, then we headed back into the party and got really high. It was my last night of freedom – at least for a week. The next day I'd be setting off to join my owner for a week, whoever in the world he or she might be.

33

'That makes artist Esther Glass worth £35 million a year. Why is this living masterpiece worth the price of a Picasso on today's art market? We all wait with bated breath to see. And now for the regional weather in your area.'

The TV stirred me. I gazed up to see a clip of Aidan and me leaving the auction. The night before seemed a long way from our Soho hide-away on this grey Sunday morning.

'I love that: a living Picasso,' I said as Aidan switched off the TV. He was standing naked by the bed, holding two mugs.

'You're going back to Manhattan,' he said categorically.

It took me a moment to connect, then my heart sank. 'Who bought me?'

He sat down on the bed and handed me a coffee. 'Name's Ben Jamieson.'

'Was he yours?'

'Sure was,' he replied, a touch smugly.

'Go on.'

'He usually deals through Greg Weiz, but apparently Jamieson gets a kick out of the saleroom. Likes to do it himself, on the phone.'

'Why'd he go so high?'

'He must have got carried away.'

'Or he's a total lunatic,' I answered, feeling slightly nervous.

'No, Est. Just knows what he wants.' Aidan leant forward and kissed my forehead. 'He obviously thought you were worth it.'

I couldn't help but feel thrilled at the purchase price. It was so much money it was going to make a significant difference to my future as an artist. It would give me the freedom to experiment, or even to stop and take stock for a while, in fact to do whatever I chose. I could set it up in trust for the future of a child, or children. It was more money than I had ever imagined having. In fact, the money side had been the last thing on my mind for the past few months. I had been too absorbed in the project itself, and in keeping Kenny Harper from my door, to think too much about its financial worth to me. I realized now that the bid made Kenny's £25,000 bribe seem like small change.

'So,' I demanded, 'tell me everything you know about him.'

Aidan lay back against the pillows. 'Well, he and Greg Weiz are good friends. There's nothing weird about him. He's a big-time collector, real keen on the contemporary Americans and also owns some post-war art – Pollock, Rauschenberg. It's rumoured he just bought some Warhols but no one's been able to verify.'

'What's he want with a purchase like me?'

'Maybe he just likes the idea of owning someone famous and beautiful.'

'Bollocks.'

Aidan looked wry. 'And I think he's interested in widening his portfolio, getting into the Brit scene.'

'Isn't he a bit late?'

'Why do you say that?'

'Well, there aren't any bargains left, are there?'

He began to stroke my neck. 'Ben Jamieson isn't a bargain hunter, Esther. He's one of the richest dealers on Wall Street. He's only interested in quality.'

I felt an anticlimax.

'What's up? You've landed on your feet. He's one of the good guys.'

'I'm sure, but it's just, oh, predictable – that I'd be bought by an American.'

Aidan shook his head in disbelief. 'There aren't many European dealers who could afford you.'

'I know, but it could have been an obscure Asian or European collector, even a woman.'

'But that's not how the art market works.'

'Some works disappear off into the unknown,' I replied, sliding down under the sheet.

Aidan slid down to join me in the dark. 'Not often and not at this price.'

'No one knows where Dr Gachet is,' I grumbled, referring to the most expensive Van Gogh ever sold at auction – now in a private collection somewhere in the world. No one knows where, or, at least, no one's saying. 'I suppose it's fitting that I should be purchased by a rich American male,' I continued. 'Most of my performances are based on women who had been bought and sold on the open market by men, after all. And I'm going across the Pond, just like poor old Frances.'

Aidan held me. 'This is one masterpiece I want to ensure comes back to London.'

'I have no plans to stay in New York,' I whispered. 'It's your past, full of hateful secrets.'

'I don't have any secrets from you, Esther. Carolyn's well and truly history and Jacqueline was nothing but a figment of your imagination.'

'I felt uneasy there last time.'

'You were stressed.'

I still wasn't so sure, but he wouldn't be drawn out and I knew it.

'What do you think this Ben Jamieson will want me to do?'

Aidan pushed the sheet back and stroked my face. 'Be his escort, make some art, impress his friends.'

'As long as that's all.'

'Whatever he wants, you know you can handle it. And anyway, remember that contractually you can always say no.'

'I'm not in the least bit concerned.'

'Good.'

'Are you jealous?' I was semi-teasing, but I knew this possession thing was personal. And that Aidan was trying hard to ignore the fact.

'He's not quite your type,' he said, too quickly. 'To be honest, I'm more jealous of Guy Coligny.'

'He was with Jeanne last night. What's there to be jealous of?'

Guy had attended the auction with his finely crafted wife. They'd come on to the party and stayed late. I'd been intrigued to meet the other side of Guy. She was about forty, exquisite, cut from the finest cloth, with neat, high cheekbones and gamine features – a modern-day Audrey Hepburn but with a deep olive complexion. Her black hair was pulled back in a classic knot. And she wore a simple, sleek cream dress. Maybe she was used to Guy's flirtations and had accepted they were part of the package. She made her position as Guy's permanent fixture perfectly clear, not by what she said, but by the way she looked at me. I was pleased about the overt display of their togetherness, both on account of the press and for Aidan's sake.

'When do I leave?'

'You're booked onto this evening's flight to JFK. You're travelling first class as per contract.'

'You going to come and wave me off?'

'Do you really think I'd allow the masterpiece from my collection to travel unescorted?'

I suddenly realized I felt exhausted. The build-up to the auction and the night itself had both been very demanding.

Aidan reassured me that all my cases were being sent direct to the airport and that I had all day to relax, to do absolutely nothing if I so chose.

'And you?'

'I don't intend to let you out of my sight,' he promised.

My face appeared on the front of every Sunday paper, broadsheet and tabloid alike. The sale had been an unqualified success. There was intense speculation about the purchaser, but as yet no one knew who he was or where I was heading. The missing pieces of the jigsaw would fuel stories over the following week, just as planned. And it seemed Aidan and I had managed to shake off reporters on the way to Soho the previous night. The following morning there was no sign of the press outside. I switched my phone to voicemail. Katie was at the gallery and the PR agency were handling all other calls. We stole these moments to be alone. At six we showered and dressed and I added my burka; Aidan put on dark glasses and a parka, hood up. Then we headed out, undetected, into China Town for dim sum. Afterwards a black Mercedes picked us up and we left for Heathrow. No one was watching.

In the back of the car I took off my burka scarves and lay with my head on Aidan's lap.

'I'm totally exhausted.'

'You can sleep in the plane, Madame. Remember, you're in first class.'

I smiled at the Ingres reference. Aidan stroked my hair distractedly, and looked out at the traffic through drizzling rain. There was a small but certain smile on his face.

'What are you thinking about?'

'I was just remembering the day we met.'

'Mmm?'

'I paid about twenty-five per cent of last night's price for your complete works.'

'That's all I am to you, isn't it? A commodity.'

'You're absolutely right.'

'Well, have I been worth the investment?'

'I would say you have far exceeded my expectations.'

I thought about his words. At this moment I found them reassuring. In many ways, so far my career had really been about us.

'Est,' he said, then paused.

'Umm?'

'I have a little surprise.'

I looked up at Aidan expectantly.

'I'm flying over with you,' he said.

'You can't.' The response was instinctive.

Aidan looked put out but his tone remained resolute. 'I thought you'd be pleased. I've got some more business to tie up with Greg. So I'll be close by just in case you need me.'

'I don't like unexpected surprises. They don't give me time to prepare,' I said equally firmly. 'I need to do at least this bit alone. For it to work, as an experiment, you know.'

Aidan sounded a little irritated. 'Think of it this way. I'm lending you to a collector for a week. And I'm delivering you. That's not such a strange procedure for an artwork of such great value.'

I suddenly felt claustrophobic. This was my bloody project. 'You may be my dealer, Aidan, but you don't fucking own me,' I growled.

He looked out of the window silently. Then his phone started to bleep. 'Hi?' I could feel his body tighten. 'Ben, sure. Congratulations. Hold on, she's right here.'

He passed me the phone. My heart picked up a beat.

'Hey, Esther. So pleased my bid was high enough.'

It was weird to hear the sound of a stranger's voice, distant yet clear and upbeat.

'I'm looking forward to meeting you,' I replied, 'but what do I do when I get to New York?'

'There'll be a car to collect you. You don't need to worry about a thing.'

The line went muffled. Ben was talking to someone, his tone urgent.

'Sorry, Esther, I got to go,' he said. 'Have a safe flight. I'll be in touch when you get here.'

He cut off before I had a chance to reply. I handed the phone back to Aidan silently and stared out at the rain.

I spent the flight alternately feigning sleep and glaring out of the window as the plane headed west through a sky darkening from brooding grey to a threatening mauve. Characteristically, Aidan ignored my mood, passing the journey devouring the Sunday papers from cover to cover. It wasn't that I didn't want Aidan around me, more that this week was about the *Possession* series and not about us. I had always imagined that I would be stepping off into the unknown. Instead, it seemed, Aidan had fixed it so I was simply walking into his domain, a place where he had all the controls.

Though these thoughts dismayed me, when we got to JFK the place was swarming with the press and suddenly I felt pleased to hold onto Aidan's arm. Extra security had been laid on to lead us to the waiting car. It sped us out and away towards Manhattan, where, to my surprise, we headed downtown, finally slowing in a dingy side street full of trash and dark shadows. We stopped at last, outside a commercial-looking building. It was unexpected and unfamiliar territory, the trendy meat-packing district squeezed between Chelsea and the West Village. I was surprised that a city guy would choose to live here. I thought he'd be another Upper East Side type, with easy access to the Hamptons for weekends.

The buildings were nondescript and industrial. But, as in London, I knew New York's surface often belied what lay beneath.

Aidan held me close, his tone tender, and I found myself responding.

'You going to be OK?'

'Of course.'

'Call me if you need to.'

'I won't.'

He kissed me hard. 'Well, you know you can.'

'I'll see you back at the airport, next Sunday,' I said with conviction as the driver opened my door.

Low lights glowed from some of the windows above my head. It was extraordinarily quiet, except for the dull murmur of machines whirring. The sound was strangely familiar. I thought hard, then I recognized its source. It was the throb of refrigeration units idling inside the lorries parked along the street that were waiting to deliver meat to the market the next morning. It was like London's Smithfield. There was even the same metallic smell of dried blood in the air.

The building was low for Manhattan, only four storeys high. The driver rang the reception buzzer, then Aidan helped him take my trunk and cases from the boot. After a few moments the front door swung open. A tall, slim man with long, thick brown hair eyed me expectantly.

'Ben Jamieson?'

'Come right in.'

I waved at Aidan and felt relieved as the car crawled away. One light bulb illuminated a wide, empty hall in which mailboxes lined the walls. There was a hint of linseed oil in the air. It was some kind of studio complex. I immediately felt more at home.

'Ben's not here. My name's Joe and I'm his studio manager.'

He looked beyond me towards my pile of luggage as he spoke. I felt slightly disappointed yet simultaneously naïve. I should've realized this hippy guy couldn't have been a multimillion-dollar player on the US financial scene.

'What is this place?'

'It's a collective of twenty-two artist studios, known as the Artden,' he said. 'Ben owns it, gives annual bursaries to students here. Oh, but you've got the penthouse.' He looked upwards. 'It's right at the top. Please, this way.'

Ignoring my protests, he picked up a couple of my cases and pointed up the iron stairwell.

'Three flights. I think you better let me.'

I looked back at my trunk, lying forlorn in the middle of the hallway.

He caught my gaze. 'Don't worry, it'll be safe,' he reassured me. 'I'll be right back for it.'

Footsteps echoing on the stone floor, we crossed to the stairs and began our ascent.

'We all watched your sale on cable. It was really cool.'

Weird to think that the hype had shot over ahead of me.

'Thanks. Has anyone been told where I'm staying?'

'No, no. The media isn't aware, yet. I guess it'll take them a while to put two and two together.' He paused on the stairs, turned and looked back at me, a smile lighting his eyes. 'They wouldn't expect Ben to spend a million dollars on an artwork then store it in the den.'

Joe's tone was matter-of-fact. It was obvious he wasn't concerned about my value. I was relieved: I could do with a bit of time out to collect my thoughts before the first performance. At a black studded door he turned a large metal key. It creaked open into a dark space.

'Well, if there's anything you need during your stay, or if you get any bother, just call me. Room 11. I'll go get the trunk.'

Joe switched on the lights. I stepped inside as he turned away and set off down the stairs.

It was a huge studio, with two large red sofas on a black woollen rug in the middle. The rest of the floor was dark mahogany, polished till it gleamed. The long windows at one end had blinds in the same red tone, pulled half down, flanked by thick cream curtains. Neon lights flashed red and green from outside. I didn't know what I'd been expecting, but now I was here I knew it wasn't this. There was an underlying smell of oil paint and beeswax. Someone had recently cleared out.

Three doors led off the space. I looked into the first, which was decked out in wood, Japanese-style, with a sunken bath, shower unit, loo and basin to one side. The second was a tiny but beautifully fitted kitchen; the last, a small white bedroom, with a large bed made up with cream linen sheets and midnight-blue wool blankets. On the bedside table a vase overflowed with blooming red roses. There was no sign of Ben Jamieson and it definitely didn't look like he was going to show tonight. It was already 10 p.m. Eastern time, three in the morning in London. Joe tapped on the door, hauled my trunk into the room, and took his leave.

I had a shower, then got into bed and switched off the light. But the jetlag combined with the sheer intensity of the last twenty-four hours left images flashing behind my eyes. I tried to put the pictures straight. Everything was going so well. In the main the press was full of praise and the money was beyond my wildest imaginings. But Aidan's journey over with me had tainted the experience already. Was it fatigue or post-travel, party, drugs exhaustion? I was all wrung out. Did I love Aidan? Did it matter? What about the series? What or who was possessing me? Finally I gave up on the notion of sleep and went back into the studio. I could hear an odd whirring sound and followed it to one of the shelving units. A humidifier was positioned underneath. It looked to be newly installed. Ben Jamieson, it seemed, really was treating me like a valuable work of art. Wearing a long black T-shirt and knee-high black socks, I saw my figure drifting like a shadow across the blinds, a negative space highlighted intermittently by neon.

I opened my trunk. Inside I'd lain the seven reproductions of my subjects flat on top of the first compartments. I slid them out, one at a time, and placed them in a line on the floor, in the order of my performances. First Marie, then Christina, Isabella, Mary, Victorine,

Frances and, finally, Judith. I immediately felt calmer. I resolved not to allow Aidan to muddy the waters for me. This week had to be about the project; Aidan could wait until the following week. It had started as I meant it to go on. I'd succeeded in becoming a highly prized commodity, as valuable as my masterpieces. And, like them, I had to remember, there was more to my surface than met the eye. I pulled another sheath of papers from the trunk, the performances' scripts. Each would last approximately seven minutes. Some were silent, others employed music and the spoken word, but I would remix sound back in London. The tapes were ready and waiting in the trunk, along with Petra's wonderful costumes. Now all I needed were the environments in which to perform them. I hoped Ben Jamieson would pull out all the stops. He was, after all, a powerful man in this city; he would be able to meet my requirements at the drop of a hat. Having reassured myself, I could feel my mood begin to lift. This, after all, was what I was here for: to work.

I discovered a pile of paper on one of the bottom shelves and some large, silk cushions underneath them. Settled cross-legged in the middle of the floor, I felt more at home and lit a cigarette. Across the top of the paper I wrote ART DEAL, paused, then started to draw. A cross between a diagram and designs for a production line began to emerge: arrows, numbers and letters spun from my black felt pen and marks appeared across the paper, until the surface became a maze of dead-ends and false starts, clear lines, charts and equations. In the top left corner I wrote my date of birth. The lines diverged and converged around further consecutive dates, each accompanied by tiny figure drawings of people and places, plus single words and phrases. The drawing culminated at the bottom right-hand corner with a sketch of a big apple with a bite out of it, next to an equation: £665,000/140 lbs = £4,750 per pound. Therein lay my financial weight and worth.

By the time I'd finished working through my thoughts, a dead light was filtering into the room. The iron radiators on the far wall had started to creak into action, the pipes hissing as they warmed up. I left the drawing where I'd made it and rose slowly. My muscles had seized up. I shook the blood back into my legs and stamped my feet. Then I headed back to bed and, at last, I fell asleep.

34

High-pitched beeping, the sound of clanking metal – a lorry in reverse ... It took a moment to remember where I was. Then the familiar sounds of New York City emerged: the unremitting bleat of sirens and car-horns above the steady, low rumble of an island humming with endeavour. I got up and wandered out into the studio, stepping over my women and the drawings left scattered across the floor, and pulled up a blind. Watery sunshine sent shafts of pale-yellow light between the buildings. The last meat lorry was heading off up the narrow street; I'd slept through the entire market. Steam was rising from an air vent in the middle of the road and cartons and boxes were piled intermittently along the sidewalk. Blood dribbled out of one, leaving a single red line through compacted grey snow.

Fresh juices, yogurts and fruit filled the fridge. I ate hungrily and looked in vain for coffee. I pushed my trunk into the bedroom and, one by one, removed the costumes, then hung all save one in the spacious wardrobe. I forced the trunk in beneath, jewellery and accessories carefully stored inside. Then I prepared for my second performance. Today Christina of Denmark would be unveiled. I didn't know when Ben would request I perform, but I'd set up my video and laptop ready. If he didn't give me an alternative suggestion, the studio was as good a place as any in which to be the virtual Christina.

I laid out her thick black velvet gown, the seven lace veils, the prayer book. The costume was a perfect antidote to my recent performance as Marie Marcoz, the scarlet woman. I intended the contrast to be startling. Marie gave everything away, while Christina would give virtually nothing. She symbolized politics and unsated desire, a suitable metaphor for a week in the ownership of a high-powered financier who bought whatever took his fancy. Holbein's painting disclosed just enough of Christina's true inner and outer beauty to ensure she was desired, but she gave very little of herself away in the process. I looked carefully over my reproduction. What had been going through Christina's mind as she stood for this court painter? Maybe he'd 'spun' the portrait to please his king and patron? After all, as court artist Holbein was being paid to do his job – to bring back a painting of a potential queen, a valuable commodity he may have felt compelled to 'tart up' a bit for her intended purpose. Given Holbein's situation, he wouldn't have wanted to disappoint Henry VIII. To give him his due, he didn't make Christina overtly beautiful, but with 'that look' he'd made her as enigmatic as *Mona Lisa*. It was clear why she was top of Henry's list. But the political stakes were high. Although it's well known that Henry VIII liked to get what he wanted from women, was she a sensible option for a king so careless with the laws of Rome?

I hoped my collector was aware of what he'd let himself in for by purchasing me. The week had already started unpredictably. And I had no real idea how it would progress from here. As I wondered what to do next, I lay on the bed and checked my phone for messages. There were three missed calls. One was from Petra. I called her in Paris. The German was there, and she still sounded high.

'You've gone down a storm across Europe,' she gushed.

'Did anyone make the connection between my costume and Marie de Senonnes?' I asked. I was hoping that piece of the jigsaw would only be filled in for the audience when the work was complete and put on show.

'No, but, even so,' she said, 'we've already had over a hundred calls placing orders for the dress.'

Petra was evidently thrilled with the reaction. After all, it was her career that was being played out in public here, too. She had worked excessively hard for this project and I felt she deserved all the rewards that were now coming her way.

'Now, how's it going over there? What's Ben like?'

I filled Petra in, about Aidan bringing me, about the lack of contact with my collector. She listened attentively.

'Don't lose your nerve, Est,' she urged, 'and don't let Aidan get in the way. He's done his bit, secured the deal; now you just need to get on with it.'

When I hung up I wandered back out into the studio and had a good look around. I hadn't missed much, other than a phone, hidden under one of the shelves. I picked up the receiver and was surprised to hear a dial tone. Maybe Ben would call me here? I felt indecisive. Should I sit and wait? I wasn't even sure that he had my mobile number. But I needed caffeine and was beginning to feel a bit uneasy here. Petra was right, however: I needed to take hold of this week and find a way to enjoy it. I wrapped up in my fake fur, put my shades on. Time, I decided, to get outside, to feel New York City buzzing around me, and to investigate the neighbourhood. I scrawled a note, just in case Jamieson showed up, stuck it under the door and headed for the street.

Cold air hit me like a fist and the sidewalk was slippery beneath my feet. I had no option but to dive into the first diner I came to. Inside it was warm and murky, the air filled with the smell of weak coffee and french fries, baseball playing on a screen above the counter. The waitress took my order without raising an eye from her order pad. I realized it was the first time I'd been out without a disguise for weeks. I sat back and read the front page of the *New York Times*, but my mind couldn't settle on the words and I only managed to absorb the forecast: wind-chill minus twenty. Then I noticed a one-paragraph story in the final column:

BritArt queen Esther Glass touched down at JFK fresh from her auction in London, Saturday. Celebrated city dealer Ben Jamieson is rumored to be her buyer for the week, at the extraordinary price of $1 million.

I was shocked by the story's front-page position and immediately felt vulnerable. I pulled my mobile from my pocket. There were four more texts: three from Aidan, one from Katie. I clicked Aidan's open in turn. The first read: RUOK? The second: RUOK2? The third: HEY, E, WHY THE SILENCE?

My initial desire to speak to Aidan flipped to irritation. It had only been a few hours, for Christ's sake. I snapped the phone shut without responding. I'd already told him that I needed to do this week alone. I forced myself to drink the coffee, hoping for a caffeine hit, paid, lifted the *Times* and trudged back out onto the street. I was tempted to scout a little further afield, to get my bearings, but decided against it. The air was so cold it burnt like acid on my skin, and I didn't want to take any risks or upset Ben Jamieson on my first day in his possession – virtual or otherwise.

The note was where I'd left it, so I lit a cigarette and smoked it lying on my back on the plush black rug, gazing at the ceiling. It was a big space for such a cramped city, but there was something weird about it. My thoughts wouldn't settle. I switched my mobile back on and threw it backwards and forwards between my hands, and jumped when it sprang to life. It was Katie, hassling me from London for some questionnaire I'd promised to do for the *Guardian* before we left.

'I did it on the plane,' I lied. 'I'll email it over later. Any other news?'

'The UK press is full of profiles of Ben Jamieson.'

'Anything negative?'

'No. They're just intrigued. No one seems to be able to get a real handle on him. Hey, thankfully it seems no one knows where you're staying – yet. Anyway, what's he like?'

I explained I hadn't seen him.

'Don't you worry, he's probably in the middle of some multimillion-pound takeover bid,' she said with a laugh. 'He'll show up.'

'It's frustrating.'

'Take a look through my notes,' she encouraged kindly. 'He seems quite sound, invests heavily in the arts. It might give you a better picture.'

When Katie rang off I felt better. She knew my neuroses and how to deal with them. Her calm confidence about Ben rubbed off on me. No doubt he would show up soon enough. There was no point in my worrying about it. So I did as she said and dug out the notes, then spread them next to my women on the floor. Surrounded by a sea of papers, I circled details and scribbled comments, building up a fractured impression of my new owner. There were dozens of pieces from the business press, going back more than a decade. He was a hedge-fund manager – whatever that meant. Our worlds couldn't have been further apart. Ben Jamieson seemed elusive. It was hard to pin down exactly who he worked for and where his deals came from. One article actually specified that enigma was one of his most effective business attributes. Others were less kind, hinting at shady dealings in the past that had helped him attain his current success. One article quoted him as saying that his greatest ambition was to deal only on behalf of billionaire clients. His was a world way outside my experience or understanding. It made my million dollars sound like pocket money.

I skim-read through the pieces without taking in much detail about finances. What I was looking for was character analysis, personality profiles. I finally came across some blurred photos of a tall, dark-haired man, snapped at a charity event or business conference. Then I found a half-page portrait giving the clearest view so far. I studied his even features, astute eyes, wavy dark hair flecked with grey. He was wearing a 'casual' shirt, hands under his chin, as if in quasi-prayer. His mouth held the merest suggestion of a smile. Behind him Manhattan was spread out like a feast. He looked wolfish, capable of devouring it whole. Finally, I found a couple of short pieces on Jamieson's art collection, one in *Art in America*, the other in the *Washington Post*. As Aidan had mentioned, he owned serious post-war American pieces. I was surprised, yet pleased to see, that he also owned several installations by Sonia Myrche. So the connections were getting closer.

Frustratingly, there was very little in the dossier about my owner's personal life. No mention of a wife or children. He was in his mid-forties, the son of an East Coast lawyer, originally from Camden, Massachusetts. Ivy League educated. The perfect résumé for the glittering financial career that lay ahead of him. Maybe he was gay? I took some more paper and placed it to the right of last night's diagrams. Then I wrote at the top of the page: GETTING TO KNOW BEN JAMIESON: TOP 10 FACTS. I lit another cigarette, lay back on the cushion and thought about him as I blew smoke into the air.

In order to survive, artists have no choice but to confront the realities of financial ownership, generally by someone very much on the inside, like Ben, and usually someone established, empowered. And through so doing, we hope to become influential ourselves. From what I'd gleaned, Ben was a classic example of the contemporary American patron. Why did he want to own art? As a philanthropic gesture, or to enhance his status? Maybe to make him appear cultured? And why did he decide to make his foray into the British art scene by purchasing me? Possibly my purchase was little more than a publicity exercise. After all, it got him a column inch on the front of the *New York Times*. Perhaps I was cheap at the price and a million dollars was no more than spare change to Ben Jamieson. Judging by the reports, he was seriously, enormously wealthy.

Until now, Aidan had totally protected me from the financial side, freeing me to concentrate on 'making' and promoting rather than selling my work. But this project had put me right inside the commercial heartland. What was there to learn? I closed my eyes. I was beginning to feel sleepy. Opening them again, I took another look around. Something here made me uneasy once more. Maybe someone had died in the studio? I was surprised to have such morbid thoughts, and tried to shut them out as I scrutinized the surroundings once again.

It was only then that I detected them: tiny camera lenses, tucked neatly into the corners of the ceiling, all pointing directly at me. Why hadn't I noticed before? Cameras are among the key tools of *my* trade. Fascinated, I stared at them in turn, wondering if they were on. I rolled onto my stomach, then back over onto my side. A lens lazily followed the move. I rolled back again and it moved into line. I was definitely being watched. I let out a nervous laugh and put my head in my hands. *He was watching me!* My mind started racing . . . was there, I wondered, sound attached?

Then the full meaning of my discovery dawned on me: Ben Jamieson already had me well and truly in his possession; I was already on display, like a real work of art. The thought was disconcerting. Nevertheless I felt right back at the centre of things. The big question was, the centre of what? I had never been one to enjoy life without an audience. But how many were in this gallery? One? Or a whole dealing floor? Either way, I thought, I had better start playing to the cameras. I hoped he – or they – hadn't noticed my discovery. It would be best to let them believe I was unaware they'd got their eyes on me. Then the fun could really begin.

No call was forthcoming from Ben Jamieson. But now I'd spotted the cameras I didn't expect one. He was already in touch. Perhaps he was getting frustrated that I hadn't performed my 'virtual view' yet – that I seemed to be spending the day lounging around, smoking, rather than doing my promised act. I took the reproduction of *Christina of Denmark* and placed it in the middle of the white performance mat. My stage was now set at the centre of the studio and I hoped it was an obvious enough sign that I was to perform. Then I went into the bathroom and checked for cameras. Relieved that, at least there, none were to be found, I took a long bath in private before starting to get ready.

Petra had prepared me different sets of make-up for each performance and I opened Christina's pouch now. It contained peachy-toned foundation, strawberry-tinted lipstick, green contact lenses and brown mascara. At drama school I'd been trained in all aspects of theatre; I was as proficient at painting myself as I was at knocking out a still life in oil. I applied her peachy oval face, slipped in her deep-set green eyes and coloured her rosy full lips. Then I slowly affected her half-smile in the mirror. Over the previous three months I'd spent more time practising make-up and facial expressions than any other aspect of my women's personalities. It was imperative I got their essential look right.

Satisfied, I then got dressed. First the crisp, white shirt, edged with fine curls of lace; next the long, black gown. I fixed the auburn wig over my hair, then attached the seven fine black veils that would hang down over my face. Finally, I placed her four rings on my fingers, slipping Dior's gift, the ruby and gold ring, onto my left hand. Then I picked up the Elizabeth I prayer book and walked slowly back into the studio, as if stepping onto a stage. While I'd been dressing up, the night sky had darkened the room; now it was intermittently lit by neon. I hoped Ben was watching, but to be sure he wouldn't miss my performance I had set my own video camera to record the event. I switched on all the lights and stood silent and still at the centre of the performance mat. I had the ability to remain posed and motionless for minutes on end – another useful skill learned at RADA. I now put the art into practice.

After what I calculated to be sixty seconds, I bowed slowly, then looked up again and began to turn in a circle, my left arm crossed over my waist, cradling the prayer book, displaying the ruby ring, the right naked hand outstretched and fluttering like butterfly wings. Once I'd gone full circle, I flicked through the book and stopped at a marked page. Then I began to read aloud, evenly:

A prayer for Marie Marcoz, Madame de Senonnes.
Good Lord deliver us from all blindness of heart; from pride, vainglory and hypocrisy; from envy, hatred and malice; and from all uncharitableness.

I slowly closed the book, removed the first veil, then repeated the cycle six more times, at each turn citing a collaborator, uttering a short prayer of forgiveness from the book, until all of my subjects had been referenced. At the last, I removed the final veil and Christina's face was fully revealed to the cameras. Standing absolutely still, I then reproduced her subtle yet knowing half-smile. Finally I bowed once more, then stepped slowly into the bedroom. I closed the door, removed the costume, washed off Christina's face and went to bed.

In my dreams I hung upside down from the ceiling like a bat and watched Esther Glass, aged sixteen, painting below me in her bed-sitting room in Maida Vale. She was naked but for a crown of thorns around her head. Her belly was extended – large and smooth and round. There was a knock on the door and when she opened it Christina walked into the room, with Kenny Harper on her arm. They were both laughing hysterically. Then, as Kenny moved forward towards the adolescent me, Christina fell to the floor and began rolling from side to side, holding her stomach, tears of mirth flowing down her cheeks. When she saw me watching her from the ceiling, her face paled, then she became absolutely still. A sinister smile spread her lips as I began to fall towards her.

35

I woke suddenly. The dream began to dissolve before I could catch hold of its threads, but throughout the morning fragments flickered inside my mind. I felt I'd been witness to something I should not – could not – have seen, and the effect made me feel nervous. I wondered if perhaps Kenny had been back in touch with the papers. I called Katie to see what more had come up in the media that morning but she reassured me things had gone quiet. Maybe it was the cameras around me that had triggered this anxiety. I wondered if Ben Jamieson had watched me sleep.

I tried to put the thought out of my mind and spent the morning replaying the video of my performance the night before. It was ethereal and ambiguous. I was pleased to see that I really did resemble Christina of Denmark, and the effect was quite chilling: she seemed to be talking from beyond the grave. The film, however, was in need of a sharp edit. The performance was interesting but the pace too regular. I decided I might speed up some of the prayers and then remix the soundtrack to combine them, so that they too would become a touch abstracted. Four hours passed without my noticing the time. But this was what I was there for: to create the *Possession* series. I was at work and felt happier for it. There was nothing to rush for. All I had to do was wait for my owner's next move. When I was satisfied with my progress, I closed the files down and switched off my laptop. Then I left the studio and went back to the diner for brunch.

The sun was stronger that day and the city felt to be in a more positive spirit. There'd been no market and the street had been cleaned. I came back and reassessed the value diagram I'd made the night I'd arrived, then turned it round so it faced one of the cameras – making it easier to zoom in on and actually read should Ben, or anyone else watching, feel so inclined. And then I worked on my 'Top 10 Facts' list about Ben. It amused me to know he might be reading it as I added adjectives. I had quickly got as far as number five and it read, boldly, in thick black capital letters: RICH PHILANTHROPIC PATRONIZING   VIRTUAL

I was toying with the next word when there was a light knock at the door. Joe lurked in the hallway. He smiled meekly and lingered on the threshold, remaining there even when I stepped back and invited him to come inside.

'I've got a message for you from Ben.'

I nodded.

'He asks if you would attend a party tonight. It's for a new journal being launched downtown.'

I asked for more details. It transpired Ben was the main backer and would be giving a presentation at seven. There'd be a slot first for my next performance. It sounded perfect: a very public viewing for Isabella d'Este, surrounded by New York's arts elite. I expressed my delight. Really, this week couldn't have started better. There could be no more appropriate an environment in which to unveil the Jackie O of the Renaissance.

It was already close to three o'clock. I asked Joe if he planned to go to the party – it would be good to have an escort on arrival – but he told me wryly that he tried to avoid occasions where his personal sense of insignificance was so effortlessly reinforced. 'Do you need anything before you go?' he added.

He had a strange knack of avoiding eye contact and I hesitated. But his modesty was appealing.

'A drink, maybe?'

He looked at me now; his eyes expressing surprise, but his tone was upbeat. 'Sure. Say, six? There's a cool bar at the bottom end of the street. We can watch for your car from there.'

I'd already laid my next costume out and was ready to dress. It was an easy outfit to wear to a party. Petra had designed a two-piece suit, reflecting Titian's masterpiece of Isabella d'Este but with a definite hint of Sixties Jackie Kennedy thrown in for good measure. Again, I painted my face first, this time with a very pale foundation, then added deep-russet blusher to enhance my cheek-bones, before lining my lips deep brown and defining my eyes with chocolate kohl. I pulled a tight-fitting wig of short russet-red curls over my hair, then placed the strange anemone hat on my head. It looked quirky but cool, contemporary yet anachronistic. Petra, I decided, was the true genius behind this work of art. I practised a steely, worldly expression in the mirror, then adjusted it, adding a touch of vulnerability for good measure. I turned the look in my eyes to glass.

Satisfied, I gathered together my accessories for the performance: a silver fox fur that would hang from my neck like a willing sacrifice, the leather-bound book listing my excessive inventory of aesthetic ownership to be held in my hand. I also had a small, beige suede money bag full of copies of Isabella's coin, stamped with my head on one side, hers on the other, and our combined insignia on both. It would hang from my other wrist, so that the coins could readily be scattered into the crowd. These small tokens of my inordinate wealth would serve to remind onlookers of the true value of my power.

Certain I was now ready, I wrapped myself in my own fake fur, switched out the studio lights and headed out to find Joe.

*

We ordered vodka on the rocks at the Gas Light, a suitably low-key but gothic bar at the end of the block. The atmosphere fitted Joe like a glove and the alcohol made me feel bold.

'How often do you see Ben Jamieson?' I enquired with a smile.

'Not so much.' Joe deliberated, looking into his glass. 'We have a quarterly meeting at the studios – a half-hour or so . . . run through general admin. Then he'll take a look around, see if anyone's made new stuff.'

'Does he buy art from the studios?'

'Sometimes, sure.' He glanced up momentarily, but as soon as I caught his eye he looked away again. 'But I've never known him to buy real flesh before.'

'Leaves that to the guys at the market opposite, huh?' I asked.

'Sure, but that's not human flesh, as far as I'm aware.'

We drank in a comfortable silence. I wondered if Joe had installed the cameras for Ben. Perhaps that was why he had refused to come inside the studio earlier: didn't want to get caught on film. I decided not to ask – yet.

'So when Ben's not around, what happens?'

'He pretty much leaves me to run the place. Once a year I provide him with a shortlist of applications for the studios and he makes his selection.'

'He must be very busy, running all those hedge funds.'

Joe smiled, irony detected. 'Sure is. Mostly I deal with his assistant, Sarah. She manages the accounts. She'll be there tonight.' At this he raised his eyebrows. 'No doubt she'll escort you when you arrive.'

While he was talking I had spied a black car pulling up along the street.

Now he acknowledged it too and nodded his head. 'That'll be for you.'

I felt warmed by the vodka – and the company – and more than ready to go.

*

It wasn't far. Soon the cab pulled up outside a ten-storey building in the heart of SoHo. I could tell I'd arrived by the crowd gathered on the sidewalk and the plush emerald carpet running up the steps to the open doors of the security-flanked entrance. New York had become awash with private police enforcers – everyone was obsessed by their safety. What kind of protection was it really? Not protection from camera flashes, that was for sure. Photographers elbowed one another for space. I made my way slowly up the stairs as lenses clicked. I was a known entity: they called out my name, begging for a pose. Only in New York would a magazine launch occasion such razzle-dazzle, even post 9/11. I wondered at the level of celebrity I'd find inside. In London you'd struggle to find the address and then discover some muscular bouncer checking your credentials suspiciously before inching you inside with a grunt. On balance, I decided I preferred it this way.

The foyer was crowded but orderly. People were queuing to be signed in by two girls dressed in red rubber minidresses, faces painted like geishas. They stood coyly, behind a little desk, checking names and handing out magazines. On the cover was a green graphic of the barrel of a revolver, accompanied by the single word SO, in the same green as the carpet outside. Obviously it was an issues-based periodical, no doubt with a splash of celebrity to get the readership figures needed to fill the advertising slots. I waited in line but was immediately approached by a young Chinese woman in a white suit.

'Esther, welcome to Manhattan.' She had painted-on charm, but intrigued eyes that had immediately seen through my disguise. 'I'm Sarah, Ben's assistant.'

Sarah gestured and I passed her my coat. She handed it to a geisha, then cast her eyes over my outfit, quasi-admiringly. 'Great costume! Ben's not here yet. The plan is that he'll go first, introduce you, then launch the magazine once you've completed your . . .' she hesitated, 'performance.'

I asked if they were planning to film the event. I saw in her eye a hint of knowledge about my venture, but it fled before I had a chance to trap it. So she knew about the cameras in the studio, too. She confirmed that they'd also be rolling here tonight.

Sarah led me through to the main room, where we were met by another red-rubber geisha with drinks. I took a champagne cocktail and glanced around. Sarah was already being beckoned away and for a moment I was left to observe the party alone. It was a vast, treble-height sculpture studio, filled with New York's arts crowd. The lavishness of the event was like nothing you'd see across the Atlantic, even today. In my mind's eye I saw snapshots of London's equivalent scene: the enormous, dark warehouses down gritty East End side streets, the smoky pub hangouts off Brick Lane and Aidan's gleaming white gallery, the alternative Mecca of the contemporary British art crowd. That all seemed less impactful: maybe we were not at the centre of things at all? There was so much money in New York, you could smell it in the very fibres of the invitees' clothes.

Dominating the space were three vast uncompleted plaster casts, huge obelisks to a generic deity, name unknown. I recognized the work and immediately knew whose studio I had entered. Why hadn't Joe told me? Jake Keene had been the subject of one of my special papers at college. It was hard to grasp that I was about to perform inside his creative domain. I looked up at the space above my head. A raised gallery encircled the lower room, dissecting long, glass windows that invited New York's skyline in. Pulleys and platforms hung tantalizingly from the ceiling, like a series of old-fashioned circus apparatus.

I was so absorbed in my surroundings it took a few minutes before my sights settled on the other guests, an amorphous mass, their conversations rising and falling about my ears. They were well-turned-out people, mainly wearing shades of black, except for the odd eccentric arty dresser with shocking dyed or funky hair. I recognized a few faces from celebrity magazines – writers, actors, artists – then spied Sonia

Myrche across the room. I would talk to her, but not right away. She was deep in conversation with a familiar middle-aged man, himself in black, grey hair slicked back. It was Greg Weiz. He was listening to her intently, rocking slowly from side to side, arms behind his back. We'd met a few times, and one thing I knew about this man was that he was never still. He moved constantly back and forth between his sturdy legs, like he was weighing things up, which, in his profession as an assessor of all things aesthetic, I suppose you could say he was. My mind turned to Aidan. When he was concentrating hard he gave the game away by tapping his fingers on his desk; otherwise he was always still and attentive. At that moment I realized I missed him, more so because I knew he was somewhere in this city, and not with me.

I looked around slowly, and found my eyes drawn to the back of a perfectly coiffured blonde head a few feet away to my right; and then I saw the object of my thoughts. Aidan was approaching her, two drinks in his hands. It was Carolyn, of course. I should have known she'd be there. I watched them as he handed her a cocktail and their heads tilted together intimately. There was such familiarity between them that, for a moment, I felt an uncharacteristic stirring of jealousy. I knew it was absurd and forced it away.

I was distracted from my observation by a voice.

'Esther, how good to meet you at last.'

I swung round to find Ben Jamieson standing there, facing me, flanked closely by Sarah – who, it seemed, retained a fixed grin at all times. I'd anticipated this moment since I touched down at JFK, but was now caught off-guard. He was taller and broader than I'd expected. Usually photographs amplify the actual but in Ben's case they'd had the opposite effect. Slowly I raised my hand for him to shake. He took it and held on a second longer than was absolutely necessary. I knew I should mind.

'I like the dress very much,' he said, looking pleased. 'Quite the First Lady.'

He hit the reference spot-on – from the auction catalogue allusion to Isabella, maybe, or from watching me dress up for this performance earlier, or perhaps someone else had worked it out for him. He must demand briefing papers on everything from his latest city deal to, in this instance, the costumes worn by me, the artist he currently owned. It was odd to think he might have watched me dress and I was disturbed to find the power compelling.

'I hope you approve,' I said evenly. 'After all, what you see, you possess.'

Ben's smile widened to display perfect white teeth. 'Are you settled into the den OK?'

'Yes, thank you.'

'Excellent. I can't wait to see your next performance.'

'I'm ready when you are.'

'Great. Once I've made my speech we'll talk some more. Oh, and I believe you have an acquaintance with Sonia Myrche?'

I glanced in Sonia's direction. She and Greg were still deep in conversation.

'I suggested that perhaps she could do an interview with you for *So*. I know you share an artistic affinity and she said she'd enjoy the challenge of writing a piece.'

Sarah now smiled at me indulgently, like the mother of a slightly mischievous schoolboy, and ushered Ben towards the stage. I glanced back towards Aidan and saw that he was watching me across the crowd. I gave him a Christina half-smile in return. He took it as an invitation and I was startled at the yearning I felt as I watched him moving gracefully towards me through the crowd. He kissed me lightly on the cheek and took hold of my hand.

'Why are you ignoring my calls?'

'I told you: I want to try and do this week on my own.'

I was tempted to ask what he was doing with Carolyn, but knowing it would be childish I made myself remain silent.

'I love you, Est, and you look amazing.'

I didn't reply.

'How's it going with Ben?' he asked.

'I only just met him, five minutes ago,' I murmured, 'but he's got cameras all over the apartment, watching me.'

Aidan laughed and his grip tightened on my hand. 'Does that mean he'd see if I snuck in to help improve Victorine's pillow book?'

Despite myself, I felt my mood lighten. 'No more pillow books, Aidan. I'm trying to immerse myself.'

We were interrupted by a ripple of applause. Ben was standing on the podium. It was time for him to perform. I could tell that, like me, he was in his element on the stage. His voice was perfectly paced, his wit wry, and he raised warm laughter from the crowd. He probably paid for most of their livelihoods with his patronage – this was Republican tax-break America, after all. Aidan placed his hand lightly on the base of my spine as we watched. I didn't move away. Ben had completed his welcome and the speech was turning to me.

'. . . and so I did something I have never done before,' he said, smiling in my direction: 'I purchased a living, breathing masterpiece. I'm sure most of you have seen Esther Glass's work, or at least read about her performances in the press. People are asking why I paid such a high amount for her. All I can say is that I believe she's one of the most important artists working today.

'In a moment, Esther will perform the third of seven acts that comprise her latest project, the *Possession* series. The entire project is eagerly anticipated by Tate Modern London, where it will be on display from May, before touring around the globe. But first, please take a few moments to enjoy with me the moment I made the finest purchase of my collecting career.'

The lights were dimmed. Then the screen flickered into life and we were back there again. The whole deal took less than five minutes to play out. I watched Marie Marcoz on the stage, and my heart pounded at what seemed very much to be her own drama. As the lights came back on I realized that the present live audience was matching the applause on the screen. I took it as a cue and walked slowly towards the stage, stepped on to it evenly, stood very still and waited for their clapping to subside. I forced my mind to focus on my next subject. Isabella d'Este was a determined intellectual, musician and politician who had the wealth, power and influence to turn her ideals into realities. She was intent on staking her claim over the works she commissioned, labelling them with her insignias and symbols. She would have adored this evening. I reminded myself of the facts. Tonight I intended to provide a view of a woman more possessing than possessed.

I stood stock still for a minute, then began to look around slowly, picking out faces among those gathered and acknowledging them, waving and pointing, as if suddenly spying friends. I could imagine Isabella now, in the courts of Italy, running her own show. She would have known everyone, been aware of who to 'work' among the crowds: who could be useful, who worth paying to provide her with whatever it was at that moment that she wanted. My act quickly raised an amused titter from the audience. They were enjoying taking part.

I now opened my inventory and began to read from its pages: 'Mantegna, Correggio, Perugino – I have their paintings, pieces of furniture, and artefacts.'

Sighing audibly, I turned my eyes heavenwards, smiled and snapped the book shut again.

'I can't help myself,' I confessed gaily, my voice glossed with a lyrical Italian accent. 'When I see a work of great artistic achievement, I have to possess it. Objects outlive us all, and without art there would be no culture to inherit. I am a woman empowered by land and by money, which afford me a certain creative control.'

I put the book down on the stage, lifted my bag and shook it. The coins tinkled inside. I undid the zip, looked out across the audience and took a handful; then I began to toss them out to people, one at a time, saying, 'Take one,' each time, until they were all gone.

Everyone was trying to catch the coins and laughter rang out as people discovered Isabella d'Este's face on one side, mine on the other. Some must have recognized the Renaissance queen. When the bag was empty, I shook it slowly and shrugged. Then I took a small bow and left the stage to a light applause.

The audience returned quickly to their conversations – my perform-ance had been only the briefest of surreal interludes. Although it seemed that they had enjoyed watching me, it was far from a momentous event. There were far too many rich and famous people about for me to be at the centre of their attention. I felt curiously re-assured by their take-it or leave-it attitude. This was not London, and within this particular elite I was one of many. I was quickly surrounded with interested parties, however. It seemed that my sale had touched a chord. Aidan tried to escort me but before long I was drawn into one conversation after another, until, fuelled by adrenalin and alcohol, I found they all started to merge into one. I was beginning to feel dis-tinctly breezy. At some undefined point Aidan was dragged away by the tide. Ben, too, had disappeared into the sea of people.

I rolled from conversation to conversation. February was a busy time in New York's art calendar. I would have loved to accept several in-vitations to dinners and openings and was even offered a couple of high-profile interviews, but I wasn't mistress of my own destiny. Katie was conspicuous by her absence; usually she would be around to sort the media side out. Surely it was up to Ben to decide where, who, how and what I should be doing with my week? A game without known rules was hard to play.

Time to switch to water. But maybe I'd have one more drink first. I took one as a rubber geisha glided by with another tray. I was sipping the unfamiliar pink liquid as Sonia Myrche joined my circle.

255

'It was a masterstroke for Greg and Aidan to persuade Ben to purchase you – quite a *coup*,' she said enthusiastically. Who else, I wondered, was on the inside track about my sale?

'Ben asked if you could interview me for *So*,' I answered, avoiding the issue.

'I'd love to. Maybe tomorrow afternoon?' she answered. 'If you're free, call me. I'll be uptown, working at the Greg Weiz gallery on my next show. We could meet for English tea? It's all the rage in New York currently.'

'I'd rather stick to coffee.'

'OK, I know just the place,' she said, glancing at her watch. 'I have to go – to dinner with Greg, if I can find him. What are your plans?'

I shrugged. 'I'm just waiting for my master to inform me of my next move. Otherwise, I expect I'll go back to the studio and sleep.'

'Don't tell me you're staying at the Artden?'

When I described the setup she let out a shriek of delight.

Sonia handed me her card and made her excuses. I decided to seek out Aidan but before I had a chance to I walked headlong into Sarah. Her grin still hadn't slipped but she did look slightly embarrassed. I felt tempted to lean forward and swipe it from her face. Memories of past parties in London swam before me. That was exactly the kind of behaviour that used to get me front-page headlines – much more often than the value of my art.

'Ben sends his apologies,' she said. 'He had some urgent business to attend to back in the office. He'd been hoping to take you to dinner. He said to tell you that he'll call you.'

I felt belittled. Was this what it felt like to be a paid mistress? I had to keep thinking of this week as a job. I forced myself to smile compliantly.

'Hey, you know, I'm exhausted,' I lied. 'Do you think someone could fetch my coat?'

'Sure,' she said sweetly. 'Your car's waiting outside.'

Before I left, I determined to say goodbye to Aidan. However, neither he nor Carolyn were anywhere to be found.

I arrived back at the studio in a bad mood, to find Aidan had sent a new text: 'Where R U?'

I decided to ignore it. He was too late. I'd already stripped off the suit and put my black T-shirt and long socks back on. But I hadn't removed the wig, which must have looked strangely theatrical as I sat and ate sushi, methodically, with a pair of chopsticks, on the cushions in the middle of the floor. I stared at the cameras calmly, as if grazing on late-night TV. Let him watch me, I thought. Eating my dinner alone.

I turned my Top Ten list round and added a fifth adjective: UNRELIABLE. Then I turned it back around to face the camera. I wondered what he'd make of that.

I was still feeling woozy from all the cocktails. The taste of raw fish was making me nauseous, too. I decided to turn in for the night. As I walked towards the bathroom, the studio phone broke the silence. I picked up the receiver in the dark. Sure enough, it was Ben.

'Hi, Esther. I hope I didn't wake you?'

'No. I was about to go to bed.'

'I'm sorry for disappearing like that. Hate to be unreliable. I had some unexpected business to deal with.'

His voice sounded a little thinner than it had at the launch. He must be tired. But the reference to my last adjective on the Top Ten list must have been intended. I felt a pang of guilt.

'Did you enjoy the performance?' The alcohol had loosened my tongue. I wanted to know how he felt. I was concerned that I hadn't managed to make a bigger impact. To be honest, I had hoped for a warmer response from the crowd.

'Well, it was–,' he paused, 'interesting, to say the least.'

'It's only one aspect of the series,' I found myself replying anxiously.

'I understand that.' His reply was measured, gentle. 'I feel we're being given scenes from a play that we won't get to understand fully until they're all worked through.'

Ben was right, and I was relieved he understood. I didn't want to disappoint, or for the project to be misinterpreted, either.

'I'm not going to be around during the day tomorrow,' he continued, 'but I'll meet you downtown in the evening. I've persuaded the curate of St Mark's Church to allow you to perform your Meditation there as one of their Tuesday-night acts. There'll be a couple of poets reading first.'

'What time?'

I could hear him turning a page. He must have been glancing at his diary. He really was back in his office, so the cameras must have been linked up to his personal computer.

'I asked Joe to accompany you. He knows all the details. The performance is booked for eight.'

My interest quickened. Aidan had done a good job: this guy understood my requirements precisely. The idea of performing as Mary in a church was tantalizing, if perhaps a little controversial.

'It sounds perfect.'

'OK, Esther, is there anything you need before I go?'

I thought quickly. 'Would you mind if I do a little exhibition-visiting tomorrow?'

'Go ahead. Maybe check out the contemporary show at the Whitney. Let me know what you think.'

I felt my spirits rising. Ben said he'd arrange for a car to be available from ten the next morning. Part of me wanted to go off alone, but I knew I wouldn't feel safe. He bid me farewell and hung up. I found that I now felt re-energized. I had been disappointed to come back to the studio early and alone and yet my mind was quickly focusing on my next performance. There was also something erotic about late-night conversations by phone, particularly with a virtual stranger. I was about to go back into the shower room to get undressed, when I had an idea.

Tomorrow's performance was about purity. I needed to cleanse myself in preparation for a day clean in thought and act. I wondered if Ben had already turned the cameras off for the night and left his office, or whether he was sitting back at his desk, watching me for one last moment before putting his suit jacket on and taking his leave. I walked back into the space and stood quietly in the centre of the room, waited for a moment as the neon lights flickered red and green, on, off, on, off, before I slowly but surely lifted the T-shirt up over my head and removed it. Then, one at a time, I slipped off my socks. Next, the black bodice and G-string I'd been wearing under Isabella's suit. I stood, naked for a moment, allowing the lights to flicker across my body, then unhurriedly I stretched an arm above my head and pulled off the wig and tossed it to the floor. My hair was slicked back underneath; my head would look sculptural in the semi-dark, my skin white as alabaster. I stood still for a few minutes, then turned in a slow circle, as I had done the night before as Christina. Then I strolled into the shower room and shut the door. Now he can see exactly what he's done with his money, I thought.

36

Ben had said, 'Let me know what you think.' As I wandered around the Whitney I realized instinctively that I was looking for something I wouldn't find. This art was nowhere near so in-your-face as the work coming out of London – it might be intellectually charged but it was devoid of wit. This lot, I thought distractedly, need to stir it up. The collective theme of the show was 'journeying'. Maybe the fundamental difference between contemporary American and British artists was to do with space? Our tiny little island has clearly defined boundaries and it felt like the artist's job to try to break out of them. In North America there's always the thought that you could pack your materials and go, start afresh somewhere else. In fact, I mused, you could keep on travelling in the US, a new state every year, for more than fifty years without ever actually leaving the country – or going back to anywhere you'd been before. Maybe that affected the limits in the art.

In Britain the options were more black and white. For me, there was only one: London. I rejected the British countryside as an irrelevance; after my escape from it, I had never felt compelled to go back. I felt a deep and determined obligation to stay in the capital. But I'd really enjoyed visiting Paris and travelling to Venice and Vienna recently. It always felt like I'd picked up a get-out-of-jail-free card when there was a plane ticket to somewhere else in my back pocket. The kickback of the turbo engines signified a fast route to outside myself, gave me a rush as satisfying as any state-enhancing drug; I felt free of my daily concerns, left back on English soil. Maybe in the US it seemed as though you could always journey but never get away?

It was already midday. My mind had wandered far into other territories – a sure sign that the exhibition had failed me. I'd arranged for Ben's chauffeur to pick me up outside. I left the Whitney, relieved to be back on the street, sucking in the icy air through my teeth. I'd woken early and my head was still feeling cloudy from the previous night's cocktails. I took the car out to Queens and the temporarily housed MOMA. I felt I now needed a fix of real masterpieces that could pull a punch. As we drove towards it, my mind was assailed by flashbacks of the evening before: the flashiness of the party, the endless smiling faces, Sonia, and latterly my late-night striptease – all caught on film, no doubt. I visualized Ben burning the midnight oil, watching. My behaviour had left me feeling slightly on edge. I knew it was a stupid thing to do, but part of me, the old rebellious part, couldn't help but quite like the sensation.

The MOMA was rehoused in a series of modern warehouses. There are few collections I'd rather visit, even in its impermanent residence. I was soon in front of Gilbert and George's cityscapes of East London and was surprised to feel a stirring for home. Then I came across a painting of Frida Kahlo, dressed in a suit, hair cut short, just after her divorce from Diego Riviera, the cut locks of her hair thrown like rats' tails across the floor. And now I knew where I'd seen Sonia before. The resemblance to Frida was startling – her Latin flesh tones, tiny scale, androgynous body, small white hands. And the suit. Maybe Sonia was busy playing the same game as I was and had actually contrived to appear like her heroine. The idea thrilled me and made me certain that the two of us could become friends. I was looking forward to seeing her that afternoon.

Buying postcards at the shop, I was unexpectedly pleased when the student behind the desk saw through my disguise of fur hat and high collar and asked for my autograph. Strangely, it reinforced my sense of self, made me feel bigger. I ordered the car back to midtown and asked the driver to stop in Fifth Avenue. I needed to walk. Then I rang. It was Sonia. We arranged to meet at a café up on the West Side.

I walked uptown, anonymous amid the throngs of pedestrians hurrying along the icy streets, on through Times Square and past skaters performing pirouettes outside the Rockefeller Center. I arrived early at the address I'd been given: a small, elegant Jewish café filled with red-covered tables and the hunger-provoking smells of pastrami and rye. Hungry now, I ordered and ate a sandwich, then sat back and drank strong, bitter coffee. Sonia was late.

I tried to take stock. However much I was enjoying the performances, would I be able to make a consolidated project from them, as I had promised on the phone to Ben the night before? My thoughts drifted to Ava. I hadn't spoken to her since the auction but she often came to my mind when I had a difficult problem to solve. I wondered what she would think of the outcome of the auction. How would she tie up all the loose ends I had created? I didn't want it to, but her appraisal mattered. However antagonistic Ava had been about my current project, ironically I knew she was probably the only one who could draw the deeper meanings from it, and that had to happen. The commissioners were expecting it, Ben and Aidan expected it, and the media would have a field-day if I failed. But I couldn't ask her for help. I couldn't bear to see that 'I told you so' smirk cross her face as she recognized my needs and prepared to deliver the solution.

I fished the Gilbert and George postcard from my bag and scribbled on the back of it: *'This cityscape makes me homesick. Hope you're well. All OK here. Back Sunday, E x'.*

When I looked up again I found Sonia grinning down at me and immediately I felt revived. I hadn't imagined it: she really was Frida Kahlo incarnate.

She didn't bother to remove her coat – just sat down and pulled her chair in. Our eyes met squarely across the table.

'Writing home?'

'Yeah,' I said with a smile. 'To my mother.'

Sonia had a way of getting straight to it.

'Are you close?' She pulled a Dictaphone out of her bag and placed it on the table.

'Oh, was that your first question?' I asked, feigning surprise.

She smiled and switched it on, her eyes still fixed on me.

'I once told a journalist that I was raised on ideas,' I told her slowly. 'What I probably should have said was: "on my mother's ideas".'

Sonia still hadn't bothered to unbutton her coat. 'Was that a bad thing?'

A waiter approached. She ordered coffee quickly, keen to get back to it.

'No, not always bad,' I answered, determined to stick within my own pre-set boundaries. It was easy to say too much and regret it later, as I had learnt over the years. 'Just unconventional. She had a lot to do with my current choice of profession.'

'How so?'

'Well, when we weren't protesting about something we were looking at paintings.'

'What did she do?'

'She was an academic – or still is, I should say.'

'Her area?'

'Political science. She's an ardent feminist.'

'Is she published?'

I nodded and filled her in on Ava's meteoric rise to fame, through her book *Raising Women*, written only a couple of years after I was born. I briefly described life at Ickfield Folly and she listened intently.

'And your father?'

I never discussed the dysfunctional nature of Ava and Simeon's relationship, or his lack of paternal responsibility towards me. 'He died when I was sixteen,' I replied.

'I'm sorry. Was he a writer too?'

'No. Another academic, of sorts.'

'Do you miss him?'

Sonia was scratching hard to get beneath the surface. My defences rose accordingly.

'Of course, but time heals.'

Sonia's coffee had arrived but she ignored it. Flecks seasoned her marmalade eyes. 'Do you see much of Ava?' she asked.

I shook my head. So, she already knew her name – knew far more than she was letting on. It didn't come as a surprise; rather, it acted as a brake on my words. My work was about the here and now. That was Ava's time. But I thought I might like Sonia, and didn't want to close her out too much.

'And what does she make of your art?'

I looked out at yellow cabs kicking grey sludge up from the gutters and laughed cynically. 'She thinks I've sold out.'

'I guess she despises the concept of you selling yourself.'

'It doesn't exactly conform to her traditional feminist ideals.'

'And it would be a male purchaser.'

'What do you make of Ben?'

My mind cast back to my late-night striptease. What *had* I been thinking of? I had hoped I'd grown out of such unpremeditated behaviour. It always worked against me. This was one aspect of the series I wasn't about to share.

'Is it all a publicity stunt for him? He's hardly given me the time of day.'

She laughed knowingly. 'Isn't Ben just living up to the character-istics of most collectors throughout history? The purchase is a value statement. He's hardly going to spend much time looking at you. Just like with any other masterpiece, he'll bring you out for public view when there's a PR opportunity for him, like last night, and then leave you collecting dust the rest of the time.'

'Is he married?' I tried hard to affect disinterest.

'God, no.' Her answer was emphatic. 'He likes women. He's been associated with a number of New York's debutantes, but doesn't seem to want to settle down. He's a strange mix of philanthropist and hedonist.'

'In what ways?'

'He likes to do things to extremes,' she said, 'like buy up an artist's entire collection. He seems to enjoy owning art *and* people. You've met Sarah? Well, he literally pays for the ground she walks on.'

'But he doesn't sleep with her?'

Sonia shrugged her shoulders.

'Do you like him?' I turned the tables on her. After all, he was her prime patron.

Although she seemed genuinely disinterested in his personal status she nodded her head vigorously. 'I can't help but like him. He's funny, bright, well-informed – there isn't much he doesn't know about. But you can't get close to him.'

'Have you ever spent real time together?'

'No, I guess not. He spends an hour here, a half-hour there. I think he goes to the Hamptons to relax, weekends, when he can.'

I asked how close he was with Greg.

Her answer was categoric. 'Real close.'

'Who's in the driving seat?'

I hoped I wasn't pushing my luck. But Sonia seemed happy enough to fill me in.

'Greg Weiz drives the deals, most definitely, and advises Ben well. But, you know, I think he also has a discerning eye of his own. I'm sure he wouldn't buy a work unless he believed in its value. I really don't think he's just buying for investment, although that must be a significant part of it.'

'And the tax breaks?'

'Of course. All American collectors have an eye on their year end.'

'So why do you think Greg persuaded him to buy me?'

'Oh, I'm sure he thinks that you're a good investment.'

She smiled encouragingly, but there was a knowingness in her tone that unnerved me. The orange flecks I'd noticed in her eyes earlier had vanished. I was certain Sonia wasn't telling me everything she knew.

I asked about Sonia's latest show at Weiz. She turned the Dictaphone off. It was called *Shadowlands*, she said, and contained a series of twenty screens, each one showing shadows of figures who were outside the screen, marking moments beyond the actual. The core concept was how the mind plays tricks on itself and, additionally, they highlighted how our recall is usually flawed.

'I can't wait to see it. I hope I get a chance before the week's out,' I said. I envied Sonia her ability to articulate her ideas.

She looked surprised. 'You sure will. Greg said this morning you're performing a "Private View" at the gallery tomorrow night.'

My mind jumped between Sonia and Ava as I journeyed back downtown. The interview had been fine, but it had also unsettled me. Sonia made me feel ill-informed about my own life, or at least about my time in New York. I understood that she was represented by Greg Weiz so was likely to know some of the dealings going on in the gallery, but in my case she seemed to know far more than was either necessary or ethical.

Since the week before the auction Ava and my telephone conversations had been no more than a series of staccato exchanges in between interviews, aeroplanes, moments with Aidan or Petra. I knew that she would be judging my current success disapprovingly. And I was sure she was sharing her views with Lincoln. Of all the people from whom I should expect unswerving support, in my mother I found my most critical observer. It wasn't so much what she said but the weight of the spaces between the words that made her views plain. It was annoying to be preoccupied with her at this stage, but I suppose inevitable, since my next performance was concerned with the ultimate icon to perfect mother love.

Joe accompanied me to St Mark's Church as planned. I was silent in the car, focusing on the coming performance, but my nerves were on edge. I realized that this was the most important, and testing, performance of the week so far. A queue was already snaking out of the churchyard and onto the sidewalk. I was wearing a long black cape over my costume, hood up. Joe guided me through to a side entrance before anyone noticed our arrival, and John, a young and clearly gay curate, ushered us inside.

'This is downtown New York's oldest church,' he explained proudly, 'and it has a time-honoured tradition of showing performance art – mainly poetry. W. H. Auden was remembered here and the Beat poets all performed in the Sixties.'

Evidently I was in good company. Ben had chosen an exemplary venue.

The church was empty, lit with candles, incense perfuming the air.

'This is a standard poetry-reading night,' John continued brightly. 'On Mr Jamieson's request we added you to the programme at the last minute. *The Village Voice* reported that in today's issue, and now there's a queue around the block.'

'How many people normally attend?' I enquired, my nerves beginning to jump.

'Normally we might expect thirty. Tonight the church will be full,' he said. 'But I'm a little concerned about the media presence. It seems a few film crews showed up. St Mark's has a policy of not allowing them in.'

'I'm sorry I've caused such a stir,' I said. I was beginning to feel anxious for my own security too. And more than a little worried about my performance. At least I had Joe by my side. He helped set up my two cameras as I rolled out my white performance mat in the middle of the church, where the pews had been removed, then we sat down next to each other in a side pew. I was fast learning that he was often silent and was relieved to be left with my own meditations.

The church began to fill up. I kept my hood on, my head bowed, hoping to remain undetected. Every space was soon taken. The curate introduced the first performance: two young writers whose drawings, poems, and related texts, he said, had appeared in many US literary journals. I was preoccupied, meditating on my own performance, and couldn't concentrate on the meaning of their prose poems, ricocheting between them like a ping-pong ball.

When their session was complete the audience clapped politely but I knew as well as they did why most had come. They were impatient for my appearance. None, I assumed, had noticed I was already there. John gave a brief introduction as a deeper hush fell over the church. It was hard to believe we were in the heart of Manhattan.

I rose slowly and walked to the centre of the performance space and again waited, absolutely still, for a minute before untying my black robe and putting it down on one side. Beneath it I was Raphael's *Madonna of the Pinks* incarnate, from her tight-fitting beige corset to the long billowing blue silk skirt, cut to draw attention to the narrowness of my waist. A fine, white veil covered my forehead and I wore a wig of braided long, blonde hair. I had made up my face with the softest of peach tones, had my mouth set in a beatific smile. I held the small spray of silk pinks in one hand, and my chosen book, *The Book of Hours*, in the other.

I stood silently and closed my eyes, then began to try to absorb Mary's core characteristics. I felt a strong consciousness-shift taking place within me. I was an ordinary woman and, although I couldn't relate to this image of unadulterated, selfless womanhood, or to Mary's virginal qualities, which hardly reflected my own moral stance, the Madonna did touch a very deep, painfully personal chord. In my own secular world I had attained a kind of cult status, though a very different one from hers, and recently my personal life had been more intensely scrutinized than the messages I was trying to convey through my art. As with Mary, my original meanings were being reappropriated to gratify the emotional and inquisitive needs of my public. That, I knew, was why the church was so full tonight. I focused briefly on these key issues as the audience waited. And then I began my meditation.

I spoke only an octave above a whisper but projected my voice easily across the congregation.

'My name is Mary. I am pure flesh, the Virgin, Madonna, Mother of Christ. My roots are wrapped inside the lives of ancient goddesses. I know all there is to know. Yet others have made me more.'

I thought I detected a disturbance in the audience, and I paused, but it was quiet so I carried on.

'These things are written. My birth was attended by prodigies. My earthly parents married me to the temple. And at six months old I walked seven steps. A party was held for my first birthday, attended by all the people of Israel. At three I danced on the steps of the temple and angels provided heavenly food. At twelve the high priest Zacharias assembled all the widowers of Israel and God betrothed me to Joseph. And for the next year I remained chaste. Then the Angel Gabriel appeared to me, advising me I was carrying God's son.'

I was certain now that I could hear a hubbub amongst the congregation, but I continued with my pronouncement regardless.

'The rest of my story is divinity made flesh through the life of my child, the Lord Jesus Christ.'

All eyes were on me, an image of projected saintliness flickering through the candlelight. And then someone began a slow clap, a sinister sound echoing around the church.

'Many people pray to me for salvation, forgiveness, love and advice, support, carrying rosaries, reciting Hail Marys.'

The clapping got louder, and so did my voice.

'They make me shrines, and say I have made visitations. My love for humanity is pure, maternal. I carry out God's will. I was born a mortal messenger, made immortal.'

I faltered as I heard someone shout, 'Shame on you!' and then another, 'Defamation!' Others began to join in, until there was a clamour of abuse ringing around the church – all directed at me. I lowered my head and let them hurl their insults. Part of me felt embarrassed, but another part of me – the analytical part – found their abhorrence of my act quite interesting. I contemplated whether or not to continue, then decided that unless someone used physical abuse I should try to see my act through to its end. I looked up and around boldly at them now and raised my voice.

'How do you see me? Am I a daughter, a bride, a mother? Or am I a simple young girl, a peasant, a courtier, a queen or a saint? What do you want me to be? Make your choice, stake your claim. I am tempera on parchment, fresco on plaster, oil on canvas. I am paint on carved wood, a statue in stone, in clay and bronze. I am a messenger and a message, an icon and a cult.'

As I spoke my final words, I was drowned out by the noise. I waited for a few moments with my head bowed and let the abuse wash over me, until I felt an arm on my shoulder. I glanced up and into Ben Jamieson's grey eyes.

'I think we better go,' he said firmly and led me through the audience as they slow-clapped me out of the church. The silence outside hit me like a punch in the stomach, and suddenly I felt the full impact of their rage. I leant against the iron railings and threw up into the gutter. Ben placed a hand on my upper back and rubbed it gently in a circle until I had finished. Then he handed me a handkerchief and I wiped my face.

'I guess I better take you home,' he said. 'Gee, Esther, you sure know how to make a statement.'

I looked up at him through watery eyes to find a face lit in a generous and unperturbed smile. For one reason or another the failure of my performance had not upset Ben Jamieson. I felt a huge wave of relief and found myself grinning in return.

'I remember the first time I saw your work,' Ben reflected calmly in the back of his black limousine as we were driven downtown. 'It was back in 1992. You'd just completed "estheris". Nothing like that had ever been done in the US. It was kind of shocking but we found it compelling.'

His words revived me and I found my interest quickening.

'It was far more successful in Britain after the edits were shown on the BBC the following year,' I confessed.

'Didn't that turn you into a household name?'

'Amongst other things.'

'Like what? That run-in with the political guy?'

I glanced across at Ben, to be met by a provocative smile.

So, like Sonia, Ben too had already done his research. There were few stones left unturned in my professional life. The media had always rolled them back.

'Strange how sensational events are far more effective at establishing one's identity with the public than aesthetic achievements,' I said, returning his smile.

'Sure, and the auction takes it to another level entirely,' he replied. 'How did it pan out in the end?'

I was sure he already knew the story but just wanted to hear it from the horse's mouth. I supposed it was his privilege. He was paying, after all.

'It all really took off when I openly attacked that government minister – "the political guy" – during a prime-time TV interview,' I said. 'I'm afraid I called him a fucking wanker. It was the main news and live on the BBC. Of course it made the front pages of all the papers.'

'And then?'

'Well, there was the running battle of words between me and the Conservative Party, reported by the media for weeks afterwards. It ended in a court case that nearly ruined my career.'

Ben was evidently enjoying the story. 'How did you take advantage of the situation?'

'The value of my art shot through the roof and I found myself in far higher demand.'

I filled him in further as the car continued its journey. It had been a time of political pacifism, and my outspoken attack on the government was heralded as the 'dawning of a new era'. Sure enough, the Labour opposition began to use me as one of its prime advocates to attract the youth vote. Meanwhile, my art became more self-deprecating, showing the most personal details of my daily life, mental and physical, and the *angst* that went with 'growing up' in early Nineties Britain. I did the *Therapy* series next, featuring me in quasi-frank conversation with my psychiatrist. I had had enough experience to explore the impact of analysis, particularly from my father's quasi-practice at the commune. That project in turn gained me a wider fan club. I was even hailed by some as the most critical female voice of my generation, the one who took the feminist cause to a new audience by learning to play laddism at its own game.

'Laddism?' Ben looked confused.

'Oh, the latest male culture that a bunch of new men's magazines advocated. If I'm honest, the problem I faced was that there were a lot of mixed messages in my early work.' I paused before adding, more seriously, 'I often bit off far more than I could chew. I saw myself as an empty vessel to fill with whatever new idea hit me. I never stepped back to consider how I might be really affected by such intimate disclosures, however fictionalized they were. Somewhere along the line I think I stopped remembering what was real and what was made up – the art somehow took over from my real life.'

'I guess it beats drugs or alcohol as a means of escape.'

Ben's words hit home. He was absolutely right. My art had always been a means of escape and until now it had been a successful way for me not to deal with the real issues in my own life.

'It used to be, but somehow recently it's stopped working that way,' I answered honestly.

'You've lost that wonderful thing called inexperience,' Ben answered, laughing kindly. 'How will you cope with the repercussions?'

It was a good question and hard to answer.

'Success is a bitter-sweet pill,' I replied, finally, 'but in my case it's mostly tasted sweet. I enjoy it. And Aidan's the best adviser you could hope for.'

He nodded in agreement. I could see we were approaching my destination. 'How do you feel about his plans with Greg? I guess that's going to have a pretty major impact on the way you and Aidan work together in the future.'

'Aidan's very much my business partner. In terms of my art, well, it's pretty autonomous. His dealings shouldn't impact on my output.'

Ben nodded vehemently. 'Aidan's always advised me that your work is absolutely of your own making.'

'Was Greg Weiz with you when you bid for me?'

I was sure a glimmer of competitive amusement flashed in his eyes.

'Far from it. He and Aidan say my bid overinflated you. But we're in the process of evening things out. They know I intend to be in it with you for the long haul.'

What did he mean they were 'evening things out'? Had Aidan started making promises regarding my future without my consent?

'Hey, Esther, I'm sorry: that was really rude.' He rightly sensed my mood change. 'I didn't mean to talk about you as a commodity. It's just that in general the art world is a business, like any other, though right at the pleasurable end, of course. But I'm forgetting my manners. It's kind of different when the artwork is human.'

I had always known that this experience would be a learning curve. It was proving to be a bigger, more cynical one than I had expected, that was all.

The car pulled up at the curb. Ben leapt out, came round to my side and opened the door.

'Esther, congratulations for shaking up the Christian reform body. I wish you a good night's sleep.'

I suddenly felt ashamed of my evening's performance. After all, it had turned into a farce. I wondered if there was anything in it I could rectify for the series. I hoped I could replace the soundtrack, turn it into a story with a message my audience would read and not laugh off the stage.

'I'm so sorry about tonight,' I said, my voice wavering.

Ben looked at me, then frowned. 'Why ever are you sorry? Didn't you expect that reaction?'

I didn't answer. I had become so immersed in the planning of my acts that I had all but forgotten that some, like this one, would be played out in public.

'I'm never sure what to expect, but that reaction was a touch more vehement than I'm used to,' I confessed.

Ben laughed and took my right hand in his. 'You've never encountered the Born Again Christians of New York City before, then,' he said, chortling. 'I commend you for confronting them: they don't take prisoners.'

I was relieved by his relaxed attitude. Ben was turning out to be quite a cool, complex character.

'Good night, Esther,' he concluded. 'Now, go get some sleep: you've got another big day ahead of you tomorrow.'

37

'What the fuck happened?' Aidan was on the phone. He'd rung insistently, six times in a row. So in the end I had picked up.

'I didn't anticipate the reaction,' I said.

'Well, you sure got it. You're all over the media. Even NBC are covering the story on the morning news.'

'Shit.'

Aidan laughed. 'That's one way of putting it. It's going to be interesting to see what the fallout is.'

I glanced out of the window into the street. 'No one knows I'm here yet, do they?'

'No, baby,' Aidan replied. 'I spoke to Ben this morning and he's got two more security guys staking out the den to make sure there are no prying eyes.'

'Are you coming to Weiz?'

'Of course,' he said. 'I wouldn't miss your private view for the world.'

'I need to know what's going on,' I said slowly. 'Ben mentioned a bigger deal with Greg.'

Evidently I had caught Aidan on the hop, and the conversation stalled.

'We're in the thick of things,' he said. 'Let's talk tonight, after your performance.'

We were getting close to the heart of the matter now. This project had started as a personal challenge to Aidan and I knew it. He had not wanted me to take it on, and I realized now that he had controlled its outcome all the way. But I wondered at what price.

I went to Weiz, trying hard to concentrate on Victorine. The timing was appropriate: she was the key model on my list who knew all about the art market and her value within it. Greg wasn't around but he'd left instructions with Carla, his exhibition planner, a keen if slightly neurotic New Yorker who darted around me like a minnow. She'd hired a scarlet chaise-longue for the performance. It was plush, more beautiful than the one I'd used back in London for *The Painted Nude* series. My Japanese screen had been sent directly to the gallery from JFK. I was impressed by their efficiency. There were some, if not many, advantages to this close liaison with Aidan and his New York friends.

Sonia had generously given over two of the three gallery rooms for the evening and her films had been removed. First we unpacked the screen. It was tantalizingly erotic with its ten concealed peepholes for viewers to watch me through from the outside.

Victorine's was going to be the hardest performance to film and I set two cameras up: one from behind the screen to give the audience's view, the other in front to provide a clear image of me as I performed. The final piece would require hours of post-production time in the cutting room.

Joe had left a note at the studio, offering to escort me to the gallery. I was ready half an hour before we had to leave, so I sat down on my bed and called Guy.

'Thinking of Victorine has led my thoughts back to you,' I told him honestly, 'and I wanted to say thank you,' I continued, 'for being so generous – with your knowledge and your friendship.'

Guy laughed kindly. I think he was a little embarrassed by

my sentiment. 'How are you, Esther?' he asked. 'Is everything OK?'

I paused, wondering if I should load him with my worries. But I couldn't help myself, and soon I had divulged the complexities I was encountering in New York.

'Think of Victorine, what she had been subjected to,' he urged, 'and remember you're autonomous. As an artist you can make whatever you want out of this experience.'

Guy's words were always reassuring. I thanked him again and was about to ring off when he stopped me.

'Esther, there's just one more thing . . .' He sounded serious.

'What?'

'It's Aidan.'

'Go on,' I said suspiciously.

'I think he loves you very much,' he replied simply.

I sat and absorbed my reproduction of Victorine for one final time. Was Guy right about Aidan? Did his love for me really come before my art? I looked at Victorine and I could read her thoughts, they were written in her eyes: 'You can fuck me, but don't fuck with me.' I wondered if that was the attitude I had projected for all these years – if I, like her, had been too wary of letting my guard down. Victorine had been abused, both mentally and physically, a thousand times. She's telling us she's been there and done it before, she'll be here and do it again, but you won't be getting anything new, anything more than you see on the surface. There's no mystery, and there'll be no surprises. I hoped that was not how I appeared. I hoped that Aidan could still see more.

I dressed with care and became Victorine reincarnated in old age, dressed in a nineteenth-century-style shabby black skirt and jacket, over a greying high-collared white shirt, wearing black leather gloves and clasping a walking stick. I had an unruly grey wig over my hair, a loose bun slipping at the back. I'd made my face up to pile on the decades and emphasize my physical decline: crimson lipstick smudged, eyes sticky with kohl, ears pierced by brash golden hoops. Joe appeared visibly taken aback by my disguise. I'd half expected him to have watched me dress, half convinced that he was Ben's 'eyes' behind the camera lenses. He urged me to tell him whom I represented, but I refused to be drawn. I wondered cynically if Ben was awaiting his call to find out the details.

I was to begin at the end of Victorine Meurent's life, work backwards to the height of her powers as Manet's *Olympia*. I was keen to show how time had destroyed Victorine's spirit just as her painted value was rising to the sky.

By the time we arrived at the gallery I felt like I'd taken a valium. Joe's quiet company had relaxed me. Maybe that was because he was so deadpan and treated me as if I were completely normal. Most people were looking for something to glean from beneath my surface: a nugget from which to form unique opinions of me – opinions that could be seen as being more insightful than anyone else's. Knowing 'Esther Glass', or anyone celebrated, for that matter, made people feel they were holding a privilege card with extra reward points added. Celebrity is, after all, a currency with an inflated value, as Kenny Harper's reappearance had reminded me all too recently. I knew instinctively that Joe would consider a street cleaner with an interesting story to tell just as worthy of his time. Greg, on the other hand, was metaphorically rubbing his hands together as he furtively took in every inch, dollar signs pinging behind his eyes.

'We're so privileged to have you here,' he said, holding out a sweaty-palmed hand.

'The privilege is all mine,' I murmured, my actress's voice smooth as cream.

The performance was planned for 7 p.m. Greg showed me to a tiny back room filled with canvases propped up against one wall. Carla had attempted to turn it into a dressing room for me, with a small table and mirror, a chair, and a couple of coat hangers hooked to the back of the door. The room was rigged up with security cameras that watched the gallery. While I ran through the act, I kept one eye on the space outside. It was hard to concentrate on Victorine as the usual suspects began to appear.

Sonia was first, dressed characteristically in a grey suit, this time over a shocking-pink shirt embellished with orange flowers. She headed straight for Joe and, as they hugged, the space between seemed to close up. They were evidently comfortable around each other's bodies. Now Ben and Sarah appeared, Ben looking more casual than usual, in jeans and a leather jacket, like a middle-aged Hollywood star: handsome but already slightly too mature for starring roles. Sarah followed him in another safe cream suit. Ben and Greg moved away from the group and I watched as they headed for Greg's office. Next Aidan appeared, followed closely by Carolyn. To my surprise, Sonia made a beeline for her, arms outstretched. Slipping an arm through Carolyn's, Sonia leant forward to kiss air with Aidan, and the three engaged in high-spirited conversation. Joe ambled over and joined their group. The atmosphere between them all was one of complete ease. Then I realized why. Surely these were the key components of Aidan's old crowd. I bet they'd been around since his early New York days. Until now he hadn't wanted to share them with me.

Soon other people began to arrive, an eclectic crowd of young and old, moneyed suits and creative types rubbing shoulders with the requisite 'black-clad' people. There was a familiarity about some of them, from the *So* launch on Tuesday, perhaps. This was Greg's chance. I watched as he reappeared and went from group to group: he'd throw his arms wide in welcome; then, as conversation progressed, he'd clasp them behind his back and the characteristic rocking would commence. Meanwhile, Ben approached Aidan. I watched with growing interest as a hand patted Aidan's back, then the two men shook hands firmly.

Even in the back room where I waited I could sense that there was an air of anticipation in the gallery. My private view was open only to a privileged few, thirty in all. Greg had asked if the media could attend and we'd agreed to allow only *Vanity Fair* inside. Their celebrated photographer was as much an A-list celebrity as the rest of them. He strolled about taking pictures of the crowd as they chattered and drank champagne.

Weiz comprises three interconnecting spaces. The guests had at first been directed through to the 'back gallery'. My performance was to be carried out in the 'middle gallery', where the screen and chaise-longue were already set up. At 6.55 I watched as Greg and Carla began ushering everyone into the front space, which was still filled with Sonia's screens. From there, they would be invited back through, ten at a time, to watch my performance.

I would repeat the seven-minute act three times, so ensuring everyone had their own private view. As planned, Carla now placed the pillow book, opened at random, on a large scarlet cushion in the centre of the space where they had been socializing. A sign next to it read: PLEASE TOUCH. The viewers would congregate back here after the view.

I got a rush moving into the middle space unwatched, knowing everybody was waiting so close by. I took up my position, behind the screen and in front of the chaise-longue, which was covered by a black velvet cloth. Carla peered around the door. I nodded. She switched on the soundtrack I'd made to back my performance, then turned down the lights. The space was spotlighted red.

The piano suite *Pictures at an Exhibition* was composed by Mussorgsky in 1874, just a year after Manet painted *Olympia*. It was his musical response to the death of his close friend the Russian artist Victor Hartmann. The piece begins with 'Promenade', a theme that returns four times throughout the music and serves to unify the whole work. 'Promenade' bridges ten larger sections, and represents the viewer moving between paintings, stopping at some exhibits, before moving on to others. It seemed an apt backdrop to my performance of Victorine Meurent.

The opening bar of the music denoted that I was ready. I listened, head bowed as the first ten viewers shuffled quietly into the space. Next to the screen was a small black box with a slit in the top, the words 'Donations, please' on its side. I could hear as each of them dropped coins and stuffed notes in. When the door closed behind them, I knew they were ready, eyes watching me greedily through the peepholes.

I was an old lady, bent double, walking erratically, tapping my stick and muttering, a bottle of gin in my hand. Before me on the floor was an old French beret with a few francs inside. I shuffled around it, try-ing to move my body in time to the music. It was a grotesque display of poverty and ill health.

I stopped still and let the stick roll away across the floor. Then, slowly, I began to reshape my posture, first straightening my legs, then my back, and then my shoulders. Finally I lifted up my head to stare at the screen, as if I had just noticed its – and their – presence. Gaze fixed, I now pulled off my grey wig and discarded it; beneath it was a second wig, of copper hair, tied back, away from my face. I picked up the beret and pocketed the change. Then I began to act neurotically, moving quickly around the space. First I picked up a vanity mirror and wiped away the make-up with a cloth, repencilled my lips and added mascara to my eyes. Then I covered my head with the Japanese shawl, took up a small black valise from the floor and began to pace anxiously back and forth.

Suddenly, I sat down on the bed, as if to compose myself, dropped the valise and picked up a guitar, which I began to play distractedly, a few chords only, over the classical music playing behind. Then I lay it under the bed and pulled back the black covers to display the scarlet chaise-longue, piled high with white cotton sheets and pillows. I stood before it then turned my head and watched the screen with a bored expression, mimicking Manet's impression of Victorine. Then, I began to remove my clothes.

When I was naked, I opened the valise and took from it a flower, which I placed behind my ear, slid rings onto my fingers and a gold bracelet onto my left wrist. Finally, I tied a black lace ribbon around my throat in a bow. Then I spread my shawl on top of the white sheet, lay down on it in the precise pose of *Olympia*, and placed my left hand flat over my lap. Finally, I allowed my left slipper to fall from my foot.

Now, the music softened and I began to speak in a hoarse whisper.

'My name is Victorine-Louise Meurent. I am an artist, a musician, a model, and a whore. I live in Pigalle, Paris. It is 1872. Name your price, state your desire. A photograph? A painting? Music – I play the guitar.' I paused for maximum effect. 'Or perhaps you would simply prefer to fuck?'

I had tried to perfect Victorine's stare over weeks of practice in the mirror at home and I used it now. It was, as hers, utterly unashamed, indecently bold. My tone changed and my words now came more harshly.

'Monsieur Manet liked to look at me, to paint me in the nude. He called me his muse. But the Salon refused to acknowledge the master-pieces he made – until it was too late and he lay in his grave. I was there to watch my rise in painted fame. His works made more money than the price of diamonds.'

I laughed demoniacally.

'Imagine! When I died, my body was left to rot on the streets of Pigalle while people queued to look at my painted flesh in museums. But however much their eyes ogled, in the end only I owned the thoughts that lived in my mind.'

After a moment, as directed, all the lights in the space switched off and the music stopped. The audience was silent behind the screen. They were led away into the third gallery and the door closed. The lights then came back on. I got up from the bed, took up the mirror and my clothes, and prepared myself to begin again.

'You know how to open my eyes wide,' said Ben, smiling wryly.

Watching Ben, Greg, meanwhile, looked slightly furtive, yet extremely pleased.

'I'm just relieved that I didn't gain the same response as I did at St Mark's,' I confessed.

'You're among friends, here,' he said with a laugh. 'Now, would you like to come to dinner?'

My mind was already focused on my proposed discussion with Aidan. I wondered if I would offend if I refused his invitation. 'Do you know,' I said tentatively, 'I am absolutely exhausted. Would you mind if I declined?'

To my relief, Ben seemed unperturbed. 'Of course not,' he assured me. 'The most important thing is that you're refreshed for each day's act, and tomorrow is particularly important. After your tea party, we're going on a long journey, so I recommend you get some sleep first.'

I got the impression he wasn't going to divulge the destination. All I knew was that, wherever we were going, my final performance, the 'Private Dinner' with Klimt's Judith, was going to be held outside New York.

In fact, my excuse was true. After my act as Victorine I did feel drained. I was still reeling from the aggressive response to the previous night's act too. At least with the latest one my reception from the guests had been overwhelming. The pages of the pillow book had been thoroughly flicked through and Ben had asked specifically if it was his to keep. I promised it was an integral part of the work. The evening felt like the high point of my career. This was a discerning group of international art aficionados telling me I was now one of them. But I still had to deal with Aidan and until we had spoken I wouldn't feel one hundred per cent assured. Aidan had already slipped away, leaving

Carolyn behind with Joe and Sonia. So I ordered the car to his apartment.

Aidan was tilted back on a Charles Eames lounger, tie loosened, beer in hand.

'What exactly have you promised Ben and Greg?' I asked, getting straight to it.

'Your performance tonight was fantastic,' he replied.

'Don't change the subject, Aidan. I want to know what's going on.'

Aidan didn't like tight corners. He got up and started to pace. 'Well, before the auction took place Greg and I discussed terms with Ben. We knew he was likely to outbid anyone else, but suggested 350k was probably enough to secure you. In return, we committed to him being first in line for new works.'

'At special rates?'

His phone beeped. He fished it out of his pocket, glanced at the screen, thought better of it and switched it off.

'Esther, nothing's finalized. Which is why I haven't talked details with you.'

'I suppose his crazy bid has made your negotiations with Greg harder and his influence greater,' I guessed.

Aidan looked out of the window and spoke slowly. 'You're right in a sense. We didn't anticipate he'd go so high. And it does affect the way we do business in the future. Of course he has greater power now, and wants tidier cuts on art he buys from Greg in return – not just yours, our other artists too. You have to remember, Ben Jamieson is Greg's greatest client – in fact, in some ways, partner too. They work very closely together to fuel the market here, so I have to play an even smarter game to ensure we get a fair deal from them.'

I came up behind him. 'Is my integrity really not too high a price to pay?'

He turned to me, his tone gentle but firm. 'I'm absolutely on your side, Esther, and your integrity is safe in my hands. But I'm determined to wipe the international board with my artists. Doing well isn't good enough. I want all of your work to dominate a generation. That won't happen if I sit in London selling a few pieces each year to Germany and the US.'

'But if my sale is the basis of a wider deal between the three of you, on behalf of the gallery artists as a whole, my purchase price at auction is shot through with subdivisions,' I suggested. I think I was beginning to understand.

'Ben's bid has raised your market value. You should feel good about that.'

'Yes, but it seems I'm to be heavily discounted against Ben's future acquisitions. Which I imagine will make it harder to sell the others, since their perceived prices will seem too high.'

'That's precisely why we have to negotiate carefully and why I'm here this week. It's sensitive but we'll pull it off.'

'I'm just sorry you didn't enquire whether I wanted to be Ben's permanent possession or not before you thought to strike this deal,' I said.

After all the research I'd done into women in the history of art, how they were dealt and dealt with, it was only now, when the subject was well and truly me, that I was beginning to understand the price of art and money, and the stranglehold of ownership.

For his part, Aidan looked visibly annoyed. 'Most universally recognized artists have one key patron,' he said. I could hear impending thunder in his tone. 'Why does the idea disgust you so?'

I didn't reply.

'Nothing's agreed,' he coaxed. 'When we fly back to London, Sunday, we can go through the details, once Carolyn's lot have finished with the contracts.'

'Carolyn?' Finally it was all falling into place. 'Carolyn's law firm is handling the negotiations?'

He affected astonishment that I hadn't pieced it all together. 'Of course. She's the best on the block.'

'Surely it's illegal for her to deal with personal business?'

'One of the other partners is taking the actual work on. She's just casting an eye over it.'

'Well, isn't that generous? A real family affair.'

Aidan opened his mouth, closed it again.

'What?'

'Oh, Esther, nothing.'

He took hold of my left hand. Victorine's ring still sat on my middle digit. He fondled it between two slim fingers.

When I came out to New York I wanted to concentrate on the *Possession* series, and by that I meant my performances. But I now saw that this deal had got far wider implications and that it was all interlinked.

'Come on, Aidan. Tell me everything,' I suggested more calmly.

Aidan held up his hands. 'Come and sit down,' he said, 'and I'll try to explain where we are.'

I went back to the sofa, Aidan to his chair. He leant forwards and filled me in.

'Greg and I want to create a foundation in Philadelphia, a US Mecca to British Art,' he began evenly, 'and we need capital. We'd like to use the auction cash as a part-investment in its development. Of course you won't be left empty-handed, but we propose reducing your share of the auction sale price to 15 per cent, giving you an actual take-home fee of around £100,000 – after Sotheby's commissions have been deducted. In lieu of payment you will have a share in the new company we're forming and give a commitment to producing a certain number of works over the coming five years. Ben Jamieson is keen to invest further but first he wants a commitment: that we still give him first refusal, at a discounted price, on all your future works.'

I watched Aidan now, trying so hard to hide his anxiety, so desperate for my collaboration, so uncertain of my hand. His fingers were back to their old habit, tapping nervously on the arm of his chair, the only outward display of an inner turmoil caused by an aching desire for something he thought he might not be able to have.

'It sounds to me like you're committing me to a future more focused on the US.'

'Well, that's the other factor, Esther,' Aidan said gently, taking my hands in his.

I looked into his beautiful, earnest face and I could see that none of this had been done in malice. He was trying to make the best of something I had created. My art had never simply been about me. All the same, I felt a sense of foreboding.

'I wanted to wait to talk to you about this back in London,' he continued, 'because it affects both of our futures so significantly, but I guess now we need to talk it through.'

I waited quietly.

'Esther, I want us to move over to New York and I want to start this foundation. I want our future to be open, loving and transparent. And most of all I want us to be together, to be doing what we love most, and I want to spend more time with Sam.'

I felt a dark cloud descending. 'I can't do that,' I said. 'I'm sorry, Aidan, but I'll never leave London.'

Aidan looked utterly dazed, then put his head in his hands and sighed deeply. I wasn't about to explain. I got up quietly and left the apartment.

As I hit the avenue I heard a familiar whirr, then a click, followed by several more. Then a voice clearly shouted out, 'Heretic bitch!' Others joined in a chorus chanting, 'Esther, go home! Esther, go home! Esther, go home!'

A group of snappers crowded the sidewalk amid a gaggle of protesters brandishing banners with photographs of my face on them, each disfigured by a red ink cross. One banner had the words 'Blasphemous

British Bitch' scrawled across it in red capital letters. Holy shit, I thought, this really was not the moment to be found. I pushed past them, jumped into my waiting car and directed it back downtown fast, hoping they wouldn't follow. I felt absolutely terrified. To my relief, there was no sign of a chase.

Joe was waiting at the door; he opened it hurriedly and pulled me inside. Two security guards were loitering in the hall. They'd had a call about the protest in the last few minutes and reassured me that no one had been snooping around the den. They also promised that from now on they would be keeping twenty-four-hour guard.

I went straight to bed, and called Aidan in the dark. He took a while to answer the phone and when he did his tone was spiritless. I told him what had happened and also said I was sorry about my reaction to our conversation, but that I needed time to think it all through.

'We'll be on the plane, Sunday,' he said calmly. 'We can talk about it then, and when we get back home to Soho too. Don't be so afraid of the future, Esther. It's going to be really good.'

After he hung up I lay in the dark listening to New York's sirens calling out to one another, and I found myself anticipating the sound of one entering our street and stopping outside. I felt anxious. Aidan was putting me on the spot, was forcing commitment from me on so many fronts. I could understand the merit in all that he said, and in many ways his proposal and future plans were perfect. Perhaps a few years in America would be good for us, would let me see Aidan on home turf, and finally make me part of his world. He was right that it really was time for us to put down roots together. The problem was, I didn't feel I could leave London, let alone England. It was my home, my foundation, and, psychologically, it was where my heart lay.

38

Over the previous few years I'd been entertained everywhere from pop-star pads on Holland Park Avenue to old-money mansions in Chelsea and Belgravia. But as my car pulled up outside Ben Jamieson's Manhattan home, I sensed that no private London residence could quite compare to this. The nineteenth-century townhouse gleamed, as if the outside were regularly hand-polished – bricks, mortar and all. Rising eight floors high and set in one of the most desirable blocks east of Central Park, it was four times the width of the neighbouring houses.

A butler opened the grand front door and ushered me inside. Its traditional exterior belied a cool, cavernous foyer which resembled an ultra-modern, hip hotel – minus reception. In its centre an apparently unsupported glass stairwell twisted elegantly to the first floor. Either side, on dizzyingly high white walls, hung vast abstract paintings – a de Kooning, a Rothko – that couldn't even begin to dominate the space. A huge, complex mobile of choreographed translucent-coloured planes danced from the centre of the ceiling, the place where one would expect to find a glittering chandelier. To the left of the stairs a smooth, duck-egg-blue obelisk towered at least twenty feet high, making the boldest challenge to the space – but even it failed to compete. The sculpture was by Jake Keene. No wonder he had hosted the magazine party on Tuesday night, I thought.

The butler guided me up the stairs and into a library on the first floor. Evidently I'd arrived first. Four pairs of floor-to-ceiling windows commanded an impressive view across Central Park, where lights were shimmering in the dusk. It was only 4 p.m. but the sky was already darkening. The walls were lined with rows of books, ranging from astrology to bio-genetics, art to technology. I glanced across their spines, taking very little in, and wondered if Ben read them, or if they were just part of the décor. Then I caught sight of myself in a mirror set above the fire. It took me by surprise.

Petra's Whistler-inspired dress made me appear bloodless and abstract. Translucent powder had rendered my complexion spectre-pale and my lips glimmered with pearlescent gloss. I looked younger and far more innocent than in recent, more provocative incarnations. The white chiffon dress was high-necked and cut on the bias, tailing off, modestly, just below my knees; the train tapered and brushed the floor behind me, like folded angel wings. I wondered, this time, if the artistic reference was too opaque, if it might be lost even on Ben. I was wearing the long auburn wig Petra had redyed after our last trip to New York. Now the colour perfectly complemented my ensemble.

I thought about Frances's role in my series, and the contrast between her and Victorine, the subject of my last performance. When Modernism was born, art was forced out of its Garden of Eden and Victorine went readily with it. She's the antithesis of innocence, has already put her foot into the future, knows it's ugly, but is resigned to all it brings. By contrast, Frances still has an eye on the past, seems poised at the brink of its loss. She represents Whistler's preoccupations with naturalness, simplicity and truth. That afternoon in Manhattan I felt an affinity with both perspectives. The evening before had confused me. I wanted to take a step into Aidan's future, but part of me was holding back – one of my eyes was still fixed on the past.

There was a light tap on the door and I turned to see Ben come in. He was dressed in a tweed jacket and jeans, and looked unusually animated. I fleetingly recalled Petra's words about my always falling for the bourgeoisie. He didn't speak, but stood still and allowed his eyes to wander across my surface. A half-smile escaped across his lips and a glimmer of warmth lit his eyes – or maybe it was just the reflection of the fire. Eventually he held out a hand to me and I placed mine in it. His was warm and smooth.

'When I was in my twenties, I lived a block away from the Frick,' he said quietly. 'Every Saturday I would go there for an hour, choose one painting only and observe it in detail. I think Frances Leyland was my favourite. Whistler chose a most beguiling muse.'

I left my hand in his.

'Your performance today will be held in the drawing room, as requested, before afternoon tea,' he continued warmly. 'The other guests were invited for four thirty. But first,' he told me, 'there's something I want to show you.'

'What have you bought?' I asked, assuming rightly that his apparent excitement must have something to do with a new acquisition.

'Esther, you've set me off on a wild spending spree,' he replied in mock despair, then instinctively he took his hand from mine and raised both his arms skyward. 'You've inspired me to purchase another very important new work.'

He ushered me quickly from the library, along a long, white hall, on through an open door and into a dark, burgundy-walled office dominated by a huge mahogany desk. Behind it hung the new painting. My eyes glued to it and stuck. My first thought was, I wonder whether or not it's the original, then I checked myself. Ben Jamieson wouldn't dabble in copies; he would only ever have the real thing.

The painting was very familiar. I felt strange, standing and admiring it, dressed as I was as her double.

'You look like you've seen a ghost,' Ben said, sounding inordinately pleased with himself.

It was true. My skin felt clammy and I found it impossible to answer.

Instead I continued to stare, first at her face, then her auburn hair, the folds in her ivory and gold dress, her beautiful hands entwined through the basket of roses.

'Do you know it?' His voice was low but filled with satisfaction.

I turned from the painting and looked at him. Ben was slightly tanned – quite a feat for mid-February in New York. Only those with serious supplies of money could achieve that genuine air of wellbeing at this time of year. I nodded my head slowly but I couldn't speak. This was the one painting I had studied for the series that I couldn't go to see. Because it was a rare commodity indeed, a masterpiece that had remained in a private collection. If Sonia Myrche hadn't mentioned it to me, I might never even have come across it in reproduction. As it was, after my last trip to New York I had actively sought it out.

I didn't need to say anything. At this point, Ben rightly registered my disapproval.

'I had to have it, Esther,' he pleaded. 'You're only temporary. I can keep this for life. As a reminder of my first live acquisition.'

'How did you get it?'

'Much in the same way as I got you.' There was a twinkle in his eye. 'I made them an offer they couldn't refuse.'

'But why? You don't collect nineteenth-century art.'

'I recognized your reference to Frances as soon as I saw the catalogue entry.' He smiled, as much to himself as to me. 'Of course, I didn't realize it was the Whistler, not the Rossetti, you'd use as inspiration.'

'Are you sure?' I thought back to my meeting with Sonia at the Frick. Of course she'd led him to the painting.

'Well, maybe I had a tip-off,' he confessed with a smirk, 'but there's no way I could get hold of that version. Masterpieces that hang in public collections are only threatened by Getty,' he said, 'as you Brits well know from the recent wrangles over *The Madonna of the Pinks*.'

Ben didn't miss a trick. My mind flitted briefly to Guy, to his insatiable appetite for art historic facts, his total commitment to aesthetics. By contrast Ben got his satisfaction from the power of not only knowing but also possessing.

'Why do you collect?' Suddenly I had to ask.

He stared at the painting before us. 'It's a very personal addiction. I guess you could say it's my refuge. Luckily, I've made enough money to feed my habit.'

'But why do you need to *own* it? Why isn't it enough to go and look at it on a museum wall?'

He stared at the Rossetti for a while before answering me. 'Art's like family to me. It makes me feel secure.'

The words seemed heartfelt.

'Surely not in my case?' I replied.

He glanced away from the painting and appraised me unhurriedly, almost teasingly. 'How could I resist the opportunity to buy the essence of the thing?'

'And you like playing games?'

He feigned a hurt expression but his eyes were still dancing with the hit. 'Buying you wasn't a game, Esther. I bought you because the concept was so original and when I saw you on the stage, well, you were exquisite. I have an unshakeable secret passion for Ingres' women. So you inadvertently hit me on two levels. It's not often that an opportunity like that arises.'

'And you paid so much for me you got your name on the front page of the *New York Times*.'

'That was an unexpected outcome.'

His words surprised me. 'You didn't want the publicity?'

'No.' The thought seemed genuinely to trouble him. 'My clients depend on my absolute discretion.'

'Who, in fact, are your "clients"?'

I could tell my questioning was distancing him again. He moved back a step and looked up at Mrs Leyland.

'Private investors,' he replied levelly, 'who have very substantial funds at their disposal, and quite frankly, Esther, I made more money in commission the day I bought you than you cost me to buy. And I had to be quick. I understood your value. I put in the figure to close the deal. Right then I had a bigger fish to fry. So I wouldn't worry too much about the price.'

His words felt like a stab in the stomach. In my book a million dollars is a million dollars. It was hardly small change, whoever's pocket it was coming out of. Ben was smiling up at Rossetti's wonderful painting, seemingly unaware of the offence he had just caused. He was flushed with triumph. I wondered if Aidan hoped to be like him one day, whether his own desire to see me succeed was in order for him to achieve a similar level of financial empowerment. I hoped not but I couldn't be sure. There was something extreme about such a cold, calculated desire for success. Ben never let his guard down.

I sensed a presence at the door and turned to see the butler hovering.

'The guests are being shown into the library, sir.'

Ben placed a hand lightly on my back. I moved to one side. He either missed or chose to ignore my reaction and continued to address me merrily. 'I can't wait to see your own inimitable take on the wonderful Mrs Frances Leyland,' he said. 'I think it's time. Let's go.'

He guided me back out of the room. I couldn't help but glance behind me. *Mona Rossa, Portrait of Frances Leyland* hung in the semi-dark, the model frozen in time, unaware of the drama unfolding around her, permanently quiet and calm, eternally focused on tending to her perfect flowers.

Ben and I stepped across the hallway and into the cavernous drawing room for my performance, which seemed fitting, I thought, considering Frances had repeatedly sat for Whistler in his own personal quarters at Lindsey Row, Chelsea. I felt thrown off course. I'd spent hours analysing my reproduction of that painting. It had such a close relationship with Whistler's later portrait of her, had been the main reason it came about. I felt like Frances Leyland had literally followed me to Ben's house. I was here, as the artist, and her medium, and here she was, the actual work of art.

A white grand piano gleamed at one end of the room; an arrangement of brown leather sofas dominated the centre, around another roaring fire with a vast gilt mirror above it; at the other end hung an immense early canvas by Jackson Pollock, the only painting in the room.

I asked for the lights to be turned low. Earlier in the day Joe had been here, setting up my cameras. We were becoming quite a team. I was as ready as I would ever be. I switched them on, then stood with my head bowed, face to the fire, my back to Ben's invited friends as they began to file into the room. I was aware of them stopping and staring at my figure, then shuffling around to ensure they all got a perfect view. I was determined not to be put off my performance by what I sensed to be a range of familiar faces staring into my back, most of whom, at this moment, I didn't trust an inch. No doubt Greg was there, Carolyn, Aidan, maybe Sonia. They all felt they had a stake in my ownership, whether psychological or financial. But I wouldn't let it rile me. Not now. I heard Petra and Guy's words: my art was more important. What I captured on film is what would remain of this long after the week was finished. Like Whistler one hundred and thirty years before me, I had to concentrate on aesthetics, even though the relation between the viewer and the viewed – both now and when he painted Frances – was far more complex than words would ever convey.

Slowly I raised my head at an angle and looked back and away over my shoulder, to the middle distance, in the precise pose Frances had adopted for the painter. My heart weighed heavily in my chest. I felt fragile, delicate and unsupported, and, at that moment, strangely in touch with her spirit. I had my hands clasped in front of me, but then

I linked them behind my back, just as Frances had done all those years ago. As I did so, I swayed slightly. The movement was intentional: I wanted to appear slightly unstable and unbearably light. On the brink. I rocked very gently, almost imperceptibly, from side to side. The room was silent but for the gentle sound of breathing and the tick of a grandfather clock.

At this point, the performance took on a new and unanticipated turn. As I thought about Frances, her unhappy marriage, her ambiguous friendship with Whistler, her uncertain future, I felt tears stinging my eyes. A single drop slid down my cheek, followed by another, then another. Then the tears flowed fast, and I wept silently, my shoulders trembling. I was crying for the others too, particularly for Victorine, for Christina and for Marie. And also for myself, for the fear I now felt in the midst of it all. I was afraid of the future, of making decisions, and I was tired of the past, and of its hold over me. I thought of my fear of Kenny, of the media, of being translucent, and then I thought of my fear of losing Aidan because I couldn't work it all out. The fire was very warm. I could feel my make-up softening in its glow. And then I found myself losing consciousness, and crumpled to the floor.

I travelled through space and time, away from Manhattan, back to England, but not to London; instead the journey took me to Ickfield Folly. I was soaring high over the commune, looking down at its turrets, swooping low over its beautiful, ornate gardens. I could see Ava sitting on a deckchair on the lawn. Beside her Simeon was lying on the grass, reading from a book held high in his hand, shading his eyes from the sun. I flew down and landed, shoeless, on the dewy grass and stood behind my mother, listening. I was very small. I had little girl's feet. Simeon was reading Ava poetry and she had her eyes closed, her face turned up to catch the sun's gentle rays.

'Where's Esther?' she asked suddenly, interrupting his verse and looking from side to side with anxiety in her pale-grey eyes. She looked very young; her hair was dark brown and flowing, her complexion flaw-less, her lips full and red. Indeed, she was beautiful.

'I'm here,' I whispered into her hair.

She turned round to the source of my voice, but didn't register me, instead looked straight through me, back towards the folly. 'Esther? Esther, where are you?' she called.

'I'm here,' I repeated.

Then she pulled herself up from the deckchair and walked earnestly through me and away, back towards the house. I watched her figure recede, then turned to look at Simeon. He lay back on the rug and closed his eyes.

'Esther! Esther! Wake up.'

I could hear the urgency in Aidan's voice and opened my eyes. I was lying on one of the leather sofas, and he was cradling my head in his arms. Faces peered down all around me. An auburn-haired woman I didn't know handed me a glass of water and someone else asked if they ought to call a doctor. Her face came into focus. 'I am a doctor,' I heard her say firmly.

I sat up slowly and shook my head. My mind was beginning to clear. I drank the water and leant forward to increase the flow of blood to my brain.

'Are you sure you're going to be OK?'

'I'm absolutely fine,' I reassured Aidan, as he stood by Ben's front door, coat and gloves on. He looked utterly dejected.

'I wish you didn't have to go.'

'Aidan, I'm looking forward to it, and the week's nearly over. Only two more days and we'll be on our way home.'

He smiled dolefully. 'Don't forget, I love you, Est,' he murmured.

It had been an emotionally fraught afternoon. Aidan seemed to have been affected as deeply as I had. I kissed him and he stroked my cheek.

'I'll see you at JFK,' I said firmly, ushering him out. 'Now go and finish your double-dealing. And remember, I won't sign a thing with Greg till I've read all of the small print.'

He smiled meekly. ' 'Bye.'

I felt a weight lifting as the butler shut the door behind him. He was the last to leave. Next it would be Ben's and my turn. The car was waiting to take us to the airport. Apparently our trip required we take his private jet.

39

What's your favourite smell?
Linseed oil.
What's your favourite word?
Yes.
What's your favourite journey?
Anywhere above the clouds.
When and where were you happiest?
17 June 1991, London, St Martin's College Degree Show.
Which phrase do you most overuse?
I'll finish it today.
What trait do you most deplore in yourself?
Not listening.
What trait do you most deplore in others?
Not hearing.
How often do you have sex?
None of your fucking business.
What's your most treasured possession?
My trunk.
What keeps you awake at night?
Illegal substances.
What items do you always carry with you?

Video camera.
How would you like to die?
Corporeally.
How would you like to be remembered?
Aesthetically.

Four hours earlier I had collapsed on a sofa in Manhattan. Now I was trying to fill in this bloody questionnaire, as I'd promised Katie, while flying through the night sky in a Boeing 727 jet. I was beginning to see that Ben's collecting habit extended outside the art world – he'd already told me this was 'one of' his planes. As soon as we took off he excused himself and went into the 'study cabin', leaving me in the plush, carpeted lounge. First class had nothing on this. I was supine in an extremely comfortable armchair, sipping a glass of champagne. After the drama of Frances's collapse, I felt slightly light-headed, but otherwise fine, almost cleansed by the experience. I had awoken from my fainting fit refreshed, as if from a very long, deep sleep.

The mystery of Sonia's relationship with Carolyn had resolved itself before my fuggy eyes as I watched them sitting, hand in hand, on the sofa opposite me, and I now understood why Sonia was so intrigued by me. Carolyn must have been keen to understand everything she could about me – and who better to find out for her than her lover and my aesthetic counterpart in New York City? It reassured me to think of Carolyn with Sonia. She and I were becoming friends and perhaps she would pave the way for me to feel more comfortable around Carolyn and Sam. Perhaps I had to take a deep breath and agree to Aidan's plans. If only I felt I could leave London behind me. Oddly, this change of heart had something to do with Frances. Her loneliness had touched a chord in me today. She was the victim of a long and loveless marriage. I knew that the core of my relationship with Aidan had been the antithesis. Any loneliness I felt was entirely my own.

We were to 'eat in the sky', Ben said, once he'd completed a little business transaction that demanded some urgent attention. I looked out over a darkened United States. We were heading west. Ben wasn't joking when he said he bought me with spare change. But I wasn't going to be the judge of it any more. I still had no idea where we were going. He promised to tell me over dinner. Apparently the trip would take five hours. I was beginning to understand that Ben was married to his work; that art was the luxury he afforded himself when he had time off.

When he reappeared I snapped my laptop shut. I still had four questions to go, but I thought I'd maybe mail it like it was: couldn't make Katie hang on any longer. She'd have to get creative on my part.

He settled into the armchair next to mine and put his feet up on the footrest in front. He seemed exceptionally relaxed. 'What were you writing?' he asked.

I explained. He persuaded me to let him read the answers.

'So you like being high?'

I looked at him quizzically.

'I mean literally – above the clouds.'

'I like the spaces in between things; not being in one place or another.'

'And what about high places?'

I was beginning to see where the conversation might be heading. 'What, like mountains?'

'Precisely.' He leant forward slightly and turned towards me. He was kind of, well, perfect – if you liked that sort of thing. Aidan was striking in a far more interesting way. There was something slightly raven-like about him, which left you on edge. By contrast, Ben was plain handsome. I couldn't think of a more subtle term to describe him.

'Where are we going, Ben?'

'To Aspen, of course. Where else does one go in the US in February? I just bought a cabin there.'

'Is it in the mountains themselves?'

'No. It's in a place called Hayden Peak, but we can look out of the windows towards the four mountains that flank it. It's beautiful. Huge landscape, fantastic snow . . . so much space and clean air. And, most excitingly, I've commissioned an extension to the property to house works of art. At last I'm getting a permanent home for my collection.'

'Is there any art at the house?'

'No, I'm afraid there's nothing much there yet. I've got an appointment with the architect to go through final drawings in the morning and then a skiing lesson in the afternoon. I thought you might like to see where I intend the *Possession* series to end up.'

I found the idea hard to grapple with, considering I was still only halfway through the work. Generally I finished pieces before they were put up for sale.

'Do you ski?' he asked.

'It wasn't – how should I put it? – part of my upbringing.'

Ben looked disappointed. 'Would you like to have a go?'

I couldn't think of anything worse. 'I fear it,' I said, with an honesty that took me by surprise.

'I'm sure we could get someone to take you on the nursery slopes for an introduction. Bet you'd love it,' he coaxed.

Skiing was a pastime that had been sneered at by my crowd at school. It was something toffs did. The idea of being out there in a Puffa jacket looking over a precipice filled me with horror. But I nodded and smiled. Whatever Ben wanted, I was determined to comply with.

I thought about Ben's evasive nature as we sat quietly, continuing our journey west; his focus on material things: jet planes, art, houses; his lack of personal relationships. Why didn't he let anyone get close to him? But there seemed to be few intimates and he wasn't the kind of person who'd readily open up. I was determined to find out a little more about him on this trip.

'What answers would you give?'

He'd been sitting back, eyes closed. Now he glanced across at me, evidently confused.

'The questionnaire. How about you answer it?'

He knew he had no means of escape. And one thing I'd already learnt about Ben was that he wouldn't readily turn down a challenge.

'Pass it over here. You can read my answers once we're at the house,' he said.

Ben tackled the questionnaire pensively. Like everything in life, he took the task seriously. Soon I fell asleep. When we landed it was gone midnight Eastern, 5 a.m. Colorado time. We were driven in the darkness, along quiet lanes flanked by fir forests, to an estate that rose out of the night to greet us. In the middle was the house: a series of modern, internally lit hexagonal glass blocks, linked by glass-covered walkways, set in formal gardens. Ben guided me gently inside. I was hardly awake.

I was led to a room with a bed set atop a high platform, looking down over a floor carpeted in beige suede, with plump plush cushions scattered around. The windows were curtainless – commanding, I anticipated, an impressive view. At the time all I could see was the white tips of mountain peaks, made luminous by the light of an emerging moon.

Looking down over the precipice, I felt very, very small – and absolutely terrified. It may have been a nursery slope to Ben, but to me this was a university education in skiing and I only had two hours to perfect the course. As it was, I honestly didn't know if I could even move forward one step. He'd brought me here and left me, in a hurry to head further up to his expert heights for some kind of super-speed lesson. If I could force myself to open my eyes and look around, I knew the view before me would be magnificent. But if I'd had it my way, I would have headed immediately to the nearby après-ski café and awaited his return there. Some action-Barbie doll in a pink ski suit had been hired to teach me and, at this moment, was smiling brightly while proffering a glove-clad hand. I hesitated, then forced myself to clamp on to her.

When it was all over I sat and drank coffee, relieved to have achieved my first lesson in the art of high-class winter holidaying. I'd never had a full-scale panic attack before. The side of a ski slope was not the best place to start. Luckily, Pink Barbie turned out also to be a trained masseuse and relaxation therapist. She had managed to calm me down enough, finally, to drag me, inch by inch, to the bottom of the slope. And, I had to admit, I felt exhilarated.

The best bit was the ski-lift back up the mountain. All around me was a white canvas, shimmering brightly under an empty blue sky. I felt pleasantly overwhelmed by the magnitude of the mountains, the sheer expanse of snow. The air was sharp and cold but the sun was surprisingly warm on my face. I sat outside, drinking my coffee and inhaling the view. I felt as though my spirit was receiving a vigorous spring-clean. All thoughts of New York and London evaporated and my mind filled with nothing but the view. Then, as if on cue, into it strolled Ben.

I smiled openly. 'That was one of the most terrifying, difficult and yet amazing things I have ever experienced.'

He looked incredibly pleased. For the first time since I'd met him, I thought I might be getting a glimpse of the real Ben Jamieson, someone who liked to do things very, very well, and who got an inordinate sense of achievement from seeing someone else benefit from his wisdom and generosity. That was an aspect of the control characteristic that was actually appealing. I thought about his words in New York, the time he told me that the money he'd paid for me was his form of patronage. Maybe that was just it. He genuinely liked to have influence over people he admired. And he was rich enough to afford it.

We made our way back down the mountain again by ski-lift, basking in the mid-afternoon sunshine as it started to fade over the spectacular view below; a lake shimmered in the valley beneath us and a river meandered its way through the ice-hardened meadows.

As we were driven home through the estate's acres of rolling hills, Ben talked with boyish enthusiasm about his summertime fishing and hiking exploits. Nature and the Big Outdoors were making him more real. We arrived back at the fantastic glass-house, which, though perfectly warmed by underfloor heating, had a fire roaring from a modernist grate in every room. The light from the snow cast a serene glow across the pale furnishings that graced the rooms. It was my idea of heaven. I loved it here. For the first time in my life I found myself revelling in the enormity of the empty space outside.

I retired to prepare for my final performance, but since there were a couple of hours to spare I first took a shower, wrapped myself in one of the thick, plush towels laid out and collapsed onto the huge suede cushions. I stared peacefully out over the landscape as the light faded and the fire crackled in its grate. I had never been anywhere so ethereal in my life. It was a long, long way from Manhattan's meat-packer district, or London's East End. The only thing sullying the snow were the footprints of wild animals and birds. And it was absolutely silent, the landscape so expansive it swallowed all sounds before they had a chance to travel more than a few metres. I felt physically exhausted, but that sensation was so different from mental fatigue. It was much, much better.

'Esther, wake up!' Ben's voice was no more than a whisper.

I came round slowly; felt warm, soft – I must have slept for a while. The room had grown dark and only the brightness of the snow created a little light, just enough to see by. The fire had burnt to orange embers.

Ben was crouching next to me, leaning close. As my eyes opened he whispered, 'I've been watching you for a while.'

I looked up into his face. 'What did you see?'

'Someone who should look that way more often.'

'What do you mean?'

'All the worry lines have left your face. And it's free of masks. Frances has gone, and Victorine, and Marie. I got to see a little bit of Esther.'

I sat up and blinked. I could feel his breath on my cheek. Then Ben leant forward and kissed it tentatively. When I didn't turn away, his lips moved to my mouth. He tasted warm and slightly salty, nice.

He pulled away. 'I'm sorry.' He paused, swallowed. 'It seemed the only thing to do.'

I didn't reply.

He pulled himself upright and made to leave, then he turned at the door and asked quietly, 'Are you too tired to perform? I'd understand.'

'What, you'd miss out on Judith? No way.'

He looked relieved. 'OK. When you're ready.'

The door closed behind him with a subtle click.

Ben had really set the scene for Judith's act, I mused, but I was surprised at myself. I didn't want this man, wasn't even sure I liked him. But my reaction to his embrace made me aware how much I'd been missing physical contact. It had only been a week since Aidan and I were last together in Soho, but it felt like years. I missed him, his touch. I suddenly realized no one else would ever do, but maybe there were too many obstacles; maybe I wouldn't ever be balanced enough to make a future together work.

After only one more day the two of us would be flying home to London, united again, away from New York, from his scene. We could talk through the whole Weiz deal. It would work out well – so long as we could stay in London, that is. It wasn't only about money, after all. If some of the auction cash was negotiated in return for my next project, perhaps that was fine too. Maybe I'd like Ben as my primary patron. As long as we continued to keep sex out of it. It would really mess things up to be sleeping with my dealer *and* my patron.

Relieved now that Ben had averted catastrophe, I pulled myself up out of the cushions and decided to get ready. If I watched my step for the next twenty-four hours, everything could still work out fine. Then I remembered: he'd filled in that questionnaire. Curious, I pulled out my laptop and switched it on.

What's your favourite smell?
Evergreens above snow.
What's your favourite word?
Juliet.
What's your favourite journey?
This one.
When and where were you happiest?
Anytime and anywhere before I was ten years old.
Which phrase do you most overuse?
Hold the line.
What trait do you most deplore in yourself?
Failing to fall in love.
What trait do you most deplore in others?
Seeing my money before they see me.
How often do you have sex?
When aroused.
What's your most treasured possession?
My mother's wedding ring.
What keeps you awake at night?
Clients.
What items do you always carry with you?
Cellphone, wallet, photographs.
How would you like to die?
Healthy at 89 years old in an avalanche.
How would you like to be remembered?
With generosity.

These were hardly the answers of the man I thought owned me. I was intrigued. So what had happened to him as a child? And who, I wondered, was Juliet?

I cast my eyes carefully about me. I was pretty confident that at least I wasn't rigged to film in this room. I took the fabric out of its muslin cover and laid it down on the bed. I spread it out flat, the long, kimono-style dress printed with pink, green and orange coils threaded with gold, hiding the minuscule, sexually explicit 'inner dress'. I put the outfit on and tied the outer strings and was pleased to reflect that now I was the picture of modesty. I placed the long, dark curling wig over my own hair. Petra had prepared a unique sheer make-up which made my skin glisten with a suggestive sheen. I smoothed it over my face, neck and chest. Next I added a single black beauty spot, just below my left eye; then I darkened my eyebrows and painted my lips an uncharacteristically deep burnt orange. I attached my long, red, talon-like fake nails, then I clasped the encrusted gold choker around my neck and slid the numerous beaded bangles onto my wrists. The weight made the jewellery feel like chainmail, as if I was preparing for battle.

Minutes before the auction, Petra had taken me to one side.

'The props for Judith,' she'd said with urgency: 'They arrived only yesterday, so I've wrapped them and placed them at the bottom of the trunk. They're heavy. Don't forget them. And be careful: remember Judith is capable of murder.'

I'd left the trunk in New York and had brought just these curious props. I unravelled the long, heavy package to find what I had half been expecting inside. A leather sheath carried inside it a miniature scimitar sword. It was a tantalizing object, with an extremely sharp, curved stainless-steel blade and a beautifully crafted wooden handle bearing my insignia interlinked with Judith's name. I had no idea where Petra'd got it from. I practised holding it, watched myself in the mirror as I slashed it from side to side. It made a slight, satisfying swishing sound as it cut through the still air. Its real danger gave me a sudden thrill. I could have some fun frightening Ben with it that night. I wouldn't mind seeing him uncertain, for a moment, of the power he wielded.

There was a slim leather belt with the sheath and I discovered loopholes around the inside of my kimono through which to thread it. So I tried it on. The curve of the knife settled comfortably into the shape of my leg. I decided there was no harm in leaving it there. I thought through my plan for the performance and was pleased to spot a moment when it could easily add to the drama of the scene.

At this point I noticed that wrapped up with it was a small glass vial, filled with a pale cloudy liquid, as well as a piece of folded paper. I opened it and read.

> Remember, Est, Klimt's predilection for the erotic was all-pervasive, whether he was painting a woman's portrait or a forest of trees. Enjoy this performance to it's full potential!
>
> P xx

I felt unnerved by the appropriateness of Petra's note, considering I was not only surrounded by the most awesome landscape I'd ever seen, but had recently been kissed by my collector. One thing was for sure: it was the perfect moment to perform as the femme fatale. And it was my last performance too. I thought back to Ben's comment about catching a glimpse of the real me. But that wasn't what this project was about – and it wasn't what he'd bought. He'd bought the *Possession* series, and in that I was not Esther Glass, I was an artist and an artwork. Tonight he would get the final theme: the woman as myth.

But what about the liquid? I turned the paper over. Right at the bottom of it, in the left-hand corner, Petra had written two words in tiny capital letters: SPECIAL K! It took me a moment to figure out their meaning. But when I did I knew she wasn't talking cereal. Perhaps this was one joke too far. I picked up my mobile to call her, then realized I had no signal. I was well and truly cut off. And there was no way I was going to use Ben's phone system to talk to her about hallucinatory drugs.

I knew what was in the vial. Special K is a legal drug, sold generally to vets to sedate animals. When used by humans the most common effects include delirium and vivid hallucinations. Too much can cause aggressive behaviour, amnesia or, in some extreme cases, coma. In recent times it has been associated with 'date rape'. I cast my mind back. The effects take ten to twenty minutes to occur and usually last less than three hours. Like all drugs, it's detectable in the system for up to forty-eight hours. The effects are enhanced by mixing it with alcohol.

How do I know all this? During our time at the Eastern Palace, Petra and I tried everything that was going – although thankfully we drew the line at crack. We used to say, 'A little K goes a long way,' particularly when used in conjunction with cocaine, our favourite party drug.

I turned the vial over and over in my hand. What was Petra's intention? I thought about Judith – how she had plied Holofernes with alcohol, leading him to delirium, then sleep. Then she had murdered him. How far was I prepared to go? Did I want Ben to experience the full effect of a femme fatale? I'd always taken risks. But maybe this was one risk too far?

Ben was a game player. He liked to be in control. I thought about his kiss. It was uncharacteristic. Or was it? Maybe he had done it deliberately, to disconcert me. It was a classic method of control – to unnerve your opponent. As he had explained to me, he took only calculated risks. I thought about the purchase of the Rossetti, the absurd sum of money he had paid for me in order to outwit his opponent, Greg Weiz.

His attitude towards ownership was repellent. It was no different from the Gettys', who had shaken their coffers at *The Madonna of the Pinks*. In both instances the value of the art lay in the power that its ownership wielded. And part of his purpose in buying me had been to flex his muscles.

I looked at myself in the mirror. I'd show him how to play games, I decided. I was suddenly determined to outwit him, give him more than he'd bargained for. Men had had the upper hand throughout the history of art – those who controlled the women behind and on the surface of the canvases they'd commissioned and owned, and the dealers who felt they had carte blanche to wheel and deal with them like stocks and shares. I had to find a way to get under his skin, make him see that, like all my subjects, there was far more to me than met the eye. Give him a little scare – only in the name of Judith, of course.

I looked at my reflection in the mirror. The costume was phenomenal: I really did look like Klimt's creation. I practised untying the outer garment and slipping the kimono open just a touch. The effect was highly erotic and it made me feel charged. Then I discovered a tiny, internal pocket, below my left breast. I took out the vial and tried it for size. Of course it slid in perfectly. Petra is the consummate designer. I looked at my reflection as I patted the pocket, then retied the outer robe. No harm in carrying it. It was legal, after all.

As I left the room, the only sound was the sigh of silk brushing against bare skin. My naked feet moved silently across the polished wood floor. Ben was waiting for me in the sitting room, curled up on a deep, white leather sofa, pretending to read *Time*. He glanced up and his expression immediately changed.

'Take a turn. Let me admire you more fully,' he said.

I revolved slowly and made a tiny mock-Japanese bow.

'Is it a Klimt?' he asked, regarding me thoughtfully.

I nodded. 'Judith was the biblical heroine who seduced General

Holofernes, then cut off his head in order to save her city.' I had two cases in my hands. I moved forward and handed him the first. 'This is your chance to collaborate,' I told him. 'You get to film me.'

He looked pleasantly surprised. His fingers quickly undid the straps and pulled the camera out. I watched as he became absorbed in its mechanics, working out how to use it. I put the other case on the floor. In it were my two portable studio lights and Holofernes' head.

'What are you going to do?'

I laughed. 'It's up to you.'

He looked quizzical.

'This is your chance to control the performance,' I explained.

With an amused smile, he started filming me, zooming in and out with the lens as if it were a new toy.

'Tell me what to do,' I suggested.

He looked up, disarmed, but quickly collected himself. 'Recount the tale,' he ordered evenly.

I asked him to move back the sofa to give me a bigger space and then he helped me set up the two spotlights, which would throw Judith into bright, theatrical focus. Then Ben moved around me, filming as I began to act.

'My name is Judith,' I began. 'I performed a terrible act for the love of God and the love of my people. I dressed to tantalize and crept from my home. I intended to bewitch the general with my female wiles.'

I stopped and smiled provocatively, staring straight into the lens. I could see Ben grin behind the camera. He seemed to be enjoying the drama, so I carried on.

'I went to Holofernes' camp and offered myself as his slave. The soldiers knew what I wanted, or at least they thought they knew. I was led to his tent. When he saw me, the general was entranced.'

I stopped again and continued to stare Ben out. He did not avert his gaze. Instead he pointed the camera at me and mouthed, 'Go on.'

'The general was hungry . . . thirsty, too.' I crouched before Ben and spoke more quietly. 'So I sat down and encouraged him to drink some wine. When he'd had enough, I suggested a little more. And when he had finished the bottle, I asked for another to be sent. At first he refused, but I had ways to make him acquiesce.'

Ben smirked as I stood back up and turned round. With my back to him I slowly undid the front ties of my robe and allowed it to fall open, so revealing the extremely low-cut dress beneath. I ensured the sword was still hidden by the robes as I swung back round. I saw the camera falter, detected a new nervousness in my owner. I leant forward closer to him and the camera's lens. I could see him zooming in on my stomach, on my bare flesh. Then I continued my story.

'I waited. Holofernes was becoming quite drunk, more desirous. But I wouldn't let him touch me. Instead, I persuaded him to drink a little more, and then a little more, until, finally, he fell asleep. Then, I took out my sword.' With this, I slowly slid the scimitar out of its sheath and pulled it out in front of Ben's face. The camera began to tremble noticeably. I took a step back and cackled with laughter as I swung the sword from side to side. 'And with two swift strokes,' I said, 'I cut off his head.'

Ben was still filming but was now watching me a touch anxiously over the top of the camera. I lunged towards him, then as he ducked I let the sword fall from my hand onto the floor. Next I took the model head from its box and swung it madly in my left hand before him. 'And then I took his head back to my people as proof that this was one possessor who was no longer possessing.'

I froze in Judith's pose from the painting and fixed Ben with her same mad, sexually erotic stare. A silence prevailed between us as the head swung back and forth in my hand.

Then Ben slowly began to laugh, and I bowed deeply and began to retie my dress.

'Cut,' he said, switching the camera off and collapsing back on the sofa, 'and put that fuckin' thing away.' He gestured towards the head, laughing. 'It's sick.'

I dropped the head back into its box.

'Now, pass me that knife, Esther. I don't trust you with it.'

I picked up the sword and handed it to him, blade first. He held up his hands. I turned it round and he took it, examined it carefully, then put it down on the table.

'You're one crazy woman,' he said, shaking his head from side to side, mirth in his eyes. 'Now, are you hungry?'

'Ravenous,' I said.

Dinner was served in a long, narrow dining room, hand-painted from floor to mid-wall on all sides with a hyper-realist image of a Midwest field of corn. The pinched, haunting faces of small ragged children peered out between the crops, watchful. I recognized the style: the artist was a contemporary American included in the Whitney show I'd seen back in New York. I was surprised by Ben's choice. The work was gauche, and it seemed out of place here. But maybe that was just the winter. I glanced outside at the snow shrouding the dead landscape and encasing us inside it like a tomb.

Directly facing me, on the far wall, was a large plasma screen. I wondered what art films he watched on it. Or maybe it was rigged to the Artden, or even to my bedroom here. Maybe his voyeurism knew no bounds. As guided, I sat at one end of the table, Ben at the other. A mountain of *fruits de mer* – lobster, oysters, crayfish, prawns – cascading over ice was set between us.

'I'm alarmed by how much you seemed to enjoy the narration of such a crime,' he said, watching my talon-like nails click-clacking across the shells as I extracted the flesh. 'I hope you see no parallels between our historic anti-heroine and your current situation?'

I was pleased to see I'd amused Ben. 'Maybe I do,' I answered, 'but if so, surely the question must be who is the general and whose head is going to end up on the block?'

'Who, would you suggest, are the potential generals?'

I put down the oyster I was about to eat. 'Let's see now . . . Of course there's . . .' I hesitated. 'Aidan?'

Ben nodded encouragingly.

'Or, of course, Greg.'

He nodded again, this time more forcefully.

'Or perhaps the real general is Joe?'

At this, Ben shook his head, a look of pity crossing his face.

'And then, of course, there's always . . . you.'

He faked a flinch. 'I'd never do such a thing. I offer myself as your great protector between feuding generals back home in New York.'

'Well, all I can say is I feel privileged to be valued so highly by you – and to spend this week as your possession.'

He raised his wine glass to me. 'The privilege, Esther, is all mine.'

When we had finished eating we retired back to the sitting room. The scimitar was still lying on the table, glinting dangerously.

'Would you like a nightcap?' Ben asked.

I was pleased the evening wasn't about to end, although I wasn't certain where it would go from here. I accepted a large whiskey and he poured another for himself, then said he was going to dismiss the housekeeper for the night.

My mind was working overtime. I guess I wanted Ben to try to seduce me, I wanted to throw him off balance and I wanted to see the project turn full circle. The first performance had been a virtual view. Christina was untouchable. Judith might be just within his reach, for a moment. But Ben had hardly touched the wine over dinner. I'd drunk practically the whole bottle. Should I do it, I wondered. I felt inside my dress and pulled out the vial.

One thing I didn't know was whether security cameras were

watching me. I held the vial invisibly in my hand and pulled the stopper out. Then I got up, moved to the table and started to pack up the video camera, busying myself with the task. A moment later I surreptitiously slipped just a couple of drops of the liquid into his glass.

Even if the cameras were on I was certain they wouldn't have caught me in the act. I sat back on the sofa, took a glug of the whiskey. It wasn't enough to do Ben any harm, I reassured myself, but it would cause him to relax more and possibly have a touch of amnesia in the morning.

I sat on the colossal white sofa, the lights turned low, and gazed at the scene outside. The snow glinted in the light of the moon. The silence was as deep as time. Soon Ben returned and sat down at the other end of the sofa. I had tucked my legs up under me, but now allowed them to stretch out, covering the space between us. My feet were still bare. I saw Ben glance down at my toes, then turn his eyes away quickly, as if he'd been caught out. He looked out of the window at the snow. He drank a little whiskey, then a little more. Soon we had both finished our drinks.

'I've enjoyed you being here very much, Esther,' he said finally. His words were slurring slightly and he yawned widely. He put his hand out and stroked one of my feet. 'And I have particularly enjoyed tonight.' He looked straight into my eyes.

I returned his gaze.

'That dress is unbelievable,' he said.

I moved nearer. 'Would you like to take a closer look at your masterpiece?' I asked.

He made no reply, but his fingers began to move quickly from my foot, along my body and up to the ties on my dress. Then he slowly undid them, one at a time. His hands were trembling and his breath notably faster. He pushed the outer garment back and ran one finger between my breasts, down my stomach, to my navel. His guard was down at last.

I pulled back, wanting to draw this out, let the drug take fuller effect. That's when the evening would become really interesting. I pushed my face close to his. 'I read your questionnaire,' I said. 'Who is Juliet?'

My words altered the mood entirely. Ben pulled away from me, moved back on the sofa and looked past me, out of the windows, at the snow. A moment passed in silence.

'Juliet,' he spoke the words incredibly softly, 'Juliet was my mother.'

'What happened to her?' I asked gently.

'She was murdered,' he replied dispassionately: 'Shot in a street robbery in Boston. When I was ten.'

I took his hand and placed it back on my feet. 'What did she do?' I asked.

He turned to me. To my alarm I noticed that his eyes were blurring, his words increasingly slurred.

'She was a painter. Abstracts in oil.'

I drew him back towards me and he acquiesced. As I placed his head on my breast, I saw a tear slide down his cheek. I stroked his hair as he began to kiss me, very lightly, along my collar bone. Then I heard his breathing slow and his head become heavy against me. The effect of the drug had been rather more sudden and extreme than I'd expected. But I was immensely relieved. I had begun to think I was getting myself into a very tight corner. It was the perfect moment for my act to end. But I felt sad, for Ben, for his tragedy. This wasn't a game any more: for a moment I had got to the heart of his matter.

I felt his pulse. It was slow and his mouth hung open as he snored. He seemed OK, just sunk in a deep slumber. I managed to move him so he was lying down, then undid his collar and belt, and loosened his shirt from his trousers. That done, I took his glass and rinsed it out, before throwing away several inches of the whiskey in the decanter. I half filled the glass again and left it on the table before him. He didn't stir.

Out of the box that held Holofernes' head I took my final prop, a small rectangular transfer the size of a playing card. I turned Ben onto his side and placed it carefully at the arch of his back. Then I began to rub, slowly, in a circular motion. After a few minutes I peeled the plastic coating away, leaving my insignia indelibly marked in permanent black ink on his bare flesh. Then I turned him back over and pulled his shirt down.

Finally, I untied the strings of my dress, took it off and draped it spread out on the sofa next to him. I gathered up the knife, camera and the head, and took myself off to bed.

40

I woke late, and sat bolt upright in bed as the memory of my behaviour of the previous night came back to haunt me. I was filled with dread. This was the kind of antic of Esther Glass of the past. In recent years I had tried hard to control my conduct. I thought I was growing up, taking more responsibility for my actions and my art. But last night I had slipped straight back into my old ways. I felt ashamed and annoyed at myself – and then very concerned. What if the drug had wiped him right out? I got up quickly, tiptoed to the sitting room and pushed the door open cautiously. The room was empty, the whiskey glass, my dress and Ben all gone.

I wandered around the house. It was still and silent. There was no one around, not even the housekeeper. Then I heard the sound of engines running and glanced outside to see a car pulling up. To my initial relief Ben got out, but then I saw he was followed by two very severe-looking men in dark suits. My stomach twisted in panic. They looked official: perhaps they were police coming to get me. I fled back to my room. Representation or reality? This time I realized I might well and truly have gone too far.

I sat on my bed and waited, but no one came. Eventually I took a shower and got dressed, hoping against hope that if I behaved normally there would be less suspicion placed on me. Then I packed my bags and waited again.

Eventually there was a slow knock on the door and my heart lurched. 'Come in,' I said.

The door opened slowly and Ben appeared, holding my dress limply by his side. He handed it to me lamely. He looked grave, his skin pallid. I took it from him and invited him to come inside. He perched on the edge of the bed, looking uncomfortable.

'Esther,' he said.

I smiled in *faux*-innocent expectation.

'I don't know what came over me last night. I'm so sorry if I did anything untoward. It's kind of weird. I just don't remember. When I woke up this morning, you were gone, but,' he motioned towards the robe now safely back in my hands, 'your dress . . .'

I felt relief flood through me. He hadn't worked it out. 'It was fun,' I interrupted quickly. 'I enjoyed myself. It must have been the Judith effect.'

He looked at me quizzically. 'At least it didn't end in my murder.'

'Far from it,' I answered ambiguously. I wondered what he was thinking. I could see he was truly disarmed, at last. But I assumed he hadn't yet spotted the tattoo. 'Where've you been this morning?' I still wanted to know who those guys were.

'The architects came,' he replied, evidently relieved at the change of subject. 'We've finalized the plans. And now, I'm afraid, it's time to go back to Manhattan.'

'As I'm pretty sure you can't buy them, I thought you might like these – as a memento,' I said as the car headed back to the airstrip. I handed Ben a pack of seven cards: reproductions of the seven masterpieces. He shuffled through them a couple of times, then he looked up at me sadly.

'They're great,' he said, 'but the most important face is missing. There isn't one of you.'

He disappeared into his study as soon as the plane took off, and worked all the way back to New York. I tried to relax but I too felt uneasy. I thought back to Lincoln's remark at the start of this project – the one about Icarus and the flames. I'd just seared my tail feathers; I was truly lucky to have come through my last performance without serious injury, on either my or Ben's part. What if he'd gone into a coma? I'd be spending the rest of my life behind American bars. It was a really stupid thing to do, and I was, I realized, too old for these games. I used to act on impulse with my art, do stuff to see what the reaction would be, and I didn't care about the repercussions. Now I was changing. I was much more concerned about the effect.

I contemplated Ben's revelation about his mother's death and wondered if he remembered telling me about it. I understood now about his passion for art. It was a way for him to stay close to her creative spirit, to feel in touch with her memory. But it had all got out of hand. He was building an art collection instead of a relationship. It was a shame.

Before we landed, he reappeared and settled into the seat next to me. I wanted to talk to him about his mother, but I could see that it was already too late. I'd ruined my chance the night before. He had already closed up.

'I've called ahead to Joe,' he said. 'He'll be waiting for you at the den.'

I felt a touch defeated. It was my last night in Manhattan and it sounded as though Ben intended to run away, to leave me to spend it alone. I must have really freaked him out.

He took hold of my hand and gripped it firmly. 'It's been an absolute pleasure to have you here, Esther. I can't wait to see what you produce from this week.'

'Will you come over for the opening show in London?'

He smiled widely. 'I wouldn't miss it for the world.'

'And how about the rest of the deal?'

'Oh, that's something for me to talk through with Greg. I imagine I'll be meeting up with some of your gang over the coming weeks. Maybe I can even persuade a couple of the other artists to do their own stint at the den.'

'With or without CCTV cameras?'

Ben affected gravity. 'I'm sure you understand. They're reserved only for works of extremely high value.'

Two cars awaited us at the airport. He embraced me with a clearly paternal affection and then, just like that, was gone. Returning alone downtown, I felt disappointed, and then a bit wistful as I thought back over the last few days. He was quite unlike anyone I'd met before. The mix of extreme ease, dynamism and sensitivity were unusual. But on one level, maybe we weren't so dissimilar; after all, he guarded secrets, a broken history, stories he didn't usually share. I was sure he was convinced we'd gone further than he could remember the night before. But he played his cards extremely close to his chest. Sonia was right about that. I couldn't help but feel pleased about the kiss; the touch of his hands on my feet. I had transfixed him, aesthetically and sexually, and he, in return, had stimulated me: as a woman and an artist. I couldn't help it: if I were honest, both of these things mattered to me. However, I could see that Ben would always remain an enigma, just out of reach, but a very useful one to know. Perhaps, indeed, Aidan was right: perhaps he really was the perfect patron.

I had to speak to Aidan. I had to tell him how much I loved him, how right it seemed he had been. I had thrown all my anxieties about this project into his lap, turned all my fears about failure into projections of rage and distrust against him. But there was another very different root to my worries, as I was all too aware. And as the days passed, it seemed I was less and less able to ignore them. It was time I talked properly to Aidan; time to make amends.

*

As the cab pulled up, Joe opened the studio door with a smile. It was as if he'd been waiting, watching for my arrival. He hauled my case out of the boot and helped me with it up the stairs. When we reached the apartment he turned and I detected a curious look of anticipation in his eyes. I moved forward and turned the key, pushed open the door and was met by a dazzling and unexpected sight. The studio had been filled with winter lilies – hundreds of large, sculptural white flowers in enormous glass vases, throwing out their heady scent.

Joe handed me an envelope. 'They arrived this afternoon.' He shrugged. 'Don't ask *me*.'

I tore the envelope open and immediately recognized Aidan's handwriting.

> *E, hope the trip was a success. Missed you in Manhattan. Sorry to say I need to stay on for a few more days. Deal nearly done. Call me when you can, from here or London. Love you to distraction, A.*

I couldn't look at Joe.

'Hey, everything OK?'

I mumbled a response and thanked him for helping me up the stairs with my bags, and felt inordinately relieved when he turned to leave.

After my all too recent change of sentiment, the note left me cold and disappointed. Maybe I was wrong; maybe Aidan was intent on putting the business before me after all. Perhaps Ben's personality was just a fortuitous piece of luck. I felt deflated. My decision to release my true self to Aidan had left me, momentarily, feeling more optimistic than I had done in years. But however could he think that a few bunches of flowers would make up for leaving me to go home alone? I thought, after our conversation a couple of nights before, that he understood how critical it was to me that we talked his plans through as soon as

humanly possible. Not only that, I'd have to deal with the chaos of
Heathrow without support. The more I thought about it, the more let
down I felt. As for the deal, well, quite frankly, he could go shove the
goddamn deal. I didn't want to be part of his bigger picture any more.
Of that I was suddenly, absolutely, sure. I paced the flat. For a start
I needed to get rid of all of these fucking flowers. Their scent was
making me nauseous. I opened one of the vast studio windows and
gulped cold air.

One by one, I began to throw the lilies from the window. They
tumbled like rag dolls and slapped softly onto the sidewalk below. The
street was empty and the action felt cathartic. Then I thought I heard
a sharp click. I listened hard: there was another, then a ricochet of
clicks and flashes. Now I noticed them – a huddle of figures in a dark
warehouse entrance slightly to the left of the building. I dived back
into the studio and slammed the window shut, cursing. They'd finally
found me. And I in return had just provided them with a spectacular
exhibition of my current wrath against Aidan. No doubt they would
have watched the flowers arrive earlier in the day, would already
have checked details of the sender with the delivery-man.
Information was cheap. They'd think my actions were intended for the
media.

I slid to the floor under the window and tried to regain my breath.
After a few moments I crawled back across the room and slipped into
the bedroom. Thank God the curtains were closed: only Joe and Ben
could see me from here – if they were watching. I slammed the door
shut and stood up to turn on the light. Then I addressed one of the
camera's lenses directly. I would know soon enough if sound were
attached.

'Joe or Ben, please come and get me. There's a media mob outside.
Knock four times and I'll let you in.'

It was not long before I heard four taps. Relieved, I crawled back out
across the floor and opened the studio door.

Joe walked quietly into the space and closed it firmly behind him. 'I'm so sorry.' He sounded upset. 'We've been keeping a watch: we didn't see a soul.'

'That's OK,' I replied resignedly. 'Comes with the territory.'

It was almost impossible to avoid discovery. I knew that all too well from my daily life in London. But I should've been more careful. One momentary slip and my frailties had been exposed once again.

'There's a fire escape out back. I'm sure we could go that way,' Joe said. 'I've spoken to Ben and he's asked me to escort you to his house. I've called a car. It'll be waiting at the end of the alley.'

I nodded my head vigorously. This certainly wasn't the moment to confront the media. I'd given them enough theatre for one night.

First we headed up one internal flight of stairs and then out of the fire exit and down the spiral metal staircase that ran down the outside of the building like an exposed spine, our feet clattering as we tripped and turned all the way to the bottom. The alleyway was full of trash from the meat market. Joe took my hand and together we ran through it, slipping occasionally on the ice. A black car was stationed at the end of the alley, engine purring quietly, lights off. We climbed into the back and it glided away, headlights now illuminating the street. I glanced out of the back window, gasping for breath. The street remained silent. No one seemed to be following.

Joe left me at Ben's. I was pleased to be back there. I hoped I might get a chance to see my patron one last time, but the butler showed me directly to a suite of rooms and asked if I'd like him to prepare me a meal. I refused the offer and turned in for the night. Ben Jamieson had already slipped from my hands back into his enigmatic world.

The next morning a car arrived to take me to the airport. Before I left I sneaked along the corridor to Ben's office and tapped on the door, but there was no answer. I slipped inside and took a final look at

Rossetti's wonderful portrait of Frances Leyland. I whispered goodbye and turned to leave. I felt sorry for Frances. It seemed that on all fronts now she was truly trapped inside New York. I, thankfully, had a return ticket to London, and home was the very place I wanted to be.

41

The Today Programme, BBC Radio Four

'Did you imagine that you'd reach such a high price?'

'No, it came as a complete surprise.' My voice was thick with sleeplessness.

'And would you say Ben Jamieson got a good return for his money?'

I paused. 'I think he'll form his opinion once I complete the series.'

The interviewer chortled. 'How did he treat you? I don't suppose he stored you away with the rest of his collection?'

'He kind of did for a while, but he made up for it by taking me on a trip to Colorado over the weekend.'

'So you weren't publicly exhibited?'

'There were a couple of private views.'

The interviewer adopted a knowing tone. 'Do you really think there's anything thought-provoking about selling yourself at auction? Or was it simply a publicity stunt?'

I wasn't sure now why I'd agreed to subject myself to this as soon as I got back. 'You know, I always say my work is self-referential, but it's about more than me. I see myself as a vehicle for my ideas – the blank canvas, if you like. My art is about look-ing again. Ninety-nine per cent of the time the first impression is only a tiny aspect of the whole picture.'

'It must be said that this week the media has been as, if not more, interested in the current status of your relationship with Aidan Jeroke as it has in the value of your project. Can you throw any light on that for us? After all, the two of you are our glittering couple on the art scene. Any fracture there would make headline news in the broadsheets as well as the tabloids.'

The question wasn't in the brief. I tried hard not to sound riled, but I know my voice rose an octave higher.

'That, quite frankly, is none of your business. He's been in New York working on a separate art transaction.'

'Esther Glass, I'm afraid that's all we've got time for. Thanks for joining us and welcome back to London.'

'That wasn't in the bloody brief.'

I was in the back of a cab and Katie was on the phone.

She hesitated. 'Have you seen the papers?'

I had them all on my lap, and I appeared on the front of every one. They'd snapped my arrival at Heathrow's media circus the previous night, dressed all in black, shades on, mouth closed in a crimson line. I had been too preoccupied to sleep on the plane. To make matters worse, *The Times* and the *Telegraph* had joined the tabloids in display-ing a second, smaller photograph next to the main one of me. It was of a poetic bunch of lilies lying, forlorn, in the snow. The captions were all along the same lines: Esther's symbolic memorial to her relationship with Aidan Jeroke. Katie, wisely, hadn't asked any questions – yet. And I didn't offer any kind of explanation.

'Have you got the *Clarion* there?' she asked tentatively.

The front-page headline read: ART TART FLIES BACK.

'Yes. So much for John Herbert being on my side. It's the worst of the lot.'

'No. I meant the story inside,' she replied edgily.

I felt sick as I opened the paper. There, on page three, were the three sketches I had bought from Kenny Harper, reproduced in a row. Beneath them the story read:

Now Esther Glass has sold herself, we give you the chance to own a bit of her art. The *Clarion* has exclusive access to fine-quality reproductions of these three early masterpieces(!) to give away to the lucky reader who can come up with a suitable title for them. The term 'blue period' springs immediately to mind.

As ever when emotional turmoil threatened to overwhelm me, I turned to my work for relief. I shut the door on the world camped outside with lenses fixed on my windows. Between now and the opening I didn't want to hear another word about, or from, the media. It was too much to contend with and I determined to keep them locked out. It seemed I had been wrong to assume I could play them at their own game. Aidan had been right: the more newsworthy my art became, the more bloodthirsty they grew, and I didn't have enough inner resources to be their primary donor. I was disappointed, if not surprised, that Kenny had sold them the copies of my sketches. I had no way of stopping him. I could try to sue, but what was the point? The drawings were out there now, for anyone to see. At least I owned the originals. I wondered how long it would be before the journalists got bored with the Aidan–Esther relationship story and began to pick at the background, the context, of the sketches instead. And then dig deeper into my youth. I knew it was only a matter of time.

It was now the second week of March. The Tate Modern show opened at the end of May. I'd need the intervening time to pull the material into shape. I had all the content I could possibly need: the research into my seven subjects, the costumes, scripts and actual films of my performances. But the task of weaving these elements together with my personal experience of the *Possession* series was on a scale I had never before undertaken. I wanted to produce a consolidated series – one that was both visually arresting and thematically clear. And I was determined that my personal sale would strongly underpin the show. It would be too easy for it to be obscured by my seven women's stories. I had to find a way to make the correlation clear.

I began by downloading all the films onto my iBook. Then I started to edit. It was a slow and, to a degree, laborious task, but the solitude required to see it through suited my fragile state perfectly. It was magical to watch the characters reappear before me on the screen. I already felt detached from my performances and, as I reviewed them in sequence, I could almost forget that it was me behind the costumes. I had been truly possessed – not only by Ben but by each of them in turn – and it showed in the resulting films.

Marie's show at auction was the most highly charged. She looked confident of her sexuality yet there was clearly a watchfulness about her; she was uncertain of her personal worth. Christina was the most phantom-like, yet engaged with the camera with the greatest intensity and awareness – maybe because of her prayers on behalf of the series as a whole. Isabella seemed to be the most in control – and to be having the most fun into the bargain, enjoying playing to her crowd. Victorine, conversely, seemed to be locked in her own lascivious world – a pitiful and condemned place – isolated and angry, with no way out. Mary was the most eccentric performance; it was unwieldy and dangerous. Her personality seemed obscure and hard to grasp. But I liked the fact that she held a certain ambiguity. After all, for centuries people have read into her world what they chose. It was not my intention to try and pin her down. As for Mrs Leyland, her performance was ethereal, at times beautiful and emotionally compelling – equally romantic and desperate. The cameras continued to roll as I swayed, then fell to the floor, and this finale to her act appeared intentional. I felt my stomach lurch each time I watched it.

Every time I replayed Judith I knew I'd had a narrow escape from calamity. It appeared highly charged and completely insane, a rash act, professionally on a par with my run-in with the politician nearly a decade before. This was partly, perhaps, because it was filmed through a viewer's eyes. Ben had experimented wildly with the camera – erratically zooming in and out on my face, my clothes, the scimitar blade, and Holofernes' head – adding to the general air of madness. Judith's eyes looked even more crazy than I had intended and her body positively oozed with frustrated sexual energy. I realized that, during that performance, the culmination of all that had gone before was now rushing through my veins. It was really no wonder it had ended so close to disaster. At that moment I had become a woman totally possessed by my art.

I could already see that, once edited, the resulting films would be startling. Each would begin with a still frame of the actual masterpiece, which would then fade into my performance, with sound attached, before fading back out again and on to a close-up of each woman's face. They were all great masterpieces for a reason. They pulled a hefty punch. But there was an element missing, the glue. At the heart of the project there needed to be a living spirit – me, and my relationship with the viewer. And therein lay my crisis. My mind was busy tracing different lines, lines of my history, etched memories in my mind that I had spent years trying to erase. It was my identity that I needed to use to stick all this together, but the problem was a fictionalized me wouldn't do this time. Somehow I had to find the real Esther Glass to place at the heart of my work.

I took calls from only Petra and Katie over the following week. Petra had fallen out with the German and was back in the doldrums. Why did her affairs never last? Perhaps I would soon be asking the same of myself. We decided to take a trip together somewhere hot before the show opened. It would be good to get a break, to feel sun on our faces, before the media scalded us once again. Since the auction Petra, too, had been catapulted into the design world limelight. And they hadn't even seen the rest of the costumes yet. After the show opened she'd be taking another meteoric leap up fashion's catwalk to success.

Katie gently coaxed me to call Aidan. He was getting anxious, she said, but I continued to hold out. I had begun to feel relatively in control and absorbed by my work and I didn't feel I could afford any distractions that might cloud my focus. He was back from New York, but I had to work out what I wanted for my future before we could discuss again the proposal he had made to me. I knew my behaviour the night before I left New York had been infantile, but I also felt Aidan was asking a lot, maybe too much, of me. I determined to ignore these worries until I had resolved the series. But then I received a handwritten letter from Ben and everything began to fall apart.

My dear Esther,

I wonder how you are, and if it feels good to be free of me. I've found it impossible to sleep easy at night, knowing I have been dishonest with someone whom I so admire, someone who herself has such integrity – personal and artistic. So I feel compelled to write with a confession – and a request.

First to the confession: I'm afraid I was watching you, all the way – well, all the way to Aspen, at least. Cameras followed your every move, and not just on the stage, or at the den. So now I can go back through film and relive those moments, there at the den, when you gave me Christina – and that very generous, unmasked view of Esther Glass, my living, breathing masterpiece. I can see you hard up as Victorine, pure as Mary, empowered as Isabella, even absorbed by other people's art as a viewer in New York's museums, or sharing coffee with Sonia in an uptown café. But the pictures I want, the ones I dream of recapturing, already seem lost to time. I can't shift Judith from my mind and wonder endlessly what it was she did to me that night, or maybe what I did to her. I found your signature, your stamp, on me, but I guess I'll never know how you put it there. The masterpiece signing her owner – a late twist in the tale. I remember your beautiful skin, those fine silver-etched lines on your stomach as you pulled back Judith's robe. Why didn't I know you had borne a child? What else do I not know about the real Esther Glass? And why, I wonder, has the sequence of these memories evaporated as soon as they were made?

That was the only time I watched you perform through your own lens and did not set up my own. And you were at your most magnificent, entrancing – and terrifying. I know I touched your warm, smooth, bare feet. But now for the request: please, dear Esther, tell me, was there more or are these other images mere fantasies in my mind?

Now I understand why you called it the *Possession* series – and why I was compelled to pay such a price for the privilege of possessing you. Little did I anticipate that I would, in the end, be the one possessed.

Finally, I would like to thank you. My week with you has taught me an invaluable lesson – that art can never replace life. We all need to engage with other human spirits in order to nurture our own.

Yours ever, patron – and friend,

Ben

PS You never finished the list. I wonder what five adjectives would sum up the series?

I screwed the letter up and threw it in the bin. My cheeks were burning and my heart was thumping wildly in my chest. Without thinking first, I picked up my mobile and hit Ben's number. It was seven in the morning in London – it would be 2 a.m. in New York, but I didn't care.

Eventually he picked up, sounding woozy from sleep.

'How dare you insinuate such things . . . make assumptions about me from the marks on my skin,' I screamed at him. 'You know nothing about me, nothing about my past, and it's none of your business.'

Ben sounded taken aback. Then he tried to placate me, but I was too upset to listen. Instead I simply hurled abuse at him down the phone before hanging up and crumpling in a woeful heap on my bed. As I sobbed into my pillow, I placed my hand on my stomach and slowly allowed my fingers to trace the barely distinct marks left from a distant past, a past from which I had disengaged for so very long. For all his searching beneath my surface, and despite all our years of stripping each other bare, Aidan had never noticed the lines. They had become so faded that even I had almost forgotten them, if not what put them there.

How had Ben noticed them? I thought back to my final performance, how I had pulled back my robe right in front of him, under the glare of my studio spotlights. For those few moments, he had zoomed the lens right in on to my body. I thought I was displaying the life of a myth. Instead, at that moment I had inadvertently paraded the biggest secret of my life before him on my skin.

I tried to calm myself, to think. I had furiously guarded this secret from the media, even from Ava and Petra – and, of course, Aidan. That's why I had hidden in the bedsit for the year, and changed my name to Emmeline to avoid detection, while I had allowed my child to grow inside me as the world outside waited for Esther to re-emerge from her period of . . . I wonder what they thought? Depression? Mourning? Sulking? I wonder what Ava really thought lay behind my insistent distancing from her and all those I knew through those months of self-imposed solitary confinement.

I'd hidden this secret from everyone I knew, had purposely lost touch with my friends from my Maida Vale days – partly because the only way I could live with what had happened was by blocking it out. Reality? I couldn't bear too much reality. Representation? Art and artifice? Dressing-up? Making up stories? Being someone else? Taking careless risks? All these activities were far easier than addressing who I really was and living with what I'd really done.

The phone now rang again. It was Ben, so I picked up.

'Esther, I am so sorry, I had no idea.'

I immediately felt guilty for my outburst: it wasn't Ben's fault.

'I'm the one who should be apologizing,' I replied weakly. 'I'm afraid your letter gave me quite a shock. You touched on a part of me that no one else has ever seen, a history that no one else is a party to. I need it to stay that way, to remain private, please.'

He gave me his promise and when he hung up I smoothed his letter out and forced myself to reread his words. It seemed that Ben and I had been at the opposite extremes of the same emotional paralysis. In the final lines of his letter there was a warning to me. Maybe it had come just in time. Like him, I knew I had hidden behind my art for far too many years. It was time I began to take control of my personal future and the human relationships within it. I needed to be in possession of myself, as well as my art – and, most significantly, I needed to take control of the past and accept it as mine.

I had made the *Possession* series with one very particular person in mind. Sixteen years had passed since my time in Maida Vale. There had been sixteen years of a certain life that I hadn't witnessed, living and breathing, experiencing the world that had been given to her. Among the daughters of the revolution to whom I was intent on dedicating this series was one very special one: my own. She was old enough now to start making her own decisions about her future, and therefore potentially about a future relationship with me. Maybe she would decide she wanted to find me and I hoped she could. But if I left London it would be harder. I felt obliged to remain available and close to where she was. As far as I was aware, the family who had adopted her still lived in the capital.

42

Ben's letter broke the lock around my heart and once I had calmed down I took a cab to the gallery. It was, I realized, the first time I had left the flat for more than two weeks and I felt nauseous and unstable on my feet. Aidan was working at his desk and I approached his office quietly. When he looked up I could see that all the joy and energy that had been pumping through his system in New York had seeped away. The crispness of Manhattan, the sharp creases he'd perfected there, were beginning to fade.

He eyed my approach and smiled ruefully.

I shut the door behind me softly and pulled down the blind. Then I quietly moved towards him and sat down in his lap. He held me round the waist and breathed into my hair.

'How ya doing, Est?' he murmured. 'I've missed you.'

Before I could respond, his phone started to beep repeatedly. For a few moments he ignored it but the insistent noise continued. It was Katie's line. Aidan picked it up with a sigh, listened momentarily, then handed the receiver to me.

'Esther, I'm really sorry to bother you,' Katie said, 'but it's John Cressfield. He's on line two. Says it's urgent.'

Ava really chose her moments. John's voice sounded distant and trembling. 'Ava's gravely ill, Esther. We're at my house, in France. I'm sorry, but I think you should come immediately.'

43

If he hadn't used the word 'gravely' I wouldn't have leapt into action. But I'd already lost one parent and felt unexpectedly distraught at the prospect of losing another. I thought I might throw up and wasn't sure if it was the turbulence or the worry. Though it was a clear, blue day, the wind was unusually strong and the plane danced a jig through the sky. We were hurtling over southwest France and far, far below, wide-roaming rivers were turned silver by the sun and shallow hills punctuated by pale houses were spread out like a contemporary Dürer, perspective skewed.

At Bergerac's one-shop airport I smoked half a cigarette, then threw up in the loo, before staggering outside into blazing heat to see John loitering by an old Renault. A young, sandy-haired man in slouchy faded jeans stood by his side. I could see from his ruddy reflection that John was half-cut. It was only mid-afternoon. The sinking feeling in my stomach deepened. The young guy, introduced as Jacques the carpenter, took my bag as John gave me a weighty hug. It was a Burgundy day. I could smell it not only on his breath; it seeped out from his skin, like spice.

'How is she?'

His explanation of Ava's ill health over the phone had been confused: something about heart-murmurs, a collapse. She was back from the hospital, at home now. But it was best I saw for myself.

We got in the car and began the arduous journey, an hour and a half rattling around in the rusty heap, first gear up gruelling hills, free-wheeling round right-angled bends, shuddering down steep declines. My nausea returned with a vengeance but I contained it with a boiled sweet found sticky in its wrapper on the back seat. I'd worn Christina's ring, Dior's gift, since returning from New York, but now I had to prise it from my finger. My hands had swollen considerably during the flight. I, too, was definitely getting sick.

No one spoke much. But I deduced that Jacques had been employed to build John a library of shelves for the vanload of journals currently wending their way from London with another 'comrade' from the commune days. We finally pulled off the A-road onto a B, then onto a bumpy track, which wound through shady pines. The car finally spluttered into a clearing and came to a halt before a remote old stone house, with steps up to a long, thin, canopied balcony and a solid oak front door a floor above the ground.

John lumbered up first and I followed resignedly. The carpenter brought up my bag, then bid us farewell and took off once more in the car. I watched him reverse away and realized I was now well and truly stranded. The sole transport that remained was a rusty old bike lying like an arthritic mongrel in the yard below. John shoved his weight against the door and it creaked open. Inside was a cool dark room, with whitewashed walls and a cavernous, empty fireplace. I noticed first a smell of sawdust and, next, Ava, lying on the sofa, a rug over her legs, smiling waterily.

I gave her a hug and felt tears welling in my eyes.

She stroked my hair and murmured, 'Darling, how good of you to come.'

Something wasn't right.

Ava was evidently weak. She remained on the sofa all evening but was unclear as to the extent or details of her illness. Apparently she'd had 'an erratic heartbeat', wasn't sure of the medical terminology, had been given stabilizing drugs. It seemed to me that she and John must have found it hard to understand what the doctors had diagnosed, the language barrier causing a degree of confusion. She refused to be drawn. I was afraid for her and hoped the real story wasn't that she had something terminal.

The night dropped over us early like a blackout cloth, the temperatures suddenly plunging. The house felt cold and soulless without the sun's rays creeping in through the shutters. I found myself shivering but there was no wood to build a fire.

Eventually John clattered around in the kitchen and produced some paté, a stale French stick, half a Camembert and a few tomatoes. And another bottle of red wine. Ava said she wasn't hungry and I still felt unwell, so we watched on as he munched his way through the food and guzzled the alcohol.

'What's the real diagnosis?'

John looked awkward. Ava had retired for the evening, taking her time to cross the room and go up the stairs to bed, adamantly refusing all offers of help. My questions simply made him reach more regularly for the bottle. I got the impression he, too, was in denial. I went to bed determined to get the carpenter to take me to the hospital when he showed up in the morning. I'd go and seek out her consultant for myself, find out what was happening. I was concerned that she appeared to have no drugs to take. Suddenly Ava seemed old and frail and helpless. I was resolved to do all I could to help her.

I woke to the sound of sawing and tumbled out of bed and down the stairs to find Jacques hard at work in the salon. He acknowledged me simply with a smile and continued filing down a plank of wood. The project was ambitious: the entire room was to be lined with shelves and he was crafting them with care. The sun was streaming in through the open windows and I looked out across the surrounding fields. The forest closed around us on all sides, but the grass in the immediate meadow was still verdant from the winter rains. I hadn't noticed the silence before, or the sweet smell of pine and wild flowers filling the air. It was a fairytale place – but along with the beauty there was something intangible but disquieting, like the invisible threat of a roaming beast. We were miles from anywhere.

I made a pot of tea with spoonfuls from a tired-looking tin of leaves in the rudimentary kitchen. There was very little food in the fridge, but a lot of red wine in the racks. I took my cup of tea and went back and perched on the edge of the sofa. I had only schoolgirl French, never having needed to use it with Guy.

'*Je veux aller à l'hôpital*,' I pronounced awkwardly.

Jacques stopped sawing and looked up at me, concerned. '*Vous êtes malade, mademoiselle?*'

I shook my head vehemently and pointed above my head. '*Ma mère, Ava. Je voudrais voir le médicin.*'

He continued to eye me uncertainly. I struggled on but curiously he still seemed not to understand what I wanted to say. Just as I was beginning to feel impatient, light began to dawn in his green eyes.

He gave a huge shrug, a gesture that reminded me for a second of Guy, then explained, in surprisingly clear English, 'I did not know your mother is ill. Since I am 'ere, she is OK: no doctors, no '*opital*.'

It was my turn to be confused. I asked how long he'd been working at the house.

'Three weeks,' he replied reassuringly. 'She 'as bin very well indeed, all zis time.'

Not a single moment of malady? I sipped my tea and thought it through. Was it really possible that he had missed the drama unfolding? Considering John and Ava had no car, it was hard to see how.

'I saw your pictures in the *journaux*,' he said, interrupting my

341

concentration with an innocent grin. He gestured towards a pile of papers and magazines on a small corner table, telephone book placed neatly on top. I pulled them all out: press clippings galore. Even here Ava had kept up to date. The last piece, in *Paris Match*, was from only two days before. For the past month in London I had determinedly ignored the press. But now I was compelled to read every word of the stories piled in front of me, like someone else's diary, left open on a page peppered with my name. I took the stack, went out onto the balcony and sat in the morning sun, reading them all, one by one. There were at least fifty. She'd carefully marked each with a red pen, picking out opinions as to my value, the worth of the sale. The intense scrutiny reminded me, uncomfortably, of that night back in New York when I'd read up on Ben. In my case, even I was shocked at the depths to which the hacks had sunk in their determination to destroy my reputation.

In the initial weeks following my return they had concentrated on my love life, my perceived affairs with Aidan, Ben and Guy. They had shredded me for sexual deviancies, for conducting an immoral and greedy triangular affair. The articles were tantamount to calling me a fully paid-up whore, a modern-day Olympia. They'd used images from my private view as Victorine as an example of my lurid behaviour. The pictures looked clandestine on paper, like they'd been taken through the window of a bedroom. How had they got hold of them? I couldn't imagine *Vanity Fair* selling on their film at any price.

Then the press had gone on to analyse the collapse of my personal and business relationship with Aidan. There was article upon article about my sale being rigged, about a bigger deal and a smokescreen to cover the public's eyes. In one instance it was even called 'Esthergate'.

Someone on the inside must have been planting the stories – some-one who was clearly out to undermine me. The press were having a really good go at ensuring he or she succeeded. But who, and why? Did I really deserve such contempt? I felt renewed sickness in my belly. I wasn't sure I could hold out against this onslaught. And all along I had honestly thought the art was worth putting myself on the line for. The press all saw it as just a bland publicity stunt, the sale value as nothing more than a faked event, however strenuously Ben had publicly denied the fact, including even a formal statement in the *Washington Post*. In it he also denied that he and I had had an affair during my week in his possession.

Then, finally, I came across a small clipping from the *Clarion*. It was the only one Ava had circled twice.

Esther Glass might always be up for self-revelation but the *Clarion* can reveal that she hasn't always been so keen on press attention concerning her personal life. Remember the artist's lewd sketches we sold off last week? Well, she made them when she was a teenager – what a child prodigy! Soon afterwards she moved to a bed-sit in London from her hippy commune home and changed her name to Emmeline Glass. What was she trying to hide? Rumour has it that there was a baby on the way and Esther didn't want the father to know about it. Well, fathers have rights too, and in this case the dad does want to know. So come on, Esther, when are you going to spill the beans?

I threw the paper down, stormed back into the house and up to my mother's room. Ava was still asleep, appearing small and vulnerable, lying quietly on her side. I opened the shutters noisily and she cocked one eye open, fast followed by the other. In the light of day I noted she had quite a nice tan coming on; that the whites of her eyes were clear and healthy.

'I was going to get Jacques to take me to the hospital – to see your consultant,' I said.

Ava looked furtive, pulled herself upright and smoothed the counterpane with nervous hands.

'But,' I tried hard not to raise my voice – I actually felt like taking hold of her and shaking her viciously – 'he informed me you haven't been ill, not for a moment. No hospital visits. No dickey heart.'

She made no attempt to deny the facts; she looked resigned to my rage, but refused to speak: just lay back on the pillows and watched me.

'So what the hell am I doing here? I've got less than two months till my show opens. And you think it's a good time to drag me to this shack in the middle of nowhere. It's just unbelievable.'

'Esther, come and sit down.'

'I'm too angry,' I shouted, like a petulant teenager. How could she make me behave like this? I stomped out of the room and went back downstairs.

'I want you to take me to the airport,' I said to Jacques.

He looked up from his saw apologetically. 'The car is broken,' he said. ' I 'ave only my moto.'

I felt hot and cold, went to the loo and threw up again.

I didn't know where I was going, but once I'd set off I couldn't stop. First I headed up the dirt track and then off on a well-worn footpath through the soulless pine forest, whose canopy overhead suffocated the barren land beneath it, parching it, denying it light. I wandered through the trees, then eventually out, across undulating hills covered in small oak trees, their roots clawing like ancient hands through shards of limestone littering the earth. Small streams struggled to find a way out between the rocks – another month and their beds would be dry to the core. I didn't think, just walked, concentrating on my breathing, the movement of my feet over the uneven terrain, ignoring the views, simply absorbing the silence.

After two – or was it three – hours, the steeple of a small church appeared on the horizon. I determined to head for it. But it was further than I anticipated and by the time I reached the outlying houses of this tiny village another hour, at least, had passed. At this point my legs had slowed down and my mouth was bone dry. 'Monde ancien' read the hand-painted wooden sign hanging like a loose tooth from its stake. I continued past the cluster of meek, one-storey homes and encountered no one. A few dogs barked lazily at me, scratched at their haunches, then gave up. Finally I came to the church. Like the houses, it was made of pale limestone, with a fine, narrow steeple pointing upwards at the clear blue sky above.

The door was open and I entered. The air inside was impregnated with incense. I sat down in a cold back pew and waited for my eyes to adjust to the dim light. It was a tiny chapel, in complete contrast to the last church I had entered, St Mark's back in Manhattan, and it was resplendent with gilt decorations and icons to Our Lady. Her presence immediately relaxed me; it was like seeing an old friend. A statue of Mary stood by the altar, cradling the baby Jesus in her arms, a beatific glow on her overly painted face. A golden crown sat in her braided hair and she wore blue and pink robes.

I walked down the aisle until she was directly before me, then stared up into her face. The Virgin had doll-like pea-green eyes and they stared straight through me. Was I really so undeserving of her attention? There was a tiny font next to the front pews and I dipped a finger in it. The water was ice cold. As I looked at her I let it drip between my fingers, then touched it to my tongue. It tasted slightly stale, musty.

The circular stained-glass window above the altar was thick and dark; a pattern of dull red, green and blue lights played over the chancel. Candles glowed, giving a more local illumination beside the pews. I dug around in my pocket for change and found only a few cents. I exchanged them for a candle. I was about to touch the wick to one already alight, but then I hesitated. For whom was my candle? My seven portrait subjects floated through my mind, but I rejected them all in turn. Next Aidan's, Ben's, and finally Ava's, faces appeared to me, but again I pushed them away. And then, for the first time in many years, I finally allowed myself to really remember Jasmine May Glass.

Did she know who I was? If so, what did she think of me? Was she, like all those other teenage girls, busy painting her innermost thoughts on the surface of her beautiful young skin? And, in so doing, making herself vulnerable, a victim to the preying eyes and dreams of adolescent boys, or maybe even of more sinister predators? Had my example, my risk-taking, resulted in making her less safe?

Of course, it was because of her that I had found the public reaction to *The Painted Nude* so utterly terrifying. It was because of her that I had experienced such creative paralysis; and it was because she was so inextricably linked with Kenny, to that day, to the sketch, that I had been so horrified by its re-emergence – and so had determined to undertake the *Possession* series.

I wanted to communicate to her that she had a value over and above that which perhaps her introduction to boyfriends, to sex, to the patriarchy, might suggest. I couldn't speak to her directly, but maybe, just maybe, if she knew my work she would recognize something of her own value through my art. It was a long shot, but the only one I had. Her sixteenth birthday had just passed. She was old enough to choose to find me now, if that is what she so desired. I believed I relinquished my right to her the moment the adoption papers had been signed, but I wanted her to know I was there for her should she ever need me. So I had to do something to try to encourage her to come forward and seek me out. I shuddered with cold as my trembling hand lit a candle with my daughter's abstract, absent self now flooding through me, easing into all the empty spaces, filling me with the warmth of her very live, pulsating being.

I looked up once more at the Madonna cradling her child. Where was Jasmine now? I didn't even know what she looked like, or what, these days, she was called. Maybe her parents had changed her name the moment they left the hospital ward. I suddenly felt overwhelmed with sorrow. What on earth had I done? How had I ever, ever, given her away? I knelt at the altar and placed my hands together. I looked up at the Madonna. People had always made of her what they chose: they took Mary's core essence and used it to respond to their emotional needs. Right now I needed forgiveness. I closed my eyes and I prayed to her for my absolution.

44

'Baby Glass', she'd written in blue ballpoint on the wrist tag, before fastening it gently around her new-born flesh.

'She's called Jasmine,' I whispered. The nurse nodded kindly and patted my hand.

For the last six weeks of my pregnancy my bedsit had been filled with the heady scent of the tiny white flowers that spilled in through the door from my little balcony. Ahmed, Clara and George, my friends in the house, had lent me their unswerving support as my belly had grown and my child had learnt acrobatics inside my womb. I was barely more than a child myself, but my body knew instinctively what to do, and I blossomed with her inside me with all the health and natural ability afforded by youth.

Jasmine arrived in the depths of a star-studded early-spring night – it was the first day of March. She slid from me with extraordinary ease, my body opening up and giving her out like a heavenly gift, perfect and untroubled, shiny and new, ready to be handed to her expectant parents, who were waiting anxiously in the wings. She had a smooth, oval-shaped head, strong limbs and an all too recognizable, if wet, mass of Kenny's thick, liquorice hair. Her eyes were squeezed tight shut against me and the world, her fingers locked into fists held tight to her chest. She twitched and grunted; then, minutes after birth, she began to clamber up my body towards my breast for sustenance. It was at that moment that I asked them to take her away.

45

Back outside the chapel I found a single tap and drank from it copiously. I was feeling weak, having not eaten since being sick again that morning. I needed food, but there was nothing to be found. So I began on my journey back to the house. Darkness thickened around me as I hurried through the forest and I felt irrationally afraid, like Little Red Riding Hood running from the wolf. My pace quickened until I found I was running, chaotically, trampling frantically through the woods. By the time I arrived back it was pitch dark. The abnormal heat of the day had been replaced by cutting chill. It was still only March, after all; the weather was erratic, on the change.

Ava was standing on the balcony in the glow of a single lantern, looking forlorn, wrapped in a large navy-blue shawl. I mounted the steps to meet her and she held out her arms silently. I suddenly remembered the day at the folly, the morning after Simeon's funeral. We were back to the beginning again. I embraced her begrudgingly, feeling dislocated, exhausted. It seemed too late now for food, but she forced me to have a bowl of soup. John was still absent and I didn't ask where he'd gone. Jacques, too, had left for the day. As soon as the soup was finished I took myself off to bed.

I fell asleep with the scent of Jasmine suffusing my senses.

*

When I woke I still felt wretched, but now deeply depressed too. And my limbs were aching from my run. I came downstairs to find Ava making coffee. But the smell only made me feel worse. I accepted a tisane and ate a piece of stale bread and strawberry jam, then another. Feeling restored, I sat next to her on the balcony, gazing out.

'Is what they're saying true?'

I looked up over my teacup at Ava. 'I didn't have an affair with Ben,' I said flatly.

'I didn't mean that.'

I shrugged. I knew what she wanted but my lips still wouldn't speak.

She looked troubled. 'What are you going to do?'

I looked across the meadow, let my imagination wander back through the forest's dark, winding paths. We had stopped sharing emotional intimacy the day she had told me to get rid of my baby. I still hadn't forgiven her for misreading me so completely. Of course it had been a long time ago, but I couldn't help but blame her for triggering the detachment. She'd been so determined that I should grasp my independence – and grasp it I did, fully, with both hands. She hadn't anticipated that the consequence of her method would be the severing of our own ties.

'I wanted everything for you.'

She had an inimitable knack of reading my thoughts.

'Maybe the price was too high,' I said.

Ava didn't respond.

'I'm sorry if you feel your experiment failed.'

She looked genuinely puzzled. 'Experiment?'

'Isn't that what we were – the children of your revolution?'

She smiled sadly. 'Perhaps your self-obsession is of our making.'

I felt the muscles in my throat contract. She still saw my upbringing as a collective responsibility. 'Ava, my work merely reflects society's self-obsession, not my own. Don't you see?'

She nodded knowingly. 'I see lots of things, as, evidently, do you, Esther. But the one thing I don't see is my daughter.'

She always was one for maudlin sentiment.

'Why have you chosen this moment to bring all this up?' I asked.

She looked straight into my eyes, fixing me with a stare of steel. 'Because, Esther, I'm frightened for you. And I want to help.'

Now I laughed aloud. 'I thought I was supposed to stand on my own two feet.'

'That's what I tried to teach you. Which makes it even more ironic that you seem to have hidden inside a million identities, and become so dependent on men – both sexually and financially – into the bargain.'

Before I had a chance to answer, the sound of a motorbike filled the air: we were to be saved from each other by the carpenter. For the moment, at least.

Since my mobile didn't get a signal and there was no phone in the house, I begged Jacques to take me into the village after lunch so I could call the airport and book a flight home. I don't know if he was in cahoots with my mother, but he refused, apologizing this time for not having a spare helmet. He promised to bring one the next day. So I had another twenty-four hours to put up with. It was scorching hot, but I still felt ill. Perhaps I had caught a chill the previous day. So I took myself off back to bed. It was, at least, one way to avoid another heart-to-heart with my mother.

When I woke up she had gone. And so had Jacques' motorbike.

'Your mother took it, to go to the market,' he told me with a smirk.

Why hadn't I thought of taking off on it myself? I spent the time rereading the press clippings. I had to turn the media on its head. Neither I nor my women should have been denigrated, reduced to such base symbols of lasciviousness. We were all worth more than that.

I had to find a way to resolve this series, for all of them, for me and for Jasmine.

By the time Ava got back, panniers full-to-bursting, it was getting dark again. John still hadn't reappeared and I determinedly didn't ask where he'd gone. I didn't care. Ava was in false high spirits, ignoring my sullenness, chattering away to Jacques in appallingly over-educated French – about the market, the wonderful produce, the low prices. She tried to persuade him to stay for dinner but he made his excuses and to my regret soon put-putted away, leaving us alone once more.

Ava had gone to town, literally, buying asparagus, *confit* of duck, wild strawberries and a kicking local red wine. She set the table with a pale-blue cloth and lit candles. I could see there was no way out, but I was still sulking. John, she said, had gone to stay with a friend in Cahors for a few days, 'to give us space'. I grimaced at the prospect. I was determined to leave in the morning, even if I had to walk to the village and ask a local for help.

Halfway through dinner, as I had anticipated, Ava suddenly put her knife and fork down. I had known we couldn't get through the meal without returning to the subject. But to my surprise, her tone was apologetic.

'I'm sorry, Esther,' she began gently. 'I was too harsh on you earlier.'

'I'm not in a mess,' I replied coolly.

'I just feel you don't value yourself as highly as you should. Your work sells you so short.'

'How?' I didn't understand what she meant.

'You hide inside other identities. They're always less valuable than who you really are.'

I could correct her on this point, at least. 'But this time they're masterpieces, Ava. How on earth can they be worth less than I am?'

'I'm not talking about money. Because they're dead, Esther, don't you see?'

I was silent. We were on to the essence of the thing: the value of aesthetics over the actual. Which was higher? I knew what I believed. Or, at least, I thought I did.

'Why do you place the value of your art over the value of your own life? Is it just an avoidance technique?'

She was at it again, second-guessing me and trying to get close to the workings of my mind – and getting quite close, but with the wires crossed.

'Avoiding what?'

'Looking into yourself, Esther. Into who you are and what you want.'

'That doesn't matter.'

Ava appraised me. She looked genuinely sad. 'You matter more than anything. You can't be a role model for others unless you know who you are and what you want for yourself. And you sell the value of the women you represent down the line if you only look backwards. You have to show how you are looking to the future, for the sake of all women who live now and those who will live after you.'

I thought back to the start of the project. How I had said I wanted to teach the children of my own idiosyncratic revolution, the daughters who were following me – my own daughter, in fact – the value of art and the value of womanhood. I hated to admit that Ava had a point. But I knew I was struggling with the latter part of my equation. I did understand the value of the art, of the real women inside the master-pieces: they had all become personal heroines of mine, and I thought, through their brief resurrections, I'd found a way to expose something of their true values. But as to my own? The future of women's lives? Here there were fewer certainties, that was true. I had never really forgiven myself for what I had done all those years ago. Instead I had cared very little for who I was, had made new costumes to redefine myself in, avoided going too deep into myself. I wondered what Ava thought of that article in the *Clarion*. I wondered if she knew.

'It had to be that way, Esther, so we could create the middle ground. And you are fortunate enough to inhabit it. But it doesn't mean that there's true equality now. You are still at the brink.'

Whistler's image of Mrs Leyland looking back over her shoulder fleetingly passed through my mind. 'My art isn't about feminism. That's just one backdrop.'

'But, Esther, you are a woman, whether you want to call yourself a feminist or not. You wrestle with the same problems of value and ownership as the next woman. If you didn't, then you wouldn't have embarked on such a daring and courageous project.'

I was surprised by her praise. 'Daring?'

She looked at me quietly, with a depth of affection I didn't remember seeing for a very long time. 'I'm so proud of what you've done. But don't let them destroy it – the media, the men in your life. Make it work, make it something to go forward from.'

'What I don't understand is why they want to destroy me in the process. I'm just trying to get to the heart of the matter.'

She laughed. 'You've just answered your own question. You've stood on the parapet. And they'll try to destroy you through pure avarice. You have a value over and above them – the media and your dealers, they want to take some of it back. What's so stupid is that, in the end, they'll be the ones lamenting your demise.'

'I don't know what to do next,' I said.

'For a start, I think you need to get some sleep,' she replied. 'Go on, up you go.'

She was right. I was so tired. The sickness in my insides was somehow consuming all my strength. But the mood between us had become profoundly calm. It was good to talk like this; it had taken years. It might only be a beginning, but at least we had started. However, at that point I had to sleep. I had no choice.

Ava smiled kindly. 'Go to bed,' she urged. 'I understand.'

She put a cold flannel to the back of my neck as I retched up bile. 'How many weeks are you?' she asked.

I looked up at her questioningly.

'I was exactly the same with you,' she continued. 'Morning, noon and night.'

With her words came a horrible dawning and the distinct memory of a taste embedded deep in the roof of my mouth. It was there again. And I knew her words struck true.

'Did you read about my pregnancy?' I asked.

She didn't answer.

'I mean my last one, when I was sixteen?'

Ava had her arm round my waist and I looked up into her eyes. They were filling with tears and she couldn't speak. Her shoulders began to shake.

There was nothing for it but to stay in bed. I didn't have the will to move. I felt literally taken over by the tiny new foetus growing inside me. Six times a day Ava appeared with little snacks to try to tempt me to eat. Each time the idea appealed but the reality appalled. My stomach rebelled and my limbs ached.

As the week went on, little by little I told Ava about Jasmine, about my determination not to abort her, and about how depressed I had been once I had given her away. Ava listened with gravity, and without judgement or comment, allowing me to find my own way to tell at last the story I had guarded for so long.

Six days passed in this way. And on the seventh I woke to a curious settling inside me; and the strength to make a decision. I would write to Jasmine. I had to let her know I was there for her if she wanted me. Every day it was becoming easier to think positively about her – partly, perhaps, because by talking to Ava I had made Jasmine more tangible in my mind, and partly because my new pregnancy brought memories of the last into clearer focus. Until I knew whether or not she needed me, I couldn't make decisions about my future.

I sat down at the small table in my room and looked out across the silent meadow, then up towards the forest. The sun's rays were growing stronger as the day took shape. Ava was returning from her morning stroll, kindling in her arms. She looked old and tired, detached from the landscape around her. I wondered if there would be time for us to rebuild our trust in each other, whether there could be a third phase to our relationship, built on mutual understanding and a shared focus and interest in my children, her grandchildren.

I picked up my pen.

Dear Jasmine,

This is a hard letter to write but no doubt a harder one to receive. My name is Esther and I am your natural mother. I don't know how much you know about your adoption or who your natural parents are and I also don't know whether you <u>want</u> to know. But now you are sixteen I feel compelled to get in touch to tell you that I love you and, if you ever feel lonely, or want to find out more about the past that shaped you, I will always be here for you.

Maybe you will feel that you don't want to meet me, that you are already happy and complete in your own world, with your mum and dad and the life they have created for you all, and that there is no place for me within it. If so, I will understand and must be happy to accept that they have fulfilled all your needs.

When you were born I was a very lonely sixteen-year-old who had just lost her father. I felt terribly confused and over-whelmed by my unexpected circumstances. Your own natural father was my first boyfriend, a beautiful, bold young man with wild eyes and a restless spirit that I couldn't contain. By the time I found I was pregnant, he had already left my life.

But please believe I loved carrying you with all my heart, and I didn't want to let you go. I just couldn't see any other way. I have thought about you every day since you came into being, and I wonder endlessly about your life, your happiness, your sense of self and identity.

Please, if and when you feel ready, call me or write.

With all my love,

Esther

I wandered downstairs at midday and, curled up on the sofa, watched Jacques' skilled hands at work. In the intervening days, between running errands for us, he had almost completed his task. He smoothed oil into the wood with a rag held gently in his unblemished hands. He looked at peace as he worked. I watched him and I realized why. There was simplicity to his actions, and pleasure gained from the smallest of things: the colour and the grain of the wood, the perfect balance of his design. This was a craft of which he had become the master and it fulfilled his spirit.

When he downed tools for lunch, my thoughts shifted once more. It was essential I returned to London. I had just under two months before the show opened and I had to complete the *Possession* series. But first there was someone I needed to see, urgently. I had to take one final trip to Paris.

46

She's more famous than any other painting of a woman – and that's precisely why I hadn't chosen her for my series. It seemed there was something too predictable about an audience with the *Mona Lisa*. Yet, try as I might, throughout the *Possession* series all brushstrokes led me back to her face. In each instance, my selected subjects seemed to have a link back to Leonardo da Vinci's great masterpiece. I had never before understood why she was so essential to the history of art, why she was so famous, so revered, priceless. I had simply put her reputation, like mine, down to over-inflation and media hype.

My selected portraits all clearly emphasized a singular aspect of womanhood, whereas now I saw that the *Mona Lisa* effortlessly encapsulated them all: beauty, politics, sexuality, power, purity, aesthetics and myth – they were all reflected in her face. Depending, that is, on your point of view. And that was the key, in my mind, to her success – and my current failure. The true value of art wasn't about the subjects on the canvas at all. It was about the effect they provoked in their viewers. There wasn't just the painter and the painted. The critical factor was the objective eye lying between them. Real masterpieces, I now understood, allowed viewers to gain a true insight into themselves.

God knows what thoughts were really going through Mona Lisa's mind when she sat for Leonardo. She was definitely a two-way mirror. Look at her and you look into yourself. Ava had fought me hard on the subject of my own self-identity. And as I lay curled up in defence for those seven days and seven nights in John's French house, agonizing about the creation of another human being inside me, Leonardo's masterpiece kept reappearing in my mind. Hard as I tried, I couldn't push her away. She was generous and assertive, calm and certain, knowing and eternal. She seemed to understand what I was going through and steadfastly led me to look deeper into myself. And it was there that I now finally began to find the answers.

Guy's wise words had come back to me from that day in Paris when we stood together before Leonardo's cartoon of Isabella d'Este. I had asked, instinctively, if Isabella were pregnant when he drew her, nearly giving my own secret history away through my sense of affinity with her. Guy appeared not to have noticed, replying emphatically that some art historians believed that both she and Mona Lisa were.

'Look at their rounded faces and figures,' he had said, 'and, look, neither of them's wearing a ring.'

Ironically, it was impossible to spend time absorbing Mona Lisa's true qualities. When I arrived at the Louvre this time, the area in front of her was swarming with tourists, cameras held high, flashbulbs endlessly going off in her face. The atmosphere around her was electric. Everyone knew they were in the presence of an icon. But no one was really seeing her – they were all too busy looking at a famous masterpiece through the lens. I thought back to all the press previews, the auction, to the cameras that had become my stalkers, my shadows, and I felt sympathy for Mona Lisa, trapped there, behind her bullet-proof glass.

Slowly, but with determination, I edged my way to the front of the crowd and managed to stand before the painting. People pushed and shoved me to get their lenses straight, but I refused to be moved. Mona Lisa seemed to acknowledge me straight on, ignoring all other eyes that observed her. She definitely represented maternal understanding and emanated inner warmth, suggestive of her expectant state. She eyed me knowingly and seemed to recognize that we shared a secret. At that moment she implicitly became part of my series. After a few moments I left her and walked through the museum's glorious halls without affording another painting a single glance. I emerged into the Paris sunshine and took a long, deep breath of air.

How to use *Mona Lisa* in the final exhibition was harder to decide. But one thing was clear: she had to be part of it. Because it was she, in the end, who had taken possession of me. And I now saw that her impact was all-pervasive. It was everywhere, not just in the Louvre, her permanent address, or even in the portraits of all my women, who, in one sense or another, took on a little bit of her as their own. She wasn't even only reflected in women's faces; she was both male and female; in fact, her spirit was present in every face in every village, town and city in the world. In her complex human values lay all of our own.

Mona Lisa has been used in more advertising campaigns than any other painting and it was in that field that I discovered the 'glue' I needed for my series. Subliminal advertising is dangerous and, in explicit cases, it is banned. But as far as art exhibitions are concerned there is, as far as I was aware, no law to say you couldn't project an image for a split second onto a wall. So that is what I determined to do. In the flatteringly cavernous room given over to my project at Tate Modern, I installed projectors to flicker on the walls the negative image of *Mona Lisa* between my films of the seven women. She appeared and dissolved again so fast that the mind didn't have the chance to react or register her presence until after she had gone.

Each film began with a first frame of the relevant masterpiece, before a fade-out and then my performance itself started to play. In between each screen I had laid out my women's own possessions for the viewers to observe: their costumes on showroom dummies, alongside their various, colourful accessories – and, in each case, their own open book. I had also written a potted history of each masterpiece, told from my perspective, not that of the art-history books. So the public could now read about Christina's long and lonely ending, discover the truth about Marie's lowly roots, her impending marriage, the knife attack in the attic. They could see Victorine ageing and alone as her aesthetic value soared, and wonder still at the true values of iconized Mary. Then they could consider the power of money in Isabella's world and the cost of love and the price of aesthetics in the salon of Mrs Frances Leyland, before, finally, examining the double-edged sword stimulated by Judith's myth.

At the end of the series was my trunk, open and laid bare. All that was left inside were the gilt engraved insignias and empty boxes. In the centre of the gallery I had installed a glass odalisque of my own design, whose sides were cut like crystals to reflect the light and the images of the audience who passed through, as well as frames from the films as they flickered ephemerally across its reflective surface. Etched into them was the equation in respect of my value: £665,000/140 lbs = £4,750 per pound.

This was me: a block of glass – a pun on my name – and an empty vessel, waiting to be filled, both by the reflections of the viewers of the show and by my seven subjects, as their films flickered colours onto my own surface and sent their prisms of light flashing through me. As to my own identity: this would be the last time I would lay myself bare to my audience. I hoped I would not fail them or disappoint any of my fans. But I knew that at last it was time to desist from meddling with representation and reality. I needed to make a statement that came just from me.

47

To my disappointment, when I arrived in London Aidan had already gone back to New York. He'd left a message saying he was staying only a couple of days, that he wanted to see Sam, and was going to stall the deal with Ben and Greg until I was ready to make some decisions. There was also a message from Billy, asking me to come and see him at the National Gallery. Billy was disorganized. He never got in touch unless he wanted something specific. I had a distinct feeling the subject of his call was Aidan.

I was right.

'You've got it all wrong, you know.'

Billy's canvas was now covered with a photo-realist oil painting of folds of fur and black velvet. The rabbit skins were no longer on the hat stand. Instead a new Barbour was hanging there. It seemed he really had become a country squire.

'Is that what you wanted to talk to me about?' I replied.

Billy busied himself, cleaning brushes in turps. I observed him from the other side of the studio. I could hear the hum of traffic passing outside. It was his last week as resident at the National Gallery.

'I'm going to miss it here,' he mused quietly. 'I've become quite accustomed to working among the masters. Every time I need to work something out, I just go into the museum and check the source. It's been fuckin' amazing.'

I sat down on a wooden chair and waited for him to finish. Eventually he put the brushes down in a neat line on a side table and pulled a stool up in front of me. He sat down and took my hands in his. His skin was surprisingly rough.

'Esther, I think you've got it all wrong.'

I was surprised to find sincerity thickening his words. I wondered how many times he'd rehearsed this scene – possibly with Aidan by his side.

'Go on,' I said warily.

'Aidan's only been doing his job. He's trying to make the best of this for you. I don't think you realize how tough it is out there. In his own way he's a genius, you know.'

I had of course anticipated the topic. Aidan and Billy had always been two of a kind. And just like Aidan, Billy was a player. It was also to Billy's advantage for me to invest in this new project. But none of it really mattered any more. I was happy for Aidan to run the business of my art, as it stood, so long as I could step outside of it for the time being and concentrate on what really mattered: our real life. But I wasn't about to tell Billy that: it was something I could discuss only with Aidan.

'Petra warned me, you know, in Paris, before the sale. She said the money would tip the balance between us. And maybe that's partly why I set up the challenge in the first place. I wanted – no, *needed* – to push us over the edge. Even if I hadn't quite anticipated the force of the outcome.'

'Maybe Petra's just jealous of you and Aidan?' Billy's tone was hardening.

I scoffed.

'I'm not joking, Esther.' He was impassioned now. 'Petra's always wanted to have what you've got. Aidan's been a big part of that for her, I'm sure.'

I didn't believe Billy. At least, I didn't want to. I wondered if he was trying to find a weakness that would cause me to falter. After all, if I pulled out of Aidan's scheme, we both knew every artist in the gallery would be affected.

'Do you remember what you said to me, a while back, about us all needing change?'

Billy let go of my hands and ran his fingers through his hair. 'Change, not fucking Armageddon.'

'Maybe you think I'm naïve,' I continued; 'perhaps I have been. But I was raised on ideals and, for the first time in a long while, they're beginning to make sense to me. I don't want to be in the possession of a dealer any more – not professionally, at any rate. You don't need to tell me that Aidan's amazing. I know that. But the whole way the art world functions, it's just not for me right now. I need to follow a new direction. Preferably without the media on my back.'

Billy took my hands again. His grip tightened. 'It'll kill 'im, Est. He loves you, you know. Adores you. He won't know what to do if you leave him.'

'Who said anything about leaving him?' I asked.

For a minute Billy looked confused, then he put a hand over his mouth to disguise a smirk. 'What, you mean you're not fucking leaving him?'

'Do you have to swear all the time?'

'Yes, I fucking do.' He laughed, then pulled me close to him and gave me a hug.

'Jesus, Esther, you've given Aidan one huge fucking fright.'

I pulled back for a moment 'Hold on a minute, Billy. I haven't talked this through with him yet. Maybe Aidan won't want to keep me on my new terms.'

I knew at this point what I wanted from my future. If I could have it all my way, I would marry Aidan and we would make our permanent home in London. I wanted to meet Jasmine and for her to become a part of our world, preferably before the baby arrived. And if we could afford to, I wanted us to get a new apartment in New York, where we could spend every third or fourth week with Sam. He could come to London, too, maybe even come and live with us, go to school here, if Carolyn and Sonia would allow it. We'd sell our two London places and buy a real home – a place with a bedroom for Sam, for Jasmine, and for their shared sibling when he or she arrived – and an artist's studio for me: something small, with good light, a place in which to start painting again.

These were my new dreams, but for the first time in my life they were like specific goals. There were two obstacles, however. The first was that Aidan was in New York, and that, it seemed, was where he wanted to be, and the second was Jasmine. A week had passed since posting my letter and there had been no sound from her, nothing at all. I knew I had to be patient, it was early days, but already a gloom was settling back inside me. Time was running out before the show opened in London and I was madly busy getting ready for the installation of the *Possession* series. Normally work would overwhelm all other concerns, but this was different: Jasmine tugged at the very root of me.

48

Lincoln Sterne handed me the DVD with a cautious schoolboy grimace.

'You'd better not have fucked me over, Linc,' I threatened, but he could see I was smiling.

He shrugged and with a smirk said: 'We just did our best.'

'I'll let you know if it was good enough when I've seen for myself.'

Petra was over and we'd planned an evening on the pink suede sofa to watch the documentary together. She arrived at the flat and promptly burst into tears. No use telling her my woes, then: evidently she was pretty wrapped up in her own.

'I never thought he was worth it.'

She shot me a hurt look.

'I'm only being honest.'

She smiled weakly, then began to cry again.

'Come on, let's watch Ava and Lincoln trying to screw my career. That should cheer you up.'

The documentary opened with a cine-film of me, aged about six, swinging from a tree, wearing a pair of flared jeans and a floral tanktop. My hair was long, brown and wavy. I could equally have been boy or girl. Fade out Jagger's smoke-edged rendition of 'Wild Horses', fade in Lincoln's voiceover: 'Esther Glass was raised by her mother, the famous feminist writer Ava Glass, at Ickfield Folly in Oxfordshire, one of the first – and longest-surviving – communes to spring up at the end of the1960s.'

I groaned and hid my head in the cushions. As predicted, Petra shrieked with laughter. The film proceeded to chart my childhood with a vigour that lent it a magical spirit. Ava had gone to town with the snapshots. There were pictures of me, of us, and the rest of the gang, throughout my childhood and adolescence. Occasionally Ava herself would come into frame, either being interviewed at the time, or the previous winter, sitting in her armchair by her fake gas fire. As I saw my childhood portrayed on film, it seemed strangely to grow in my affections. Ava's words were kind, generous. She looked absolutely beautiful in the old films. I began to remember things about her I had forgotten: the way she used to stroke my hair back from my face when she woke me in the morning; the way she used to walk with me to school singing silly rhymes we made up on a whim. In the film Ava talked of my passionate love of liberty, my loathing of hypocrisy, my tireless search for the essence of life and my insatiable appetite for art. She described how these attributes had manifested themselves at a very early age. Her words were strong, proud and loving. As I listened to them I began to see emerging the portrait of someone I didn't seem to know.

Was I as she projected me? If so, when had I lost that confidence she spoke of so enthusiastically? In the public's eyes, it was probably still there. But Jasmine had happened along the way and made me question my sense of self. Was it simply that reality, not representation, had taken its invisible toll, knocked the edge off my idealism? I suddenly remembered all the games of make-believe we used to play, and saw that as a child I had – for a time, at least – been immensely, immeasurably happy.

49

Aidan sounded weary. He had just got in from New York.

'Can you meet me?' I implored.

'Of course, Esther. Where?'

'The flat, in Soho, tonight,' I replied.

Once more I dressed in my burka and made my way from Bow. Ten days had gone by since my letter had been sent, and still there was no news from Jasmine. Although I knew the process it had to go through was arduous – first the adoption agency would receive it, then pass the letter on, and who knows, perhaps, even, her parents had intercepted it – I was feeling dejected.

I rang the bell and Aidan buzzed me in. I took off my burka and we lay on the bed together in silence. Aidan didn't try to touch me; he held his hands above his head. He looked like he'd lost weight.

'I've come to say thank you, and to tell you I'm sorry,' I began.

Aidan didn't reply. He sighed deeply and closed his eyes.

'Aidan, there's so much I've hidden for so long.'

His eyes opened again and he looked at me quizzically. 'Is there someone else?'

I shook my head sadly. 'There's no one, Aidan; there never has been.' I paused. It was hard to start. 'For one, there's the real me,' I said quietly, 'and with that person comes a whole history, a story about someone who was there before you came.'

As the night grew old, I tried to tell Aidan about Jasmine. It was very, very hard, because it seemed there was so much to tell, and yet so little. She had slipped out of my hands so long ago, and I had only the barest of fragments upon which to recount her own tale. When, finally, I felt that maybe I was done, I could hear the sounds of late-night Soho creeping under the door. And as light strained to get in through the blinds, I remembered another night, many, many years before, when we had lain together on another bed, just around the corner, in Beak Street, and Aidan had shared with me the pain of his recent history, had let me witness his own wounds. Why had it taken me another decade to trust him and myself enough to return the confidence?

'So what do you want next, Esther? Can I help you to find her?' he asked once I was finally through.

'I need to know she's OK, that she doesn't need me, before you and I make any major changes,' I said.

'I understand that, and I'll do all I can to help you. Ben's keen to develop his patronage wherever you are,' he answered, 'but I'm still very focused on the foundation plan.'

We were still lying propped up on the bed, but now Aidan was behind me, legs around my body, with the weight of my back leaning into his chest.

I was silent for a while. Then, 'And I want you to be a full-time and permanent father to our child,' I added.

'You want another baby? Are you sure you're ready?' he replied quietly.

'It's too late for us to ask the question.'

I could feel Aidan's body tensing.

'You're pregnant?'

'Sure am.' I turned round and looked into Aidan's beautiful eyes and saw that they were full of tears. 'Why does everyone cry when I tell them good news?' I asked. Then I realized that I too could not contain my emotions. For a while, sobs racked my chest.

When, finally, we were both calm enough to talk again, I told Aidan of my dreams. Somehow, he promised, we would make them become a reality, even if we couldn't manage to put every last element in place. Some of the decisions, we both had to accept, were simply out of our hands.

50

'What are you going to wear?'

'I want to go out with a bang.'

'Out?'

'Don't worry, you'll soon understand.'

'Do you want me to design something new?'

'What, with five days to go?'

'You know I'd pull out all the stops.'

'No, don't worry, Petra. It's got to be Marie. She's where it all began.'

There was nothing from Jasmine, not a sound.

The crowds were cheering as Aidan and I stepped from the car and walked down the red carpet laid out for VIPs before Tate Modern's jaw-stretched entrance. I stopped and posed, first left, then right. The media were hungry and uninvited crowds outside were making a huge amount of noise. If I weren't mistaken, they were chanting my name.

It felt good to be back with Madame de Senonnes. I was determined to enjoy this moment with the press and the public, too. It might well be the last for a very long time. I felt strangely at home dressed in Marie's outfit, although the seams were tighter, my breasts being more prominent than when I had last forced them into Petra's ingeniously designed bodice. I was even more grateful than before for Ingres' wonderful antique shawl. It was wrapped around me like a talisman, keeping me safe.

Invited guests were milling around the vast turbine hall. No one was allowed into the show before the exhibiting artists had arrived and been given their own private view. We were led through them. Aidan had one hand flat against the base of my back and I could feel it trembling. We went by escalator to the second floor, which was given over to The International Contemporaries show. I thought back to my last public appearance here, that time with Guy. The space was empty but for the director of the Tate, along with the six guest curators who had taken part in planning the show. They were taking a turn round the exhibit before the marauding masses were allowed to come in and disturb their serious contemplation of the works.

The director spied me and smiled with uncharacteristic warmth. He moved quickly towards me and took my hand. 'Esther, I must commend you on an exemplary series,' he said firmly.

I had come in with Jane and Petra that morning to put the finishing touches to the exhibit. But walking around it later with the professionals, I realized with satisfaction that, in the intervening hours, the *Possession* series had gelled. Everything had come together perfectly. At that moment Mona Lisa's face flickered through my mind.

People began to arrive. I saw Ava walk in with Lincoln on her arm. She was sizzling with an excitement that made her skin glow and her eyes shine bright like they used to.

As she embraced me she asked, nervously, 'Was it all right, really?'
I nodded.

Lincoln looked tickled pink. 'Darling, I knew you'd see the light.'

I was distracted by the crowd, who were turning in unison towards the door. Someone important must have arrived. Sure enough, with the eloquence of a metaphysical poem, Petra glided into the room. In the design of her outfit she hadn't missed a trick. She looked startling, dressed in a creation that somehow resembled the inside of an oyster shell, within which she was very much the pearl. Her entrance was greeted with a round of applause. She wore her new-found fame with the ease of one of her latest creations. For her, celebrity would never prove a problem. Unlike me, Petra was born to be famous.

Next appeared Ben. He looked smaller, more meek, away from his own world. As he spotted me, a broad smile stretched wide across his face. He approached and gave me a reassuring hug. We'd met up earlier in the afternoon and had talked my future through. He knew what was on my cards and certain commitments had been set, to his and my satisfaction. Then I noticed an auburn-haired woman by his side. She had an almond-shaped face and sage-green eyes. There was something of Isabella d'Este about her.

'I'd like to introduce you to Penny,' he said.

The woman smiled adoringly as she looked up at Ben. He put his arm around her and squeezed.

Guy arrived next, with Jeanne, and, hard on their heels, the New York team: Carolyn, Sonia, Sam and Greg had all flown in, much to my great surprise. Aidan had kept their visit a secret from me. It was hard to know whom to greet first. Really, I wanted to talk to Guy, but somehow he got lost in the crowd. I found myself instead with the Manhattan circle closing in around me, and was amazed how reassured I was by their presence.

'We want you back,' Sonia implored.

'When are you guys coming home for good?' Carolyn added, laughing; then, to my amazement, Sam put his arm around me.

'Are you and Dad going to get married?' he asked boldly.

Everyone looked at me expectantly.

'Well, if we do, Sam, I promise you'll be the first to know.'

He pulled me down close to him and whispered in my ear, 'He told me about the baby. It's our secret. I haven't even told Mom.'

I could see my curator, Jane, approaching. I held onto Sam's hand and looked around for Aidan. He saw me and quickly approached.

'Are you ready to give your speech?' Jane asked.

I nodded and with Aidan on one side of me, Sam on the other, I followed her to a small podium set up with a mike. Seeing our move, the crowd began to gather to hear what I had to say. First of all the director of Tate Modern got up and made a short speech about the exhibition in general, then he explained that I had asked to say a few words and handed me the mike. Slowly, I stood up on the stage, knowing that this would be the hardest performance of my career to date.

I looked around the audience and smiled, then I began.

'The *Possession* series has been a personal voyage for me,' I said, unintentionally softly. 'Before now, all my art has enabled me to hide inside the identities of fictionalized women, women I have made up, told stories about, had a whole lot of fun playing. And then came *The Painted Nude*. That series took me in a new direction, because in it I was myself, the writing on my skin projecting only my own personal thoughts. But it also projected me into the limelight in a way that I hadn't anticipated. The *Possession* series is my response to that experience. Beneath my surface and the surface of the masterpieces featured are the lives of very real women, who represent core values we all share – and values that have been manipulated, or misconstrued, by the public and the press.'

I paused. I seemed to have gained the audience's undivided attention, for the moment at least. My mouth felt dry. I caught sight of Aidan and he smiled encouragingly.

'I was hoping to find their true identities beneath the surface of the paint. But there was also a very personal reason for me to do this project. I fast realized I was also looking for my own identity in the mix. I thought that somehow, if I looked inside the lives of other women, I might also find out some facts about myself. As a woman and an artist, I have spent many years mixing fact with fiction, and somewhere along the line I think I lost a sense of who I really am. And, if I'm honest, that loss felt, for a very long time, like a release – and a relief. But recently I have begun to see that I have taken many careless risks, perhaps because I have never seemed able to really care for myself.'

The hall was silent. People like nothing better than a heartfelt confession, I thought. Aidan locked his eyes with mine.

'And now for some home truths.'

At this I smiled and the audience responded in kind. I was among friends.

'This is the last series I will be producing for the foreseeable future. Aidan Jeroke, my dealer, and I are expecting a child. I plan to embrace my new role as a mother, and I hope I will be allowed to savour the experience away from the prying eyes of the cameras.'

There were a few murmurs across the room and I held up my hand once more.

'And finally, and most importantly,' my throat felt as if it might contract, 'I am dedicating this show to a young member of my family. Her name is Jasmine. The *Possession* series is ultimately for her, and for all the women of her generation. I hope, through this work, they will learn something it has taken me thirty-two years to understand – that is, the importance of valuing self-possession, of being strong, bold and independent, but also of loving and respecting yourself, whoever you are and whatever your history has made you.'

My attention was broken by a sharp sound from the audience, a slow, regular hand-clap. I looked around and spied the source; it came from a young woman, standing alone towards the back of the audience. She was tall, shaped like a pear, with long, dark, curling hair and an ethereal oval face. The audience turned, too, and stared.

I stepped down from the podium as other people began to join in her applause and, as the crowd parted, I quickly made my way towards her. As I got closer her face became clearer. She looked similar to

Christina of Denmark, who was projected on the gallery wall next to her. Perhaps it was the enigmatic gaze, or her full bottom lip; or maybe what they shared was an inherent vulnerability, generated by their evident youth and, possibly, by their fear of what the future might reveal. After another few steps I could see the colour of her eyes. They were an indeterminate grey-blue, cut through with fine splinters of green. As I stopped before her she fixed those eyes on mine. Holbein's masterpiece was to her right, art and life now existing side by side, and I knew immediately which was the greater creation. I also knew which had been made in my own image.

I took her hand in mine and it was as though I were holding my own, or indeed my mother's, hand, for this one was made of the same flesh and blood. As I touched it, I felt complete. I looked long and hard into her eyes and the young woman allowed her mouth to quiver on the edge of a smile. Immediately I knew with perfect certainty that I had finally found what I had spent so many years searching for: I had just come face to face with my very own, living, breathing masterpiece.

Author's Note

Although Esther Glass's journey is a pure work of fiction, the paintings referred to in the text are all real works of art. The stories about the women in the portraits are based on facts, but in some instances the fictionalized world nudges its way in. Particular examples include the faux-sale of Rossetti's wonderful painting of Mrs Leyland, *Mona Rossa*, to Ben Jamieson. Rumours abound about photographs of Victorine Meurent. Sadly, I came across none in my research: Guy's discovery is simply wishful thinking. In contrast, the Ingres-style shawl found on the internet by Petra really was for sale when I was writing. If only I, like Esther, could have afforded to buy it.

Bibliography

Archer, Michael, *Art Since 1960* (Thames and Hudson, 1997)

Buck, Stephanie, and Jochen Sander, *Hans Holbein the Younger: Painter at the Court of Henry VIII* (Thames and Hudson, 2003)

Hope, Charles, *Titian* (Chaucer Press, 2003)

Kovachevski, Christo, *The Madonna in Western Painting* (Alpine Fine Arts Collection, 1991)

MacDonald, Margaret F, Susan Grace Galassi, Aileen Ribeiro and Patricia de Montfort, *Whistler, Women and Fashion* (Yale University Press, 2003)

Neret, Charles, *Klimt* (Taschen, 2000)

Ribeiro, Aileen, *Ingres in Fashion: Representations of Dress and Appearance in Ingres' Images of Women* (Yale University Press, 1999)

Sassoon, Donald, *Mona Lisa: The History of the World's Most Famous Painting* (HarperCollins, 2001)

Warner, Marina, *Alone of All Her Sex: Cult of the Virgin Mary* (Vintage, 2000)

Museum Websites

The Frick Collection, New York: www.frick.org

MoMA The Museum of Modern Art, New York: www.moma.org

The National Gallery, London: www.nationalgallery.org.uk

Kunsthistorisches Museum, Vienna: www.khm.at
The Louvre, Paris: www.louvre.fr
Musée d'Orsay, Paris: www.musee-orsay.fr

Other Museums
Musée des Beaux Arts de Nantes
10 rue Georges Clémenceau
44000 Nantes
Tel: + 33 2 51 17 45 00

Cà Pesaro International Gallery of Modern Art
Santa Croce, 2076 – San Stae
30135 – Venice
Tel: + 39 041 72 11 27

Picture Credits